Hebridean Meeting

Patrick Wetenhall

PATRICK WETENHALL

authorHOUSE®

AuthorHouse™ *UK*
1663 Liberty Drive
Bloomington, IN 47403 USA
www.authorhouse.co.uk
Phone: 0800.197.4150

Published by AuthorHouse 01/29/2015

ISBN: 978-1-4969-9626-8 (sc)
ISBN: 978-1-4969-9621-3 (hc)
ISBN: 978-1-4969-9627-5 (e)

CHAPTER ONE

Susan Dalmane, the Countess of Saint Helens, raised herself slowly to a sitting position in the bed while she considered her situation. Lord Dalmane was dead. Her husband, John, the Earl of Saint Helens, had died in his sleep four days ago, and today was the day of his funeral. Susan was still in a state of shock following her husband's unexpected death, which had hardly ever been out of her mind since it had happened. This morning, however, her thoughts were confused as she recalled a vivid and disturbing dream from which she had just woken. She had been thinking of Jim Sandy, the former Guide of Rhodes Castle, who had featured prominently in her dream, but now a picture of a coffin came into her mind's eye. In the little chapel of the Castle, a small room on the second floor, a coffin covered by a richly embroidered purple pall lay before the altar. The coat of arms of the Earl of Saint Helens was worked in gold on the purple pall, and four candles in huge candlesticks were burning beside the bier, and two more candles were burning on the altar. Susan saw these details for a moment in her mind's eye before her attention was distracted by noticing something else.

A table stood in front of the bedroom window, and on this table there laid, among other things, a map. It was a map of the Isle of Skye. The sight of it caused Susan to tell herself that she must ask her maid to remove it. She and John had been planning a Hebridean cruise for that summer in John's yacht, the OSPREY, but now of course it was unthinkable that she should go there without her husband. The holiday was off, for that year at least.

Susan's sleepy thoughts returned at once to the one absorbing interest of the moment, that dream, which had ended so recently that it, was almost as if it was still going on. The face of Jim Sandy, her former lover, again appeared in her mind's eye. Jim had been the Guide at Rhodes Castle until last year, but Lord Dalmane had been forced to dismiss him when he had discovered that Susan had become, to all intents and purposes, his mistress. He had, in fact, confessed to having an affair with her. The dismissal of Jim had happened some eleven months earlier, in April of 1962; and now it was early March, and very cold, with little sign of the approach of spring.

"Hello, Sam!" Susan had not heard her maid's quiet knock on the door before she entered the bedroom, but suddenly she saw that she was there.

"Good morning, Sue," said Samantha. The pretty, fair haired Samantha Burton was standing in the open doorway, looking with concern at her distressed and sleepy mistress. "Have you had a bad night?"

"Yes, a very bad night." Susan had no intention of saying anything to Samantha about that dream.

"Oh, I'm sorry to hear that, Sue; but your morning tea's there. I brought it in earlier when I pulled the curtains, but you were still asleep. Then I thought I'd better look in again to wake you, if necessary."

Susan looked sleepily at her bedside table, and noticed that a cup of tea was there, resting on a saucer. It was funny that she had not noticed it before, or realized when she had looked out through the window that Samantha must already have been in to pull back the curtains and to bring in the tea. Samantha always brought her a cup of tea in the mornings, and drew the curtains for her.

"Thank you, Sam," she said. She picked up the cup.

"Right, I'll go now," said Samantha.

"Just a minute!" said Susan, remembering something, and putting the cup back on its saucer without taking a sip of her tea.

"Yes?" Samantha stopped, her hand on the door handle.

"Could you take that map with you, Sam, if you're going downstairs, and put it away? The map of Skye on the window table. I shan't need it now."

"Yes, of course." Samantha came in, picked up the map, and then opened a fold or two to peep inside. "Where should this go?"

"In the map drawer in the Tower Library. John's maps are all stored in there in the top right hand drawer in the desk in the window. Put it in there. The maps are all jumbled up in no particular order."

"All right," said Samantha. But if I may say so I think you should go to the Isle of Skye sometime, Sue not perhaps this year.

It's such a beautiful island. You'd really love it, I'm sure."

"Well, sometime, perhaps, I'll go there," said Susan dully, "but I can't think about that now."

"Very well, I'll just put it away." Taking the map with her, Samantha left the room.

She was a Scot, Susan remembered, and had been born somewhere in Scotland Edinburgh, was it? and she had told Susan before about holidays on the Isle of Skye with her parents. But such a subject held no interest for Susan now, and in a moment her thoughts slipped back to considering that upsetting dream as she began listlessly to drink her morning tea, sitting up in bed, and staring with unseeing eyes through the window towards the wintry-looking front garden of Rhodes Castle.

Outside there the early morning sun was lighting up a pale-blue sky, and was casting long shadows of the cedar and the smaller trees over the white lawns and the ice on the ponds.

But Susan was unmoved by the brightness of the morning. She was dimly aware of the whiteness on the ground outside, but did not know or care whether it was a light covering of snow or just a heavy white frost. It was, in fact, merely frost; there had been no snow lying on the ground the day before, but that winter had been a very cold one with a great deal of snow, and Susan had rather expected more snow that night as it had been cold and cloudy at sunset. But the sky had cleared during the night to give this bright, crisp morning.

For some minutes Susan remained where she was, with a woolen shawl loosely draped around her shoulders to cover her nightdress (the room was reasonably warm with a large radiator in front of the window giving off a good deal of heat). She drank her tea slowly, her mind lost in her gloomy thoughts.

Suddenly her dreamy speculations were distracted as she heard footsteps approaching.

"Susan! Are you awake?" It was a pleasant female voice which spoke to her through the closed door. Someone tapped gently on it.

"Yes, Mother," said Susan. "Come in!"

The door opened, and Susan's mother, fully dressed in a black outfit for the funeral, walked into the bedroom. Susan, who had been rubbing her eyes, slowly removed her hands from her face and blinked a few times at her second visitor of that morning; but she made no attempt to move.

"What a beautiful morning it is!" Lady Ardell, Susan's mother, was standing by the window, looking out. "It's very cold outside, but delightfully bright. Most invigorating, although I dare say you haven't felt that yet. You will, though, I think, when you get out into the sunshine presently."

"Will I?" murmured Susan weakly.

"Now, my dear," said her mother, turning to face her daughter, "it's high time that you were getting up and coming down for your breakfast. It's ten to nine, you know." Susan had no idea of the time until that moment, but now she looked at the watch strapped round her wrist, and was a little surprised to note that it was indeed ten minutes to nine. "And remember," continued her mother, that you asked the Vicar to call sometime for a talk, and he said he'd be here this morning at about half past nine."

"Oh, heavens, yes, so I did!" said Susan. "That's why I asked Sam to wake me in good time, and she's been in twice, actually: the first time to bring in my tea when I was asleep, and then a second time to check that I was awake."

"Sam's very good to you, isn't she?" Susan's mother now came and sat down on a chair near the bed so that she could sit facing her daughter to talk to her. Like Susan she was a tall, dark haired, good-looking lady. Her name was Elizabeth (her maiden name was Bellingham-Smith), and she was the wife of Richard Ardell, The Marquis of Walton, which, of course, entitled her to be called Lady Walton. She had come over to Rhodes Castle from her home in north-east Essex, Soken Hall, immediately on being informed by telephone that Lord Dalmane had died; the death had occurred in the early hours of the morning, and Lady Walton had arrived by car to console and help her daughter by tea-time that same day. As she now sat by Susan's bedside she held out some small thing made of black lace.

"What's that you've got there, Mum?" asked Susan.

"A veil for you to wear at the service, my dear," she said.

"Oh dear!" sighed Susan. "The funeral. I almost wish I didn't have to go to it. I feel so well, ill, almost. And I've got such a headache."

"You've had a bad night, I expect. Have you had any sleep apart from when Samantha brought in your tea?"

Susan shook her head slowly. "Very little," she said. "Last night's been the worst so far. I don't think I had a wink of sleep until some time, perhaps, between seven and eight this morning. And then I had a rather worrying dream I've just woken up from."

"What was it about?"

"Oh about John." Susan decided as she said it that she would not tell her mother that she had also been dreaming about her other lover, Jim Sandy, and that she was the more upset on that account. She looked at her teacup, saw that there was still a small mouthful of tea in it, and drank it, although it was now quite cold. Her mother nodded her head thoughtfully on hearing that Susan had been dreaming about John, but now she looked more closely at her daughter, as if worried about her health. No doubt Lady Walton was thinking that the signs indicated that Susan was, understandably, under severe nervous stress following the shock of her husband's death. After a few seconds their eyes met, although Susan on this occasion only saw her mother's face mistily, for tears were swimming in her eyes. Lady Walton's eyes were not like Susan's, although they were also attractive eyes; they were of a hazel brown hue, nothing like as dark as Susan's, which she always described as "black".

Elizabeth Ardell had the same shade of dark, almost black, hair as her daughter and, like Susan, had it cut fairly short. She had a decidedly youthful look about her too, and in this way again she was like Susan; one might have thought, looking at her face, that she could hardly have been over forty, whereas in point of fact she was forty-nine years old, and looking forward to her fiftieth birthday in August of that year.

Lady Walton looked at her watch, and then rose at once to her feet and held out her arms to Susan, who was now in a half-reclining position in the bed.

"Come on, my dear," she said, "you must make the effort to get up and get dressed. That way, I expect you'll find, will be much better for shrugging off the memory of an unpleasant dream than just sitting there brooding; and I expect you'll find your headache will go too as you get busy. I should think some coffee would help it along, so you hurry along for your breakfast, Sue."

"Yes, it might," said Susan. While Lady Walton had been speaking she had helped Susan to rise from her bed by taking hold of her hands, and gently pulling her up.

"They're waiting for you in the breakfast-room, you know," added Lady Walton.

"Waiting?"

"Jane and Dick didn't want to start their breakfast while you, their hostess, were not there, but I told them they'd better start while I went to find you.

"Oh dear!" sighed Susan weakly, "there'll be those two to make polite conversation to at the breakfast table."

"Of course!" said her mother. "Buck up, Susan, dear; it's nearly nine now." Lady Walton knew how to speak to her daughter with just the right mixture of kindness and firmness.

"All right," said Susan. She was now walking slowly across the room with her mother to collect her dressing gown, which was hanging on a hook behind the door. "Is Father waiting for me too in the breakfast-room?" she asked as she and her mother left the room together. "And Denise?" Denise was Susan's older sister.

"They're up, but they weren't in the breakfast-room when I came up here," said Lady Walton, "but they may be there now."

"I'll be down as soon as I can," said Susan. She headed for the bathroom while her mother descended the stairs to return to the breakfast-room.

About three minutes later Susan, now back in her bedroom, took off her dressing gown and nightdress and began to dress herself. She found that already her headache seemed to be receding, and that she seemed to be waking up properly. I wish Jane and Dick weren't staying here, she thought, as she fastened a brassiere in place over her large breasts. At least, I hope they'll leave after the service. Dick Dalmane was John's brother, Richard, and Jane was his wife. They had arrived at Rhodes Castle the previous evening for the Earl's funeral that day; it was going to be at twelve noon in Rhodes Church.

Essentially the funeral was going to be a private service for the family only, but a few close friends of the late Earl, including some senior servants of the Castle, had also been invited to attend the service in church and the burial. The burial would be in the special plot in the Rhodes Churchyard reserved for the Earls of Saint Helens and the Dalmane family. Virtually all of the Dalmane and most of the Ardell families would be gathered for the Earl's funeral later that day in the little church in the Rhodes Park. Most of these people were due to arrive at the Castle that morning.

Susan, when she had pulled on a dark skirt, looked for a moment out of the window and saw two figures in overcoats walking on the large lawn in the bright early morning sunlight; they were her father, the marquis of Walton, a short figure with dark hair, and her sister, Denise, a tall, slim woman with long red hair. Like Jane and Richard Dalmane, they had arrived by car the previous evening, driven by Lord Walton's chauffeur. Susan also had an older brother, Paul, who had married a Dutch girl, and who now lived and worked in Holland; but they were not coming to the funeral as it was too far to travel for the funeral of one who was not of their own family. And Lady Mary Dalmane, John's mother, would also be present at the funeral, Susan remembered, and at the reception in the Castle afterwards. She was very shy and anti-social, and so was seldom seen in public; but today, of course, she would be there. Yes, there'll be Mary, and Dick, and Jane, and a lot of other relations and friends of John's, thought Susan; and then, of course, they'll all be here to eat a hearty lunch after the burial. How awful! I'm really dreading that!

Suddenly, as she was about to leave her room for the breakfast-room, that worrying dream came back into her mind again; worrying about other things had temporarily put it out of her mind. I wish Jim were here to comfort me, she thought. He knows nothing about poor John having died, of course, and I don't think I'll write to tell him about it. No, better that he should know nothing about it. Only, if he were here now he could be a tower of strength and a great comfort to me.

With that thought she left her room, and closed the door behind her. With a sinking feeling of despondency and apprehension she set out to meet her breakfast guests, and to greet them just as if it were another cheerful, ordinary day. I'm no good at being a widow, she said to herself as she descended the stairs. I need you now, Jim, to comfort me as I've never needed you before.

CHAPTER TWO

It was getting on for eight o'clock on the evening of the second of March (which was a Saturday) as a very cheerful Jim Sandy, having crossed the Jubilee Bridge over the River Cocker, approached the top of the hill at Victoria Road in Cockermouth. In another minute or two he would have completed his walk home from the station at the end of his day's work. Jim lived with his father and his twin sisters, Carol and Victoria, in a house which was one in a row at the end of Lorton Road.

The night was fine but cold, and he was walking up the hill at a good pace, although he was not hurrying. The moon was at first quarter, and was visible in a clear sky over the roofs of the houses to his right, but it was not high, and did not seem to cast any noticeable light, so Jim's way was lit only by the yellow glare of the street lights.

Jim was feeling cheerful because, after he had eaten his supper, he meant to go round to the house where his girlfriend, Jill Rose, lived with her sister, Julia, and their parents. He felt that he could well afford to go out that Saturday night because he did not work on Sundays, and so had a whole day of rest or leisure ahead of him. He had a new job nowadays, working for British Railways as a porter at Cockermouth station. His hours of work from Mondays to Saturdays were necessarily long as he had to report for duty at seven-fifteen in the mornings to be at the station for the early train to Carlisle (the 7.25); and he was not allowed to go home in the evenings until a quarter to eight, after the 7.33 train had left for Carlisle (that was not the last train of the day, for which he was not required to wait).

The job was inclined to be a little boring at times between the infrequent appearances of trains at the station, but Jim was, on the whole, happy to be a porter, at least temporarily. He thought that with a job in his home town of Cockermouth he must be better off than if he were to remain unemployed, even if, as was certainly the case, the work was of a very dull nature.

But that evening as Jim came back to his own front door, and went in, he was thinking not of what he had been doing at the station that day, but of what possibly might lie ahead in a few hours if he should find his girlfriend, Jill, at home. In the hall he took off his coat, scarf, and porter's cap, and hung them up on a hook. That evening the house seemed oddly quiet. "Hello, Dad!" he shouted, and then opened the door of the sitting-room on his left, while at the same moment he heard an answering "Hello!" from inside the sitting-room. His father was sitting on the settee, reading a newspaper.

"Oh, hello, Jim!" said Mr. Sandy, putting down his newspaper. "How's it been at the old station today, then?"

"Much as usual," said Jim. "Nothing particular happened today. It was my turn again to be on duty in the Booking Office between one and two, but as usual no one came to buy a ticket." There were no trains from Cockermouth between the hours of one and two o'clock in the afternoon in those days, so the Booking Clerk was given his lunch break during that hour, while another member of the station staff looked after the Booking Office for him.

"H'm, yes," said Mr. Sandy. "The slack hour in the middle of the day, eh? Well, Jim, supper's ready, if you're ready for it. Carol and Victoria are both out this evening, so there's just the two of us in for supper."

"So that's why the house seems so quiet this evening," said Jim.

"Carol's gone out with one of her boyfriends, has she?" Carol and Victoria, the twins, were aged nineteen, but Carol was the older of the two by some fifteen minutes; she worked in a bookshop, while Victoria had taken a job as an assistant in sweetshop.

"Indeed, yes," said his father, nodding his head. "'One of her boyfriends', you say! She does seem to keep several young men interested in her, doesn't she?"

"But where's Vicci?" asked Jim.

"Jazz Club," said his father. She'll be back about ten, she said." Jim remembered that on the first Saturday evening of each month Victoria went along to the local Jazz Club, where she played the saxophone.

"I'd like to go out to see Jill after supper tonight, Dad, if I may," he said as he followed his father into the kitchen. "If she's at home, of course, as I expect she will be. So I might be back here rather late; perhaps midnight or later if you don't mind, Dad."

"Not a bit, Jim," said Mr. Sandy kindly. "No, you go out and enjoy yourself for as long as you like. You've no work tomorrow, so I'm sure you could afford a late night, if you want one. And look here, Jim, if you do meet Jill tonight, why not ask her to come round here for supper sometime?"

"I say, Dad, could I really do that?"

"Of course you could! We'd be delighted to entertain her here one evening, wouldn't we?"

"Which day should I ask her to come for?"

"Oh, almost any day would be all right. But, let me see: perhaps Wednesday evening of next week would be best. Ask her if she'd like to come to supper with us on Wednesday. I should think we'd have both your sisters in too that evening, so it would be more of a party."

"All right!" said Jim happily. "Yes, I'll do that."

Mr. Sandy had been taking food out of the oven while they had been talking, and about half a minute later he and Jim were seated at the kitchen table, beginning their evening meal. Jim was thinking that it was odd that he had not before that evening thought seriously of asking his girlfriend to a meal at home, but then he thought that he had not liked to ask her because he did not yet really know her.

He had, in fact, only met Jill for the first time some three weeks earlier, and so far had only been round to see her at her home twice.

Somewhat less than an hour later Jim was on his way to Mr. Rose's house on his bicycle. Luckily he had not far to ride; the Roses lived only about a mile away in a big house in the country to the east of Cockermouth. Jim, well wrapped up against the cold night air in plenty of clothes, and with a scarf around his neck to keep out the wind, was feeling very happy as he pedalled off up the first stretch of Lorton Road from his home towards the railway bridge; then he would turn left onto Strawberry How Road just past the cemetery.

The bicycle he was riding was one which Susan Dalmane had given him at Rhodes Castle on his birthday nearly two years ago. It was a fine, light machine to which Jim had added lights so that he could ride it at night. For a moment, as he was setting off, he was reminded of Susan, who had given it to him against her husband's wishes. But he thought about Susan only very infrequently nowadays, and when he did think about her it was with only a shadow of the infatuation he had felt while he had been living at Rhodes Castle. This evening, predictably, as Jill was very much in his thoughts while he was riding to see her, the memory of Susan soon slipped away from his mind, leaving his feelings almost unmoved. For a long time he and Susan had kept in touch with each other by frequent writing of letters to exchange news, but this winter, as if by some mutual agreement, their correspondence had become less and less frequent until a day had come when Jim had not been very much surprised to receive a letter suggesting that the time had come for their regular correspondence to cease. By a strange chance that letter had come just after the day when he had first met Jill; and since that day he had not written again to Susan.

★

It had been on the day of the interview for the porter's job at Cockermouth that Jim had first met Jill. He had travelled to Carlisle to talk to the Area Manager, and for this journey, as it was on British Railways business, Jim had been issued with a free pass to travel by train that day between Cockermouth and Carlisle. The interview over, Jim had returned to the platforms from the Manager's Office in Carlisle station to wait for the next train to Cockermouth, which was the 5.42p.m. But as it was only five minutes past five he decided that he would first visit the Refreshment Room on Platform 3, and have some tea and a snack to pass the time.

At half past five Jim went along to Platform 5 to get into his train. He found it waiting there at the platform, but at the first glance, even before he boarded it, he saw that the two-car diesel multiple-unit already looked crowded with passengers. He entered the forward car, and looked around for an empty seat; he looked all round the carriage but could see no empty seats anywhere except right up in the front section, which in this train was marked as a First Class seating area. Bother it, he thought, if only I hadn't stayed so long in the tea room I could probably have got myself a seat. But now there's only the First Class section with some spare seats . . . and I can't sit there, of course. But then another thought suddenly struck him. On this journey he was, for once, not the holder of a second class ticket, but of a free pass. He looked again at those First Class seats up at the front.

Well, why not? He thought. Why should I have to remain standing when those seats are probably going to be wasted with no one to sit in them? And with that thought he went boldly into the First Class seating area.

Even up there at the front there were a fair number of passengers sitting down, but Jim saw that the seats in his favourite position, the right-hand side at the extreme front of the carriage, were vacant. He thought vaguely that a man sitting with his wife on the opposite seat, an elderly gentleman with grey hair, looked somewhat familiar to him, but he was really only thinking of sitting down in the seat with the best forward view in the whole train, and he quickly did so.

"Hello, Jim! First-Class passenger today, eh?" said a voice close to him. It was the grey-haired elderly gentleman who had spoken, and Jim saw that after all he was an acquaintance.

"Oh, hello, Mr. Ruddock," he said. "I haven't seen you travelling as a passenger before on one of these trains. You were driving the train the last time I met you." He saw that Margaret Ruddock was looking at him, a rather quiet, shy woman. "Hello, Mrs. Ruddock," he added.

Mr. Ruddock looked backwards for a second or two, as if he were trying to see whether there were still any vacant seats in the crowded second-class area. "Aye, but I've retired now," he said, turning back to Jim. Last summer I retired, having completed my fifty years on the railways."

That's a jolly good record to achieve!" said Jim.

"Aye, I've had a grand life, working on the railways," said Mr. Ruddock. "But today the 5.42 is pretty full, isn't it? No second-class seats left in there?"

"I don't believe there are," said Jim doubtfully, wondering whether the old driver was going to advise him to leave his First-Class seat.

"Well, I dare say you'll be all right, Jim, to stay where you are. I shouldn't think Tim will want to order you out of that seat."

"Tim? Is Tim Blencow the Guard on this train?" asked Jim.

"Aye, he is. I've seen him in his compartment in the rear carriage when we came along here. But you see, Jim, it's all right for me and Margaret to sit up here on account of me being an old employee of British Railways."

Jim remembered again that he had that free pass in his pocket.

"Yes, of course. And today I reckon it's all right for me to sit here in the First Class as there's nowhere else to sit."

"How do you reckon that, Jim?"

"I've got a free pass to travel by train today!" said Jim happily.

"You see, I've just been for an interview at the Manager's office here for a job they advertised at Cockermouth station."

"The porter's job?"

"Yes. Apparently there've been very few applicants for it."

"Good for you, Jim!" said Mr. Ruddock. I've heard you were living back at home in Cockermouth again. But I certainly hope you get the job, my lad. You'd make a good porter, I reckon, to start off with.

And what do you hope to progress too presently? Does the idea of driving appeal to you? Or would you rather see yourself as a guard? Or a signal-man? Or station-master, maybe?"

Jim had not the heart to let the old railway man know that he was not thinking of starting a life's career on the railways, but that he was only thinking in terms of some temporary employment which might last, perhaps, for a year or two until something better turned up. He thought for a moment, and then answered.

"Well, yes, I realise that it would be very dull to remain just a porter for long. But I'm not sure whether I'll look for promotion to a better railway job, or not. I think I might well go into signaling if a job in a signal-box comes vacant soon."

"It's fascinating work, the job of a signal-man, Jim. Of course, first you'd have to learn the work thoroughly as an apprentice, and it would take quite some time before you'd be put in charge of a box a rural signal-box somewhere, maybe. I was in charge of Plumpton Head signal-box that's on the main line between Penrith and Carlisle for the four years while the first Great War was on - the 1914-18 War -but that's going back a bit!"

"Yes, isn't it!" agreed Jim. "Hello, here comes our driver." The driver of the 5.42 for that February evening, carrying a little black bag in his hand, was coming up the platform towards the cab. He climbed into his cab, shut his door, and then, turning round for a moment, recognized Mr. Ruddock.

"Hello there, Tom," said the driver, half opening the door through into the carriage.

"Hello, Bill," said Mr. Ruddock. "We're just going through to Cockermouth, Margaret and I, to see our grand-daughter."

"Oh yes," said the driver. Well, come through into the cab presently if you'd care for a crack with me while we're going along."

He shut the door and sat down in the driving seat.

While Jim had been talking with Mr. Ruddock passengers had still been boarding the train. It seemed as if some of the new arrivals, seeing Jim sitting in a first-class seat, but not looking at all like a first-class passenger, had decided to follow his example rather than have to remain standing for the journey. By the time when, a few minutes after the driver had boarded his train, Mr. Blencow, the guard, gave the signal on the buzzer to start, there were no empty first-class seats left except the one immediately beside Jim. The heavily loaded train rumbled noisily out past the green light of the starting signal, and set off on its run to Penrith, the first stop.

★

It was twenty minutes later when the train drew into one of the platforms of Penrith station. Jim saw people waiting on the platform to board the train, but here there was no great crowd; he thought that there were no more than about a dozen folk waiting. As the train stopped Jim saw that a pretty, fair-haired girl happened to be standing close to the door nearest to where his seat was, but he also noticed that she was the only person close to that door; the other new passengers were going to enter the train further back. He saw the fair-haired girl open the door, put a foot on the mounting step, and enter the train. Then he saw that the girl was quickly looking around in all directions, trying to see an empty seat in that crowded train. She looked as if she might be about twenty years old or roughly the same age as Susan Dalmane. In fact, Jim immediately recognized this girl as someone he knew by sight, although he knew nothing else about her.

She probably lived either in or near Cockermouth, he thought, as he had occasionally noticed her walking along a pavement in the town, perhaps doing some shopping. He had noted her mentally as an attractive-looking girl, although, because of his love for Susan Dalmane, he had never felt any real attraction towards her.

This time, however, was quite different. He felt an instant interest in that girl, and his eyes watched her carefully for the few seconds while she stood by the partition where the first-class seats began, and looked around for a seat. She was wearing a short overcoat, and had a colourful scarf loosely draped round her neck, while below the overcoat pale coloured trousers were visible. Jim saw her take off her scarf and unbutton her coat as she looked around, and these actions reminded him how hot the inside of that train felt with the heating fully turned on, although it was a cold day of early February; but he had already removed his own coat and scarf.

Jim was longing to offer that girl the empty seat right beside his own, but somehow, most maddeningly, he felt suddenly quite overwhelmed by a ridiculous shyness, and could not make himself either speak to the stranger, or even stand up for her. But before he knew what was happening she was coming up to him; she had seen that empty seat for herself.

"Is that anybody's seat?" she asked, looking at it.

"No, it's free, if you'd like to sit here," said Jim, feeling that he was probably blushing slightly, but hoping that no agitation showed on his face.

"Thank you," said the girl. Do you mind if I take off my coat? It's very hot in here as usual."

"Do, please feel free to take it off," said Jim. "It is very warm in here; positively stuffy in fact." He stood up to be ready to assist the girl to place her coat and scarf on the luggage rack; she was carrying no baggage with her.

The girl quickly slipped off her coat, and Jim almost gasped with pleasure at the sight which met his eyes. Gosh, what a beauty! He said to himself. A white pullover had been revealed to view by the removing of the overcoat, a pullover which, as Jim instantly noticed, fitted the girl's slim figure very tightly. He noticed too that the white pullover together with the off-white trousers made up a striking outfit which, he thought, looked very smart indeed on this slight, slim, fair-haired girl. For a second or two his gaze, after taking in her trousers, became focused a little higher up where he saw the outlines of an attractively shaped bust. She's gorgeous! He said to himself. Aloud he said politely: "May I put your things on the rack for you?"

"Thanks!" said the girl, handing him her coat and scarf, while Jim took them, and then reached up for the luggage rack. The next moment, as he turned round before sitting down again, he saw that the girl had already sat herself down beside him; then, as he sat down, their eyes met for a fleeting moment. Jim saw lovely blue eyes under well-formed eyebrows; altogether, he thought, the face of a girl who was shy and took a serious view of life.

She was small too; much later, when he had had time to think about her appearance, he came to reckon that she was probably no taller than around five feet.

"It's very crowded in this train today, isn't it?" said the girl, with a quick look into Jim's face; but Jim at that moment shifted his gaze slightly away from her face.

"It certainly is," he agreed. "That's why" He broke off suddenly. He had been about to say: "That's why I came up here to sit in the first-class"; and, of course, the last thing that he wanted just then was that anything should make that girl get up and look for another seat.

He saw that she was looking at him with a look which clearly meant: "Yes, do go on. What were you going to say?" But she remained silent.

"That's why I'm sitting in the first-class," he finished lamely.

There was no need to say anything to her about his free pass; in any case he was not at all sure that he was entitled because of it to sit where he was. He glanced across to the other front seat, and saw that Mr. Ruddock was smiling at him almost mischievously. The next moment they heard the sound of the buzzer, and saw the driver push the brake lever into the "off" position and move his gear-selector lever; they were off again, moving out from the dim lights under the platform roof into the darkness of the February evening outside.

At first, however, there was enough light from street lamps and other lights round about for Jim and his new companion, looking forwards through the right-hand side of the driver's windscreen, to be able to see the rails and various points of red and green light which were the signals. The rails appeared, wherever light fell on them, as black lines on a white ground, for hereabouts, as Jim had noticed on his outward journey in the daylight, there was a good thick covering of snow on the ground, perhaps some three inches of it, he thought.

He was trying hard to think of something to say.

"There'd be a jolly good from here, at the front, if it was day-time, with all this snow lying about," he said as the train moved off into the darkness on its branch line to Keswick and Cockermouth.

"There is," said the girl. "I saw it coming here this morning, you know but not from this front seat."

"Are you travelling far on this train?"

"To Cockermouth."

"You live there, do you?" Jim was feeling a little surprised at his increasing boldness in questioning the girl.

"Yes at least, we live near Cockermouth. And I think you must live there too? I've seen you quite often before now."

"That's right," said Jim. "I live in Cockermouth in Lorton Road, actually."

There was a pause in the conversation for a few minutes. Jim felt a little disappointed that the girl had not revealed her address, but had only said, very vaguely, that she lived "near Cockermouth". He would have liked also to have asked her what her name was. But perhaps she'll tell me that later, he thought, if we manage to get a proper conversation started. Bother it, I wish I could think of something else to say to her.

At that time, however, Jim could think of no other opening conversational gambits, and anyway his thoughts were distracted a moment later when Mr. Ruddock got up, winked at him, and said: "I'm just going through to have a word with Bill."..With that Mr. Ruddock went through into the driver's cab and closed the door behind him. They saw him sit down in the guard's seat immediately in front of their front seat, on the other side of the glass. Jim remembered how Susan Dalmane had once sat in that special seat while Mr. Ruddock had been driving, and the trouble that had come to him when an inspector had caught him breaking the regulations in that way. It had happened on the day when he had first met Susan, when she had happened to be travelling by train with him; but he soon forgot about Susan again. With a slim and pretty blonde girl sitting right beside him it was little wonder that he could not for longer than about a minute think about his former love, Susan, the Countess of Saint Helens.

After the train had started from Carlisle Jim had been thinking mostly about the interview he had just attended, and he had been weighing up in his mind, quite optimistically, his chaces of success.

As the train now began the journey along the branch line through the snowy northern part of the Lake District, heading for Keswick and Cockermouth, Jim's mind was still turning from time to time to the interview and his chances of getting the porter's job; but mostly he was thinking about his new companion, as he wondered who she was, and why she happened to be travelling at that time between Penrith and Cockermouth. The nearness of such an attractive girl excited him considerably, but he was being careful to see that he did not reveal this excitement in any way.

There was little conversation for most of the way to Cockermouth between Jim and the girl in the white pullover and pale trousers. He had been afraid that he might lose her company at Keswick, where quite a number of passengers had left the train, but she had not moved, even though after Keswick there were some empty seats in the first-class end of the leading carriage. Then Jim thought that he would try talking about the weather; he knew it was often a good way of opening a conversation with a stranger.

"I think there might be some more snow tonight," he said.

"Yes," said the girl, "there might be."

"They've got more at Penrith and Keswick than we have at Cockermouth, but there's hardly any at Carlisle, I noticed."

"Carlisle?" said the girl. "Is that where you've come from today?"

"Yes, I was there this afternoon."

"Do you work there?"

"No; but I'm just on my way back home after an interview for a job in Carlisle a job working for British Railways, actually."

"I work in Penrith for British Railways," said the girl. "I'm in the station-master's office, where I do the secretarial work typing letters, and so on. But what about you? What job at Cockermouth have you applied for?"

"Porter; but perhaps I'll be promoted to work in the signal-box presently, if I decide to stay and if I get the porter's job, of course. I'm quite optimistic about that, though."

"Are you? What's your name, by the way? Mine's Jill: Jill Rose."

"And I'm Jim Sandy."

"I say, weren't you once in the police at Cockermouth?" Jill was looking at him keenly, almost as if she had suddenly recognized him as an old acquaintance.

"Yes, I was, but that was quite a few years ago. I was a cadet. But then I left the police; that was back in 1959 because I found a much better job down in the south, in Dorset."

Then, of course, Jill wanted to know what that better job down in Dorset was, and Jim immediately felt that the conversation had taken an awkward turn. He would have to be very wary in what he told her concerning Rhodes Castle, and particularly about how he came to leave his position there as Guide; he would certainly not tell her that he had been dismissed, in effect, in disgrace.

So he only told Jill, in answer to her question: "When did you leave Rhodes Castle?" that he had returned to Cockermouth in April of the previous year, because he had become homesick for the North after residing for so long in Dorset as the Guide of Rhodes Castle, working for the Earl and the Countess; he did not even tell Jill their names, merely saying that he had worked for Lord and Lady

Dalmane. Jill seemed satisfied with his sketchy answer, and asked him nothing more about Rhodes Castle or the Dalmanes, instead moving onto a different topic for talk: the last occasion she had noticed him in Cockermouth, which, she said, had been on a dark, wet day shortly before Christmas.

Mr. Ruddock did not leave the cab until they came to Cockermouth, but when the train was already slowing down as it crossed the bridge over the river, immediately before arriving at the station, he opened the door into the carriage, and came back to help his wife out of her seat. Jim and Jill had just left their seats, and had gone to the nearest door on the left-hand side to be ready to step down onto the platform. The train stopped, and they got out, and some others immediately behind them also disembarked through that door, and the Ruddocks behind them. Mr. and Mrs. Ruddock did not immediately make for the exit via the subway; instead they waited a minute or two to wave to Bill, the driver, as he took his train out of the station on its way down to Workington. By that time Jim and Jill had passed through the subway, climbed the steps at the other end, and handed over their free passes to the station-master, who was waiting at the top of the steps.

Jill seemed to be in a hurry to get out to the yard, as if she expected to see someone there to meet her, but she did not object to having Jim walking beside her.

Just outside the entrance to the station Jim saw two people who were apparently waiting to meet someone off the train; they were a man, perhaps in his forties, and a girl, both with brown hair and blue eyes.

He discovered later that the girl's name was June Stannley, and that she was eighteen, but he immediately guessed that this was the grand-daughter whom Mr. Ruddock was expecting to meet, together with her father, Mr. Ruddock's daughter's husband. At the same moment, however, Jill spotted her father sitting in his car, waiting for her in the station yard. Mr. Rose waved a hand through the window towards his daughter. Jill quickly turned to Jim.

"Why not come and see me at home sometime, Jim?" she said. "I'm usually at home in the evenings, or else you could come at any time on Sundays. We live at Westray Hall, if you know where that is."

"Oh yes," said Jim eagerly. "I know. Quite near Westray Farm, off the Strawberry Howe road to Embleton, on the left."

"That's it. Well, good-bye for now, Jim."

"Good-bye, Jill, and thank you very much. I'll come to Westray Hall sometime soon."

So that's where she lives, thought Jim as he watched Jill climb into the front passenger seat, and saw the car being driven off into the street. He did not hear or notice the meeting which was taking place behind him of the old Ruddocks and their grand-daughter, June, and her father, Mr. Stannley. I must go to Westray Hall this Sunday, said Jim to himself, unless the roads are too snowy for cycling; and they won't be if there's no more snow. There's really none left on the roads around here now.

★

So had started a friendship between Jim and Jill. The interview at Carlisle had been on a Monday, and on the Wednesday morning of that week Jim received a letter from the Area Manager, confirming that the porter's job was his. The following Monday he started work at the railway station, having spent some very happy hours on the Sunday afternoon talking with Jill at Westray Hall, where he had also met the rest of her family: her sister, Julia, and Mr. and Mrs. Rose. Julia Rose was a little older than Jill, and had dark hair; she also was small and pretty, but Jim did not at first see much resemblance between the two sisters. Anyway, on that Saturday night when he set off again for Westray Hall to give Jill his father's invitation to come to the house in Lorton Road, Jim was thinking only of Jill, and very much wanting to be with her. He thought that he was in love with her, but did not realize that his infatuation was only skin-deep. It seemed as if the fire of his great love for Susan Dalmane had gone out; but that fire was, in truth, not extinguished, but merely subdued. It was like a fire of glowing embers which was only awaiting a draught to make the flames of passion spring again into joyful life.

CHAPTER THREE

One thing which Susan had not expected to happen during the funeral service of her husband, John, was that anything should remind her of her cancelled Hebridean cruise, but she was nevertheless reminded of it for a moment during the Vicar's address

"Will ye be seated, please," said the Vicar in his soft Scottish accent, stepping out from his stall as he prepared to address the congregation from the chancel step, with the Earl's coffin immediately behind him.

Susan sat down without any conscious thought of what she was doing, but as suddenly as if her legs had given way beneath her. The last full chord of the organ had just ended, and the last lines of the hymn, "The Lord's my Shepherd," were still sounding in her head, although she had not tried to join in the singing of it. She had been standing there almost unaware of what others round about her were singing, while she remained sunk in her own sad thoughts. For a second she turned her head to the right, and saw that her sister, Denise, was looking keenly around, and obviously enjoying herself; she was not sitting next to Susan, but was between Lord and Lady Walton, while Susan herself was sitting on her mother's left in the outermost position in the front pew, next to the carpeted nave.

"What a pity we couldn't have had the Bishop instead of this chap drawling on in his Scottish accent!"

Susan heard her mother's loud whisper to her father, but felt that she could not in the least care that it was only the Vicar who was beginning to preach, and not the Bishop.

She did not turn her head again, and so did not see her father nod his head thoughtfully by way of a reply. The Suffragan Bishop of the diocese had been a close friend of Lord Dalmane, and so had been asked, at very short notice, to preach at his funeral; but he had not been able, because of other commitments, to attend the service, and so the address, naturally enough, became the Vicar's responsibility together with the rest of the service.

If it had been someone else's funeral, and she had not been the widow at the centre of it, Susan might well have noticed the way in which Denise kept looking at the Vicar with great interest. As it was, she noticed nothing of this. But the Vicar was, by all accounts, an exceptionally handsome man; and so, although Denise was a married woman who had two children, it was perhaps not surprising that she kept looking at him so keenly (she had left her two young children at home with their nanny). David MacHassock, the Vicar of Leigh-with-Rhodes, was a tall man in his mid-forties, who had curly brown hair and a full brown beard and moustache. He looked even more imposing when he was wearing his clerical robes than he did when he was wearing an ordinary suit. That day he was immaculately dressed in a clean white surplice, over which he wore an equally clean black stole. His soft Scottish accent seemed to complement perfectly his rugged, masculine appearance; but Susan had grown so used to hearing his accent that it now meant nothing to her at all. Mr. MacHassock had been born and brought up in Glasgow, where he had also started his ministry in the Church. After remaining in the city for some years as the minister of a Church of Scotland church in the city centre he had moved with his wife and family to a remote rural parish in the Highlands.

Then in 1957 he had moved again, this time deciding to leave Scotland altogether to go south to Dorset, having read of the vacancy for an incumbent in the Dalmanes' parish of Leigh (in which Rhodes

Church was situated). Now he had been the Vicar at Rhodes Church for nearly six years, and apparently he was quite content to remain there Susan had gathered as much only that morning when he had been talking with her in the Castle

I must try to listen, she said to herself. But she had already missed a sentence or two of what the Vicar was saying.

"This sad occasion today reminds me of another occasion when I was Minister of the wee Kirk at Ullapool, in north-western Scotland," she heard the Vicar saying. "It was my privilege while I was there to conduct the funeral of the local Clan Chief . . ."

"What's all this got to do with John?" Susan heard her mother mutter savagely under her breath.

She missed most of what followed next in the Vicar's brief account of the funeral of the Clan Chief, but managed nevertheless to gather the general drift of what he was saying. The whole Clan had gathered around their Chief's graveside for the burial, the Vicar said, very much like a family gathering for a much loved father. Susan realized that the Vicar was comparing this gathering of a Scottish Clan for the laying to rest of their Chief to her husband's own funeral. He was saying that it was as if Lord Dalmane were the father of everyone present in Rhodes Church that day, and that they were all his children, come to mourn him.

For a brief moment Susan had been reminded by the mention of Ullapool, the little port on the coast of Wester Ross, of the cruise she and John had planned to make in the <u>Osprey</u>. Ullapool was a place which they might well have visited. They would have been very happy cruising in the Hebrides, or along the coast of north-west Scotland, but now she was painfully reminded that John would never again make such a trip, or go sailing anywhere on board the yacht, <u>Osprey</u>, which was now her yacht. Bother it, she thought, why must I be reminded of these things now, when I only want to forget them? But on the instant another idea flew into her mind; and quietly and easily it pushed aside the first unwanted thought, only to replace it by a much more harrowing idea.

"All his children." He said all of us here might be John's children, his family, she thought. He said he was like a father to all of us here in church, and I dare say he is . . . was . . . but, of course, really we had no children. That's the saddest thing of all; I've no child by him, no heir, no son or daughter. And we tried so hard to conceive a child until John became too weak and ill to make love to me, but it was no good because the doctor said that John was infertile. I suppose meant that I could never bear his child, never give him a son. . . or daughter. Oh dear, oh dear! If only we'd had an infant son perhaps he would have grown up like John; but, in any case, for me John would have lived on, in a way, in his child, whether it was a boy or a girl.

Part of his life would have passed on into his child so that, although he's dead, he wouldn't really be gone . . . What's that the Vicar's saying? Oh yes, I know there may be a Resurrection, but John's still gone from <u>me</u>, hasn't he?

She had heard very little of the sermon so far, but she had caught a few snatches of it, and now a few more sentences came to her ears.

"John was a man of faith: of that, my friends, I am convinced. He knew his New Testament well, and he endeavoured to lead a Christian life according to the way of faith set out in those pages. I was talking with him a few days before he died we were having a very frank talk about spiritual things and he shared with me some of his thoughts about death. And what he said, my friends, is that in death we come to a change, not an end. A change, and not an end. Then he quoted those lovely lines which we heard read in our Lesson, from Saint Paul's First Letter to the Corinthians: 'For the trumpet shall sound, and the dead shall be raised incorruptible, and we shall be changed'."

"We shall be changed," thought Susan. I wonder if John <u>really</u> believed that believed that that's what'll happen after death? I dare say he probably did, though. And things are changed for me too, now that he's gone.

Susan did not realize that she was slipping back into the dark pool of her sombre thoughts, and that she scarcely listening any more to the Vicar's words. How shall I manage without him? She thought.

Now Susan heard absolutely nothing of the Vicar's sermon; nor was she aware of the bright sunshine which was streaming in through the windows. She did not see how the sun was lighting up the colours in the little stained-glass window to the right and a little in front of their pew, behind the organist's bench, where Tracy Symon, the organist, was sitting and listening carefully to the sermon. Tracy was a serious-looking student of music, who lived in the nearby village of Yetminster; at twenty-five years old she had recently completed a course in composition at the Guildhall School of Music in London. She had long blonde hair (paler than that of Jim's new friend, Jill) and, unusually for a blonde, she had yellowy-brown eyes. But Susan had hardly looked at her since she had walked slowly into the church behind her husband's coffin.

Susan's thoughts had become concentrated into a kind of mental groove as she bemoaned in her mind the fact that she had no child by John, but suddenly another thought unexpectedly entered her mind. This new thought was horribly inappropriate at her husband's funeral, but Susan did not see it that way. She simply thought suddenly: If Jim were to marry me then, surely, I could have children. <u>He</u> could be the father of my children, and now that I'm a widow, what is there to prevent us from getting married . . . sometime? But perhaps it's sinful of me to think such a thing when poor John's just going to be buried . . . I don't know . . . but in my dream last night Jim was making love to me. Of course, he could become my husband if we can meet again sometime next year, perhaps, or later.

The end of the short sermon took Susan by surprise the Vicar had only spoken for about ten minutes, as he had promised that he would at the beginning of his address. Susan saw that people around her were rising to their feet. She stood up herself.

"And now, before our prayers, we'll sing the second hymn on your service-sheets," announced the Vicar. "'Let Saints on earth in concert sing with those whose work is done'."

Tracy Symon began to play over the fine old Scottish hymn tune, "Dundee", a smile of satisfaction on her face at the pleasant music she was producing on the organ. It was a small pipe-organ, electrically blown, and played from a console which stood separately from the organ itself; wires ran under the floor to connect the console, on the right, with the organ on the left-hand side of the chancel.

Susan looked up for a moment, and saw the smile on Tracy's face. All very well for her to smile, she thought in a rare moment of bitterness. She isn't mourning anyone. This is just another job to her . . . But Susan forgot her thought a moment later as the congregation lifted up their voices, and began to sing the hymn.

★

They were standing at the graveside, the Vicar having lead the procession out of the church, and along the path through the churchyard to that special plot, enclosed within a brass fence, wherein the former Earls of Saint Helens lay buried.

Susan had held back her tears with difficulty as she had stumbled along, her mother's arm holding her's, beside the four undertakers who had wheeled the bier to the graveside. At the appropriate moment the coffin was lowered in slings into the hole in the ground prepared for it.

"We therefore commit his body to the ground; earth to earth, ashes to ashes, dust to dust; insure and certain hope . . ." The Vicar was reading the words of the Committal in a strong, steady voice. The Chief Undertaker threw a handful of loose earth over the coffin.

Susan now wept openly. Oh, John . . . John, my darling! was all the thought in her head as she looked down, standing there in the bright sunlight of that cold spring day to take her last farewell to her young husband, John, the tenth Earl of Saint Helens. But it was all too much for her. Weakly she dabbed at the tears in her eyes and on her cheeks with her handkerchief. However, she was not the only one there who was weeping. Close to her stood Lady Mary Dalmane, John's mother, who was also applying a handkerchief to her face as she watched her son being buried; but Susan did not even know that Mary was there.

"Come, my dear," said a quiet voice, and at the same moment Susan felt a gentle pressure on her arm. Her mother knew that she was unable to tear herself away from the grave.

The funeral and the burial were over. Now the Chief Undertaker walked with Susan and her mother as they made their slow way back to the waiting cars, while Denise and her father, Lord Walton, walked immediately behind them.

The undertaker offered Susan a supporting arm as a respectful gesture of comfort, while she made an effort to control her emotions, and to stop crying. But she hardly heard the single bell which was tolling mournfully through the bright, crisp air for the departure of Lord Dalmane. The day was so beautiful that it was as if the brightness made an incongruous setting for such a solemn occasion, but that idea did not occur to Susan.

★

A few days later Susan was talking with Samantha one morning in the Green Drawing Room of Rhodes Castle. Susan had spoken first of her husband's funeral.

"Did it upset you all the more that it was such a fine day?" enquired Samantha, sitting beside her on the sofa for a few minutes' break. Both women were drinking mid-morning cups of coffee.

"No. Why should it upset me?" said Susan.

"Oh, I just thought, with all that lovely sun we had last Wednesday at the funeral I thought perhaps it had upset you that it wasn't cloudy and dark you know, to . . . to match your mood." Trying to find the right words, Samantha had finished her sentence clumsily.

"Oh no," said Susan, "I didn't feel that at the time. I just thought how much John would have liked it like that all bright and sunny. I expect it pleased him . . . wherever he is now."

"I expect so." agreed Samantha.

CHAPTER FOUR

When Jim came home on the next Wednesday evening after his night-time cycle ride to Westray Hall he found that two surprises were in store for him. The first of these was in the form of an unexpected visitor at the house in Lorton Road.

Jim came in thinking about Jill Rose; it was that evening that she was invited to come to supper at the Sandys'. Jim was looking forward to a very pleasant evening chatting with Jill, but at the same time he was a little apprehensive about how things might turn out. He had now visited Jill at Westray Hall three times, but this was to be her first visit to the house in Lorton Road; and because it was the first time Jim could not quite dispel a certain nervousness.

He closed the front door behind him, hung up his porter's cap on the peg in the hall, advanced a pace or two, and then stopped abruptly.

Jackie Rothwell, his father's attractive young secretary, who worked with him at the mine, suddenly appeared out of the kitchen, followed a second later by Mr. Sandy himself.

"Hello, Jim!" said Jackie Rothwell cheerfully.

"Hello, Jim," said his father. I think you know Jackie Rothwell, don't you?" This he said jokingly, with a hint of laughter in his voice, knowing that Jim knew perfectly well who Jackie Rothwell was, having met her before on various occasions.

Jim was considerably taken aback by the unexpected appearance of Jackie.

"Oh, hello," he said awkwardly. "I had no idea –I mean, I didn't know you'd be here, Jackie."

"But I am!" said Jackie, smiling at him mischievously, holding out a hand as she spoke. They shook hands.

Jim felt that the surprise of meeting Jackie Rothwell when he had least expected to see her had given him a severe emotional jolt. Every time he met her he was staggered anew by her beauty, and this time was no exception. That he had, until that moment, been thinking about Jill Rose did not in any way diminish this reaction; if anything, it increased it. However, his surprise had left him temporarily speechless. Jackie was certainly very pretty, with curly brown hair and sparkling brown eyes. Jim knew that his father was in love with her, and that he and Jackie were even thinking in terms of getting married.

First, however, divorce proceedings between Mr. Sandy and Jim's mother (who lived in London) would have to be completed; but Jim knew that Jackie often appeared at his father's house in the evenings nowadays, although somehow it had never entered his mind that he might meet her this evening.

"Let's go through into the kitchen," said Mr. Sandy. Jill hasn't arrived yet, Jim, but then supper isn't quite ready; and anyway, we asked her for eight o'clock, and it's only five to eight now, so she could be here at any minute."

"Are Carol and Vicci out?" asked Jim, as he followed Jackie and his father into the kitchen. He was still feeling a little dazed by the pleasant shock of meeting his father's secretary, and his eyes were following the back of her head closely; but he had expected to see his sisters when he came in.

"They are out," said his father, "but they <u>ought</u> really to be back here by now. They promised me they'd be in before eight, so . . . we'll see if they make it!" He looked at his watch.

"But where are they?" asked Jim.

"Only next door but one. Called in on their friends there."

"Oh, I see." Jim was not really interested in the whereabouts of his sisters, the Twins, but he wondered who would come in first through the front door. Would it be the Twins, or would Jill arrive first?

"Now then, if you two would like to sit down, I'll just put the finishing touches to our supper," said Mr. Sandy. "No, I don't need any help at the moment, I promise you." Jackie sat down in an armchair in the corner of the room. Mr. Sandy moved a wooden chair so that Jim could sit beside her. "That's right, Jim, you sit down there and keep Jackie entertained until Jill arrives."

As Jim sat down he was looking at Jackie, and for a moment their eyes met. Jackie had big, greeny-blue eyes and attractive eyebrows. She was rather short, and had a large bust; her shape always pleased Jim greatly, as it did this evening. She was wearing an outfit which he had seen her in before, and which he thought looked very becoming on her: a navy-blue, V-necked jersey, and a matching navy-blue skirt.

There was an awkward silence for a few seconds while Jim was desperately trying to think of something to say which would start a conversation. He glanced at his father, but he had his back to them, and was busy with something in the oven; there was no help there.

But Jackie seemed to be perfectly at her ease sitting in a very relaxed position in the armchair, and, after she had met Jim's look, she seemed to be staring at a picture on the wall opposite her. Gosh, thought Jim, what can I say to her? If only the Twins would come in, that would make a diversion, and then conversation would be easier with several of us here. Or if Jill would arrive now it would be easier.

But the seconds passed, and no one arrived, and there was no ring on the doorbell.

"How are things getting on at the mine?" he asked suddenly, remembering that his father's mine was a subject for conversation on which he could always fall back when he was with Jackie. The Leadthwaite Mine was an old lead mine in the fells near Keswick, but nowadays it only produced barytes (barite). Mr. Sandy was the Manager, and was in charge of a small workforce.

"Oh, not badly," said Jackie. "Your father and I have been doing a bit of prospecting recently."

"For barite?"

"No, for lead and zinc. Our early results seem very encouraging: it seems as if there could be a lot more ore, of zinc particularly, than we thought possible in our first estimates so we could soon be mining sphalerite as well as barite."

"How exciting!" said Jim. "When?" He broke off suddenly. His father, perhaps hearing steps approaching the front door, had just left the kitchen and gone out into the hall.

At that moment the front door opened with a crash and two girls, both rather breathless, rushed into the house.

"Sorry we're late!" panted Carol.

"If we are late," added Victoria. She closed the front door behind her.

Mr. Sandy looked again at his watch.

"My word!" he said. "You've made it with just half a minute to spare! You promised you'd be back by eight remember?"

"Yes, Dad. Sorry we've cut it so fine," said Victoria.

Carol looked at her watch. "I make it right on eight o'clock now," she said. "You see, Dad, we got talking, and we didn't notice how the time was passing. Has Jill arrived yet?"

"Not yet," said Mr. Sandy. "But I have another guest here, as we're having a bit of a party tonight."

"Someone else here?" said Victoria.

"Come into the kitchen and be introduced." Mr. Sandy was already walking back to his kitchen. He had left the door open, and inside the kitchen Jackie and Jim were watching the arrival of the Twins. "You've both met Jackie Rothwell before . . ."

Jackie stood up for a moment as the Twins, one after the other, shook her hand. Carol and Victoria were not identical twins, and, although they were rather alike, one could easily distinguish between them. Both girls had honey-blonde hair with a hint of red in it, but Victoria had her's cut short, while Carol had left her's long, so that it hung untidily over her shoulders. Both girls had hazel-brown eyes, and both had good figures, but their faces, although broadly alike in the main features, were quite recognizably different in the more subtle details.

If Jim had been asked what he thought of his sisters he would probably have replied that he thought they looked very ordinary, or perhaps even very dull; and they were, perhaps, all things considered, a very average-looking pair of nineteen-year old sisters.

Having shaken hands with Jackie, and said "Good evening", the Twins went upstairs to their bedroom for a few minutes. Jim tried again to think of something to say to Jackie, but this time could think of nothing at all, so he remained silent, watching his father, who was again busy at the cooker with his final supper preparations; but he also kept taking sneaky glances at Jackie, close beside him in her armchair.

A couple of minutes passed, and there came a ring at the front door. Jim instantly sprang to his feet

"Hello!" he said as he opened the front door, and saw Jill Rose, heavily wrapped up against the cold in coat, scarf, and woollen hat; she was holding her bicycle. "I thought you were being brought here by car."

"Father was going to bring me," said Jill, "but I said I'd go on my bike to be independent so he wouldn't have to come and fetch me later on."

"Come in, Jill!" called Mr. Sandy from behind Jim in the hall.

But Jill looked doubtfully at her bicycle.

"Where can I put my bike?" she asked. "I don't really like the idea of leaving it here on the street, even if it's locked."

"You can leave it round the back of the house, where my bike is," said Jim. He noticed with pleasure that tonight she was again wearing those pale trousers which he thought suited her so well; she had trouser clips on the legs for cycling.

"You show her the way, Jim," said Mr. Sandy. "Now, if you'll excuse me for a moment, Jill, I must get back to the kitchen.

"Yes, of course."

Jim lead Jill, wheeling her bicycle, along the little garden path which ran round the south side of the house to the back of the building, where there was a small area of garden and also a wooden shed. An outdoor electric light was already illuminating the back area, and by its light Jim opened the door of the shed, in which were stored various things, mainly gardening implements and Jim's bicycle. There was room for another bicycle beside Jim's, and now he took the handlebars of Jill's bicycle, and carefully propped it beside his own machine.

"I think you'd better lock it," he advised her. "There's no lock on the door of this shed. Was it awfully cold biking here in the dark?"

"It was pretty cold," said Jill. She took a bicycle padlock from the basket on the handlebars, and locked her cycle with it. "But at least it's a fine night and it looks as if it'll stay fine"

"Well, come in and get warm, said Jim

★

Ten minutes later they were all seated at the rectangular table in the middle of the kitchen while they began to eat their soup, which was the first course of that evening's party. Mr. Sandy had taken a great deal of trouble to make the occasion into a party, rather than a mere supper. After he had welcomed Jill at the front door he had returned at once to the kitchen, and had taken from a cupboard a couple of seldom used silver-plated candlesticks with candles in them. These he had placed on the table, on which there was a tablecloth; then he had lit the candles. Jim, meanwhile, was in the shed with Jill, parking her bicycle; then he had brought her into the house through the back door, which opened directly into the kitchen. The Twins had re-appeared from upstairs at the same time; Jill had been introduced to everyone; and then she had been offered a choice of things to drink, and had chosen beer. Jim had invited her to remove her outdoor clothes: coat, scarf, and hat, and she had done this when he had shown her the way to the cloakroom and the bathroom. About five minutes after that they had sat down to their meal.

Mr. Sandy was sitting in his usual place at the head of the table. To his right, as the principal guest, sat Jill, and on his left was Jackie. Jim was sitting next to Jill on one side of the table, and Victoria was sitting next to Jackie on the other, while Carol was at the other end of the table.

Jim was feeling very pleased that Jill was there in his own home for the first time, and sitting beside him at the supper table, but he kept looking across the table at Jackie. There was no doubt about it. For him Jackie had stolen the limelight from Jill. It was to have been Jill's evening, but now Jim was rather shocked to find that, because she was there, it was really Jackie's; it was as if Jill's presence beside him was superfluous. He thought that Jill was looking very sweet and charming that evening, again wearing her white jersey with those pale trousers, a combination doubtlessly chosen especially for his benefit at Westray Hall he had told her how attractive she looked wearing that outfit but such was the strength of the fascination which Jackie seemed to arouse in him that he felt quite powerless to prevent his gaze from staring at her for much of the meal. He felt almost angry with his father for ruining his evening (in a way) by inviting Jackie to the party, yet at the same time his infatuation with her was making him feel very light-headed and happy simply because she was there. These two contradictory feelings were struggling for supremacy in his mind for most of the rest of that evening, but his crush on Jackie was certainly turning out to be his dominant emotion. It was in fact proof, if proof were needed, that the infatuation he had felt for Jill that day when he had met her in the train had been only skin-deep; but Jim, of course, did not understand that, nor did such an idea occur to him.

★

After they had finished their meal a excellent three-course dinner and done the washing-up, the whole party retired to the sitting-room. Mr. Sandy seated himself in his armchair, took up his newspaper, and began to read it. In spite of his job as a mine manager he was well-educated and literary man; he liked <u>The Times</u>, so that was the newspaper he bought. While Mr. Sandy read, Carol, Victoria, and Jackie (having finished work in the kitchen) were sitting on the settee, talking and drinking cups of tea.

Jill had borrowed the page from Mr. Sandy's paper on which was the crossword puzzle, and she and Jim were squatting on the floor with the <u>Times</u> crossword, Jill filling it in, and Jim trying to help her with the clues. He was not much good at this, but Jill was fairly skilled at crossword puzzles, and was managing mostly without his help. From time to time Mr. Sandy would read aloud some passage from the newspaper which he supposed might be of general interest, temporarily distracting Jill's concentration.

Presently Mr. Sandy came across a small passage in his paper which really startled him.

"Good heavens!" he said. Listen to this, Jim. 'Earl dies', it says. 'The funeral of John Dalmane, the Earl of Saint Helens, who died last Saturday, takes place today . . . '"

"Not Lord Dalmane . . . dead!" gasped Jim. He was so shocked by this staggering news that for a second he thought he felt sick; but that passed, and left him simply incredulous.

"It says here that Lord Dalmane's dead," said his father, "and that his funeral was held today. The announcement goes on: 'Lord Dalmane, who was 37, leaves a widow, Susan, but had no children. The funeral will be a private service in Rhodes Church, but it is expected that a memorial service will be held next month in Salisbury Cathedral'. Then it says: 'Obituary, page 22'."

"Gosh!" said Jim. "I can't believe that Lord Dalmane's dead. He was quite young!"

"The man you used to work for at Rhodes Castle?" asked Jill.

"Yes, it must be him," said Jim slowly. "But I didn't know that he was ill. . . or likely to die!"

"Perhaps he wasn't ill," suggested Carol.

"He may have died suddenly an accident, or something?" said Victoria. They were all suddenly full of interest in the startling announcement of the Earl's death.

Mr. Sandy was turning over the pages of his newspaper.

"We'll see if the Obituary says anything about how he died. Ah, here it is! 'Obituary Lord Dalmane of Saint Helens. Lord John Dalmane, who was until recently a Junior Minister at the Foreign Office, died last Saturday, March 2nd, aged 37, at his home, Rhodes Castle.

John Louis Dalmane was born on January 15th 1926. He was educated at. . .

'Yes, yes, it goes on with the usual short biography, but it doesn't tell us anything more about his death."

"It's incredible, quite incredible," murmured Jim. "I mean, there didn't seem to be anything wrong with him the last time I saw him."

"When was that?" asked Jackie.

"Oh, let me see about eleven months ago, in April of last year just before I left Rhodes Castle."

"Ah, but that's really not a long time, Jim," said his father. "He may have looked healthy enough to you at that time, but perhaps he already had some disease that didn't show any obvious symptoms. And then, maybe, that disease became very much worse."

"Maybe," said Jim.

"But if his widow had no children, who'll be the next Earl?" asked Carol.

"I suppose Dick Dalmane will be the next Earl," said Jim. "Dick was his brother, and he was baronet."

"Presumably that's what'll happen," agreed Mr. Sandy.

"But, you know, I can still hardly take it in: that Lord Dalmane's dead," said Jim. "It's really shocking news, somehow. And I bet Susan must be feeling terribly shocked by what's happened."

As he said this the thought came to Jim that, now that Susan's husband had died, he was at last free to marry her himself.

Obviously, though, he would have to wait quite some time for her to get over her shock, but then . . . what would there be to prevent him and Susan marrying each other, if she still loved him? Nothing, said Jim to himself. Yes, surely it should be possible, if he and Susan could meet again, to make his long-cherished dream come true. He had dreamed of the possibility that Susan might someday become his wife ever since the day when he had first met her, and gone with her to Rhodes Castle. However, he had known that such daydreams were but ridiculous fantasies, as Susan had a husband, Lord John Dalmane. Now, however, all that was changed.

Jim considered these points during a few moments of thoughtful silence in the sitting-room. However, such considerations raised no further emotions within him. He was emotionally drained, first by the contradictory feelings he had been experiencing towards Jackie Rothwell, and then by being suddenly shocked at hearing that Lord Dalmane had died; and so he found the thought that Susan, as a widow, was now free to re-marry, held no particular pleasure for him. He told himself that it was unlikely to happen anyway, as it seemed unlikely that he would meet Susan again

The conversation in the room presently turned to other things, while Jill resumed her crossword puzzle; but Jim could no longer think of crossword clues, although he made a faint-hearted attempt to continue to help Jill. He kept on thinking about Lord Dalmane being dead, and about Susan being left on her own. Even the attractively rounded figure of Jackie now held little fascination for him as he wondered what had been happening at Rhodes Castle. How could he have died? He asked himself. Will I ever know what he died of?

CHAPTER FIVE

Thirteen months passed, and then, one fine April evening, there came a ring on the doorbell of Mr. Sandy's house. It was a quarter to eight, and Mr. Sandy, who was expecting Jim to come in from work in a few minutes, was just finishing the preparation of the evening meal.

Victoria was helping her father in the kitchen.

"Could you see who it is at the door, Vicci, please?" said Mr. Sandy. "I'm rather busy at the moment." The doorbell had rung just as he was about to draw a shepherd's pie, which he expected to be cooked, out of the oven.

"Right, oh!" said Victoria. She put down the three plates in her hand on the table beside the gas cooker, and went into the hall. She opened the front door. "Hello!" she said.

A rather good-looking lady with shoulder-length blonde hair was standing outside the front door; she might have been almost any age between twenty and fifty, Victoria thought afterwards.

"Good evening," said the lady. "Does Mr. Sandy live here? I think I've come to the right house?"

"Yes, he's my father," said Victoria, who did not recognize the lady as anyone she knew. "He's here now, if you want to talk to him."

"May I, please, just for a few minutes, if he's not too busy? My name is Mrs. Burton."

"Just a moment, I'll tell him." Victoria went back into the house, leaving the good-looking blonde lady outside the front door on the pavement. "Dad, there's a lady at the front door who wants to see you, a Mrs. Burton."

"Mrs. Burton?" said Mr. Sandy in a puzzled voice. "Whoever can that be? I don't know anyone. . ." But he had finished moving the pie, which, he considered, would be ready to eat when Jim came in, so now he proceeded to the front door, followed by Victoria.

The front door stood open, and Mr. Sandy, looking out, saw that the blue of the sky in the east was beginning to darken, as it was almost the time of sunset. He saw the lady called Mrs. Burton standing there, holding a small suitcase.

"Good evening," said Mr. Sandy politely. It seemed to him that he had never met this Mrs. Burton before, and was very puzzled to know who she was, and what she could want.

"Good evening, Mr. Sandy said the lady. "I'm Samantha Burton, and I work at Rhodes Castle in Dorset for the Countess of Saint Helens, but I'm just up here for a short holiday."

"Ah, Rhodes Castle!" said Mr. Sandy, suddenly understanding that this strange lady must be some old acquaintance of Jim's from his days at Rhodes Castle. "I see. So you've come to see my son, Jim, have you?"

"Yes, indeed, if he's at home if it's no trouble, Mr. Sandy?"

"Not at all," said Mr. Sandy kindly. "Come in, please, Mrs. Burton. Jim hasn't come in from work yet, but I'm sure he'll be here any minute now. Do come in, though, if you'd care to wait a few minutes for Jim." He stood politely aside while Mrs. Burton entered the hall of his house. Then he closed the front door, and switched on a light in the hall.

"This is my daughter, Victoria Jane," said Mr. Sandy, pausing a moment to introduce Victoria. "She's a twin with my other girl, Carol Anne, whose out until later this evening."

After the introductions Mr. Sandy lead Samantha Burton into his kitchen, and drew out a chair from the table for her.

"Do please have a seat, Mrs. Burton."

But Samantha hesitated before sitting down. "Look here," she said. "I'm afraid I'm interrupting you just when you're very busy getting a meal ready. Now, if you like, Mr. Sandy, I could call back later?"

"Quite all right," said Mr. Sandy. "That's quite all right, I assure you but if you'll excuse me, I'll finish getting things ready, and we can talk at the same time."

Samantha sat down. Mr. Sandy nodded to Victoria, who was standing in the doorway, and she left the room. "So you work at Rhodes Castle, but you're on a short holiday at the moment?" continued Mr. Sandy.

"Just a few days off work," said Samantha. "I've been up to Glasgow by train to see my grandparents, who live there. Grandfather hasn't been too well lately, but he's better now. I'm on my way back to the South now, but I thought I'd just call here this evening on my way through Cumberland to see you and Jim, as Susan had given me your address."

"Did you have any difficulty finding the house?" asked Mr. Sandy, who had been continuing to work while he was listening to what Mrs. Burton was saying.

"No, I found the right house quite easily, thanks to Susan's very exact directions. You see, I've just walked here from the railway station."

"Oh! So you must have come by the train that arrives here at about half past seven, the last one that Jim has to wait for? Jim's working at the station as a porter these days. Perhaps you noticed him there when you stepped off the train?"

"Well, I believe I did," said Samantha. "I saw a porter busily moving some load of heavy stuff out of the guard's van of that train, and I immediately thought: Heavens! That porter looks very like Jim Sandy! But he was busy, and I hadn't time to stop on the platform to look around, so I thought as I left the station that it couldn't have been Jim after all; maybe I'd just thought that because I'd seen a tall, fair-haired man."

"That was my son, Jim, all right," said Mr. Sandy. "They allow him to come home after that train's gone, so he must be here any minute now."

"Here he is!" A shout came from upstairs where Victoria had been keeping a look-out for her brother from her window; the Twin's bedroom was one which overlooked the front of the house, giving a reasonable view of a stretch of the road outside. They heard Victoria come running down the stairs, jumping the last few steps into the hall. "I'll tell him the moment he comes in that there's a visitor here to see him!" She opened the front door.

About half a minute later, Jim arrived.

"Hello, what's up?" he asked at once, wondering why his sister should be standing in the hall as if to greet him.

"There's someone here who's come to see you," said Victoria. "Mrs. Burton."

"Who?"

"Mrs. Burton from Rhodes Castle. You know her don't you?"

"What? Rhodes Castle? What are you talking about, Vicci? I don't know anyone at Rhodes Castle with that name." He had come into the hall while he was talking, shut the front door behind them, and hung up his cap. He had forgotten that Susan's maid at Rhodes Castle, Samantha Villers (as she had been called then), had been planning to marry her fiancé, Roger Burton, soon after he had left Rhodes Castle, so the name "Mrs. Burton" now meant nothing to him. As he followed his sister towards the kitchen he wondered for a moment whether she was playing some trick on him. But, no, he thought, Vicci sounded quite serious about this.

"Oh, Samantha!" he exclaimed in joyful surprise, recognizing Susan's maid the moment he entered the kitchen.

"Hello, Jim!" said Samantha, rising from her chair as she spoke.

"How nice to see you again." They shook hands warmly "So you're a porter at your local railway station nowadays?"

"That's right," said Jim. "I've just come from the station now. Have you come here by train, Samantha?"

"I have; in fact, I saw you, Jim, as I was getting out of the train, only you were busy, and I don't think you noticed me."

"I didn't."

"Mind you," said Samantha, "I didn't really recognize you in porter's uniform."

"Mrs. Burton was just telling me that she's come from Glasgow by train today after visiting her grandparents," explained Mr. Sandy. "Do please sit down, Mrs. Burton. Now, we're just going to sit down to our supper, so we hope very much that you'll stay here and eat with us while we talk."

"Yes, do stay, please," said Jim. "I'd love to know how things are going on at Rhodes Castle."

"Well, that's very kind of you, Mr. Sandy, to ask me to stay to supper," said Samantha, "but I really can't do that. I didn't know you'd be having a meal now, or I shouldn't have come, as I really only meant to drop in to talk for a few minutes."

"No, but do stay to supper, Mrs. Burton, now that you're here," urged Mr. Sandy. "You'll be most welcome, I promise you, and there's plenty to eat; more than enough, in fact, for the three of us, so we certainly hope that you'll eat with us don't we, Jim?"

"Indeed we do," said Jim. "Yes, please stay, Sam."

"You people are very kind," said Samantha, "but I do feel that I've been very rude in barging in unannounced and unexpected like this. You see, Mr. Sandy, I rather thought that you'd have had your evening meal earlier."

"Never mind about that," said Mr. Sandy. "We eat late because Jim only gets back from work now; and Victoria and Carol and I wouldn't like to start our supper until he is here. So tonight we really want you to stay to supper, Mrs. Burton. You will, won't you?"

"Thank you very much," said Samantha. "Yes, I will stay, as you press me to."

★

Supper was more or less over when the conversation turned to the subject of holidays. Jim had just asked Samantha whether she had come up to the North on holiday, but she had told him that she was not taking her holiday yet; she was only taking a few days off work. She had already explained earlier that she would have to leave Cockermouth early the next morning in order to get back to Rhodes Castle that evening, so she was going to travel on the 7.25 train from Cockermouth to Carlisle, the first train of the day. Mr. Sandy, on hearing this, had managed to persuade her to abandon her idea of staying that night at the Lakes Hotel, and to stay overnight with them instead. He had pointed out that from his house there was not so far to walk to the station for that early train, and had assured her that it would be no trouble for her to have an early breakfast, as they all ate early since Jim had to get to the station to start work before that same train came in. In the morning she could walk to the station with Jim, he had said; and in the end Samantha had agreed to this plan.

"I'll probably take my holiday when Sue decides to go away," said Samantha, in answer to Jim's question. "We thought we might go away together this year for company, as it wouldn't be much fun for poor Sue to go away all by herself, wouldn't it?"

"No, I'm sure it wouldn't," said Jim seriously. "But has Sue decided where she wants to go for a holiday?" He was hoping as he said this that Samantha was going to tell him that Susan was thinking of coming to Cockermouth, or at least to the Lake District for a few weeks.

"No, we haven't made any definite plans yet. But Sue is considering the idea but only considering it, mind you of going cruising in her yacht, the Osprey."

"Gosh!" said Jim. "So the Osprey belongs to Susan now? And you'd be going with her in it?"

"Sue has asked me to come along as a passenger on board the yacht if we decide to go somewhere this summer, as I dare say we will, perhaps in June and so I said, Yes, I'd love to come too, if she really wants to have me for company. And the <u>Osprey</u> is her own yacht now, and it's still kept up here in the North."

"At Maryport?"

"Yes, at Maryport, at Doctor Himmel's boathouse, where it always used to be kept while Lord Dalmane was still alive. Sue's never been up North, though, to sail her since Lord Dalmane died; I suppose the summer of last year was still too soon after that really tragic death for her to think of doing anything like that. But, as I told you before, she really seems to have got over the shock of all that trauma now, and she says she'd love to go sailing this summer, so I dare say she will."

"Oh, well, she must be feeling happy again if she's thinking of going cruising in the Osprey," said Jim. He paused a moment, and then, remembering a question which had been on his mind since he had heard of Lord Dalmane's death, he added: "By the way, Sam, what did Lord Dalmane die of? Sue never told me that in the letter she sent me after the funeral."

"Terminal cancer," said Samantha, suddenly looking at him gravely; up until then she had been mostly smiling. "A very sad way indeed, it was, for Sue to lose her husband. . . when he was still so young.

"Yes, really it was very sad," agreed Jim quietly.

There were a few seconds of silence at Mr. Sandy's kitchen table. Then Jim spoke again, when he had drunk a mouthful of water.

"But about your planned cruise in the <u>Osprey</u>, Sam: you two wouldn't be going alone in the yacht, would you? Or are you a good sailor, Sam, who could help Sue with the steering, and handling the sails, and all that sort of thing?"

"Good heavens, no!" said Samantha, almost breaking into laughter at the thought of herself as a sailor. "Me, a good sailor? Why, I don't know the first thing about sailing! I tried to tell Sue that it would be no use bringing me, because I'd only be a useless passenger to get in the way, but she said, No, if we go, she'd be very glad of my company. But we wouldn't be going alone, Jim, although I believe

Sue could handle that yacht entirely by herself very proficiently, if she wanted to. But we'd be going with Martin Himmel and his wife: the four of us, with Sue as skipper, Martin and Anne Himmel as mate and crew and me as useless lumber!"

"Oh, don't say that, Sam!" said Jim. "You'll learn as you go along."

"Yes, I'm sure you would, Mrs. Burton," said Mr. Sandy. "No doubt the Countess of Saint Helens would be a good teacher of sailing, if she's good at it herself. She's a very splendid young woman, I thought, in many ways."

"Indeed, you may well say that, Mr. Sandy," said Samantha. She looked thoughtful as she paused for a moment, considering how much she might learn about sailing in the <u>Osprey</u> for a fortnight or so with her mistress, Susan Dalmane, as skipper and teacher.

"And what about your husband, Sam?" asked Jim presently. "Wouldn't he go with you too?" He had forgotten that Samantha was now a married woman, but his father, by calling her, "Mrs. Burton", had reminded him that she had a husband; Roger Burton had been only her fiance when Jim had left Rhodes Castle.

Roger certainly won't be coming sailing," said Samantha. "He's no sailor like me only he says that he definitely wouldn't <u>want</u> to go sailing in a small yacht. Anyway, he can't because of his work." (Roger Burton was a solicitor, working in Sherborne.) "But he's taking a holiday later in the year August or September so we'll maybe go away together then."

"I see," said Jim. "But if you do go on this cruise with Susan and the Himmels, where would you be heading for?"

"We haven't decided that yet. We'd have to set sail from Maryport, of course, which would mean coming up to Cumberland first"

"Oh!" interrupted Jim, his eyes suddenly lighting up at the thought. "Do you think that perhaps Susan might decide to call <u>here</u>, at Cockermouth, on the way to Maryport? I'd so love to . . ." His sentence faltered into silence.

"To see her again?" said Samantha, smiling knowingly at him. "I've no doubt you would, Jim! But, no, I don't see how we could fit that in. You see, we'd be travelling, Sue and I, up from the South by train, and Sue was explaining to me the other day how we could get to Maryport station with only one change (after Crewe, where we get off the 'Pines Express'): we change at Carlisle, she said, and go direct from there to Maryport which, I gather, is not via Cockermouth. So I'm sorry, Jim, but I don't think you could count on meeting Sue if we do come up to the North." Samantha saw a look of disappointment come over Jim's face as she told him this, but it quickly disappeared as he continued to question her about the proposed voyage.

"And you've no idea where <u>Osprey</u> would be heading for?"

"Well, hardly. We had talked vaguely of heading for Scotland from the Solway Firth, but I don't think Sue had made any more definite plans than that."

★

There was a break in the conversation at this point. Mr. Sandy handed round a box of chocolates, and then suggested that they should leave the washing-up until later and adjourn to the sitting-room, where they would be able to continue their discussion about holidays in more comfortable surroundings. They rose from the kitchen table, and Mr. Sandy lead the way through to his sitting-room in the front of the house, but Victoria did not come with them.

She did not mind being left out of the conversation, and said so when Samantha apologized for ignoring her while she had been deep in animated talk with Jim and his father.

When Samantha Burton, Mr. Sandy, and Jim had made themselves comfortable in the sitting-room the conversation was resumed after Mr. Sandy had pulled the curtains to shut out the yellow glare of the nearby street light.

"How about you, Jim?" asked Samantha. "How much holiday do British Railways allow you as a porter?"

"Two weeks in the year," said Jim, "and I can take them when I like. That doesn't include days like Christmas Day, of course, when there are no trains run and I'm off work on all Sundays as well."

"I think that's not too bad," said Samantha. "And are you going away anywhere this summer?"

"Yes, Dad and I are going to Skye for a week in early June."

"Oh, but how delightful for you! Do you mean you'll be on the Isle of Skye for a week, or that you'll be away from home for a week altogether? Because it may take you a few days' travelling, you know, to get to Skye from here, depending on how you choose to travel."

"We'll be away from home for a week well, no, only for five days, actually. We're going to set off on June the first, which is a Monday."

"We're going to travel up to Mallaig by train," said Mr. Sandy, "on the West Highland Line, which, I'm told, is very beautiful. Then we'll take the ferry across to Armadale."

"And then we're going to get a bus if there is one to Portree, and stay a night there. And we're hoping to hire a car so that we can tour around the island for a couple of days before we have to leave Skye on the Thursday afternoon of that week."

"Well, well, you lucky people, you <u>are</u> set to enjoy yourselves!" said Samantha. "In fact, I'm really rather envious of you. The West Highland Line certainly is scenic; very scenic indeed, most of it and Skye is a most beautiful island."

"You know Skye, do you?" said Mr. Sandy.

"Oh yes, I know Skye, but it's a long time since I was last there. In fact, I haven't been back to Skye since we used to holiday there regularly when I was a child. It may surprise you to know, Jim, that I'm a Scot really, by ancestry."

"You, a Scot, Sam!" exclaimed Jim in surprise. "Well, I never would have thought that!"

"I dare say you wouldn't think so, as I've really no Scottish accent to speak of, having lived most of my life in the south of England. But I was born in Scotland."

"Where?"

"In Edinburgh well, in a suburb of Edinburgh, to be precise. My mother's a Scot, you see, but father was an Englishman."

"What clan do you belong to?" asked Mr. Sandy. He knew very little about the Scottish clans.

"MacCarron of Glen Brittle," said Samantha. "Mother's a MacCarron, and Grandfather is too; that's my mother's father, whom I've just been up to Glasgow to see. Glen Brittle, by the way, is in the Isle of Skye, so I suppose that's really our ancestral territory."

"How very interesting," said Mr. Sandy.

"Well, I digress somewhat by telling you about my family, but I mentioned that to explain how it was that, for some years when I was a very little girl, we used to take our summer holidays on Skye. But then Father changed his job, and moved down to London. I suppose I must have been about eight, or nine, or ten years old at the time but since then I've never lived in Scotland, and I've not been back there all that often for holidays."

"But were you living in Edinburgh up to the time of the move to London?"

"That's right: we lived in Gilmerton, which is a suburb of Edinburgh. Most years while we were there we went by train to Skye, going up to Inverness, and from there to Kyle of Lochalsh, but once I think it was only once we went the other way by the beautiful West Highland Line to Fort William, and then on to Mallaig. I believe that was our last holiday on Skye, and I still have some recollections of it that are still vivid after so many years.

"And that would be back in the Thirties . . . or was it just after the War that you took those holidays on Skye?" asked Mr. Sandy.

"It was in the Thirties. You see, I'm thirty-six now," said Samantha. "But to come back to your holiday plans: do you reckon to reach Skye by the evening of your first day –Monday the first of June, I think you said it was?"

"No," said Mr. Sandy. "I know we could do that, but we've decided that we'd rather not rush things like that, so we reckon to stop the Monday night at Fort William, and to go on again the next morning."

"And that way," said Jim, "we'll get to Armadale on the Isle of Skye around midday on the Tuesday. What time does that ferry come into Armadale, Dad?"

"One o'clock, I think it is."

"Yes; and then, you see, we want to go on at once, if we can, by bus to Portree, because that's where we're going to stay on the Tuesday night. Is there a bus to connect with that ferry, Dad?" Jim knew that his father had been sent some timetables, along with brochures on accommodation, and other material, from the Tourist Information Office at Portree.

"There is," said Mr. Sandy, "but I can't remember the times now. Anyway, we get by bus to Portree that afternoon, around four o' clock, I think."

"And have you anywhere in mind yet as a place to stay that night?" asked Samantha.

"Well, yes, we have; our plans seem to be already well advanced," said Mr. Sandy. "In fact, only yesterday I sent off a letter to the 'Harbour View' Hotel at Portree, asking them to reserve for us a room for two nights on the second and third of June. I dare say it may have been unnecessary to do that, as I don't foresee any difficulty over hotel accommodation in Portree so early in the season, but I never like the idea of leaving things to chance on these occasions so we're booking in now to the 'Harbour View' Hotel. Jim and I have read the brochure, and we've agreed that that one sounded like the best hotel for us. I wonder if you know it, Mrs. Burton? You know Portree well, I expect?"

"The 'Harbour View'," said Samantha thoughtfully. I'm not too sure . . . but, yes, I remember Portree well enough from our holidays. It's a most charming little town. You'll enjoy staying there very much."

Then Mr. Sandy remembered that in an inside pocket of his jacket he had a little street map of the town of Portree, which the Tourist Information had sent him. He drew it out.

"I've a map of Portree here," he said, unfolding it, and smoothing out the creases. "The 'Harbour View' Hotel is marked on it, if you'd like to see where it is."

Samantha said that she would be most interested to see whereabouts the hotel was, so Mr. Sandy stood up and showed her the map. Around the edge of the street plan there were some small pictures, including one of the "Harbour View".

"Why, yes, I do remember the 'Harbour View' now" she said when she had looked at the picture, and seen its position marked on the map. "In fact, we stayed there one year. And there really is a splendid view over the harbour, if you get one of the front rooms."

After that the talk turned to the subject of touring the island by car. Mr. Sandy said that it was a pity that he could not ask Mrs. Burton to come with them to Skye to be a guide as she seemed to know the island so well, but he asked her advice on what places she would particularly recommend them to include in their tour. Samantha told them that she thought it would hardly be possible to go all over the island on such a short visit, but she recommended him not to miss seeing the Cuillin Mountains from the best vantage points: Glen Brittle, and the neighbourhood of the village of Elgol on Loch Slapin.

"You could do them both in one day easily," she said. "I should say that, starting from Portree in your hired car, you could first take the Glen Brittle road, and go right down to the end of it, and have a look at Loch Brittle. But to get to Elgol you've got to go back over the same road as far as the Sligachan Hotel, and then take the main road to Broadford. The Elgol road turns off there by the bridge, close to the Post Office. It's a gorgeous drive down that road past Loch

Slapin, with magnificent views of Blaven if you get a good day. It's quite a long way, but very well worth doing all the same."

Mr. Sandy had turned over the street map of Portree; on the other side of it there was a general map of the Isle of Skye. He had shown it to Samantha, and now he was following the route she was describing with his finger. "And Glen Brittle?" he asked. "Are there good views on that road too?"

"Oh yes, most definitely! I'd advise you not to miss it, Mr. Sandy."

"We won't," he said.

★

Jim, as he sat in his armchair listening to the talk about Skye, and often joining in the conversation himself, was thinking about Susan once again. He was wishing that somehow he would soon be able to see her again. Recently he had all but forgotten about Susan, while he had been seeing a good deal of his new friend, Jill (and occasionally Jackie also); but now, not without arousing a certain painfulness, his old yearnings for Susan were being stirred up by Samantha's talk. Jim liked Samantha: he was enjoying himself looking at her pretty face and her lovely sweep of shoulder-length golden-blonde hair, and by listening to the particularly mellow sound of her very distinctive, clear voice. Yet even the way she spoke tended to remind him of Susan: Samantha had a habit of speaking out of the side of her mouth which Jim, however, found attractive to watch. All these reminders of his old life at Rhodes Castle made Jim feel almost as if Susan herself were there in the room with him, together with her maid, Samantha. I'll have to see Sue again, he said to himself. I'll have to see her soon, even if it means going down to Rhodes Castle, if she doesn't drop in here to see me when she comes north with Sam to go sailing in the <u>Osprey</u>.

★

After a while they heard the sound of a car drawing up outside the front door. About half a minute after that Carol, wearing an anorak, was standing in the sitting-room doorway. Her boyfriend had taken her to the cinema that evening, and had just returned her home.

Mr. Sandy introduced her to Samantha, and when she had said, "Good evening", Carol left the room.

"You seem to allow your girls a good deal of freedom so far as boyfriends are concerned, Mr. Sandy?" said Samantha, with a grin at Jim, as soon as Carol was out of earshot behind the closed sitting-room door.

"Yes, maybe I do, admitted Mr. Sandy. "But they know that I trust them to behave sensibly when they're with boys and, so far as I know they do behave sensibly."

★

Soon after that Samantha retired to her bedroom. As soon as she had closed the door of the spare room Samantha opened her suitcase, and took from it a notebook, which had been packed on top of the clothes and other things in the case. She sat down on the bed, and immediately began to make some hasty notes in the notebook, using the pencil from her pocket diary.

★

Next morning Samantha and Jim walked together to the railway station in time to meet the 7.25 train. As they walked they were again talking about Scotland; Samantha had clearly been moved by the reviving of her old holiday memories of the Isle of Skye; and Jim too, although he had been thinking so much about Susan, had been stirred by all this detailed talk of holiday plans. He was, indeed, greatly looking forward to his Scottish holiday. But when they arrived, rather early, on the station platform, and found no one about, he spoke of Susan for the first time.

"You'll give my love to Susan, won't you, Sam?" he said rather shyly.

"Of course I will," said Samantha. "And why not write to her? An exchange of news. I'm sure Sue would <u>like</u> to hear from you, Jim."

"Why, yes, what a good idea! I'll do that. Ah, here come the station-master and Bill, the signal-man." The station-master and the signal-man, chatting together, strolled onto the platform.

The train arrived in the station on time, but there were no other passengers waiting for it. Jim quickly moved the wooden mounting-steps into the right position for Samantha to enter the front carriage of the two-car diesel train (at Cockermouth the platforms were too low to board a train easily without these steps). Samantha boarded the train, and then Jim handed in her suitcase after her, and they said their good-byes, and shook hands, and kissed each other. Then Jim closed the door as Samantha chose a seat and sat down. When the train pulled away from the station Jim waved to Samantha, and she waved back through the window. He had nothing in particular to do just then so he stood where he was, wistfully watching the train rumble away past the sidings and over the river bridge, after which it disappeared round the curve of the track. Sam's gone! he said to himself. Oh, but I wish, I <u>really</u> wish I could have gone back to Rhodes Castle with her to see Sue again!

CHAPTER SIX

Right on the dot!" said Jim, looking at his watch, as at exactly half past four the 4.30 train began to move.

Jim and his father had come into Queen Street station in Glasgow about an hour earlier, and had boarded the evening Fort William train when it had arrived at its departure platform. There had seemed to be quite a large number of people boarding that train, but Jim and his father had nevertheless managed to find themselves an empty compartment. Now a whistle had been blown for the departure of the train, and they were off, and still no one else had come into their compartment.

"Yes, it's a good start," agreed Mr. Sandy, "especially as so far we're still on our own in here."

The train left the platforms, and plunged into the darkness of the tunnel under the northern part of the city, as it headed up the incline towards Cowlairs Junction.

"Isn't it hard to believe that presently we're going to be seeing lochs and mountains from these windows?" said Jim a few minutes later when they were once again in the strong daylight of the June afternoon.

"Indeed," said Mr. Sandy. "Within the hour, I suppose, we'll have exchanged these dreary streets and suburbs for a very different country."

It seemed to Jim to take a long time until those dreary suburbs of Glasgow were left behind; in fact, it took about twenty minutes.

Then they saw the widening water of the Clyde estuary to the left of the train.

★

There was a mini-buffet on the train so Mr. Sandy suggested that, as it was nearly five o'clock, they had better go along there for some tea. They stood in the mini-buffet for some time, eating sandwiches and drinking cups of tea while they watched the changing view; after Craigendoran the railway left the Clyde and, passing Helensburgh, began to wind its way along the hillside above the Gare Loch. The afternoon was rather cloudy, but every now and then gleams of the sun appeared, sometimes picking out gleams of colour on the hiilside, purple rhododendrons, or bluebells. The bluebells reminded Jim that Samantha had said, when she had visited them on that April evening, "Keep a look-out for the bluebells". She had said that one of her holidays must have been in late May, or early June, because she remembered seeing some marvellous bluebells on Skye, flowers that were both bright and deep in their colour; and the best ones of all, she had said, were on the Sleat Peninsula around Armadale. She had told Jim that he might expect to see them almost anywhere from a train on the West Highland Line. Indeed, it's true, thought Jim, the blue colour <u>is</u> marvelous. But I wonder where Sam and Susan are now? Perhaps they're cruising somewhere in Scotland in the <u>Osprey</u>, but, of course, they may be still at home.

They were thinking of returning to their compartment when Jim sighted Loch Long. Far below the level of the railway line, to the left of the train, the narrow, fjord-like finger of salt water thrust its way northwards into the mountain massif between steep wooded hillsides.

"Half a moment, Dad, look at that!" said Jim. "I suppose that must be Loch Long down there?"

"Yes, I dare say it is," said Mr. Sandy. The country was all new to both of them; neither had ever travelled north of Glasgow before.

"Shall we stay here a little longer?" said Jim. "We wouldn't be able to see that loch so well from our compartment with the corridor on this side." He drew his camera out of a jacket pocket while he was speaking.

"It looks very dark and deep, doesn't it?" said Mr. Sandy. The sun had disappeared behind dark clouds a few minutes earlier, and the lack of sunlight seemed to add to the dramatic effect of the sombre water. "But well worth taking a photo," he continued. "Look, there's a motor boat down there." A small motor cruiser was heading northwards up Loch Long, and the train was overtaking it.

Jim took a photograph of the loch. "But that boat'll only be a tiny speck in my picture," he said.

"I wonder whether your friends from Rhodes Castle are afloat anywhere in their yacht now?" said Mr. Sandy, and Jim knew that the sight of that boat moving on the loch had reminded him of Samantha Burton, and of how she had told them that she and Susan Dalmane were planning a cruise in the Osprey.

"They may be; but we won't see them, of course."

"No, I suppose there's no chance of that; at least, it would be an incredible fluke if we did come across the Osprey on this holiday."

It did not seem to take much time until they came to the place where they had a last sight of Loch Long; and very soon after that they were seeing Loch Lomond on the other side of the train. The sun had by now come out again, and the handsome peak of Ben Lomond and much of the loch were resplendent in the sunshine.

Jim was often amazed at the steepness of the drop down towards the main road which ran at the lochside. Mostly it was a well wooded hillside with many patches of bluebells, which appeared to float like a deep blue mist above the green of the grass and the undergrowth of the woods, but here and there were rocky crags and precipitous drops to the road at the edge of the loch.

"The bonny, bonny banks of Loch Lomond!" said Jim happily. "Gosh, Samantha was certainly right about the bluebells being a gorgeous colour!"

The journey continued, passing the junction at Crianlarich, and then proceeding by valleys and mountains until they came to the wide desolation of Rannoch Moor. Jim and his father were astonished to see those two lonely outposts of civilization, Rannoch and Corrour stations, serving, apparently a barren and unpopulated wilderness: a region of badly drained peat bogs and bare rock, with here and there small lochs and dark sluggish streams crossing the moor. Soon after passing the summit of the line at Corrour station (where there are no houses, and not even a metalled road) they saw lonely Loch Treig lying in a deep valley between the high mountains of the Western Highlands. However, when they arrived at Fort William at about twenty minutes to nine, Jim was disappointed to see that the higher parts of Ben Nevis, looming behind the town, were lost behind dark clouds.

★

Next morning the Sandys continued their journey by rail, taking the morning train to Mallaig, having spent a comfortable night's rest in a guest-house in Fort William. The train was again rather crowded, and this time Jim had to make do with a backward-facing seat, whereas yesterday he had been facing forwards. He soon found, however, that facing backwards had its advantages on that run; after Corpach there was a superb view along tidal Loch Eil towards Ben Nevis. That morning it was still cloudy, but the cloud seemed to be thinning out. There were Ben Nevis and its surrounding peaks behind Fort William.

Their lower parts were veiled by misty white clouds, while higher up they stood clear of cloud, although the summit of Ben Nevis was still hidden from Jim's view. He saw, however, that the clouds around those high peaks of Lochaber were lifting and breaking up rapidly, and he was waiting to take a photograph, his camera ready in his hands. He was hoping to take a photograph of Ben Nevis showing the whole mountain clear of cloud before the train, rounding a curve, left that view behind; and near the halt at Locheilside he had the view he wanted, and quickly clicked his camera shutter.

The morning continued to improve as the train headed west towards the coast. Jim had thought that the scenery on the previous evening's journey from Glasgow could hardly have been improved upon, but now, when the train came to the pretty Loch Eilt, and the railway began to hug the shore of the loch closely, he thought that the country was more spectacular than ever. Then they reached the west coast at Loch nan Uamh. Jim was astonished at the beauty of the scene revealed to him through the train windows, as was his father. The sun was shining, and sparkling off the blue water of the sea; they saw very clean-looking white sand on a beach, and small islets off-shore in the tidal loch seemed to be floating on the dazzling water. The train had never been moving very fast, but now Jim wished it would move a little more slowly, so as to give him longer to survey that scene.

There was another glimpse of the coast at Arisaig, and then Jim, who had now changed his seat for a forward facing one, saw that the railway was again turning inland. The scenery now changed abruptly. To the left of the train he saw flat, boggy country, the low-lying region called Mointeach Mhor between Arisaig and the mouth of the Morar River, but when he looked the other way he saw that the railway line, curving all the time to follow a contour line, was skirting the flank of the hilly country. A little further on the country became relatively flat on both sides of the railway line. It was possible for Jim to see both sides from his seat without moving as they were in an open carriage with a central gangway

"We must be almost at Mallaig," said Mr. Sandy some ten minutes later. Jim looked out through the left-hand windows, and saw that the line was again close to the sea. Some way out there he saw an island with a curious and distinctive skyline; it was the Isle of Eigg, but he did not know this until later. The sea looked bright and blue under the now clear blue sky, and from inside the train it appeared to be smooth. Jim noticed a white speck on the water between the coast and the northern end of that island skyline: clearly it was a boat, perhaps a white-sailed vessel, but it was too far away for him to be sure of that, and not worth digging the binoculars out of his suitcase, he reckoned, as they must be almost at the terminus. Yes, the train was slowing down; a siding appeared; they were approaching Mallaig station. He and his father stood up, and prepared to leave the train. Then the platforms of Mallaig station appeared, and the train drew to a standstill.

★

Jim and his father were walking the short distance from the railway station through the street down to the jetty in the harbour where the Skye ferry was waiting at the quayside. But they were in no hurry to go aboard the ship. It was only five minutes past twelve, and the ferry, they knew, was not due to sail until one o'clock, so they decided to spend a little while wandering around the harbour, looking at things. But the most interesting view, Jim thought, lay out to sea. Out there, over the water, was an outline of hills, the Sleat Peninsula of Skye, to which they were bound. Then he noticed that white speck again, nearer this time; he could see clearly, without using the binoculars, that it was a small boat with white sails. It was sailing northwards up the coast, clearly making the most of a good breeze from the south-west; for now that they were out in the open air it was evident that the sea was not so smooth after all; in fact it looked rather choppy in that fresh breeze that was blowing off the sea. Oh! he thought suddenly, could that boat possibly be the <u>Osprey</u>?

No, he said to himself, it won't be the <u>Osprey</u>. Why, I don't even know whether Sue and Sam are still at home, or not. They could still be at Rhodes Castle. However, for the next few minutes Jim's eyes followed the steady northward progress of that boat, taking no notice of the many fishing vessels moored in the harbour.

"Come on!" said Mr. Sandy suddenly. "We'd better be getting our tickets, and then going aboard that ferry."

★

Fifty minutes later Mr. Sandy and Jim were standing on the deck of the Armadale ferry as it left the harbour and headed out into the Sound of Sleat. They were standing on the starboard side of the vessel, where the bridge afforded them some shelter from the fresh wind, and looking around them, mostly watching the receding shoreline of the mainland of Scotland. It was soon possible to see well up the broad inlet of Loch Nevis, but then Jim remembered something else. He stared intently for several seconds to the north, up the Sound of Sleat, towards the point in the distance where the Sleat skyline and that of the mainland appeared to converge. Was that a white speck on the water far away up there, or was it not? Jim, remembering roughly what the map looked like, realized that the white-sailed yacht (if it was that yacht) must be heading into the narrows around Glenelg, where the island of Skye was separated only by a very narrow channel from the mainland. He took his binoculars out of their case, hung the strap around his neck, and for a minute or two tried to focus them on the distant yacht. This he found difficult enough, in spite of the smooth motion of their vessel; he kept seeing that boat in the binoculars for a second or two, and then losing sight of it again. But he had soon seen enough to be sure that the boat was indeed a yacht, obviously the vessel he had seen from the train, and seen again nearer when it had crossed the harbour entrance at Mallaig.

Mr. Sandy had seen what his son was watching through his binoculars.

"That boat?" he said. "I should hardly think it could be your friends sailing their yacht but what do you think?"

"I was just trying to see whether I could read a name on that boat," said Jim. "But I can't. It's definitely a yacht, though, with white sails, like <u>Osprey</u> but it won't stay in focus long enough for me to read the name on the stern, if there is a name on the stern. Hello!" (He was still staring through the glasses). "I caught a flash of something red just then – there it is again –could be someone at the tiller wearing something red, perhaps?"

"Perhaps," said Mr. Sandy. He was silent a moment, but then added: "But we're getting well out into the Sound now. Must be nearly half way across, I should think. Have a look at the coastline ahead of us, Jim."

"Okay." Jim re-focused the binoculars, looking now straight ahead towards Armadale. Anyway, he said to himself, even if that boat was the Osprey, I'd have lost sight of it altogether in another minute or two, and we're not likely to see it again. He caught sight through the binoculars of a single grey pier ahead of them, a pier jutting out from a wooded, hilly outline of land. He put down the binoculars; it was easier to look at things without them. Now he could clearly see houses here and there on the land ahead with his unaided eyes. "Over the sea to Skye!" he said to himself. What fun! Of course it's ludicrous to speculate on whether or not that boat was the Osprey. It probably wasn't.. Anyway, we're having a super holiday so there isn't really much point in thinking about the Osprey. Sue and Sam will have a lovely time cruising in her, no doubt.

When the ferry had tied up alongside the Armadale Pier, and the Sandys, taking their turn in the queue by the gangway, had disembarked, they found that a bus for Portree was waiting in the car park adjacent to the pier. They presently took their seats in this bus, which at a quarter to two left on the long drive to Portree, much of it being along a narrow but very scenic road. The bus finally brought them to Somerled Square in Portree at half past three.

★

Jim woke the next morning to bright sunlight in the small hotel bedroom. He saw that the time was five minutes to seven, and sat up in the bed. The head of Jim's bed was almost underneath the window of the small room, while the other bed, in which Mr. Sandy lay, was close beside the door; and Jim, looking at his father, saw that he was still asleep. Jim thought of getting out of bed, but then changed his mind. He could see what the morning was like, and have a look at the view through the window, by simply turning round and kneeling on the pillows at the head of the bed. He immediately did so, and thus was able to see out through the window, and his spirits rose at once as he saw how bright and clear the morning was. However, the view from that window was a little disappointing, although the weather that day promised to be magnificent for sight-seeing and photography, even if it did feel decidedly cool for early June at that early hour of the morning. But the day'll warm up very nicely in the sun he thought.

They had not been able to book one of the front rooms of the "Harbour View" Hotel, from one of which there would indeed have been an unimpeded view over Portree Harbour. Instead they had been given a room on the top floor of a side wing of the hotel. It had been late when Jim and his father had come into their bedroom last night after they had taken an evening stroll, following their supper, and, although it had not been dark, Jim had not bothered to study the view through that window when he had decided to retire to bed (there is hardly any real darkness at night in June in northern Scotland).

Now he was looking at the view carefully for the first time. The foreground was filled with a roof: the ridge of a steeply-pitched roof of grey slates, which must have been the roof of another part of the "Harbour View' Hotel. Peeping over the top of this roof was the top of a tree; he saw bright green young leaves on the topmost branches fluttering in a strong breeze off the sea. And there, immediately behind that tree, was blue water. The sun was shining down on Portree Harbour from the left, as Jim looked at that view, and picking out a trail of golden specks which seemed to dance on the surface of the water. It was almost too bright to look at steadily. The view was completed by the hills which rose straight up from the further shore of the broad inlet of the sea. The sky was cloudless and very bright.

Jim remained silently where he was, kneeling on the pillows, for a few minutes while he looked out thoughtfully at the delightful scene before him. It's a really grand day, he thought, just the sort of day for good adventure! If only Sue were with me it would be perfect! Then another thought struck him. Why not take a picture? A photograph from this unusual angle, he told himself, would be different, would be unique in his collection: Portree Harbour seen over a hotel rooftop, and with the topmost branches of a tree also in the picture. It would make a charming and original photographic study.

His suitcase lay open beside the bed, and on top of the things in it lay his camera in its case. Quickly he took out his camera, and then settled himself again, kneeling on the pillows, leaning over slightly to his right, with the lens of the camera pointing out of the window. Although it was very bright he thought that there would not be too much light to take a photograph. Ah, what was that he saw out there in the bay? A boat? There was a white speck out there which had not been there a minute earlier. Jim considered for a moment what to do next. At first he did not think that this boat could be the same one that he had watched so keenly yesterday because there were no sails set (but it was very hard to be sure of that as the water was so dazzlingly bright). The binoculars! he said to himself, laying his camera down on the window shelf. He dug the binoculars out of the suitcase, and presently, not without some difficulty, managed to bring them into focus on that boat. "Oh!" he said, without meaning to speak his thought aloud. "It *is* a yacht with its sails down loose on the cabin top."

The yacht was coming straight towards him, heading for the pier which he could not see; obviously the people on board were meaning to moor it at the quayside. Jim thought he could see someone on the cabin roof of the yacht, doing something with the sail. But in about another minute that boat was going to disappear from his view. With feverish haste he flung the binoculars down on the bed, took up his camera again, and pressed the shutter just in time to capture that boat in his picture; a few seconds later it had gone, hidden behind that roof.

"Hello, Jim!"

Jim turned round to see that his father was awake. Mr. Sandy was propping himself up in bed with one elbow while he rubbed his eyes sleepily with a hand.

"Good morning, Dad!" said Jim.

"Taking a photograph, were you?"

"Yes. There's a roof out there which rather blocks the view of the harbour, but I thought it would make an interesting picture all the same. And there was a boat out there."

"A boat? What sort of a boat?" Mr. Sandy was sitting up now; he swung his legs down onto the floor as he spoke.

"A yacht with white sails like the one we saw yesterday."

"And you thought this might be the same one?"

"I thought it might be, but it was very hard to be sure because they hadn't got the sail up; it was lying loose on the cabin top. I could see that through the binoculars. They must have been using an engine."

"Let's have a look," said Mr. Sandy. He walked over to the window bare-footed in his pyjamas.

"Oh, you can't see it now, Dad. It was coming into the harbour here, but it's hidden now behind that roof.

Mr. Sandy looked out at the view. He opened the window a little wider, and breathed deeply, not seeming to notice the coolness of the air. There was silence for several seconds. "My, what a gorgeous morning it is!" he said presently. "Just the day for us to go motoring, eh, Jim?"

"I should say so!"

Mr. Sandy returned to his bed, and sat down. He took a pair of bedroom slippers from his suitcase, and put them on.

"I say, Dad?" said Jim a moment later.

"What's that?"

"Would there be time to go down to look at the harbour after breakfast? Perhaps we'd see that boat tied up there?"

"Ah!" chuckled Mr. Sandy. "I know what you're thinking! You're wondering if that boat could possibly be the <u>Osprey</u>, aren't you? And if it is, you'd very much like to go aboard and see Susan Dalmane for a few minutes."

"Well," said Jim, "I was thinking that; at least, that is, if by any chance that boat *is* the <u>Osprey</u>."

"It won't be, Jim. At least, let me put it this way: what do you think the chances are of that boat being the <u>Osprey</u>? About one in a million, perhaps?"

"Oh, come, Dad, the chances can hardly be as remote as that!"

"Well, perhaps not. But you've got to remember that we don't even know for certain whether Lady Dalmane and Mrs. Burton are cruising at the moment, or whether they're still at home. And then there must be hundreds of yachts with white sails. Do you know what sort of a rig the <u>Osprey</u> has?"

"She's a cutter," said Jim. "A Bermuda Cutter with white sails. Sue told me that herself."

"But do you know what that sort of rig looks like?"

"No, not for certain. It's one mast, I think, and two sails . . . or is it three?"

"So you don't really know quite what you're looking for? Well, Jim, time's going on, and this speculation is getting us nowhere. But we'll certainly go down to the harbour right after breakfast, if you like, and have a look at that vessel, if she's there, and read her name."

"Thanks, Dad, I'd like to be certain, one way or the other."

"Well, we'll do that, and then go along to that garage they told us about. Now then, I'm going along to the bathroom, and then I think we'd better get dressed, and go down to the dining-room to see about breakfast. I think they told us it was served from eight o'clock."

★

At his first glimpse of the quayside from the wall by the Square, overlooking the harbour, Jim felt a pang of disappointment. That yacht did not appear to be there unless, perhaps, it was lying somewhere where it could not be seen from the Square. They walked quickly down the steep little road from Somerled Square, and so came to the quayside. But there was no sign of a yacht. Jim looked everywhere carefully, but could only see small motor craft, fishing boats, and some rowing boats. Two motor vessels were moored to the pier, and others were riding to mooring buoys further out in the harbour. The morning breeze had died down, and now there was only the slightest of ripples breaking the long golden path of the sun on the water.

Jim and his father walked right down the gravelly beach to the edge of the water. Jim took the binoculars, which were hanging round his neck, and carefully searched the further shore of the harbour (which was about a mile away). The bright light bothered his eyes, but he could see no boats moving further out.

"Well, Jim, I'm afraid we've come too late to see your yacht," said Mr. Sandy. "Obviously she's gone if, indeed, she ever came in here. Are you sure about that?"

"Oh yes, Dad, I'm absolutely positive that yacht came in here," said Jim. "But it really doesn't matter at all that she's gone; she wouldn't have been the <u>Osprey</u> anyway."

"No, I'm afraid that's probably true. I'll tell you what, though. Isn't that the Harbour-Master over there, talking to those fishermen? We could go and ask him if he's seen a yacht in here this morning." Mr. Sandy was pointing to one of the fishing boats tied up to the pier, where they could see that there was a cargo of fish being unloaded.

"Yes, let's do that!" agreed Jim eagerly.

"And then we ought to be on our way to that garage."

They strolled round to the pier. A man with a bushy black beard, wearing dark blue nautical uniform and with gold braid on his cap, was standing close to the edge of the quay, chatting with a sailor. Just beside them a ladder lead down to the deck of a fishing boat, where two more men were busily packing herrings into boxes.

"Good morning, Harbour-Master," said Mr. Sandy, walking up boldly with Jim at his side.

"Mornin' to you, sir," said the Harbour-Master, politely touching his cap. "Aye, and a grand mornin' it is too!"

"Have you by any chance seen a yacht this morning? Was there a boat with white sails in here earlier?"

"A wee boat wi' white sails? Och, aye, there was such a one came in here about five past seven, but she sailed again soon after that. The Osprey, she was called, I noticed."

"Osprey?" said Jim eagerly. "Do you know where she'd come from?"

"From Loch Sligachan."

"Where's that?"

"Och, maybe some twelve miles down the coast to the south." The Harbour-Master pointed vaguely towards the south. "Were there friends o' your's on board her, then?"

"I think so," said Jim miserably. He had been terribly disappointed to hear that the Osprey had indeed put into Portree Harbour that morning, and had already sailed again, but now a doubt crept into his mind. Where, exactly, was Loch Sligachan? Perhaps this Osprey was not Susan's yacht after all?

"Did you gather where they were bound for?" asked Mr. Sandy.

"Tarbert. That's what the young man said, whom I spoke to. They were going to cross the Minch later today, and hoped to make Tarbert on the Isle of Harris by this evening and I reckon they should do that. They will find a good wind, I think, once they're clear of the Isle of Skye."

"A man?" said Jim doubtfully. "You didn't see anyone else on board that yacht or did no one else come ashore?"

"Aye, a man," said the Harbour-Master. "A youngish chap wi' curly fair hair: he was the only one I saw come ashore from the Osprey. If there were any crew on that yacht, I reckon they must ha' stayed in their cabin. Anyway, that chap came into my office to ask where he could get fresh water, as he was voyaging afar, I gathered.

And when he'd got his water I came wi' him to the quayside, and had a quick look at his yacht, but I didn'a see anyone else aboard her. And then he were off at once, using his engine; that was, maybe, shortly before eight o'clock this morning."

"That must have been Doctor Himmel," said Jim to his father. Mr. Sandy nodded. Jim had never met Martin Himmel, but he had heard Susan talking about him, and knew that he was a sailor and a friend of the late Earl; and now he remembered Samantha telling him that the Himmels would be sailing with her and Susan on their cruise in the <u>Osprey</u>.

"I see," said Mr. Sandy. "There were friends of our's on board that yacht; at least, they're my son's friends, to be exact but I'm afraid we've missed them."

"Aye, ye've missed them."

"But did you gather where they'd come from?" asked Jim suddenly. "Did that man tell you where they'd *started* their voyage from?"

"England," said the Harbour-Master. "Aye, he told me they'd come all the way from the North o' England. They'd set off, he said from a wee place called Maryport over the Solway Firth."

"We know it," said Mr. Sandy. "We come from near there ourselves; and that means that they definitely *were* our friends. But they couldn't have been expecting to meet us here."

"Ye're not sailing yerselves?" asked the Harbour-Master.

"No, we're motoring: touring the Isle of Skye on our first visit. Look here, we'd better be getting a move on. Thank you very much for your help, Harbour-Master."

"Ye're welcome! Good day to ye!"

They said good-bye to the Harbour-Master, and walked away, silently at first.

"Well, that's that," said Mr. Sandy when they were trudging up the steep brow to the Square. "I'm sorry we've missed them, but I hope you're not *too* upset about it, Jim."

"I'll try not to be," said Jim. He had been looking very glum as he walked along in silence, but now he began to look a little more cheerful.

"After all," said his father, "you never expected to meet Susan Dalmane, or Samantha Burton, on this holiday, did you?"

"That's very true, Dad; of course I didn't. I'll try to forget about them again. Where are we going, Dad, when we get our car? Glen Brittle?"

"I think we might as well do as Mrs. Burton suggested, and start by motoring to Glen Brittle. Everything's new to us on this island, except only the road we came on yesterday in the bus, so there's nothing to lose by going anywhere else, it seems to me."

They came again into Somerled Square, and now took the main road southwards out of the town which lead to the bridge over the river. Immediately beyond this bridge Dunvegan Road branched off to the right, and it was in this road that they expected to find the garage which hired cars. But Jim could not easily forget how narrowly he had missed an opportunity to see Susan. Now, if only we'd come down to the harbour *before* our breakfast, he said to himself, then surely I'd have seen Sue. It might have meant asking Dr. Himmel, or knocking on the cabin door, but I'd have seen her. I think I'm tired of Jill. I *must* see Sue again soon, so perhaps I could go down to Rhodes Castle later in the summer. But I must try to forget about what's happened this morning, if I can.

CHAPTER SEVEN

"I say, Dad, what an incredible view those mountains make, seen from here!" said Jim. "Couldn't we stop somewhere around here so that I could take a picture?"

"Why not?" said Mr. Sandy. "We're in no hurry, and I'm sure you should have a picture of those jagged peaks; and I expect round about here would be as good a place as any for your camera. But this road's so narrow that we can't park just anywhere. I'll pull in at the next passing place."

About half a minute later Mr. Sandy swung the hired car into the next lay-by on the left of the road. He switched off the engine, and they both stepped out, Jim taking with him only his camera in its case, and Mr. Sandy taking from the back seat of the car a flask which had been filled up with coffee at the hotel.

There was by any accounts a superb view to the south-east across the rolling moorland from the rough little mountain road which lead from the top end of Loch Harport over a shoulder of the moorland down into Glen Brittle. The morning had remained perfect since breakfast time for Hebridean sight-seeing, but by now, at around a quarter to twelve, it seemed to be better than ever; also it was becoming decidedly warm in the strong June sunshine.

Mr. Sandy and Jim crossed the road (there was hardly any other motor traffic about). They began to walk over the uneven lumps and tussocks of rough moorland grass on the western side of the road.

"Mind where you put your feet, Dad," said Jim a moment later, when he had just managed to save himself from tripping over an unnoticed step made by a peat cutting.

"Ah, yes," said Mr. Sandy. "This moorland must be all good peat just below the surface, with a bedrock I suppose of gabbro underneath it. His geological instincts surfaced for a moment as he glanced ahead at an outcrop of dark rock. "No doubt the natives could dig peat for centuries to come, to burn as a fuel."

"Yes," said Jim, "there's a really big peat cutting just there, close to the place where we've parked the car."

"Where are we heading for, Jim?"

"I thought, if I could just climb up onto that little knoll over there, the view of the Cuillins would make a really superb photo with this road in the foreground, winding over the moor."

"Right. And we can sit down there too, and have some coffee."

As Jim advanced over the rough ground with his father at his side towards the little rocky knoll, some few hundred yards ahead of them, he kept glancing backwards towards the imposing line of blue peaks along the eastern horizon. in spite of having all his life been a native of the English Lake District, Jim thought that never before had he seen such dominant colours in mountain scenery. A long line of fantastic, deep blue peaks rose up dramatically over there from the brownish and olive-green tints of the peat bog into the cloudless, blazing blue sky.

At one point, on the side of a bowl-shaped corrie between two peaks, there was a conspicuous patch of white on the blue background, the remains of a deep drift of snow hard-frozen into the corrie.

When they were on top of the little summit, which was only about fifty feet higher than the surrounding tableland of peat bog, they found that there was plenty of convenient bare rock on which to sit down; luckily it was quite dry too. Mr. Sandy chose a good place, and sat down on it, but Jim remained standing. He pulled their map of Skye out of a pocket and opened it, standing facing the summits of the Cuillin range, and wondering whether he could see the highest peak, Sgurr Alasdair, and which one it was if he could see it.

Jim had by now all but forgotten the intense disappointment he had felt on learning that the Osprey had put into Portree Harbour that morning, and had sailed again for the Outer Hebrides while he and his father had been having their breakfast. He had been thinking of Susan and Samantha on board the yacht, probably somewhere off the north-eastern coast of Skye, and sailing northwards, while he had been walking up Dunvegan Road in Portree to the garage where cars could be hired. But once he was sitting beside his father in the hired car, driving along the main road southwards from the town, he had quickly forgotten about the Osprey and her crew. Now, after another study of the map, he took out his camera, and presently took a picture. There was a handsomely triangular-shaped peak which stood a little in front of the other summits, a spur of the mountains jutting out towards the moorland road, and Jim carefully positioned this peak to be exactly in the centre of his photograph. To the left of it was a serrated line of points which appeared to be of a slightly paler blue because they were a little further away, and there was that north-facing, snow-filled corrie also included in his photographic composition. To the right of Sgurr Thuilm, the boldly triangular summit which made the centre of Jim's picture, another knife-like top could be seen, although most of it was hidden behind the shoulder of the nearer hill. My word, he said to himself, Samantha was right when she told us there were superb views of the Cuillins from the road to Glen Brittle! I'm so glad we've taken her advice, and come this way!

Looking to his right, it was evident to him that a valley lay between those blue mountains and the rolling country in the foreground; the valley itself was hidden, but by following with his eyes as far as he could the zig-zagging line of the road, he could see that beyond the point where it disappeared over the top of a brow there had to be a sharp drop down into a glen. His map confirmed for him that this was so, and that the valley was called Glen Brittle.

They were going to motor down there to the place where the road ended under the Cuillins by Loch Brittle.

Then Jim looked to his left, where the road wound its way uphill for several miles from Loch Harport, following the valley of a small burn. He thought that as there was no one else in sight, and as no cars were visible other than their own hired car, all that idyllic scene stretched out in front of them was somehow even more pleasing to survey. Oh! he said to himself, no, I'm wrong! There are two people walking up the hill no, not walking; I think they must be on bikes.

He remembered that they had overtaken a couple of cyclists on the road perhaps five minutes before his father had parked the car. These two, a red and a blue moving speck, must be them. He made an instinctive move with his right hand for the binoculars, forgetting, for the moment, that they were not hanging round his neck, but were still in the car. He could, however, see without the binoculars that those bright specks of colour on the road were moving too fast to be people on foot unless, perhaps, they were running. No, they were cyclists; he could now see bright glints of metal where the sun was catching the polished chromium of cycle handlebars, but they were still too far away for Jim to determine whether they were two men, or two women, or one of each. He watched them pedalling along the hot, dusty road, gradually drawing nearer as they approached the passing place where their blue car was parked; and after about a minute he noticed that each figure was carrying a rucksack on its back.

"Ready for some coffee, Jim?" called his father from somewhere behind him. They had only one plastic mug with them for drinking, and Mr. Sandy had already drunk some coffee from it, and now he poured out some more. He was sitting quite comfortably on a table-like bluff of dark rock, dangling his feet over a convenient ledge.

"Yes, thanks, Dad." But before he sat down beside his father Jim glanced back again at the road. He saw that the cyclists had come to the passing place where their car stood in the hot sunshine, and that they had stopped there for a rest. He could see the two bicycles lying on their sides and the two cyclists sitting on the rough grass at the edge of the road.

About ten minutes later the Sandys stepped back into their hired car to continue their journey. The cyclists had also moved off, but they were not far ahead; they could see a red and a blue spot toiling uphill about two curves of the road ahead. But when, about a minute after that, Mr. Sandy carefully overtook the cyclists for the second time Jim, as before, only had time to notice that the one wearing blue clothing had long fair hair under a blue peaked cap, which made her a female, he reckoned. She was again lagging a little behind the other cyclist, who seemed to be wearing a red anorak, with a white cap on his head; but both of them had their heads well down as they were evidently pounding slowly and laboriously up the last uphill stretch of the road, so that Jim had no chance to see them properly. He thought, however, that they were probably husband and wife, assuming that the one in red was a man. It seemed that they also were bound for the end of the road by Loch Brittle, or else for the Glen Brittle Youth Hostel, but Jim knew that they were following a dead-end road; so it was quite likely, he thought, that they would meet them again at, or near the end of the road.

★

Soon after overtaking the cyclists the Sandys found themselves down in Glen Brittle, a green, flat-bottomed valley, with the River Brittle flowing down it to the sea. Mr. Sandy was driving slowly so that they could look at things easily as they motored. Presently they crossed a small burn and passed the Youth Hostel, a dark, wooden, two-storeyed house beside the road.

"That'll be the Youth Hostel, I expect," said Mr. Sandy. "What a beautifully remote place to stay!"

"Perhaps those cyclists are staying there," said Jim.

In another minute or two, driving the car through an open gateway, they reached the end of the surfaced toad at Glen Brittle

House. Not far away on their right was the river; they had just passed a footpath or track leading off in that direction, and crossing thr river by a footbridge. Thr road over which they had just driven crossed over a smaller burn immediately before the gate, and Jim remembered that a waterfall was marked on his map where that burn came down from the Cuillins, the Eas Mor, Gaelic for Great Waterfall. There was a wall on their right, and a house on their left, and plenty of space for parking and turning cars. Ahead of them they saw another gate, closed, where a rough road went down to salt-water Loch Brittle.

Mr. Sandy parked the car alongside the wall.

"This seems to be the end of the road," he said, switching off the engine.

"No, I think it goes on," said Jim. He picked up his map, which was lying on the back seat, opened ready at the correct folds to show the Minginish Peninsula of the Isle of Skye. "Yes, the map shows this road going down to the sea at the head of Loch Brittle," he said. "It must be about another mile or a bit less, perhaps and it's marked as a rough, unfenced track."

"Right," said Mr. Sandy, "I'm all for exploring to the end of the road, but we might as well get out here and look around as we've stopped."

They stepped out of the car, Jim this time taking the binoculars with him in their case.

"Hello!" he said "There's a post-box here. I'll post my card here." He took from his pocket a postcard to Jill Rose in Cockermouth:

he had written the card that morning before leaving the hotel, but had then forgotten to post it.

The message he had written on the card (a colour photograph of Portree Harbour) was a very shallow one, two simple, stark statements:-

"Having a lovely time. The weather here's gorgeous. With all my love, Jim."

He looked at the red post-box in the stone wall, and noted that there was one daily collection made there at one p.m. It pleased him to know that he was in time for the collection, but as pushed his postcard into the box he could feel no interest in Jill. Of course, I *must* send one to Sue at Rhodes Castle, he said to himself. I'll buy one at the next shop we come to that sells postcards, and she'll get it when she comes home from cruising. The thought reminded him again, for a moment, of Susan and Samantha, now at sea on their way to Tarbert.

After a short debate on which way to walk, Jim and his father decided to continue on foot through the second gate on the road down to the loch, and then to look out for a track leading off to the left, up the hillside. They would ascend the foothills of the mountains a little way in order to admire a wider view, but they were both agreed that the day was much too warm to do any serious climbing of the Cuillins; and, in any case, they had not brought with them the correct footgear for mountaineering.

★

"There's a pretty good view," said Mr. Sandy, "although we haven't climbed more than about a hundred feet from the road."

They were sitting on the green slope of a hillside on which there were patches of bright yellow where the gorse was flowering, and wide patches of brown and grey scree and dried-up earth. Behind their backs jagged blue peaks loomed ominously over the ridge of the long green foothill.

Jim took the binoculars out of their case. There certainly was a good view; first he focused the glasses on the inlet of the sea called Loch Brittle, where he could see a stretch of greyish beach at the head of the loch.

"Ah!" said Mr. Sandy a moment later. "There are those two cyclists again."

"Where?" asked Jim. He took the glasses from his eyes, and looked quickly round to the right where a stretch of the Glen Brittle road could be seen. He had looked that way for the cyclists as soon as they had stopped climbing, but had not seen them. "Oh yes, there they are again!" he said as he saw a blue and a red flash of colour coming along the road towards the bridge, the gate, and the house where they had parked the car. He managed for a moment to get his binoculars focused on the two moving figures before they disappeared by the trees and buildings. They appeared now to be riding side by side, the blue one with fair hair being the nearer one to their vantage point. Then he lost sight of them by Glen Brittle House. "I wonder if they're going to stop there?" he said.

"They're not," said Mr. Sandy. "There they are again." He pointed to the road on the near side of the house, where they saw the cyclists again now that they were a little nearer. "They must be going down to the beach."

Jim trained the binoculars onto those two figures again. They were the only people they had seen riding bicycles that day, but he did not know why watching them had become such a fascination. Perhaps it was partly due to a natural desire to see the face of the fair-haired girl, who, he thought, must be pretty; and perhaps he thought that to indulge such a curiosity would in some way compensate him for his shocking disappointment at so narrowly missing his chance to see Susan while the <u>Osprey</u> had been at Portree. But, whatever the reason for his motivation, he watched the two cyclists keenly. He saw the fair-haired girl in blue come to the sharp bend in the road beside a small white cottage which was directly below their observation point, and he distinctly saw long fair hair blowing in the breeze.

Yes, she *must* be a girl, he thought. She was now slightly ahead of her companion. But the next second he had a closer glimpse through the binoculars of the other cyclist, who was wearing a red anorak. I believe she's a girl too, he said to himself, as he caught a glimpse of a distinctively female bust outline; but almost immediately she too had rounded the bend, and was pedalling away from him along the rough road down to the beach

Jim took the binoculars away from his eyes.

"Well, shall we be going on?" said his father.

"We might as well," said Jim. "Why don't we go down to the sea, Dad, to have a look at the beach where the road ends?"

"Okay, we'll take the car down there."

They walked back to the car, and just as they came to the gate they saw a red Royal Mail van arrive and pull up by the pillar-box in the wall. A moment later the postman was turning his van round to drive away, the mail collected, including Jim's post card; and he was pleased to think of it starting back on its long, slow journey to Cockermouth. He thought, however, that he would have returned to Cockermouth himself before that post card would reach Jill.

Mr. Sandy drove the car slowly in low gear because of the ruts and holes in the unsurfaced road, but it only took them a few minutes to reach the place where the road ended by simply widening out into a large gravelly flat above the beach at the head of Loch Brittle, where they noticed that the tide appeared to be quite a long way out. As soon as they stepped out of their car Jim noticed that they were close to a stile in the fence, and beside this stile he saw two ladies' bicycles propped up against the fence.

There seemed to be no sign of anyone round about, but the two ladies' cycles confirmed Jim's latest opinion that both the cyclists were women; and clearly they were on the beach which he could not yet see properly.

A minute or two later Jim checked himself suddenly as he came out of the rough grass onto the top of a bank of grey shingle on the beach of that sheltered bay. At the same moment a sensation went through him which was rather like missing a heartbeat, or perhaps it was more like a sudden, momentary catch in his breathing, as he looked up and saw a woman in a bathing costume standing at the edge of the sea. He had been looking down until that moment;

having climbed over the stile after his father, as it would have been very easy to have been tripped up, walking across the very uneven ground between the fence and the beach. There were sand-filled hollows in the short, dried-up grass, and coarse dune grasses and, here and there, patches of sea-holly. But Jim hardly noticed his sudden bodily reactions of shock; he was only aware of the figure which was the cause of this surprise. The girl, who was now beginning to wade cautiously into the shallow water, was undoubtedly the cyclist who had been wearing the red anorak; even without the binoculars he could see her short, dark hair. She looked fairly tall, and was now only wearing a black bikini-type of swimming costume. The girl was walking away from Jim, striding slowly out into the sea water on what was clearly a beach with only a very slight slope, for already she was several yards out into the water, which was not yet up to her knees.

However, she was not directly presenting a rear view to him; every now and then he had glimpses of a full, shapely figure with a slim waist.

In fact, this sight of a girl wading into the sea was, one would have thought, in no way extraordinary. She might indeed be attractive, but Jim had not yet had a glimpse of her face, and even if she had turned round at that moment to face him (which she did not) she would have been too far away for him to make out the features of her face without using the binoculars. But he was quite unaware that there might be something irrational in being suddenly attracted by the sight of a young female stranger in a way powerful enough to bring about an instant increase in his pulse rate, and a very sharp increase in the attention he was paying to the sight of that girl.

Quickly Jim looked to his left and his right. Where was his father? Then he saw that his father was strolling along the beach to his right towards the place where the river ran out into the loch; and he said "Good!" to himself, as his father was clearly minding only his own business at the moment. Jim also saw the other girl when he looked in that direction. A girl was lying on her back sunbathing some way off on the shingle, by the place where the two beaches of the cove drew together into the mouth of the River Brittle, a widening channel between gravelly banks. However, she failed to hold his attention for more than a second or two; almost immediately his gaze turned back to the girl who was still wading slowly into the sea.

The next moment Jim was running back in the direction of the car, the thought of the binoculars having come into his mind. But he had only gone a few steps when he pulled himself up sharply. He had suddenly changed his mind, telling himself that it would be wrong to stare at a strange girl through binoculars, no matter how attractive she might be. Instead he would take a picture. His hand went into his jacket pocket, and again took out his camera. Then, without actually running, he was hurrying down the beach in order to be near enough to the bathing woman to take a photograph of the loch with her in it. But it looked as if, at any moment now, she might begin to swim, when a photograph to show what she was like would be useless, with only her head showing above the water. There she was, almost up to her middle, and still wading outwards. But she *can't* be going to swim! he said to himself. It must be piercingly cold, that sea water. He was being as quick as he could in getting the picture he wanted composed in the viewfinder of his camera. The girl was going to appear very small in his picture - he had no telephoto lens on his camera - but no matter; the main thing was to snap the picture quickly before it was too late. He pressed the trigger of the shutter, and heard it click; his photograph was taken and straight away a smile of pure pleasure came over his face. The top half of the girl was still showing, standing up in the sea water; she seemed to have stopped wading for a moment, and was, perhaps, making up her mind to take the plunge to go in for a swim.

Jim was becoming obsessively fascinated in watching the bathing woman. His father was quite forgotten, and even the other, blonde-haired girl was forgotten for the moment. Then, a few seconds later, he saw the dark-haired girl go down into the water and begin to swim, apparently moving with effortless ease in the smooth water, and with hardly any splashing.

Jim stood where he was, gazing spellbound for a few more seconds, while he saw that the swimmer was still heading outwards into deeper water, but bearing round to the right, as if she were making for the beach on the western side of the loch, where a green promontory of the hillside ran down into the water, ending in a long, gravelly point. Heavens! He thought how *can* she do it? She makes it look so easy, but she must be finding that water positively freezing! He had never considered going swimming himself that day in spite of the warmness of the air. For one thing he and his father had brought neither towel nor swimming trunks with them; but for another, the weather had only that day turned warm after a prolonged spell of cold, but mainly dry weather; a Buchan's Cold Spell, his father had said.

A few more seconds of standing and watching, and then Jim decided, quite suddenly, to take further, rapid action. He hurried down the beach almost to the water's edge, until he was near the place where the bathing woman had left a large, orange-coloured towel lying on the sand. It was a beach of rather unusual sand; he had seen from the hillside above Glen Brittle a grey beach, and now he found himself running over wet sand that was indeed not yellow, or orange, or white, but decidedly grey: much the same colour as the bank of grey shingle and stones further up the beach around the high-water mark. For a moment, before he took off his shoes, he thought, looking at the orange towel, that the girl had been foolish to put it down so close to the edge of the water, and he wondered whether it would be safe to leave his shoes and socks where they might quickly be covered by the incoming tide. Then, seeing that the sand was all more or less wet, he realized that the tide must still be going out. Nevertheless, to be on the safe side, he put his shoes and socks, when he had taken them off, a few yards further back from the edge of the sea water. Then, as quickly as he could, he rolled up his trousers above his knees, and paddled boldly into the shallows. He had considered taking off his trousers, but had at once rejected the idea; he was not going to swim, but only to wade into the shallow water a little way after the stranger who had so thoroughly captured his attention. In his first few steps he was pleased to find that the water was nowhere near as cold as he had feared that it might be indeed, it was almost warm there, where it was only a few inches deep, ebbing over smooth sand which was easy to walk on, barring the occasional sharp stone which his bare feet encountered now and then. The water was very smooth, and only the most miniature of wavelets were breaking silently on the sand.

But where was that swimming woman? For a moment he thought that he had lost her as his eyes desperately scanned the water of the loch further out. "Ow!" he said involuntarily, as his left foot descended under water onto a sharp-edged stone which moved with an unexpected jerk as he trod on it, almost throwing him off his balance. But he did not fall over and, recovering himself, spotted again the dark head of the swimming girl. He thought that she had gone a long way out into the loch, but she had now changed course, and instead of heading for the spit of shingle protruding from the western shore, she was now swimming the other way, to the left, as Jim saw her, and roughly on a parallel course with the near shoreline. With the water now covering his ankles, Jim was content to stand where he was for a few seconds to watch that girl swimming. He saw her strike out powerfully, using the crawl, as he watched her; until then she had been quietly using the breast stroke.

My word, she's a powerful swimmer! he said to himself. He reasoned that she must, sooner or later, come back to the place where she had left her towel on the sand, close to where he was still standing. Without having made any conscious decision about it, he meant to be somewhere quite close to her when she came out of the water close enough, indeed, to exchange a "Hello!" or a "Good afternoon!" with her.

He glanced back for a moment towards the beach. Yes, the tide was still going out; the towel and his shoes and socks were further from the water's edge. If he were to continue to stand in the same place for another minute or two he would find that the water would no longer cover his feet. Further away, at the top of the beach, his father was still sitting on the same flat stone where he had first sat down, apparently calmly surveying the peaceful scene before him. Some distance to the left of Mr. Sandy the other girl had also not moved; she was still lying on her back, soaking up the warm rays of the sun. Jim turned again, and continued to wade into the sea roughly in the direction of the swimming girl.

Why had it become such an absorbing passion to continue to stare at that young woman out there with such an intense interest? Why did he feel so excited? These were questions which Jim might well have given a moment's consideration, but he did not consider them at all. He walked slowly and carefully, step by step, with deliberate purpose into deeper and colder water; and as he walked he did not even realize that he *had* become considerably excited. The only thought in his mind was to get nearer to that woman in order to get a proper look at her, and, in particular, to see her face. Although she was a stranger whom Jim did not know from Eve some primeval force was undoubtedly in operation like a magnetic field, attracting him to her. The water was above his knees now, and he knew that it would not be possible for him to walk out much further, but perhaps there was no need for him to go further. He only wanted to keep her in sight until she should decide to come in to regain her towel, when he would see her face. She was again using the breast stroke, and now he noticed that she was slowly swinging round through an arc of a circle to swim back towards the shore. He took a few more careful steps towards the woman, and then stood still, the water lapping gently around the middles of his thighs. It was a decidedly cold sensation on his skin, but he hardly noticed it. She was coming in now, swimming straight towards him.

Suddenly into the feeling of mounting excitement a new idea came to him like a flash of inspiration, for he realized that this girl reminded him of Susan, his own beloved Susan: that was why he was becoming so excited. As he began to see glimpses of her face he thought that there was indeed an uncanny resemblance in this woman's features to those of his true love, Susan.

Jim had forgotten for the moment that he was being rude by staring at the swimming woman. Then he saw that she was slightly altering her course, so as not to pass too close to him as she swam in towards the shore and her towel. He waited breathlessly, his heart beating strangely fast. A few seconds went by, and then the girl suddenly turned her head towards him, an expression of great surprise on her face; but he did not notice it, for at the same moment a feeling not unlike a mild electric shock passed through him as he thought he recognized her. She was standing up in the water now, having found that she could touch the bottom with her feet. She was hardly any further out than Jim, but the water came up almost to her breasts, while it was only lapping around his thighs immediately below his rolled-up trouser legs.

"Jim!" called the girl.

"SUE!" he gasped in a sudden burst of joy and astonishment too great for any further words as he recognized the young woman beyond all possible doubt. He held out his arms towards her, but she was already splashing rapidly through the water towards him. Another moment, and Susan Dalmane was standing beside him, the water dripping copiously off her black hair and trickling down her front and back

"Good heavens!" she was saying.

"So it really *is* you, Jim, the man I saw following me into the sea! I thought at first it couldn't possibly be you!"

"But it is!" said Jim, grinning at her happily, "Although *I* couldn't believe that the girl out there swimming really was you, until you called my name."

They clasped each other closely for a moment, and kissed rapturously. Susan's lovely dark eyes were alight with a mixture of joyful surprise and ecstatic delight.

"Sorry, Jim, my darling," she said, "I'm dripping water all over you."

But Jim hardly noticed in his joy that he was getting rather wet by embracing Susan. "But, Sue, how ever did you get here?" he asked.

"We came ashore from the <u>Osprey</u>," she explained simply. "We're on a Hebridean cruise, Sam and I, with Martin and Anne Himmel. We came ashore with our bikes, and then I went in for a bathe."

"We passed you twice on the road in our hired car," said Jim. "But when...?"

"Not now!" interrupted Susan, cutting him short with a playful wave of her hand. "Let's get out of the water now. It's rather chilly just standing here, Jim, my darling, so I'm coming out to dry myself."

"Of course!"

Clasping each other's hands, they began to wade together through the shallow water to the shore.

"I'll tell you more about how we got here when I've dried and dressed," said Susan happily as she splashed along beside Jim. "But, Jim, *you* should have taken your clothes off, and come out for a swim!"

"I thought it would be far too cold to swim."

"Oh, nonsense! It wasn't too cold at all, once I'd really got going. Can you swim?"

"Oh, yes," said Jim. He looked down regretfully at his clothes. If only he had thrown caution to the winds, and had flung off his clothes, what fun it would have been to have gone in swimming with Susan. He would certainly have done so, he told himself, if he had recognized her sooner; but it was too late now.

Splashing rapidly through the shallows they regained the wet sand of the beach. Susan ran on a few yards, grabbed her towel, and began to rub herself vigorously with it. "Hello!" she said, noticing a fair-haired man walking towards them from the top of the beach. "Isn't that your Dad, Jim, coming down to meet us?"

"Yes, said Jim, looking round. "We're holidaying here, you know."

"Are you? Here, would you like to borrow my towel a moment to dry your legs? It's rather damp, but it might do." She thrust the orange-coloured towel towards him.

"Thanks, Sue." Jim gave his wet legs a rough rub down with the towel. "I say," he added, "this towel's got awfully wet with lying on this wet sand. Will you be able to get yourself properly dry, Sue?" He handed the towel back to her.

"Oh yes," said Susan. "No problem. Sam's got a dry towel with her where she's sitting up there on that bank of shingle."

Jim glanced up the beach, and saw the fair-haired girl, whom he now knew to be Susan's maid, Samantha, and saw that she was now sitting up. She gave them a cheery wave.

Susan waved a hand to Mr. Sandy, who raised his right arm to return her greeting as he came on to meet her, while Jim went on to pick up his shoes and socks.

"Hello, Mr. Sandy!" said Susan, holding the towel in front of her in the interests of modesty.

"Good afternoon, Lady Dalmane," said Mr. Sandy politely. They shook hands (Susan was clasping the towel in her left hand). "What a very pleasant and surprising meeting this is!" But Jim thought that his father's voice showed little surprise at the meeting.

"It's absolutely staggering!" said Susan cheerfully. "I can still hardly believe that we've met you and Jim here."

"It seems like an incredible co-incidence, doesn't it?" agreed Mr. Sandy. "Now then, Jim, we'd better leave Lady Dalmane while she gets herself dried and dressed. We'll go back to the place where I've been sitting; and I dare say that you two could talk again in a little while?"

Jim was about to speak, when Susan spoke first.

"Of course we must have a good talk. I'm longing to know how you've got here, Jim, and, of course, we can tell you more about how we've come here in the <u>Osprey</u>. Look here, you must come and share our lunch picnic; we've got far more than we could eat just by ourselves. But if you could just give me ten minutes or so to dry and dress and get things ready would that be all right?"

"That's very kind of you, Lady Dalmane," said Mr. Sandy. "Of course it would be all right. Thank you very much. But Jim and I have a bit of a picnic of our own at least we've got some oatcakes on the back seat of our car, and a little coffee in a flask and we could bring what we've got to add to your picnic, if you like."

"What a good idea!" said Susan. "Yes, you do that, and we'll have a joint picnic. We'll give you a shout when we're ready."

"See you again, Sue!" said Jim joyfully.

They parted, and went up the beach in different directions, Susan with her wet towel running over the wet sand towards Samantha, while Jim and his father made for the place where Mr. Sandy had been sitting on a large flat stone. Mr. Sandy and Jim did not run, although Jim almost wanted to, and walked merrily up the beach with a light, springy step which faltered only occasionally when sharp stones hurt his still bare feet. But he hardly noticed such slight discomforts. It seemed to him that all that charming bay of Loch Brittle, with the hills coming right down to the sea on the western side, beyond the river mouth, had become far more beautiful on account of the fact that he had now met Susan Dalmane there. Even the sunshine seemed to have become brighter, the colours more vivid, than when they had arrived, when, Jim thought, the sunshine had been a little hazy. He was feeling so happy that he could not keep silent as he walked.

"It's *wonderful*, what's happened!" he said "Incredibly wonderful! Nothing more lovely could have happened today than this meeting with Sue."

"Indeed it has been a wonderful stroke of luck for you," agreed his father. "A Hebridean Meeting, as you might say. I can't think *how* they can have managed it, but they *have* managed it somehow; and no doubt they'll tell us all about it."

CHAPTER EIGHT

Mr. Sandy had chosen to sit down and look at things when he had come onto the beach at Loch Brittle, and having seen a large and conveniently flat-topped stone at the top of the bank of shingle he had at once sat down on it, leaving Jim to wander about where he would.

Like Jim, Mr. Sandy had been quick to see that the girl standing in the shallow water at the edge of the loch was the cyclist who had been wearing a red anorak; he saw the anorak lying with a number of other cast off garments further along the beach in an untidy heap beside the other girl. He had seen even before he had sat down that this other, fair-haired girl, who had been wearing a blue outer garment for cycling, was now lying on the beach, sunbathing. However, after one glance at the sparsely clothed female figure, lying on her back, he had turned his gaze aside, and had firmly resolved that he would not peep at her.

He was sitting at a respectable distance away from her, about fifty yards, and he realized that she evidently believed that she was alone on the beach; so he would respect her privacy.

If he had not been so strict with himself in this way Mr. Sandy might well have recognized the sunbathing figure as Samantha Burton before Jim had discovered that the swimming girl was none other than his love, Susan Dalmane. However, as things turned out, when Mr. Sandy had stood up to walk down the beach to meet Jim and the bathing girl, he had still had no idea of who the two ladies were. Then, when he had come near the water's edge, he had recognized Lady Dalmane, and it had immediately dawned on him that her companion must be Samantha Burton.

But how could they have got there if they had sailed for the Outer Hebrides that morning? He wondered. That was certainly something to puzzle over.

★

"We're ready!"

It was Susan Dalmane's voice which called across the beach to the place where the Sandys, father and son, were sitting on their flat stone, waiting for the ladies from Rhodes Castle to be ready with their lunch picnic. Jim had been back to the car to pick up the provisions.

They had bought themselves some Scottish oatcakes immediately before leaving Portree in the hired car, thinking of eating them somewhere for a lunch-time snack.

Jim had brought the packet of oatcakes, together with the flask which still contained some coffee, and their plastic mug, in a strong carrier bag, and had set it down on the shingle beside his father. He had remembered what an open place that beach was not exactly the best of places for a lady to change after bathing and, like his father, he had firmly resolved to resist the temptation to be a peeping Tom. In point of fact, he felt so light-hearted that he knew he had no need of any further excitement, so he did not look round at Susan as she peeled off her wet bathing garments and applied a dry towel to her skin before putting on some clothes.

"Coming!" shouted Mr. Sandy.

Jim hastily picked up the provision bag containing their contributions to the lunch picnic, and he and his father set off to join the ladies for the picnic.

"Well, well!" said Samantha, rising to her feet. "What an amazing co-incidence that we should meet you here!"

"It really is!" said Mr. Sandy.

There was a hearty shaking of hands, but Jim was thinking, as he shook Samantha's hand, that there was something a little odd about her greeting. It had not sounded so much as if she were surprised at meeting him and his father at Loch Brittle, as if she were *pretending* to be surprised. Jim was a little puzzled about this. It almost sounds as if Sam had been *expecting* to meet Dad and me, he thought, in spite of her talking about an amazing co-incidence. But how could she have expected to meet us? However, he very quickly forgot about this little problem, if problem it was. He had glanced at her face, as if he had expected that her expression might give away some secret of her thoughts, but he only saw a happy smile of genuine pleasure on it.

"Come and join the jolly picnic!" said Susan happily. "Do sit down, everyone. That's right, Jim, you can sit beside me. She caught his eye for a second, smiling at her, and she beamed back at him radiantly. "And you can be here, Mr. Sandy. I say, those oatcakes look jolly good!"

"They look most appetizing," said Samantha. "Better than anything we've got here in our food parcel which is just a packed lunch from the Sligachan Hotel."

"From where?" asked Jim.

"From the hotel where we stayed last night."

"What! Weren't you on board the Osprey last night?"

"No!" said Samantha mysteriously, a mischievous twinkle in her eyes.

There was a second or two of astonished silence. Jim and his father looked questioningly at Samantha while she brought out of her open knapsack (which lay beside her) a large parcel wrapped in aluminium foil, and placed it on the rug which had been spread out over an area of the shingle to make a dry place to sit on. They were all sitting down on the rug.

"We spent last night on dry land at the Sligachan Hotel," explained Susan. "It's about how many miles away, would you say, Sam?"

"About fourteen, I should think," said Samantha.

"Yes, it's about fourteen miles from here. You see, we came ashore yesterday afternoon from the <u>Osprey</u> in Loch Sligachan, on the east coast of Skye."

"Ah!" exclaimed Mr. Sandy. "You came ashore *yesterday* from the <u>Osprey.</u> I see . . ."

"We thought you were still on board this morning," said Jim, "when I saw the <u>Osprey</u> come into Portree."

"You saw <u>Osprey</u> this morning?" enquired Samantha.

"It was just after seven this morning when I saw a boat that I thought might be the <u>Osprey</u> coming into Portree Harbour," said Jim. "And then, after breakfast, the Harbour-Master told us that it *was* the <u>Osprey</u>; but she'd gone then, so naturally we thought that you two were on board her."

"The Harbour-Master told us that the <u>Osprey</u> was sailing for Tarbert in the Outer Hebrides," said Mr. Sandy.

"That's right," said Susan . . . "Martin said that they were meaning to cross the Minch today, heading for Tarbert. The idea is that they'll pick me up again tomorrow at Loch Sligachan, and then we'll have to head for home but, of course, it'll depend on the wind whether they manage to make it back to Loch Sligachan by tomorrow morning. If they get in there earlier than breakfast time they're going to wait for me, if I'm not there, they said."

"Only for you, Sue?" asked Jim.

"Yes, only for me. You see, Sam's going to travel back by train."

"I'm returning to Rhodes Castle first," explained Samantha, "so I'll be going back to the mainland on the evening ferry tomorrow."

"We'll be on that same ferry tomorrow evening," said Jim eagerly. "We'll probably see you on it, Sam."

"Yes, I expect we'll meet again tomorrow. But let's get on with our picnic, shall we?" Samantha had by now unpacked a number of packages of food, and had spread them out on the rug. The packed lunch from the hotel consisted of various kinds of sandwiches and two pieces of cake.

"Certainly we'll get on with the picnic!" agreed Susan.

"I suppose," said Jim, after he had eaten his first mouthful of sandwich, "you've biked this morning from the hotel you mentioned?" There were scores of questions waiting in his mind to be asked about the Hebridean voyage of the <u>Osprey</u>, but first he wanted to know more about Susan and Samantha's bicycle ride of that morning.

Susan swallowed a mouthful before answering.

"Yes, we've biked from the Sligachan Hotel on our own bikes."

"And a good, long, hard ride it was too!" added Samantha.

"But through such wonderful country," said Susan. "And then, it's turned out such a marvellous day, so it really was great fun pedalling along these roads, and getting off to push up the hills."

"It must have taken you a long time!" said Jim, with a private grin at Susan. "How early did you start this morning?"

"We started biking very soon after we'd finished breakfast."

"At about half past nine," said Samantha. "And it was just after one when we finally got here, after about three and a half hours on the road. I suppose that makes it a pretty slow average speed, doesn't it?"

There was silence for a few seconds while both the Sandys tried to do the arithmetical calculation in their heads. Jim, however, very soon gave it up; his present buoyant state of mind gave him no inclination towards mathematics. Susan and Samantha went quietly on with their eating.

"I make it four miles an hour, your average speed, said Mr. Sandy, when he had worked it out in his head. "I think you said it was about fourteen miles?"

"I did," said Samantha.

"I suppose that was quite a reasonable average speed," said Susan. "Not that we were trying to get here quickly, or anything like that far from it. And I know four miles an hour sounds awfully slow, but when you take into account that we were slowly pushing our bikes up hills quite often, and that we stopped a few times to rest, I think it wasn't a bad average speed."

"I'm sure it wasn't," said Mr. Sandy.

"Our last stop, in fact, was near the summit of the moor," said Samantha, after we'd toiled up the long hill from Merkadale, by Loch Harport mostly walking, pushing the bikes.

"We saw you stop there," said Jim.

"Did you?"

"Yes, you put your bicycles down just where our hired car was parked in a passing place," said Jim. "We were sitting on the top of a little knoll, not far away. You didn't see us, did you?"

"I did notice two people sitting on some rocks not far back from the road," said Susan, "but never for a moment did I think that it might be you two from Cockermouth! Really, what's happened today, you know, is quite amazing the sort of co-incidence you'd think couldn't happen because it's just too fantastic!"

There was a short pause in the conversation. Jim saw Samantha smiling quietly at Susan's mention of the co-incidence, but she said nothing.

"We saw you pass by on your bikes again, after we'd overtaken you a second time," said Jim. "It was when we'd reached the end of the road at Glen Brittle by the post-box in the wall. We'd climbed a little way up the hillside to look at the view. We were up there." He turned round, and pointed. "Behind that little white cottage."

"And you saw us go past on our bikes?" said Susan. "Well, fancy that! This really *has* been a strange and delightful day! Will you have a sandwich now, Jim? There are several different sorts here to choose from, but they all look rather dull to me; not like your delicious oatcakes! Are you ready for a sandwich, Mr. Sandy?" (They had started their picnic by eating oatcakes.)

Mr. Sandy and Jim thanked Susan, and took sandwiches, and the picnic went on. None of them were in any hurry; they all had a great deal to say to each other, and were happy enough to take their lunch picnic at a leisurely pace while they chatted and exchanged news. Jim soon asked Susan to tell him more about Osprey's voyage from Maryport.

"I suppose it took you several days to get to Skye from Cumberland in the yacht?" he said.

"Oh yes," said Susan "We were at sea for almost four days. It was about five o'clock yesterday afternoon when we dropped anchor in Loch Sligachan."

"When did you leave Rhodes Castle?"

"Friday morning of last week."

"And when did you set sail from Maryport?"

"Saturday morning. You see, we travelled north last Friday in the 'Pines Express' and changed at Crewe, as we'd done before, to catch a Glasgow train from Euston. Then at Carlisle we took a local train down to Maryport, and we stayed that night with the Himmels at their house in Maryport."

Susan went on to give a rough account of the voyage of the Osprey. They had divided the long voyage into easy stages, she said, and with mainly light winds their speed had not been great. The first day's sail had brought them to Portpatrick on the coast of the Rinns of Galloway, where they had spent the night in the shelter of the harbour. On Sunday (May 31st) they had sailed up the Firth of Clyde, passing the eastern side of the Isle of Arran, and then up the lower part of Loch Fyne to reach Tarbert.

That's Tarbert in Argyllshire, of course," explained Susan. There are several places in the Highlands and Islands called 'Tarbert'. It might have been slightly shorter to have sailed up the western side of Arran, but I reckoned that we'd get a better wind up the much wider channel of the Firth of Clyde to the east of Arran. You see, we had northerly winds throughout the entire voyage except for the last day, when a fresh south-westerly breeze came in very useful; but the northerly winds were mostly contrary winds except for sailing westwards from Maryport on the first day, when we actually had a light breeze from the north-east, not a bad land breeze."

Susan continued her sketchy account of the voyage with Monday's sail, which had taken them as far as Tobermory on the Isle of Mull. They had sailed on up Loch Fyne and Loch Gilp, and had motored slowly through thr Crinan Canal. ("A very useful short cut!") They had sailed between the islands of Scarba and Luing into the Firth of Lorne, and up the Sound of Mull, and so had spent Monday night at anchor at Tobermory. In the morning, having sailed early at a quarter past seven, they had rounded Ardnamurchan Point, and so, with a good south-westerly wind, they had set a course for the Sound of Sleat.

"Do you remember roughly what time you passed Mallaig?" asked Jim.

"Around mid-day," said Susan. "Did you see us?"

"Yes, a boat I saw from the train windows when we were nearly at Mallaig must have been the <u>Osprey</u>. Then we saw it again from the harbour at Mallaig. It was a yacht with white sails."

"And we saw it again later when we were on board the one o'clock ferry, crossing to Armadale," said Mr. Sandy.

"That was us all right," said Samantha. "Sue was steering, while I was down below in the cabin looking at the views through the portholes."

"Yes," said Susan, "we were making good progress there with one of the best winds of the entire trip until we came to Glenelg Bay and the narrowest part of the channel just after it."

"They call the straits Kyle Rhea," interposed Samantha. "The Isle of Skye almost touches the mainland of Scotland there."

"We motored through the narrows to Loch Alsh, where it widens out," said Susan, "and then we were off again, close-hauled on the port tack, past Kyleakin, and so to the wide waters of the Inner Sound. Are you quite lost, Jim? I suppose you can hardly follow all this without a map?"

"Oh!" said Jim. "But I *have* got a map only I must have left it in the car." He quickly checked his pockets, and found his camera, but no map. "I've no idea where those places are that you mentioned, Sue, without the map: Kyleakin, and the Inner Sound, and the rest of them."

"Well, I wouldn't bother about getting the map just now," said Susan impatiently. She wanted to finish her account of the voyage, and went on at once.

"You can show me it presently. Then we sailed between the Isles of Scalpay and Raasay - that was tacking again - and so into Loch Sligachan. We lowered the sails, and I brought her slowly in, using her engine. Actually, we've used rather a lot of petrol on this voyage so far, as we were becalmed more than once. We had to fill up with petrol at Tarbert. Anyway, we didn't venture too far into Loch Sligachan because I wasn't too sure about the depth of the water. So we anchored, and put our little dinghy over into the water, and then Martin rowed Sam and me ashore at that little village by the waterside, called . . ."

"Sconser," said Samantha.

"Sconser. We were rowed ashore there, and then Martin had to row back to the yacht to fetch our two bikes."

"Was it very awkward, bringing bicycles with you?" asked Mr. Sandy."

"My word, yes, it was *frightfully* awkward!" laughed Susan. "But it was Sam's idea . . ."

"Yes, it was my idea to bring our own bikes from Rhodes Castle," admitted Samantha. "I knew we'd need them to get about on Skye; and of course it was use thinking that we could hire bicycles at the Sligachan Hotel."

"That's true," said Susan. "But, yes, it was very awkward having two bicycles on board the <u>Osprey</u> as well as four humans. There really wasn't any room for the bikes, but we managed to cram them in all the same and, I must say, I'm very glad we *have* brought them."

"You wouldn't have been able to get here without them," said Jim. "And then we wouldn't have had this meeting!"

"Dear me, what a thought!" said Susan. "Oh, how lucky we've been . . . ! Well, to get back to yesterday; we set off biking along the main road from Sconser in the Portree direction, Sam leading the way, of course. I've never been on Skye before. It was about half past five by this time, and I was disappointed that by then it was cloudy, and looking like rain."

"Yes, it did get very cloudy yesterday evening, didn't it?" said Jim. "We had some light rain at Portree too."

"It was beginning to drizzle as we set off on our bikes for the hotel," said Susan. "But we didn't have time to get very wet as we only had about a couple of miles to go on a fairly level road. I thought it was going to rain, mind you, when the wind went round to the south-west yesterday morning. That's usually a sign of rain; and the barometer was falling too. Then, much later, at around ten o'clock, we saw that the rain was over, and that it had cleared up. But I never would have thought that it would turn out as good as this today. No doubt, if we'd stayed on board the <u>Osprey</u> we'd have seen our barometer rising considerably."

"No doubt you would," said Mr. Sandy. "Did the yacht stay overnight in Loch Sligachan?"

"Oh yes, she stayed last night where I'd anchored her."

"How do you know that?" asked Jim. "Could you see the yacht from the hotel?"

"Yes," said Susan. "I could see her from the window of our bedroom by using binoculars although she was anchored some two miles away in the loch. Luckily they gave us a room which faced in the right direction."

"*We* brought binoculars with us too and they came in very useful for looking at <u>Osprey</u> yesterday and at you and Sam today on your bikes, although we had no idea at the time who the two cyclists were."

"I brought binoculars for sailing, Jim, and perhaps I should have left them on board the <u>Osprey</u> for Dr. Himmel to use, while he's acting skipper. But he'll manage all right without them. They must have been off frightfully early this morning, though. I looked out of the window at half past six, and there was not a sign of the <u>Osprey</u>. I thought Martin might have waited for high water this morning at around seven-thirty, but obviously he didn't."

"It was about five past seven when I saw the <u>Osprey</u> from our room in the 'Harbour View' Hotel at Portree," said Jim.

"Gosh!" said Susan. "Martin must have been in a tremendous hurry to get started for Tarbert in the Isle of Harris. <u>Osprey</u> must have sailed at about half past five, I should think. Of course, at this time of the year there's no real darkness here, even in the middle of the night."

"The Harbour–Master at Portree told us that the <u>Osprey</u> called there for fresh water; and he said that they'd sailed shortly before eight o'clock, and that they'd come from Loch Sligachan." Thinking back to the morning, Jim remembered the Harbour-Master's words when they had spoken with him on the quayside.

"So you see," said Mr. Sandy, "we went away from there thinking that the <u>Osprey</u> had sailed for the Isle of Harris with you two ladies on board. We never guessed that you'd come ashore at Loch Sligachan. Jim was very despondent about missing you . . . at first."

"Well, why not?" said Jim.

"Why not, indeed?" said Susan. "But, in actual fact, we were probably setting off on our bikes about then . . . What time was it?"

"It was about half past nine when we left the Harbour-Master."

"Yes, we were setting off about then to ride here from the hotel."

"And shortly after that we set off to drive here," said Jim.

"And so we've met here by the shore of beautiful Loch Brittle," said Susan. "It really has been extraordinary . . . What are you smiling about, Sam?"

"Oh, nothing!" said Samantha quietly.

Susan looked at her watch."

"Twenty past two," she said. "I don't think we need think about going yet, do you, Sam? But I suppose we ought to get moving at least by three o' clock."

"Yes, I should say so," agreed Samantha. "If we reckon it'll take us roughly three and a half hours again, we'd get back to the hotel at about half past six, if we start at three."

"And I don't think we should aim to arrive any later than half past six," said Susan. "They start serving dinner at seven o' clock, I think. I suppose we've all eaten enough by now on this picnic?" They had all by now finished eating, and they had drunk the remains of the Sandy's' coffee and some water which Susan and Samantha had brought with them in a bottle from the hotel.

Everyone agreed that it had been an excellent lunch picnic, but none of them were in a mood to move; they all wanted to stay where they were, and continue to talk. Jim thought it had been the most enjoyable picnic he had ever eaten. The thought brought a broad smile to his face, and made him turn to Susan, at his side, and whisper in her ear, "I love you, Sue!" He felt that it did not matter at all that his father and Samantha Burton were there to see and hear him express his love for Susan; they all knew about it, and he knew that they both thoroughly approved of the love between them.

"Bless you, Jim, my darling!" Susan whispered back to him. "Isn't it lovely that we're together again today?" She put an arm around Jim, and clasped him to herself in a loving embrace. They kissed.

"Oh, I wish I wasn't going to have to say good-bye to you so soon, Sue. I wish I could stay here with you for the rest of today and then come back with you and Sam to your hotel."

"But I'm afraid, Jim, that we'll *have* to part company soon for this time, because of having our bikes here. We couldn't possibly load them into your hired car, and ask for a lift back."

"Yes, you'll have to ride back," agreed Jim rather sadly.

"Never mind, my darling, we must meet again soon. Why not come down to Rhodes Castle later this summer?"

"But I'd simply love to!" said Jim eagerly. It was odd that he had been thinking earlier of a trip to Rhodes Castle, and now here was Susan issuing the very invitation he wanted to hear.

"Then you must come sometime when I'm back at home," said Susan. "Now, Jim, I'd like to hear more of what you've been doing at home recently, and about how you came up here. But first, I'm going to lie down and rest a while as this is such a good opportunity for a sunbathe."

"I'll lie down too," said Jim.

"Then you'd better put on some of my sun-tan lotion, Jim," said Samantha. "Even if you're not going to take anything off it'll protect your exposed parts from further sunburn."

"I believe my face is rather sunburnt already."

"It does look as if it is. We fair-haired people ought to be very wary of lying in the sun, you know."

"You're quite right, Sam. Thank you very much."

★

It was some twenty minutes later when Susan, after a glance at her watch, raised herself slowly to a sitting position, and said that it was time for her and Samantha to be on their way. She had been lying on her back with her eyes shut, mostly listening to the things Jim was telling her, but occasionally answering him or making some other remark. Jim had been lying beside her talking, mostly on his back, with a hand shading his eyes from the strong sunlight, but for part of the time he had been lying on his side, facing Susan. He would almost have thought that she was asleep but for her occasional remarks. The other two were also lying down, quietly resting. Jim was feeling blissfully happy, and it pained him to hear Susan talk of going, but, of course, he knew that she had to go.

"Must you really go now?" he asked.

"Yes, it's time we were off," said Susan. "Come on, Sam! Wake up!"

"I'm not asleep," said Samantha, opening her eyes and sitting up, blinking in the strong light of the afternoon sun, which was still clear and hot.

Mr. Sandy also sat up.

"We'd better be on our way too," he said.

"Where will you be going now, Mr. Sandy?" asked Samantha. "Elgol?"

"Yes, we were thinking of taking the Elgol road, weren't we, Jim?

I believe you suggested it Mrs. Burton, that evening when you called on us at Cockermouth."

"I did, and you really shouldn't miss it, especially on such a marvelous day as this. I think if anything, the views on that road are even finer than those from this one."

"Then they must be very well worth seeing," said Mr. Sandy.

Susan and Samantha began to gather up the picnic things, and pack them into their rucksacks.

"It's a pity we've drunk all our water," said Samantha, looking at the empty water bottle.

"There's nowhere to refill it here," said Susan. "At least I'll tell you what; we could call at that Youth Hostel we passed, and ask them to fill it up for us."

"Yes, we'd better do that." Samantha pushed the bottle into an outside pocket of her rucksack. "It's pretty hot, thirsty work, cycling in this hilly country, you know," she added, turning to Jim.

Half a minute later they were ready to leave their picnic site.

The four of them began to walk slowly along the top of the beach over the grey shingle. On their right the tide was now coming in over the wet sand, but as yet the place looked much the same as it had looked when Jim had first seen it. He looked wistfully at the smooth water, thinking again of the beautiful figure of Susan standing at the edge of the shallows in her black bathing costume, as he had first seen her.

What a romantic place it was in which to have met her again, when he had not seen her for - he did a little calculation in his head - over two years. It had indeed been about two years and one and a half months since the day in April of 1962, when he had said a tearful good-bye to Susan in the Servants' Common Room of Rhodes Castle at lunch time. He had left the Castle the next morning to return home, and had not seen her again until today. "A Hebridean Meeting", his father had said, he remembered. And why not call it that? It made the occasion seem even more romantic to call it a "Hebridean Meeting".

"Come on, Jim!" shouted his father, standing beside the stile in the fence. Susan and Samantha had already climbed over the stile, and were standing by their bicycles.

"Just coming!" Jim shouted back. He had not really meant to stop, but now he found that it was hard to tear himself away from that quiet, idyllic scene, which now was going to hold a very special place in his memory for the rest of his life.

"I can hardly bear the thought of leaving this place," he told his father frankly as he reached the stile, and climbed over it.

"I know what you mean," said Mr. Sandy. "It's such a beautiful place, isn't it?"

"And so quiet and peaceful," said Samantha.

"It seems an enchanted place," said Susan. "I think it's the feeling of remoteness that appeals to me particularly: the feeling of being remote from civilization, and the peacefulness. No one else has come here to disturb our privacy."

"I think we've been a bit lucky that way," commented Samantha. "Later in the summer, probably, there'll be more people about here, especially if there are any more days as fine as today. We've been incredibly lucky in our weather today, it seems to me."

"Now, Jim," said Susan, "if you could spare a few minutes, just before we go, perhaps we could have a look at that map you said you had."

"I'll get it," said Jim. He went to the car, opened the driver's door, and picked up the map from the back seat (they had not locked the car as there were no other people about).

Jim and Susan studied the map together for a few minutes when he had spread it out on the bonnet of the car. Susan indicated for him with a finger the approximate route over which the Osprey had sailed after passing the Mallaig pier-head. Then Samantha, who had been looking over their shoulders at the map, put her finger on the village of Elgol on Loch Scavaig.

"That's Elgol, at the end of the road from Broadford," she said. "You'll find it's a marvellous drive, especially where you get a good view of Blaven across Loch Slapin from here and there are wonderful views of the Cuillins across Loch Scavaig."

Mr. Sandy and Jim and Susan were looking at the map with interest.

"It looks a fascinating drive," said Mr. Sandy.

"If only you could come with us," said Jim, looking round hopefully at Susan. "Couldn't you, Sue? Supposing . . ." He stopped, seeing Susan slowly shaking her head.

"Impossible!" she said. "Sorry, Jim, but that really would be *quite* impossible. You see, we'd get back to our hotel ridiculously late if we were to take a lift with you to Elgol in your hired car because you'd have to bring us back here much later to collect our bicycles . . . and then we'd still have the cycle ride back to the Sligachan Hotel. Heaven knows how late we'd arrive back there . . . perhaps by half past ten tonight, or even later? That simply wouldn't do."

Jim nodded his head by way of reluctant agreement with Susan, but he said nothing.

"But you'll enjoy going there with your Dad, Jim, even without me and Sam," continued Susan. "It can't be helped that we can't come with you. You've got your camera with you?"

"Yes, I've got it."

"Well then, you can show me the pictures you take at Elgol when you come down to stay at the Castle, and you can tell me all about it then. You are definitely coming down to stay for a week or two, aren't you?"

"Oh yes, Sue. I'm certainly going to! When would you like me to come?"

"Oh, shall we say some time next month, or in August depending on when you can get away for a week's or a fortnight's holiday?"

(Jim had told Susan about his job as a porter.) "I'll tell you what, I'll write to you soon, Jim, and give you a few dates to choose from."

"Thanks very much, Sue; that'll be something really nice to look forward to."

Then Susan again said that it was time that she and Samantha were getting on their way. Samantha was already sitting astride her bicycle with a foot on the ground, and with her packed rucksack slung on her back..

"It needs to be fairly light with all the hard work we've got ahead of us!" she joked.

"I might see you on the ferry tomorrow evening," Samantha reminded Jim when he said good-bye to her, "but good-bye for now, Jim. Good-bye, Mr. Sandy. It's been a super picnic!"

"It's been first-rate," agreed Mr. Sandy. Good-bye, Mrs. Burton.

Good-bye, Lady Dalmane. I hope you have a good voyage back to Maryport."

"Thank you, Mr. Sandy," said Susan, shaking hands with him.

When Jim said good-bye to Susan he felt, as he held her for a moment in a close embrace that it was more than he could bear to let her go. Their lips touched in a kiss of hot passion. For a second or two he stared into the seductive delights of her superb eyes; then their embrace slowly broke apart.

Susan mounted her bicycle. Samantha was already beginning to pedal slowly away.

"Good-bye!" shouted Susan, raising a hand for a moment from the handlebars as she began to pedal after Samantha.

"Good-bye!" shouted Samantha, also raising a hand.

The Sandys called out a final farewell, and both the cyclists rang their bells by way of a reply.

"We'll give them a minute or two to get on their way, shall we, Jim?" said Mr. Sandy, as they stood watching the departing cyclists ride away towards the white cottage along the rough road.

"All right," said Jim.

They saw the two cycling figures, one in blue, and one in red, disappear from their view around the bend by the white cottage. But Jim felt only a momentary sadness when he could no longer see Susan. He would soon be seeing her again.

CHAPTER NINE

Jim and his father were standing on the top of a little rocky headland, looking down on the smooth water of Portree Loch. Around them were pine trees, most of them standing, although a few had fallen down, blown over by gales.

"Let's have our picnic here," said Jim. "There's a nice view of the water through the pine branches."

"Right," said Mr. Sandy, "we'll sit down here."\

They sat down not far from the edge of the cliff, where they had a good view of the little bay of Portree Loch, where a small river ran into the sea. On the far side of this bay they could see some white houses and bungalows dotted about on the lower hillside. The headland jutted out into the loch, leaving Portree Harbour well sheltered on its eastern side, and the little bay of the river mouth on its western side.

The Sandys had approached the headland from a strip of beach by the mouth of the River Leasgeary by clambering up a very steep path.

Jim's first idea had been to walk right round the base of the headland between the high and low water marks until he should come to the harbour pier, but this he had found impossible. The tide was already well out and still falling, and there were plenty of beaches on the river side of the headland, but he saw that the shingle and sand ended by the point of the promontary. Round the point he expected to see the cliff descending straight into the water. That way was clearly not a practical route for the average pedestrian, so Jim changed his plan, and followed his father up a precipitous footpath towards the trees on the top of the headland. The path proceeded by zigzags, and Jim occasionally climbed up on all fours for greater safety; it would not do to have an accident in a place like that but soon he and his father had reached the top in safety.

They had been filling in time since they had returned the hired car to the garage shortly before midday. Encouraged by the success of the previous day's motoring, they had set off again in the hired car soon after breakfast on the last day of their short stay in the Isle of Skye, and had motored to Dunvegan. After a visit to Dunvegan Castle, where they had walked in the gardens and grounds (which Jim had admired very much), they had motored back to Portree, and had handed over the car at the garage. Thursday the fourth of June had dawned almost as bright and sunny as Wednesday had, and they had seen the water of Dunvegan Loch looking a sparkling blue under a blue and nearly cloudless sky. Back in Portree they had walked slowly back to the town centre; slowly because they had too much time. Their bus was due to depart from Somerled Square at two-fifteen, so they had decided that, as they were now proceeding on foot, there was not enough time to go anywhere else. They had again visited the shop where they had bought the oatcakes for the Loch Brittle picnic, and this time they had bought some pies and some more oatcakes for another picnic. Then they had made their way to the beach by the mouth of the River Leasgeary, where Jim had said that the best place for their picnic would be on top of the headland among the pine trees; and so, at about one o'clock, they had arrived there.

"The harbour's a lovely view, seen through these pine branches," said Jim as he sat down on the short dry grass.

"Yes, isn't it?" agreed his father.

"And it's a good place for looking down on the boats in the harbour or the loch, whatever this water's called. Only from here we can't see any boats that are moving out at sea."

"We probably wouldn't see the <u>Osprey</u> again even if we *could* see the open sea," said Mr. Sandy. "Perhaps she's already returned to Loch Sligachan and Lady Dalmane's on board her by now. Tell me, Jim, when is it, exactly, that you've been invited to go to stay at Rhodes Castle?"

"Susan said that I was to come next month, or in August, but I haven't got a definite date yet. She's going to write to me, and suggest some dates in a letter."

"I see; and you would use up the rest of your fortnight's holiday for this year staying at Rhodes Castle?"

"I certainly mean to. Let me see: I've got . . . about another ten days of holiday due to me, as this holiday will use up only five days altogether. And then there'll be a Sunday as well, which doesn't count as one of the days."

"You've been awfully lucky, Jim, you know, meeting Susan Dalmane yesterday, haven't you?" said his father. "One is tempted to say that fate must have meant you two to get together again, and arranged yesterday's 'co-incidence', if that's what it was, accordingly." He smiled meaningfully at his son.

"Yes, it does seem to have happened like that," said Jim. He took a mouthful of pie, and ate it thoughtfully.

There was not much more talking after that. Jim was remembering as he ate that he was now very near the end of his short stay in Skye, and he wanted to savour every last minute of it, especially while they remained seated where they were. The prospect of the smooth, blue water, seen through the pine branches, was too quiet and peaceful, and too beautiful, to be wasted by unnecessary talk.

Presently their lunch picnic was over, and they picked up their suitcases and their carrier bag, and began to stroll back through the trees to pick up a path which would lead them back, past the cottage-hospital and a small church, to Somerled Square in the middle of Portree.

They came into the square, and found that their bus was already waiting there; but there was no one in it yet, so, to fill in a little more time, Jim and his father did some more shopping for holiday souvenirs. At around two o'clock they approached the bus. They paid their fares to the driver as they boarded the bus, and he gave them their tickets, and told them to change at Broadford; his bus was going to Kyleakin. "The four twenty-three from Broadford Post Office," he told them in answer to Mr. Sandy's question about the time of the departure of the connection to Armadale Pier.

It felt decidedly hot sitting in the stationary bus in the strong sunshine, waiting for the start. The door was open, but that did not seem to make it any cooler. Mr. Sandy and Jim had taken seats towards the rear of the single-decker bus, and Jim was occasionally fanning his face with the map of Skye in an attempt to cool himself. The bus was slowly filling up with passengers as the time crept on towards a quarter past two. Although Jim felt rather sad at the thought of leaving Portree, he found himself wishing that the time for the departure of the bus would come quickly; once they were moving it would, of course, feel cooler. Finally the driver started his engine, closed the door, and drove the bus out of Somerled Square. It was just after a quarter past two.

Some twenty minutes later the bus slowed down as the driver prepared to stop at the Sligachan Hotel. Jim saw that they were going to turn off the main road to pull into the forecourt of the hotel. He looked ahead, and saw a passenger waiting for the bus, someone wearing something of a bright blue colour, with fair hair, and with a rucksack slung on her back . . . it was Samantha Burton. The bus pulled up beside her, and Samantha boarded, and stopped a moment to buy her ticket from the driver. Then, for a second, she turned round, saw Jim and his father, and waved a hand. But the bus by now was almost full of passengers, and Jim felt a sharp pang of disappointment as he saw Samantha choose a seat right at the front of the bus, immediately behind the driver. The bus was already moving off again. Samantha took off her rucksack, placed it on the seat, and sat down beside it. Jim was longing to be able to talk to her, but he knew that he would have to wait until they were off the bus before it would be possible to ask her about Susan. Had Susan already left the Isle of Skye, or had the <u>Osprey</u> not yet returned to Loch Sligachan?

In a minute or two he would be seeing Loch Sligachan, where the main road ran alongside the loch, so he would be keeping a sharp look-out for the <u>Osprey</u>. Soon, however, they reached the village of Sconser, where the bus stopped; but there was never a sign of a yacht on the loch.

At Broadford Samantha left the bus, carrying her rucksack, as soon as the driver had pulled up and opened the door. Jim and his father were already standing in the gangway, waiting to disembark, but they were compelled to wait for an elderly lady who was also getting out and temporarily blocking the gangway in front of them. The old lady slowly and carefully negotiated the three steps down to the ground through the open doorway of the bus; she was followed by Mr. Sandy, and then by Jim. He looked around at once for Samantha.

"Where's Samantha disappeared to?" he asked.

"She went into the post office," said Mr. Sandy, pointing across the road. The bus had pulled up nearly opposite the Broadford Post Office.

"Shall we wait for her to come out? I want to ask her whether Sue's gone yet."

"I don't think we'd better wait here for her," said Mr. Sandy. "You never know, Jim, but she might be quite some time in there perhaps with a letter or a post card to write, and then post. And I don't want anything in the post office."

"Nor do I," said Jim.

"Well then, shall we go for a walk? You can talk to Samantha later. Remember, we know for certain that she'll be travelling with us on the four twenty-three bus to Armadale, because she told us she'd be coming with us on this evening's ferry to the mainland."

"Oh yes, I'll be able to have a word with her either on the next bus, or on the pier at Armadale, or, failing that, on board the evening ferry. Okay, Dad, where shall we walk?"

Mr. Sandy looked at his watch.

"Ten past three. We've over an hour to wait for this bus. We might as well go down to the beach. You can see it's only about a hundred yards away, down that road to the left."

Jim agreed with his father that they ought not to go too far away from the spot where they were now standing, on the pavement of the main road, assuming that their next bus would pick them up there. They walked a few paces beyond the little road to the left, until they stood on the bridge over the Broadford River, where they stopped a minute or two to look down at the water. It was a smallish river, and they were looking down at the place where it became tidal, and began to widen out into a little estuary, although the mouth of the river in Broadford Bay was less than a quarter of a mile away. Immediately beyond the bridge another road turned off the main coastal road on the other side, and was signed to Elgol. It was the road over which the Sandys had motored on the previous evening, but, although Jim glanced at it, and recalled briefly the beautiful mountain colours they had seen across Loch Slapin and around Elgol, he was mostly thinking of something else, and his eyes kept turning to the post office. She *must* be writing a letter in there, he said to himself, or she'd have come out by now. But Samantha had not re-appeared when the Sandys set off walking again.

The small road lead to a few new houses and a hotel, but at the first bend the Sandys left it, seeing a path down to the shore. Almost immediately they found themselves on the top of a grassy bank, overlooking Broadford Bay and a beach of shingle. They descended to the stony beach, turned to their left, and began to saunter along, not aiming to reach any particular point, while they looked leisurely at expansive views of sea, land, and sky. There was some cloud in the sky now: overhead were wispy cirrus clouds, but to their right, over the sea, there were lines of fleecy white clouds. However, there was still plenty of blue sky, and the clouds looked high and thin, not threatening; and the sea was of a spectacularly deep blue colour, reflecting the light from the sky. Looking across to the other side of the bay, they saw that the village of Broadford straggled along the coast for a long way; white houses could be seen here and there by that coast a mile or more away. Jim's eyes followed that coastline towards the point at Kyleakin where it appeared to join that of the mainland of Scotland.

They soon stopped walking. Jim and his father kept looking at their watches frequently, keeping in mind the departure time of their bus for Armadale Pier. With such excellent views to admire there was little point in walking any further. Jim looked at the distant mountains of the mainland. Those peaks were of a deep blue shade that afternoon, and appeared to rise abruptly from the sea.

"I think I'll sit down here," said Mr. Sandy presently. "What are you going to do, Jim? Sit down until it's time to go back for the bus, or walk about?"

"Oh, I think I'll just wander about on the beach around here," said Jim. "I'll see if I can find any interesting stones on this beach."

"Right, but we'd better leave here not later than four o'clock."

There was a very good place to sit down out of the wind (although there was very little wind) at the foot of the steep bank at the top of the beach. Mr. Sandy sat down on one of a number of large boulders of grey rock, and made himself reasonably comfortable. Jim walked slowly down over the smaller, tide-washed stones of the beach towards the edge of the water. It was a little after the time of low water, and the tide had turned, but there was still plenty of shingle uncovered. As he walked he kept his eyes mostly on the ground, on the look-out for any stone which might be interesting enough to take away as a souvenir, but he also kept looking up at the marvellous views. However, after ten minutes of wandering about he had found nothing of interest.

"Hello!"

Jim looked up, startled by the sudden voice, and saw Samantha Burton coming towards him.

"Oh, hello, Sam!" he said. "Where have you come from?"

"Just from round the corner," said Samantha. "There's a little pier round this corner but you can't quite see it from here." Jim was looking the way she was pointing. "And there are some houses there at the end of a small road, and a hotel."

"Dad saw you go into the post office when you got off the bus."

"Yes, I went in there to write a short letter to my mother, and to post it. She lives in Edinburgh, so, you see, I feel I *ought* to call and see her on my way home, but I wrote to explain that I really haven't the time for that on this trip to Scotland."

"I see. Has Sue gone, Sam?"

"Oh yes, hours ago. The Osprey sailed from Loch Sligachan with Sue on board at about ten o'clock this morning, so they'll be miles away by now, no doubt."

"Yes, they must be well on their way," said Jim, "so I needn't think any more about keeping a look-out for them. But I don't mind much about that after meeting you and Susan yesterday."

"Wasn't it a super picnic?"

"My word, I'll say it was! It was a day I'll remember all my life, Sam; I'm sure I will."

"I know you're *very* fond of Susan, Jim," said Samantha seriously, "so I've no doubt that yesterday's reunion was important to you."

"It was it was an absolutely wonderful day altogether!"

"And the weather was wonderful too, and it still is," said Samantha, "although" (she looked up) "there's a little bit of cloud in the sky now the beginning of a change, perhaps. But that's a very pretty sky all the same, isn't it, with those fleecy white clouds over the sea?"

"Yes, there are gorgeous colours in the sky," said Jim, looking up at the lines of white cloud, and the gaps of blue sky between them. "And the sea's a lovely colour too."

"And what about yesterday afternoon when we left you?" asked Samantha. "Did you get to Elgol?"

"Yes, we went there, and I took some pictures which ought to be very good ones when they're printed."

"Which would you say you liked seeing the best: the Elgol road or the Glen Brittle road?"

Jim thought for a moment before answering.

"There are delightful views from both roads," he said, "but I think perhaps the views from the Elgol road are the better of the two.

The mountains looked particularly splendid when we came to that first sea loch, which the road skirts around . . ."

"Loch Slapin, you mean?"

"Yes, that one. The water was so smooth it looked just like a mirror, and that splendid peak on the other side, Blaven, had a sharp, clear reflection in the loch. I've never seen anything quite like it before."

"Did you stop there to get a photo?"

"Oh yes, we couldn't go past without stopping to take a picture."

"Well, I *am* glad you enjoyed your trip to Elgol so much," said Samantha. "It's an awful pity that Sue and I couldn't have gone with you. Next time I come to Skye I really *must* include a drive over that lovely road again; no doubt it'll bring back memories of holidays long ago just as Loch Brittle did."

"That's a place I'll never forget!" said Jim wistfully.

There was a pause in their conversation, while they stood looking out at the fine prospect of Broadford Bay, and over the sea to the Scottish mainland around Balmacara and Loch Carron. Jim, however, was also seeing Susan again in his mind's eye, bathing in the sea at Loch Brittle.

"Did <u>Osprey</u> come back very early to Loch Sligachan?" he asked presently.

"I suppose she did," said Samantha. "At any rate, we saw her anchored in the loch before we had our breakfast this morning. Then, after breakfast, when we'd paid our hotel bills and packed our things, we cycled off at about a quarter past nine and rode to Sconser, and went down onto the shore exactly adjacent to the place where the <u>Osprey</u> was anchored in the loch."

"But how did you let them know that you were waiting there for Susan to be picked up?"

"We were going to hail them, but there was no need. Anne Himmel was sitting on the cabin roof, no doubt keeping a look-out for us, and she saw us as soon as we appeared at the water's edge. She waved a hand, and shouted to Martin, who must have been in the cabin, and he came out at once into the cockpit, and saw where we were standing, waving to him. Then he rowed over in the dinghy and picked Sue up. It needed two trips again; first to pick up Sue, and then back to the shore to pick up the bikes. Then I saw them set the sails, and raise the anchor; and they were off at about ten o'clock while I waved to them from the shore."

"Didn't you feel a little sad at being left behind this time?" asked Jim.

"Well, I suppose I did a little, but not too much. To tell you the truth, Jim, I'm rather glad in a way, to be returning to England by land, except for the ferry over to Mallaig. I managed to feel awfully seasick for most of the outward voyage, although the sea was mostly fairly smooth, with never more than what Sue would call a 'gentle swell'."

"Oh, I see," said Jim thoughtfully. "But what did you do when the <u>Osprey</u> had sailed away out of sight? Walk back to the hotel?"

"Yes, I did that, as there were several hours to fill in before I could catch that two thirty-six bus to Broadford. I was back at the Sligachan Hotel before eleven, and then I took a walk by myself up Glen Sligachan as it was such a lovely morning. You get a superb view, you know, from the hotel up the glen towards the peak of Marsco, on the left and Glamaig too, looking east." She paused a second or two before continuing.

Jim could not remember without consulting his map where Marsco and Glamaig were, but he did not ask Samantha about them.

"And then?" he asked her.

"Then back for lunch at the hotel. Then I just mooched around for a bit to fill in time until it was twenty-five past two, when I went outside to wait for the bus, the one you came on from Portree." She paused a moment, and then added as an afterthought: "By the way, Jim, I've got something to hand over to you."

"Something from Susan?" said Jim eagerly.

But Samantha did not answer him directly. She consulted her watch.

"The lady in the post office told me the bus goes from there at four twenty-three," she said, "so I don't think we need leave this beach just yet." She started wriggling out of the straps of her rucksack.

"Yes, I've got a letter for you from Susan in my rucksack."

"Gosh, so Sue's already written to me! I wasn't expecting to get a letter from her for at least a fortnight!"

Samantha set her rucksack down on the stones at her feet, and began to open a pocket of it, and to dig about in it for the letter.

"Susan wrote this for you last night. You'd better have it now."

Samantha handed Jim a white envelope with the one word "Jim" written on it. "I was going to give it to you when we met on board the ferry, but as we've happened to meet here . . ."

"Am I allowed to open it now?" asked Jim keenly, his fingers poised to open the envelope.

"Yes, of course you may; but shall we sit down first, Jim?"

"Let's go and sit down beside Dad," said Jim. "There'll be plenty of time to read Sue's letter before we have to go back for the bus."

When the three of them were sitting reasonably comfortably on large rocks at the foot of the steep bank at the top of the beach Jim opened the envelope, and took from it the following letter:-

Sligachan Hotel,
Wednesday evening, June 3rd.

My darling Jim,

What a lovely surprise it was to meet you and your father yesterday at Loch Brittle! It was one of the most delightful picnics I've ever had - it really made my day!

I know you probably weren't expecting to hear from me so soon, but I thought it would be a nice surprise for you to get this tomorrow, so I've written this letter tonight, and I'm giving it to Sam to hand on to you. No doubt you'll be meeting Sam tomorrow when you travel back on the ferry to Mallaig. By that time, if all goes according to plan, <u>Osprey</u> will be well on her way with me back on board as skipper.

I'm very much looking forward to hearing how your trip to Elgol went yesterday after you left us. If you took any nice photos you must bring them with you, Jim, when you come to stay at Rhodes Castle, if you can get them developed and printed in time.

Now, about the dates when you could come south to stay with me. It would be nice if you could stay for a fortnight, but perhaps you won't be able to do that because of your job. Anyway, from the 29th June to 13th July is free, or you could come on the 4th August, or the 10th, or the 17th. The days are all Mondays except August 4th, which is the Tuesday after the August Bank Holiday. I wouldn't advise you to try travelling on Bank Holiday Monday because the trains might be very crowded.

I hope you can come on or round about one o f those dates, so do write to me soon, Jim, when you get home to let me know what you think. But remember, I definitely want you to come to Rhodes Castle!

Well, I think that's all for now. I hope you have a good journey home on the train; probably you'll find Samantha on the same train from Mallaig, so perhaps you could all travel together to Glasgow, or to Carlisle, depending on Sam's plans. She may want to stay in Glasgow to visit her grandparents, or she may not; I really don't know about that. Anyway, I'll be looking forward to getting a letter from you, Jim, telling me when you'll be coming.

With all my love,
Sue.

When Jim had read Susan's letter through slowly and carefully he put his hand into a jacket pocket, and drew out his diary for 1964. He began to turn over the pages until he came to the end of June, when he saw for himself that June 29th was indeed a Monday. I think that'll be too soon, he said to himself; I'll have to give the Station-Master at Cockermouth plenty of notice of when I intend to go away on this next holiday. He turned over some more pages of his diary to look at the August dates.

"Well?" said Samantha, who had been sitting near him, quietly admiring the view. "Has Sue invited you to the Castle on a particular date?"

"She's given me various dates to choose from," said Jim, "and I think I'll go south on August the fourth, just after the Bank Holiday."

★

The bus from Broadford pulled up in the large car park by Armadale Pier, and Mr. Sandy, Jim, and Samantha stepped down from it. They had been sitting together at the front of the bus, and had seen that the MacBrayne ferry was already tied up alongside the pier before the bus had stopped.

"What do we do now?" asked Jim. "Go aboard the ferry?"

"It's a bit early to do that, isn't it?" said Samantha. "It's only five past five."

"Yes, perhaps we'd better fill in time once again for a little while," said Mr. Sandy. "Shall we go for a walk?"

"Didn't we pass a cafe on our way into this car park?" said Jim.

"That building over there. Shall we go in and have some tea? I'm thirsty."

"That's a good idea!" said Mr. Sandy. "Will you join us for a cup of tea, Mrs. Burton?"

Five minutes later they were sitting at a cafe table, waiting for the waitress to bring them tea and cakes. The cafe was almost empty, so there had been no difficulty in finding seats. The waitress came with the things they had ordered on a tray.

"Doesn't it seem a pity to be leaving the Isle of Skye now after such a short visit?" said Samantha a little later.

"That's just what I was thinking," said Jim. He took a mouthful of tea, and then added: "Actually, I suggested coming in here so that we could put off going on board the ferry for at least another ten minutes. Once we're on board it we're no longer on the island, so I thought it would be nice to prolong our stay here by ten minutes, or so."

"But that's not very much!" laughed Mr. Sandy. "Time will catch up with us all too soon, I fear, while we sit here having our tea, pleasant though it is to be here."

★

The ferry was well on its way across the Sound of Sleat on the evening crossing to Mallaig. Jim, his father, and Samantha Burton were all standing on the open upper deck on the port side of the vessel, watching the receding coastline of Skye and the approaching coastline of the Scottish mainland. It was still fine, but now they had lost the sun, and it was rather more cloudy, although there was still some sunshine to be seen ahead of them, over mainland Scotland. They could now see far up the broad inlet of Loch Nevis, and Jim, looking that way, was pointing out to the others the sun shining on a distant peak.

"That peak's called Sgurr na Ciche, I believe," remembered Samantha, who was also staring at the remote jagged peak, whose steep-edged top appeared to pierce a layer of white cloud.

"It looks very beautiful, doesn't it, with the evening sun full on it, while the nearer hills are in deep shadow?" said Mr. Sandy

"Yes, it's a lovely sight," said Samantha dreamily. She was silent a moment, and then went on to explain that Knoydart, the mountainous part of the mainland at which they were looking, was a very remote and roadless part of the Western Highlands. "It certainly brings back old memories, seeing those mountains of Knoydart from the sea," she said, "and in such an exceptionally pretty light too."

Jim said nothing. He was staring ahead, like the others, at Loch Nevis, at the mountains of the Knoydart peninsula, and particularly at the bold shape of the far-off peak of Sgurr na Ciche; and he was thinking how delightful it would be some day to explore that remote and rugged country on foot. It would be really wonderful if Sue and I could come here again some time, he thought. We could stay on the mainland, and perhaps climb that mountain Sgurr na Ciche although it looks *impossibly* steep from here!

Then he turned to look once more at the receding coastline of the Isle of Skye. This has been my best holiday ever, he thought, and my most abiding memory of Skye will surely be of Sue and me at Loch Brittle - our Hebridean meeting!

CHAPTER TEN

It was a grey, cloudy morning with a hint of dampness in the air when Jim and his father came into Mallaig station to catch the early morning train to Glasgow.

"Here's the train," said Jim, seeing three carriages standing at the platform behind a large diesel locomotive.

"It looks almost empty as yet," remarked Mr. Sandy.

"Well, there are still ten minutes to go until departure time," said Jim. "I wonder if Samantha's already in it?"

They walked a little way down the platform, looking through the windows of the train, and noticing that there were hardly any passengers sitting inside it; Jim was looking for Samantha, but could not see her. They had not seen her since dinner time on the previous evening in the dining-room of the West Highland Hotel, where they had all spent the night. The hotel had refused to give them anything for breakfast at a quarter past six, but early morning cups of tea had been brought to the Sandys' room. Jim, however, felt more than ready for some breakfast, and hoped that some sort of refreshments would be provided on the train, although they had seen no sign of a buffet when they had walked along the platform.

"We'd better get in," said Mr. Sandy. They walked back a few yards, and entered the rear carriage of the train.

"Why, there's no one at all in here!" said Jim in surprise as they walked along the corridor, and looked at one compartment after another, all of them empty. "I don't believe Samantha's here yet. She'll have to hurry up, or she may miss the train."

"I expect she knows what she's doing," said Mr. Sandy. He opened the door of a compartment. "We might as well sit in here, eh, Jim? All these compartments are empty so one's as good as another."

They entered the compartment, closed the door behind them, and placed their suitcases on the luggage rack.

"Which way do you want to face, Jim?" asked his father.

"Backwards this time, I think," said Jim. He sat himself down in the window seat facing backwards.

"No doubt the train will fill up as it goes along," said Mr. Sandy, "especially at Fort William, I should think. I didn't see any sign of a buffet car, but perhaps they'll attach one to the train at Fort William."

"I hope they do! I'm hungry, and we can't have any breakfast unless there's a buffet on this train."

"We've a few biscuits left. We could eat those now."

Mr. Sandy took the remains of a packet of biscuits from the carrier bag which was lying beside him on the seat, offered Jim a biscuit, and took one himself. For a while they ate biscuits slowly and in silence. At ten minutes to seven the train began to move. They were off.

Jim waited a few minutes longer before going to look for Samantha, nibbling pieces of broken biscuit, and looking out of the windows at a grey sea with white foam breaking on the rocks. That morning the visibility was poor, and the outline of the Isle of Eigg could only just be made out. Soon the view of the sea was temporarily lost as the railway took the train a little further inland.

"I'm going to look for Samantha now," said Jim when the last of the biscuits had been eaten. He got up, and opened the door of the still empty compartment, and at once saw Samantha Burton. She was standing at a window in the corridor at the end of that carriage, next to the toilet, where the gangway lead through to the middle carriage of the train. Jim saw that she had not noticed that he was there, so he shut the compartment door and set off up the corridor to meet her.

"Good morning, Jim!" said Samantha as she turned and saw him.
"Hello, Sam!"

"It's disappointingly grey this morning, isn't it?"

"It is rather. Ah, we're slowing down for the first station.
Morar's the first stop, isn't it?"

"I don't know, Jim. Its ages since I last travelled on this line, and I can't remember things like that now. But this might well be Morar."

It was, as they saw for themselves a minute later when the train stopped at the platform of Morar station.

"There's a passenger getting into the next carriage," said Jim.

"Only one," said Samantha. "I suppose this carriage will stay fairly empty until we get to Fort William."

The train began to move again.

"I wonder if we could get a glimpse of Loch Morar?" said Jim. "I forgot to look out for it on our outward journey."

"I don't remember seeing it when I last came this way," said Samantha, "but we may as well look out for it."

Jim and Samantha were still standing in the corridor at the end of the carriage, but now they were looking out on the landward side of the train, rather than the seaward side. They had a quick glimpse of the Morar River as the train crossed it, but they saw no sign of a loch.

"Obviousy you can't see the loch from a train," said Jim a minute later. "Shall we sit down now, Sam?"

Instead of answering him Samantha turned from staring out of the window, and looked at him seriously.

"Jim," she said, "tell me: when you go down to Rhodes Castle are you going to propose to Susan?"

"Why, yes!" said Jim, his face suddenly brightening into a smile at the thought. "Yes, I suppose I could do that now."

"Hadn't you thought of doing that?"

"Well, no I hadn't. I suppose I've got so used to thinking of her as a married woman that I'd forgotten that she has no husband now, since Lord Dalmane died last year."

"Yes, she's unattached now. I think you should propose to her."

"I shall!" Then the smile vanished from Jim's face as another thought occurred to him. "But supposing that I propose to Sue, and she rejects me? Do you think she might reject me, Sam?"

Samantha shook her head slowly.

"No, I don't think so," she said. "I should say that rejection of a proposal of marriage from you, Jim, is very unlikely."

"Then I'll certainly ask her if she wants to marry me!"

Samantha smiled at him.

"You're still very much in love with Susan, aren't you?"

"Oh, I am, I really am. Sue means *everything* to me, Sam. I couldn't think of marrying anyone else. I feel as if . . ." He hesitated, a little uncertain of how to express the thought in his mind. "As if my life won't really be *complete* until Sue becomes my wife." He looked earnestly into Samantha's face. "You know what I mean, Sam, don't you?"

"Oh yes, Jim!" she said. "I know very well what you mean." She nodded her head thoughtfully, as if she were considering what Jim had told her, and then added: "And I believe that Sue feels very much the same way about you!"

"Gosh!" said Jim excitedly. "Does she? Does she really . . . *want* me to be her husband?"

"I think she does. I don't think that Susan will think of *her* life as complete until you, Jim, are a part of it."

"Oh, I hope so, I *hope* so! But do you think she'll be expecting me to make a proposal of marriage to her?"

"I do think she'll expect it," said Samantha. "Only consider, Jim: what do you think she's inviting you to come and stay with her for, if not to give you the opportunity you want to propose to her?"

"Oh . . . well, I suppose she may have that in mind . . ."

"I believe she does," said Samantha.

There was a short silence. Jim noticed that the train was skirting the edge of the hilly country as it passed Mointeach Mhor, and approached Arisaig.

"Let's go and sit down," said Samantha suddenly, changing the subject. "I'm getting tired of standing here in this noisy corridor."

"Me too," said Jim. "Why not come and sit in our compartment, Sam, where Dad is now?"

"Yes, I'll do that," she said. "Lead on, Jim!"

"Where were you sitting when you first got into the train?"

"In there," said Samantha as they walked past the first compartment door. "You see, I left my rucksack in there. Half a minute, I think I'd better just pick it up in case I go and forget it when we get in to Glasgow."

Samantha went back, and entered the empty compartment where her rucksack was lying on a seat, and picked it up. Jim had forgotten how many doors he had to pass until he should come to the compartment which he and his father had chosen, so, as he walked along the corridor, he had to look into each one to see that it was empty.

"Here we are!" he said, seeing his father sitting in a corner seat of a compartment. Jim opened the door for Samantha to go in before him. Mr. Sandy, suddenly seeing Samantha Burton entering the compartment, politely rose to his feet.

"Good morning, Mrs. Burton," he said.

"Please don't stand up for me!" said Samantha quickly. Mr. Sandy sat down at once.

"I was sitting there," said Jim, pointing to the backward-facing window seat, "but perhaps you'd like to take that corner seat, Sam?"

"Oh no, don't let me turn you out of your seat, Jim," she said.

"But perhaps I could sit beside you?"

"Please do." Jim closed the door, and they sat down.

"It's disappointing to see it so grey outside, isn't it?" said Mr. Sandy.

"It is disappointing," said Samantha, "but we've been very lucky. The last two days, and Wednesday particularly, have been, I suppose, so good that they've been quite un-Hebridean; not typical days for early summer in these parts. you know."

"Quite so."

"But this morning, perhaps, it doesn't matter so much what it's like now. I think it's going to rain fairly soon."

"Before we get to Glasgow, do you think?" said Jim, looking out of the window at the grey sky. The train was slowing down to stop at Arisaig.

"Probably long before we get to Glasgow by the look of it," said Samantha.

The train stopped at Arisaig, and in the momentary quietness Samantha whispered in Jim's ear.

"Shall we tell your Dad what we were talking about?"

"Yes, we'd better," whispered Jim. "I'm going to ask Susan if she wants to marry me when I go down to Rhodes Castle," he announced.

"Are you, indeed?" said his father. "Well, good luck to you, Jim!"

"I think you'd be ideally suited to each other as husband and wife, you and Susan," said Samantha.

"I must say, I'd be really delighted to hear of you and Susan getting married, if she accepts your proposal, Jim," said his father.

"That would be most delightful news!" Then Jim saw his father's expression change slightly as another idea seemed to occur to him. The smile did not leave his face, but it became a rather different smile as he added: "But there is just one thing, Jim, which you may not have considered!"

"What?" asked Jim, suddenly bothered at the thought of his father already raising an objection to his splendid plan of proposing to Susan.

"What about Jill?" said his father. "You've been going out with her lately, haven't you?"

"Oh, well . . . er . . . ." began Jim awkwardly. He had no idea what to say to answer his father about his friendship with Jill Rose, and felt annoyed that her name should have been mentioned.

"You weren't thinking of simply dropping her, were you, because you've met Susan, and want to marry her?"

"Oh no, Dad, of course I won't drop Jill. She'll still be my friend, and I expect I'll see her occasionally." But of course I *shall* drop her when Sue and I get married, he said to himself.

"I see. I'm sorry if I've upset you, Jim, by mentioning Jill." Mr. Sandy had detected the note of resentment in his son's voice.

"Oh, that's quite all right."

"I think Jim should be free to make up his own mind on such an important matter as this," said Samantha helpfully. "Don't you think so, Mr. Sandy?"

"Indeed, yes, I certainly do. It's your decision, Jim, whom you want to marry, and yours alone. Remember, you don't need my consent to get married, as you're now twenty-three."

"Oh, I know that," said Jim, "but I'd like to think, all the same, that you approve of this idea."

"I do," said Mr. Sandy. "I approve very much indeed if you're certain that a proposal to Susan is the right thing for you to do. I think it is."

"Actually, Sam only suggested the idea to me a few minutes ago," confessed Jim, "When we were talking in the corridor."

"Oh yes; but, good heavens, Jim, this is no *new* idea of your's to marry Susan Dalmane, is it? It's something you've dreamed of for years!"

"Of course I have. No, I only meant that I'd temporarily forgotten about it forgotten that now Susan and I are free to get married if she wants to marry me."

"You'd forgotten about it? Well, fancy that!" chuckled his father merrily.

"Anyway," said Jim, "my invitation to Rhodes Castle has only come about because of this amazing co-incidence that's happened; this wonderful stroke of luck that Sue and Samantha happened to be on the Isle of Skye just at the same time that we were there."

"Yes, it was a co-incidence all right!" agreed his father.

"Was it?" said Samantha. Jim looked at her, and saw that a sly smile had appeared on her face.

"It must have been a co-incidence," said Jim. "I know that we were thinking that we *might* meet the <u>Osprey</u> when we came up to Mallaig in the train, because you told us that evening you called on us at home that you hoped to go cruising, heading for Scotland."

"And you told me that you and your father were going to the Isle of Skye for a few days at the beginning of June," said Samantha. "Don't you remember?"

"Yes, I do; but all the same"

"Why, you told me the exact dates of your holiday, and even some exact timetable details! And you said that you'd be staying at the 'Harbour View' Hotel at Portree on the nights of Tuesday, June the second, and Wednesday, June the third; and that you meant to hire a car. Don't you understand? I *knew* all these things, Jim and had them in mind when planning the cruise in the <u>Osprey</u> with Susan and the Himmels."

"Gosh!" A sudden simple explanation for the apparently extraordinary meeting at Loch Brittle began to dawn in Jim's mind; his face was a picture of surprise. "In other words, you deliberately *planned* that Sue and I were to meet on the Isle of Skye?"

"That's right!" laughed Samantha. "I planned it as far as such a meeting *could* be planned in advance."

"Well, well! I think we've been a little dim not to have seen this before, when we were talking together at the picnic by the loch," said Mr. Sandy.

There were a few seconds of startled silence as Jim considered the implications of Samantha's staggering revelation of a master-plot for the meeting on the Isle of Skye of himself and Susan.

"All the same," he said a little later, "there must have been *some* element of co-incidence about it. Skye's a pretty big island. How could you have known in advance where you were going to meet us?"

"Well, we did speak about your motoring plans too on that evening when I came to Cockermouth," said Samantha. "If you remember, I suggested to you, Mr. Sandy, when you asked me where would be best to go, that you shouldn't miss seeing Glen Brittle; and you said that you wouldn't."

"Ah, but how did you know that we'd motor there *first?*" asked Jim, recalling some of the conversation of that April evening in their sitting-room. "We might, after all, have gone to Elgol first, and perhaps we might not have gone to Glen Brittle until *yesterday* morning and then there would have been no meeting."

"Oh, well, Jim, I'm not psychic! Of course I couldn't foresee exactly how you'd plan your motoring so, yes, I grant you there was certainly some element of luck and co-incidence in the meeting."

"Anyway, I think it was a wonderful idea of yours to plan that we should meet," said Jim. "And now it's all worked out so splendidly, and Sue has invited me to stay . . . Presumably she hasn't realized either that you'd been planning and plotting for us to meet?"

"Oh, I don't think Sue knows anything about it yet!" said Samantha. "But I'll have to enlighten her when she comes home about how I've plotted for her to fall into your arms, as you might say and I dare say she'll forgive me for that!"

After that Jim pressed Samantha to reveal more details of how her master-plan had been conceived and carried out. Samantha told him that she could not take all the credit for herself for what had been planned; she had discussed things with Roger, her husband, and together they had done much planning and calculating. The most difficult thing to calculate, Samantha said, had been the number of hours or days to allow for the <u>Osprey's</u> voyage from Maryport to Loch Sligachan. They had spent a good deal of time poring over maps, using a map-measurer, and doing arithmetical calculations to try to arrive at an approximate figure for the number of hours. "But I knew that our estimate of four days for the voyage was at best likely to be only a rough approximation," she said, "because, of course, we had no idea what the wind was going to be like, and neither Roger nor I had the slightest idea of how to allow for the effects of the tide on <u>Osprey's</u> speed, so we had to overlook the tides altogether in our calculations. But on the basis of our rough and ready calculations I advised Susan in the end that we should set off from Rhodes Castle on the Friday, so that we could set off in the Osprey on Saturday morning, May the thirtieth. And by tremendous luck, Osprey's voyage *did* take about four days, and we arrived at Loch Sligachan, as I'd hoped we would, on Tuesday afternoon, as I told you before."

"But if *you* planned all the dates and the destination of Osprey's voyage, Sam," said Jim, "how did you get Susan to agree with you? I mean, how did you do it without arousing her suspicions that something special was being planned?"

"That turned out to be fairly easy," said Samantha. "Susan said that she was quite happy to leave all the planning to me. She seemed content to agree to every suggestion I made; I think because she was still feeling a little depressed following her husband's death."

I don't think she's feeling at all depressed now! thought Jim. Can it really be that she wants to marry me, and is eagerly awaiting my proposal? Oh, if only I could propose to her *now*, and hear her say, "Of course I'll marry you, Jim!" Then we'd get married as soon as possible . . . What was Samantha saying? He had missed a few words by slipping into a happy daydream, but he heard her next two sentences.

"When we'd settled the dates Sue got in touch with Dr. Himmel, and it was arranged that he and his wife, Anne, were to come with us in the Osprey. It was lucky for us that they could come because it meant that we could go ashore on Skye, leaving the boat in the hands of two capable sailors."

"There's been a lot of luck altogether in the way that things have worked out," observed Jim.

★

When the train reached Fort William Jim got out, and hurried along the platform to see whether a buffet car was going to be added to the train. He knew that the train was going to stop there for twenty minutes; his father had asked the guard about this to be sure

that Jim could safely leave the train for a few minutes. It was still
a grey, cloudy morning, with rain threatening and the clouds well
down on the mountains; but still no rain was falling as Jim made his
way forwards along the platform. The next moment he saw that three
carriages were standing at the end of the platform, and that one of
them had a buffet compartment in it. Hopefully those three carriages
were going to be coupled onto the train during the twenty minute
stop at the station. Then, cheered by the thought that they would
soon be able to have some breakfast, he hurried back to re-enter the
train where he had left it.

Jim had already seen that a fair number of people were boarding
the train, and one reason for his hurry to get back to his seat was
the thought that someone else would find it, and want to sit in it.
But Dad and Samantha will look after my seat for me, he reminded
himself. He opened the door of his compartment, and was glad to
see that it was still empty except for Samantha and his father.

"Well?" asked Mr. Sandy as Jim sat down again in his corner seat.

"There is a buffet car," said Jim. "I saw three more carriages,
including a buffet, and it looks as if they'll couple them onto the
train."

"Let's hope they do!"

A minute later they felt a bump, followed a second or two later
by a jerk, and they knew by these signs that the second portion of
the train was being coupled onto the short train which had brought
them from Mallaig.

The rest of the journey was uneventful and even a little dull
because it was wet; with very low clouds swathing the mountains
there was little to be seen. Jim, Mr. Sandy, and Samantha went
through to the buffet car soon after the train left Fort William,
and bought themselves coffee, sandwiches, and cakes, and began to
refresh themselves. It was not exactly breakfast, Jim thought, but at
least it was better than nothing at all to eat and drink. At Roy Bridge
it started to rain. By the time the train came to Tulloch a light drizzle
had thickened to a steady rain, driven by a fairly fresh south-westerly

wind. After that, as the railway climbrd slowly along the side of Loch Treig, the rain became heavier, but before they reached the summit of the line at Corrour they were in the clouds. Now the heavy rain had been replaced by a swirling white mist, and there was little to be seen through the windows but a few yards of high moorland and mist.

★

It was getting on for midday, and the train was approaching Helensburgh, when the rain finally eased off and stopped. They had been travelling in very heavy rain from Rannoch onwards, when they had again been below the level of the clouds. By the time when the Firth of Clyde appeared by Craigendoran Junction gleams of sunshine were beginning to brighten the sky; but although the cloud had become somewhat broken the day did not clear up any more than that. Soon the train was moving rapidly through the outer suburbs of Glasgow.

"What are your plans when we reach Queen Street?" Mr. Sandy presently asked Samantha.

"I'm going to get the next train to London from Central station," she said.

"We're going there to catch the one-thirty to London, the 'Midday Scot', which we leave at Carlisle."

"Then we might as well continue to travel together as far as Carlisle," said Samantha. "I'll come with you to Central station."

"Will it be awfully late when you get to London?" asked Jim.

"I expect so, but I really don't know. It'll be too late, I suppose, to think of going on from Waterloo down to Sherborne, so I'll have to stay tonight in a London hotel, which will be expensive but it can't be helped. The alternative would have been to take a train from Queen Street to Edinburgh, and stay with my mother tonight, but that way I'd still have a long journey to do tomorrow. By going on to London today I'll be back home sometime tomorrow morning."

★

The train stopped at the terminus of Queen Street station in Glasgow at twenty minutes to one. Samantha lead the way, and they walked together along the platform, and showed their tickets at the barrier. When they came out of the station at the corner of Dundas Street and West George Street Samantha paused, and asked Mr. Sandy which way he thought they ought to go.

"We could go by the Underground from here," she said, pointing to the entrance to Buchanan Street Underground station, "but probably it would be quicker to walk."

"Perhaps we'd better walk," said Mr. Sandy. "You know the way?"

"Yes, I know the way. It'll only take us about ten minutes on foot to reach Central station."

Jim then said that he would like to see what the Glasgow Underground was like, but Samantha told him that she thought it was "not very remarkable", and that in any case they could only go by tube train to St. Enoch station, from where they would still have to walk the short distance to Central. Jim then agreed that it would be better to walk from where they were now. "But what about lunch?" he added, as a feeling of hunger reminded him that it was lunch time.

Mr. Sandy consulted his wrist-watch.

"There won't be time for lunch in Glasgow, will there?" He looked at Samantha, and saw her shake her head. "Sorry, Jim, but we'd better wait for lunch until we're on board the 'Midday Scot'."

"There'll be a restaurant car on it," said Samantha. "Right, we'll walk this way."

A minute later they had to wait for the traffic lights to change at the corner of Buchanan Street and George Street in order to cross the street.

"How did you cross Glasgow on your outward trip?" asked Samantha as they waited for the lights to change.

"By bus," said Mr. Sandy. "We didn't know the way, you see, so we found a bus, and took it."

"Quick, we'd better cross now!" said Samantha as the red lights held up the traffic for them. They crossed to the other side of the busy Buchanan Street.

Jim thought that it felt a little odd to be in the midst of the lively bustle of a large city, having just travelled from the wild, remote regions of the Western Highlands. However, he did not dislike what he saw of the centre of Glasgow. Samantha lead the way along Buchanan Street, but they were not hurrying, and there was plenty of time to look around as they walked; Samantha even stopped briefly once or twice to look at expensive items of ladies' clothing in shop windows, although she had no intention of buying anything. Jim thought that the tall buildings fronting Buchanan Street - he counted one eight storeys high -looked impressive: not like the rather more squalid mental picture of Glasgow which had somehow been his idea of the city.

Samantha lead them into Central station up the steps from Argyle Street, where the railway tracks in the station pass above the street on a wide bridge.

"Now, where exactly are we?" said Samantha, stopping to look around as they came out onto the platforms of the large terminus. "I always find Glasgow Central a rather confusing place when it comes to finding the train you want."

"That's Platform Thirteen quite near us," said Jim helpfully, "and there's Number Twelve next to it, but that train standing there doesn't look like a main line one."

"We're at the wrong side of the station," said Samantha. "I remember now that I've caught London trains from the platforms with low numbers over there. Come on!" She lead the way again and, still not hurrying as there was plenty of time, they presently found the train they wanted waiting at Platform One. The "Midday Scot" for London Euston was a very long train, so they walked some way along the platform and chose a second-class carriage near the middle of the train. The carriage looked fairly empty so they climbed into it.

"The restaurant car is the next one forwards," said Jim. "I saw it just before we got in."

"Good!" said Mr. Sandy. "We'll have some lunch as soon as the steward comes round and says 'lunch is served'."

They were called to take their seats for lunch in the restaurant car even before the train left the station. Mr. Sandy, Jim, and Samantha sat down at a table laid for four people, and looked at the items listed on the lunch menu card. It was not long before a waiter appeared and took their order, but after that they found that the service in the restaurant car was rather slow. They were still looking at the platforms, and waiting for the soup, when a whistle was blown, and the train began to move, punctually at half past one. In a minute they were slowly crossing the Clyde on the great bridge just outside the Central station.

"I wish that chap would hurry up with our soup!" said Jim. "Ah . . . Here he is!"

The waiter appeared, skillfully carrying a tray laden with three bowls of soup. The restaurant car was still somewhat empty; not many passengers were taking advantage of the expensive lunch served there.

★

"What time should you get back to Cockermouth?" asked Samantha later, when they had all finished eating their lunch.

"About ten past six, I think?" said Jim, looking at his father.

"Yes, at ten past six," confirmed Mr. Sandy. "Let's see what our other trains are." He put a hand into the inner pocket of his jacket, took out his wallet, and drew from it a piece of paper. "The four-fifteen from Carlisle, change at Penrith, and the five o'clock from Penrith," he read out from the notes he had made for their holiday travelling.

It did not seem to be very long after that when they realized that the train was slowing down for the stop at Carlisle. Mr. Sandy and Jim stood up, took their suitcases down off the luggage rack, and made ready to leave the compartment.

"I wish there weren't all those weeks to live through until I can come south to Rhodes Castle to see Sue," said Jim. "I feel I'd like to go on with you, Sam."

"Never mind, Jim," said Samantha. "It isn't really all that long until August the fourth, just eight weeks and a bit. We'll see you then! Good-bye for now!"

"Good-bye, Sam, and thanks a thousand times for your splendid plot to bring Sue and I together!" Jim was smiling broadly as he hugged Samantha warmly to himself for a moment, and kissed her on the cheek.

"Good-bye, Jim," said Samantha again, "and good luck with your proposal when you come to the Castle to make it! Good-bye, Mr. Sandy!"

Mr. Sandy bade Samantha good-bye, and he and Jim left the compartment. The next minute the train drew to a halt, and the Sandys stepped down onto Platform Four of Carlisle station.

"Let's wait to see Sam off," said Jim the moment his feet touched the platform. "We've got about three quarters of an hour before our train to Penrith is due out."

About three minutes later a whistle was blown, and the "Midday Scot" began to move again. The Sandys waved to Samantha from the platform, and saw her waving back to them through the window.

"What an ingenious young woman she is!" said Mr. Sandy merrily when the express had left the platform. "Now then, Jim, let's go and look for our next train."

CHAPTER ELEVEN

A few days after his return to Cockermouth Jim received a telephone message while he was at work at the railway station.

It was slack time of the morning. The 8.17 to Workington had left the station, and there was not another train due until the 10.05 to Carlisle arrived. The Station-Master sometimes set Jim a menial task to do when there was a long slack period between trains, and on this particular Tuesday morning at half past eight he had gone along to the gents' toilet armed with a mop and a bucket of hot, soapy water to give the place a good cleaning-up. He did not mind doing such jobs as this at times when there might otherwise be nothing for him to do, so he had set about the job cheerfully enough, humming a little tune to himself.

The station was a very quiet place that morning. The only people there were the Station-Master, who was in his office, and Bill, the signal-man, who was in his signal-box, and Jim himself. As he had expected, he had met no one by the time he had finished washing the floor. Then, as he came out of the gents' toilet, he dimly heard the telephone ringing inside the Station-Master's office, but he took no notice of it. He began to walk back along the platform with his mop and bucket, but at that moment he heard the Station-Master shout for him.

"Jim!" The Station-Master appeared on the platform. "Telephone!"

"Coming!" he shouted back, putting down his mop and bucket, and running towards the entrance to the booking-hall.

"Miss Julia Rose for you, Jim," said the Station-Master.

Julia Rose? Thought Jim as he hurried into the office to answer the telephone. Whatever can she want to talk to me about at this time of the morning? He picked up the receiver.

"Hello . . . Yes, speaking . . . No, that's all right. I'm not busy at the moment . . . What? . . . A party this Saturday? . . . Seven o'clock on Saturday evening? Yes, I can come then . . . Thank you very much, Julia! . . . Good-bye." He hung up the receiver. Well, fancy that! he thought. It's Julia Rose's twenty-first birthday this Saturday, and she's inviting me to the party. But I'll be seeing Jill there, of course, so that's good!

He went slowly back to pick up the bucket and the mop, thinking about this invitation to Westray Hall to Julia Rose's twenty-first birthday party. Clearly he had only been invited because Jill wanted him to be there; Jim hardly knew Julia well enough to be invited to a party as her friend. In fact, he rather disliked Julia, but he felt, nevertheless, that the party would be an occasion for some fun.

★

The party at Westray Hall for Julia's twenty-first birthday was nearly over. Already the drawing-room was looking less crowded as some of the guests had left; and there was Jim also thinking that it was time to go home. He had cycled the mile to Westray Hall from his home in Lorton Road, Cockermouth, and it had taken him about seven minutes.

Yes, it was certainly time for him to say good-bye to his hostess, he decided; he looked at his watch, and saw that it was nearly half past eleven.

A record came to an end, and the record player switched itself off, making, Jim thought, a sudden, welcome silence. They had been listening to continuous music on records for the past two and a half hours, mostly pop-music of the early sixties, and Jim knew that he was tired of the sound of loud pop-music, and, indeed, that he was beginning to feel slightly bored with the evening, although for some time he had enjoyed dancing with Jill. But now Jill had said good-night to him, and left the room, saying that she felt tired. For the past ten minutes Jim had been sitting in a corner by himself in an armchair, rather sleepily watching the remaining guests, a few of whom were still making half-hearted attempts to keep up the dancing.

The room had been prepared for dancing: the carpet had been taken up, and the larger pieces of furniture, a settee and some armchairs, had been moved from the middle of the room to stand alongside the walls.

Everyone present in the room had at some time that evening taken a partner, and taken part in the dancing.

As the music came to an end Jim stood up. Where was Julia? He must now find her, take his leave of her, and set off for home on his bicycle. He looked around, and when he did not see her he realized that she must have left the room, perhaps to go to the kitchen. He decided to look for her there, and at once walked boldly out of the drawing-room, along the passage, and into the kitchen. Here he found his hostess stirring a large jug of a steaming liquid on the table, while a very pleasant smell of hot punch filled the room.

"Ah, have another drink before you go, Jim, won't you?" asked Julia straight away, as if she guessed that he intended to leave.

"No, thanks," said Jim. "I must go now."

"Must you really go now?"

"I think I'd better, so I won't have another drink, thank you."

"Are you driving?"

"Oh no," said Jim. "I'm on my bike tonight, but all the same I'd rather not feel that I've drunk too much, and maybe ride my bike into a ditch!" He spoke jokingly, although he knew that he was, in fact, still reasonably sobre. Jim did occasionally drive his father's car, and had recently passed his driving test, and liked driving, but on this night he had preferred to cycle. His father had offered to lend him the car, but Jim had said that as it was a fine, warm night he would use his bicycle.

"Are you sure you can't stay a little longer?" persisted Julia.

"I really *ought* to go now," said Jim, "as I told Dad I'd be back home by midnight."

"Oh, well," began Julia, "if you really must go now . . ." She broke off her sentence, picked up the jug of hot punch, and made for the door. Jim watched her, uncertain of what to do next.

"I'll tell you what," said Julia, pausing in the doorway with the jug in her hand, "if you could wait just a few minutes more, I wouldn't mind having a word with you as you've been with Jill all the evening, and I haven't had a chance to talk to you."

"All right," said Jim dully. He was beginning to feel decidedly tired, and he knew that all he wanted was to ride home at once, and retire to bed.

"Just a moment; wait here while I take this jug through to the drawing-room," ordered Julia. "I'll be back in a sec!"

Jim sat down on a wooden chair and thought about Julia for the short time that she was out of the room. He did not like her, he told himself again, but he had to admit that she was quite attractive, in a way. At only four feet, eleven and a half inches tall, she was even smaller than her sister, Jill; and she had a slight, slim figure.

Unlike the fair-haired Jill, Julia had long black hair and heavy, dark brown eyebrows, and her dark brown eyes were rather elongated in shape.

She always used to say that she was five feet tall, maintaining that the odd half-inch below that figure needed to be "rounded up" to the integral figure of exactly five feet.

Julia was very soon back in the kitchen. Jim rose wearily to his feet, meaning to repeat that he really ought to be setting off, but before he knew what was happening Julia was at his side, having closed the door, and he caught a mischievous sparkle in her dark eyes.

"Don't be in such a hurry to be off, my darling!" she said. Then she startled him very much by suddenly throwing her arms around him, and kissing him passionately on the cheek; but no passion was aroused in Jim by the kiss. She's jealous because I've been with Jill all evening, he told himself.

"Why not come upstairs, Jim?" she whispered seductively in his ear.

"What?" murmured Jim, alarmed at this suggestion.

"Why not come up to my bedroom?"

For a second Jim was so staggered by this totally unexpected invitation that he could only stare stupidly at Julia, alarm and doubt showing in his widely opened blue eyes, while he remained speechless.

"They won't miss me for a while in the drawing-room," she added a moment later, sensing that her sudden amorous advance had shocked Jim and taken him off his guard. "And Mother went to bed about an hour ago, saying that she was tired, and Father's away. No one will bother us."

"Oh!" gasped Jim. "Well, er . . . thank you very much, Julia, but . . . er . . . I must be going! Thank you for a super party. I've enjoyed it very much."

He hurried to the door, and opened it, but Julia hurried after him into the passage. There was no one else there. He saw the front door of the house standing open (for it was a warm night), and more than ever he longed to get away from Julia and her party. He now realized that she was rather drunk, and that she wanted nothing less than to entice him into her bed. Jim, however, was in no mood for sex with a girl who, in any case, held little attraction for him.

He felt her hand on his shoulder, holding him firmly.

"Just for a few minutes, Jim!" he heard her whisper urgently to him. "Come on . . . I *want* you!"

Then Jim's desperation to escape from Julia's clutch turned to a sudden madness; a wave of panic seemed to sweep through him, and he acted impulsively and instantly. Hardly knowing what he was doing, he tore himself free from Julia, and rushed down that passage, making for that open front door. As he fled he put out a hand, and grabbed his coat off a hook where he had hung it up on his arrival. He dashed out of the front door as if he was running for his life, and as he did so he heard Julia's shout from behind him.

"Hi! Jim! Stop!"

Jim flung his arms into his coat without attempting to button it, and seized his bicycle from the wall near the front door where he had propped it up. In spite of his feverish haste he remembered to push his trouser clips roughly onto his trouser legs; and then, wobbling very much at first, he was off on his bicycle, pedalling away as hard as he could, as if he thought that Julia might pursue him, and try to drag him back into the house. He did not look round as he left the house behind, and so did not see Julia standing in the open doorway, shaking her fist at him, nor did he hear her final words addressed to him.

"You rotter, Jim! I'll make you pay for this!"

After about two minutes of hard riding Jim looked behind him, and eased off the pace of his flight. It was a dark night, as there was no moon, and as he was riding along a small country road, well away from the street lights of Cockermouth, which he could see ahead of him as a yellow glow in the sky. However, when he glanced behind him he could see no sign of anyone following him, either on foot or on a bicycle; and apart from the occasional calls from owls it was very quiet. He decided that he could take the rest of the ride back home at a reasonably leisurely pace, while he reflected on how his evening at Westray Hall had ended so abruptly. Did he regret what he had done? He was not sure, but he suspected strongly that he might have made a serious mistake in deciding on an instant flight to escape from Julia Rose. It was quite clear that he had annoyed and offended her very much by suddenly running away when she had suggested that he should accompany her to her bedroom; and no doubt that meant that it would be unwise for him to show himself again at Westray Hall for some time. But that means I won't be able to see Jill any more, at least not at home, he said to himself. Then he told himself that it did not matter that he could no longer go to Westray Hall to see Jill; the main thing, he reminded himself, was that he would shortly be making a proposal to Susan; and surely she would agree to marry him.

Then he began to wonder how the events of that evening had affected his relationship with Jill. He had enjoyed dancing with her, but it had not excited him violently, nor had he felt much moved when he had parted company from her. He knew very well, in fact, that he was not in love with Jill, although he had once thought that he was in love with her. However, he could not escape from the feeling, as he thought carefully over the evening again, that Jill was very much in love with *him*. Yes, she loves me, he said to himself in a matter-of-fact sort of way. But I can't do much about that as Sue and I are (hopefully) going to get married. Jill will remain my friend, perhaps, but that's about the limit of it.

Soon Jim was riding his bike along roads lit by the yellow glare of street lamps as he came into the outskirts of Cockermouth. As he pedalled up the last stretch of Lorton Road he saw a car parked outside his Father's front door, but it was not his Father's car. He read the rear number-plate of the car as he free-wheeled up to the house on his bicycle: yes, it was Jackie Rothwell's car. And although it was twenty minutes to midnight he saw that the light was still on in the sitting-room.

Jim propped up his bicycle against the low wall surrounding the tiny piece of garden between the front of the house and the pavement. Then he looked for a moment at the light coming through the sitting-room curtains, and as he looked he noticed that the curtains were not quite completely closed across the windows. One curtain must have become caught on a chair inside the room so that it had not fallen properly into place at the bottom; a narrow chink of window was not covered over. Drawn by a sudden irresistible curiosity Jim moved silently up to the window and, stooping slightly, applied an eye to the chink between the curtains.

"Oh!" he gasped quietly.

Jim could see through the tiny gap between the curtains that his father and Jackie Rothwell were lying together on the rug in front of the hearth, where a small coal fire seemed to have burnt out. They were lying on their sides, facing one another, while they were locked together in a very close loving embrace. In fact he could see little more than their faces for the rest of them were hidden from his view under another rug. They were lying there so still that it looked as if they might both be asleep, but there was no doubt in Jim's mind as to what they had been doing. He was fascinated by what he saw, but after staring intently for about half a minute he forced himself to move away from the window. Then he tried the front door and, as he had expected, found it locked. But the back door will be unlocked for me to come in he reminded himself.

As he wheeled his bicycle along the garden path towards the shed at the back of the house Jim was thinking of what he had just seen through the window. It was, of course, a pointed reminder to him of how he had finished his evening at Westray Hall, and of how differently he could have finished it if he had given in to Julia's request, and gone upstairs with her. There was no doubt in his mind that, under the influence of too much to drink, she had been hoping for "a little fun" in bed with him. But Jim still thought that he had no regrets in leaving the party when he had left it; only the abrupt manner in which he had done so now troubled him. Julia will be angry with me, he told himself as he parked his bicycle in its place in the shed. She'll be angry, but no matter. I'll have to keep away from Westray Hall for a while, until she's forgotten about what happened tonight.

Jim let himself in through the back door, which was not locked, and walked quietly through the kitchen so as not to disturb the lovers in the sitting-room. He made no further attempt to intrude on their privacy, but climbed thoughtfully up the stairs, and went to his bedroom.

CHAPTER TWELVE

The train from London was slowing down to stop at a station. Susan, who had been sitting opposite Jim in the compartment, and facing backwards, stood up for a moment to look through the window.

"Here's Thorpe-le-Soken "she said as a platform name came into view. "Our's is the next station"

The train stopped, and Susan sat down again.

"You know, I can't help feeling almost a little nervous about this," said Jim in the momentary quietness while the train was not moving.

"About what, my darling?" asked Susan. "Surely you're not feeling nervous about meeting my mother, are you?"

"Well I did mean that, actually. But perhaps I'm not really feeling nervous so much as feeling shy . . . at the thought of meeting your mother, and your father too. After all, they *are* the Marquis and Marchioness of Walton!"

"Oh, Jim!" laughed Susan. "You needn't feel a bit shy about meeting my parents - your future parents-in-law, remember! You needn't feel at all shy about meeting them, my darling." Susan was smiling broadly at Jim as she said this. Then, as they heard a whistle blown, she added: "Good, we're on the move again. We'll be at Kirby Cross in about five minutes." The train began to move again as she was speaking.

"About five minutes," repeated Jim doubtfully.

"Yes, and Mother said she'd be there on the platform to meet us." Susan rose to her feet again in order to sit down beside Jim. She took his hands lightly between her's, and looked for a moment straight into his large blue eyes, in which she had detected visible signs of his nervousness. Now, however, Jim relaxed immediately as he felt the gentle. reassuring pressure of her hands on his hands, and he broke into a happy smile as he saw the lovely light in her dark eyes. "Do you know," she said quietly, "it rather amuses me, the thought of you feeling nervous, or shy, at the prospect of meeting my Mum, because she's a marchioness? Have you forgotten, my darling, that *i'm* a countess? You're not afraid of me because I'm a countess, are you?"

"Oh, of course not, Sue! But you're different."

"I'm not, you know. Listen, Jim; I'm sure you're going to find that my Mum's a very sweet, charming person. And if you're wondering about how to address her, just call her 'Lady Walton', or you could say 'My Lady' for the first time, but she likes to be 'Lady Walton', not 'Lady Ardell' and Father likes to be called 'Lord Walton'; or just plain 'Sir' would do very well in conversation."

★

Jim and Susan were travelling in a first-class carriage of the 1.35 train from Liverpool Street to Walton-on-the-Naze (in those days one did not always have to change at Thorpe-le-Soken for Walton, as one does now). They were going to spend a few days at Soken Hall at the invitation of Lady Walton, Susan's mother. Three days earlier (August 4th) Jim had travelled down from Cockermouth to Sherborne by train, by way of London.

Susan herself had met him at the station at Sherborne, and had driven him home to Rhodes Castle. When the time had come for Jim to make his all-important proposal it had seemed a perfectly easy and natural thing to do.

"How lovely that we're together again!" Susan had said. They were sitting on their own on a sofa in the Green Drawing-Room of Rhodes Castle.

"Let's stay together always," Jim had said. "Will you marry me, Sue?" The words had seemed to slip out with hardly any conscious effort.

"You will, Sue?"

"Of course we'll get married, Jim, my darling! Let's get married as soon as we can."

And so, on the first evening of Jim's stay at Rhodes Castle, before dinner had been served, Jim and Susan had become engaged to each other. They had wasted no time in finding Samantha to tell her the good news, and her delight in hearing it had been obvious and genuine. After dinner Susan had telephoned her mother at Soken Hall to give her the news. She knew, even before she rang up, that her mother was going to be pleased to hear of the engagement as she had written to her a few weeks earlier, and had told her that news of an engagement was quite likely, she thought, in the near future. In her letter of reply Lady Walton had told her daughter that she would be very pleased to hear of an engagement to Jim Sandy. When Susan had rung up Lady Walton had expressed her delight at the news, and had invited Susan and Jim to come to spend a few days at Soken Hall. It had been arranged over the telephone that they would travel to Essex from Dorset that Friday (August 7th) by train, as Susan did not like the idea of driving so far in her car, and that they would arrive at Kirby Cross, the station for the Hall, on the train that was due there at ten past three, so that they could be at Soken Hall in time for afternoon tea.

★

When the train stopped at the little country station of Kirby Cross on the Walton branch line Jim and Susan were standing by a door, ready to step down onto the platform.

"There's Mother!" said Susan as soon as she was standing on the platform. She waved a hand, and Jim, looking where Susan was looking, saw a smartly dressed woman standing near the "Way Out" sign wave a hand to them in return.

"Hello, Mother," said Susan. "Here we are on time, I think." She glanced at her watch, and saw that it was just after ten minutes past three. Susan also gave Jim an encouraging smile at that moment, but Jim, now that he had seen Lady Walton, and was about to shake her hand, was feeling suddenly confident.

"How lovely to see you, my dear!" said Lady Walton to Susan. "Hello, Jim, how nice to meet you!" She held out her hand towards him.

"How do you do, Lady Walton?" said he, shaking her hand. He was smiling at her as he saw her sparkling brown eyes smiling merrily at him. Jim immediately felt that he liked Lady Walton very much. Sue was right! He said to himself a moment later. She *is* a sweet and charming person!

Susan kissed her mother, and Jim looked again at Lady Elizabeth Ardell, the Marchioness of Walton, and then at Susan. Lady Walton was wearing a light grey jacket and skirt, and had a string of large yellow beads hung around her neck, while Susan had on a white cardigan over a blue blouse, and was also wearing a pale-coloured skirt. But they don't look very much alike for mother and daughter was Jim's first thought, apart from the black hair they've both got.

"Well, my dears, your news has really delighted us!" said Lady Walton.

"Oh yes!" said Susan happily. "Jim came down to Rhodes Castle, you see, *especially* to propose to me!" She gave him a radiant smile, but Jim grinned back at her a little sheepishly, and said nothing. "And now we've got to talk about our plans for the wedding with you and Father this weekend."

"Indeed we shall talk about your plans," said her mother. "Ah, thank you, porter. You could carry those two cases for us."

The porter, who knew Lady Walton, was politely waiting to carry the two suitcases.

"Very good, m' Lady," he said respectfully, touching his cap, and advancing to pick up the cases.

Lady Walton lead the way to the place in the station car park where she had parked her car. That day she was driving herself; she had a chauffeur, of course, but preferred to drive her car herself on short journeys. When the porter had helped them in, and handed the baggage into the back seat of the car, Lady Walton drove off. Jim was sitting beside her in the front passenger seat, and Susan was sitting on the back seat beside the two small suitcases they had brought. Kirby Cross is a village in the north-east of Essex, about a mile from the resort of Frinton-on-Sea; but Lady Walton turned left off the Frinton road at the crossroads in the village. Their road, she told Jim, lead to the village of Kirby-le-Soken, and it also lead to the drive entrance to Soken Hall, the seat of the Marquis of Walton.

"But where are we going, Mother?" asked Susan a minute later as the car passed the lodge and the gates of the Soken Hall main drive. "Are we going into Walton first?"

"We are," said her mother.

"For some shopping?"

"Well, I want to call at the Post Office, but the main thing is that we've got to pick up your Father at the Yacht Club. He's taken to lunching there regularly on Fridays when he's at home." The Marquis was the President of the local Yacht Club.

Jim had been looking out keenly for the drive of Soken Hall, and as they came to a sharp bend to the right, not quite half a mile from Kirby Cross, he had noticed some very imposing stone gateposts on the left, and a roadway which ran between them, and a lodge near the gates, and had immediately guessed that this was the drive of Soken Hall. He discovered later that the stone of which the gateposts were built, and of which Soken Hall itself was built, was full of flints, like many of the churches in that part of England.

"Did you see the Hall, Jim?" asked Lady Walton a moment later.

"Yes, I just had a quick glimpse of it," said Jim. But already the car had rounded another bend, and now he could no longer see the large grey house, which he knew, was Soken Hall. The view of it had been too fleeting to notice any details. Now the car was coming down the hill on a straight stretch of road into the village of Kirby-le-Soken.

Lady Walton turned her car to the right at the junction with the village main street. Jim saw an attractive-looking village, strung out along both sides of the road.

"There's Quay Lane," said Lady Walton as they passed the opening of a small road on the left. "That road leads down to the tidal water where there's a quay which used to be an old barge quay at the head of Kirby Creek; and our boathouse is down there too. You're going to do a little sailing with Susan, I believe?" She half turned her head to Jim for a second, a smile flickering around her pretty, hazel-brown eyes.

"Yes, I hope so," said Jim.

"I thought we could teach him the basic skills of handling a small sailing boat here," said Susan. "And maybe Father could come with us too for some of the time. Look, Jim, we're just coming to the road which leads over to the Island there, the road past New Brick Mill Farm."

Jim, looking to his left, saw the entrance to a farm lane, a sign with "New Brick Mill Farm Only. Dead End" printed on it, and, only a little way back from the main road, brick outbuildings and the farmhouse itself.

"That's the road over the Wade, isn't it?" he said. He had made a careful study of Susan's large-scale Ordnance Survey Map of the Walton area the evening before, and had a good idea in his mind of the local geography.

"That's it," said Susan; "but the dead end is really at Horsey Island Farm, not at Brick Mill. The sign's worded like that to discourage people from trying that road, as the causeway can be dangerous."

"Yes, it can be if one isn't careful about the tides," said Lady Walton. "Are you going to walk over to the Island that way?"

"I thought we could do that tomorrow morning after breakfast, if there's a low tide about then."

"Low water tomorrow morning is around ten to nine, I believe."

"Well, that's not too early for crossing the Wade," said Susan.

"We could get down to this end of the causeway by about half past nine, but, of course, we wouldn't be able to spend long on Horsey Island because of the tide; but that doesn't matter there's really not a lot to see once you're over there. Anyway, we might as well do that tomorrow morning as it'll be no good for sailing until the tide's up around lunch time."

Jim already knew that the channel between Horsey Island and the mainland, called the Wade, was about three quarters of a mile wide where the road crossed it, and that one could walk across the mud to the Island when the tide was out; and he was particularly looking forward to doing this. It seemed to him that this might well be just as interesting as being taken out rowing or sailing in the Ardell's sailing dinghy. "Ah, there's the Wade!" he said. Lady Walton was driving her car deliberately slowly so that Jim would have more time to see things as they passed them; luckily the traffic on the road was light, and no one was following them. He had caught a glimpse of water with the sun on it away to his left: there was a channel of water edged by grey mud, and more flat, marshy-looking land beyond the channel. The vision of the Wade over the fields from the road was brief, but Jim caught a glimpse of a large number of masts over that way: yachts or sailing dinghies.

The next minute they had passed a turning-off to Frinton on the right, and were coming into the outskirts of Walton-on-the-Naze. On both sides of the road were pavements and new houses. They reached the junction with the High Street, and Jim saw on the opposite side of the street the handsome grey tower of the attractive Parish Church of Walton.

Lady Walton turned her car to the left into the High Street, which looked very busy and crowded with people and motor traffic; pedestrians thronged the pavements, and wandered about in the road where the pavements were narrow. The next moment they turned off High Street to the left into the narrow opening of Mill Lane. Lady Walton parked her car at the end of the short street.

"Aren't you going to drive down to the Yacht Club?" asked Susan.

"I'm going to walk back to the Post Office first," said her mother. "Then I'll drive down to the Yacht Club; but it's no good thinking of parking in the High Street when it's so crowded at this time of the year. Look here, why don't you two get out here? You could walk from here to the Yacht Club while I'm buying stamps and posting letters, and I could meet you there in, say, ten minutes? Jim would see more on foot than travelling in the car."

They all got out of the car. The Post Office was in the High Street, so Lady Walton walked back up Mill Lane and round the corner to reach it, while Jim and Susan looked around them. The pavements and the surfaced street ended a few yards beyond the place where the car was parked, but a rough road ran on to the Yacht Club, past the head of a muddy creek, and on down the side of it. Jim and Susan walked a few paces down the road, and then stopped as a sudden prospect of boats and water sprang into view. Jim rested a hand on the gunwhale of a small motor fishing boat which was leaning on its side on mud right beside the edge of the road.

"Gosh!" he said. "This creek must be the top end of Walton Channel?"

"That's right," said Susan. "This is the creek of sea water *behind* the town; and there's the open sea on the other side, on the front, where the Pier is but that's not nearly so interesting."

"Where's the Yacht Club?" asked Jim.

Susan pointed. "Just over there. That red-roofed building you can see on the top of the bank over there, beyond all those masts . . ."

She looked at her watch. "Ten minutes, Mother said, to meet her there, and it's just gone half past three now. There'll be time to have a quick look at the Mere, and then we'll walk along to the Yacht Club by twenty to four."

"The Mere? You mean that bit of water behind the town streets marked the 'Old Mill Pond' on our map?"

"That's it, Jim, and it's just this way, a step or two up this grassy bank." Susan was leading the way as she spoke up the bank on the right-hand side of the creek. "There, that's Walton Mere or the Old Mill Pond, if you like, which is just another name for it." She and Jim were standing at the edge of a lake or pond of very shallow water.

A path ran along the near shore of the Mere, and on the further side of it they saw the back of a row of houses.

"Is it deep enough for sailing?" asked Jim, looking at tufts of grass standing well out into the water, indicating a depth of only a few inches. There were no boats to be seen on the Mere.

"You can sail a dinghy on it," said Susan. "They draw only a few inches with the centreboard pulled up. But look here, let's go on down to the Yacht Club to meet Father. The Mere isn't really all that interesting."

They returned to the road, where the fishing boat was lying on the mud of the creek, and walked on down the road towards the Yacht Club.

At the extreme end of the channel, where the fishing boat lay, there was only a trickle of water left by the receding tide, but a little further down this water widened considerably. The high tide that afternoon had been at about half past two, so that the tide still had a long way to fall. Jim saw a line of sailing boats, small yachts and dinghies, lying afloat at the side of the channel, several of them protected from the weather by coloured plastic awnings. Jim and Susan were looking at each one as they walked past it, and they were drawing near the Yacht Club building when they saw Lady Walton drive past them in her car.

Susan had timed the walk well. As they came to the door, Lord and Lady Walton emerged from the Club House.

Jim's first impression of Lord Walton was of a man who looked like a keen sailor, as indeed he was. The Marquis of Walton was a small man with dark hair and a narrow fringe of dark beard encircling his face.

"Ah, here you are!" said Lady Walton as soon as she saw Susan and Jim. "Jim, this is my husband, Richard; and Dick, this is our future son-in-law, Jim Sandy."

Jim and Susan were standing holding each other's hands. For a second, before he held out his right hand to Lord Walton, Jim turned to smile at Susan, and saw her return his smile as he felt her for a moment squeeze his left hand a little more firmly; but he did not feel at all nervous of meeting the Marquis.

"How do you do, my Lord?" he said.

"I'm delighted to meet you, Jim," said the Marquis, shaking his hand heartily. "And may I congratulate you on your engagement to my daughter!"

Jim saw deep-set, dark brown eyes in a well sun-tanned face: Lord Walton's eyes were sparkling at him and Susan in obviously genuine pleasure. "Thank you, sir," he said, and again turned his head to Susan at his side.

Lady Walton then suggested that they should all return at once to Soken Hall for a cup of tea, as it would be nearly four o'clock by the time they arrived there, and Susan and Jim, she said, must be in need of some refreshment after their long train journey. On the car journey back to the Hall Susan and Jim sat beside each other in the back seat of the car, while Lady Walton drove, as before, and Lord Walton sat in the front passenger seat, where Susan had made Jim sit on the first trip, the better to see things. Jim was in a particularly light-hearted, happy mood, and was thinking that his new parents-in-law, Richard and Elizabeth Ardell, Lord and Lady Walton, were both splendid people. He was soon chatting easily with the Marquis, sitting in front of him in a smart dark suit which did not look in the least nautical. Jim gathered that the Marquis was by no means an honorary President of the Yacht Club, in name only; he sensed that he was speaking to an expert yachtsman, and soon forgot that he was also a senior Peer of the Realm.

Lord Walton explained that, having recently celebrated his sixtieth birthday, he had retired from most of his public duties so that he could give more time to sailing. Later he learned that Lord Walton was indeed an expert yachtsman who had taken part in the Fastnet Race several times, and in other important races and regattas, and had sailed his yacht right across the Atlantic to America.

When they had arrived at Soken Hall, and were drinking cups of china tea in the elegant drawing-room, Jim said politely that he reckoned that he had come to the right place to learn how to sail. Lord Walton agreed with him that the Walton Backwaters were a splendid place for a beginner in a small sailing dinghy.

"With your expert guidance, sir, I'm sure to learn quickly," said Jim, "if you'll be coming with us."

"Ah!" said Lord Walton with a playful glint in eyes. "But you won't really want *me* in the dinghy, will you? I'm sure you'll find, Jim that Susan is an excellent teacher of small boat sailing and as you'll be going out with her, naturally there would hardly be room in the boat for anyone else, would there? I expect you and Sue will manage best on your own!" He winked cheerfully at his daughter, who was sitting beside Jim on a sofa, but Jim caught Susan's eye, smiling at him, and he felt an immense surge of love for her.

★

After tea at Soken Hall Susan had borrowed her mother's car, saying that she wanted to take Jim for a walk on the Naze (Jim, of course, knew very well that the aristocracy always took afternoon tea at four o' clock). He already knew, having studied Susan's map thoroughly, that the Naze was the only piece of relatively high ground in that region of very flat, watery country, and so he was expecting a good view from there. Susan had confirmed that up there was a splendid place for getting a good view all around: for seeing both out to sea, and inland over the Walton Channel and Hamford Water.

A path lead from the car park down to the sea front, and a few minutes later Jim and Susan, having walked that way, found themselves standing at the edge of the sea. Luckily for them there were not many other folk about, and in the quietness they were relishing each other's nearness while they looked around and out to sea.

"The visibility's not very good," remarked Jim.

"True," said Susan. "On a clear day you can see much further, but, of course, you can't see right across to Holland."

"Holland?"

"The other side of the North Sea from here is the Dutch coast, but you can't see it, even on a clear day. But I was reminded, by looking out over the sea, of my brother, who now lives in Holland but he and his wife are on holiday in England at the moment, Mother says."

"Your brother? I never knew you had a brother, Sue!"

"Ah, yes, I don't think I've ever mentioned Paul to you before. It's ages since I last saw him, and, with him living in Holland, I suppose I tend to forget about him. You see, he met a Dutch girl, and married her, and now Paul has a job in Rotterdam, and they live there."

"But you said they were in England at the moment?"

"They're on holiday here. I don't know exactly where they are, but I heard Mum saying something about them seeing the sights of London. Of course, they're bound to come to Soken Hall sooner or later, before they return to Holland so, you never know, you might meet Paul and Kirsten - that's his wife's name."

"Oh yes, I suppose we might see them," said Jim, who was not interested in anyone else he might meet at Soken Hall, so long as he and Susan were there. "Have you ever been over there, Sue? Over to Holland, I mean?"

"Yes, but the only time I've been there was many years ago, while I was still at school. My parents took me and my sister, Denise, over for a summer holiday in Holland. We took the night ferry from Harwich to the Hook of Holland. I'd like to take you there sometime, Jim."

"I'd love to go with you to Holland sometime, Sue," said Jim dreamily. He was silent for about a minute, staring out intently over the misty sea, as if he were trying to make out the Dutch coastline, in spite of knowing that this was impossible. Then, remembering Susan's mention of her sister, Denise, he asked her another question.

"Is your sister, Denise, older than you, Sue?"

"Yes, she's two years older than me, and Paul's a year older than Denise. That's our complete family in order: Father and Mother, then Paul, Denise, and me. Look here, Jim, shall we walk on for a bit, and perhaps climb up onto the Naze for a view? I know it's a bit misty over the sea, but I think there should be a good view the other way, over Hamford Water and Horsey Island."

"That's the view I'm interested in seeing," said Jim.

The Naze is a flat-topped sandstone promontary to the north of Walton-on-the-Naze, between Walton Channel and the open sea. On the north side it falls to flat, marshy saltings (Stone Marsh) which end at Stone Point, where the broad opening of Hamford Water runs in from the sea. Following a path, they climbed up the soft, crumbly sandstone cliffs, and walked on until they were standing on the highest part of the Naze. Jim thought that it was, in its way, a beautiful place.

Looking around he saw a wide expanse of short, dried–up grass, crossed by various sandy paths, and dotted about with gorse and other shrubs and windswept bushes. They met a few other people strolling about up there, but there was plenty of space, and Jim felt that he and Susan had the place more or less to themselves that evening.

But the views were disappointing. Jim quickened his pace as he walked onwards, drawn by an increasingly eager curiosity to see the channels and marshes of the Backwaters from their good viewpoint at a height of some seventy feet above sea level. Susan, understanding the reason for his quickening steps, hurried along at his side. Presently, however, Jim pulled up. Not far ahead of them the grassy plateau dropped quite steeply, it seemed to the salt marsh which was hardly higher than the high-water mark; but the saltings appeared as dim and hazy flat country. At first they could hardly make out any water down there; the marshes seemed to melt gradually away into white mist.

"Oh dear!" said Susan. "The view isn't very good after all! I thought that mist was only lying out to sea, but it's creeping inland over the Backwaters as it often does here."

"We can't even see the Walton Channel," said Jim. "At least . . . no . . . isn't that water over there?" He pointed.

"Yes, it is," said Susan slowly, staring steadily north-westwards in the direction of Jim's pointing finger. She had excellent eyesight. "That's the upper part of Walton Channel. And that blur beyond it might be the north-eastern corner of Horsey Island. And that flat bit down there is the saltings around Cormorant Creek, on the near side of Stone Marsh to where we are now. We can't see the creek from here, but if we were to go down the slope towards the marshes we'd come to a dyke hard against the creek. But today the visibility's so poor that we'd have to walk almost right down there to see what it's like but there isn't time to do that."

They were both silent for a few minutes while they continued to stare into the haze. Jim was trying very hard to catch a glimpse of the broader channel of Hamford Water, which he knew lay hidden beyond the dimly visible corner of Horsey Island.

"It's no good," said Susan, guessing his thoughts. "We can't see Hamford Water today."

"Maddening, isn't it?" said Jim. "We must be almost seeing it but this mist won't let us!"

"Never mind, my darling, we'll see it tomorrow. I'll take you sailing tomorrow afternoon unless it's a dead calm again, like this in which case it'll be just rowing. But if there's a little wind tomorrow afternoon we could slip down Kirby Creek, and out into Hamford Water between Skipper Island and Horsey Island."

"I say, that'll be tremendous fun! And we're going to walk across the Wade tomorrow morning, aren't we, while the tide's out?"

"Yes, we'll do that after breakfast tomorrow."

"Good! Gosh I'm really looking forward to tomorrow!" said Jim happily.

CHAPTER THIRTEEN

Jim and Susan set off to walk the last stretch of Island Lane, leading to the dyke along the south side of the arm of the sea known as the Wade, which separates Horsey Island from the mainland. They walked on at a brisk pace (although without deliberate hurry) towards the dyke which they could now see ahead of them. Beyond New Brick Mill Farm the road had been lined by trees for some distance, but now on either side of it were low hedges, with blackberry bushes here and there, and ditches, and fields beyond the hedges.

The day had begun with an earliest breakfast in the Soken Hall dining-room. Then Lord Walton, who was not busy that morning, had taken Susan and Jim in his car on the short trip to Island Lane. He had driven his car slowly on past New Brick Mill Farm for some way, until he had come to a field gateway where it was possible to turn the car. Here Susan and Jim, having thanked Lord Walton for the lift, had left the car, and begun to walk. It was a fine morning, but cool, almost cold for August, Jim thought and cloudy; however, there were breaks in the cloud, particularly to the north, where the sky looked brighter.

"You see, Jim, the mist and fog's gone with the ebb this morning, as we hoped it would," said Susan, "so we should have better visibility today."

"That'll be good," said Jim, "but it's rather chilly, isn't it?"

"It is rather!"

They walked briskly on, and soon came to the place where the road went over the dyke built to protect the land from flooding by sea water. Here they paused a few minutes to admire the view, and to change their shoes for rubber boots before proceeding onto the road over the mud.

"My word!" said Jim. "What an amazing sight it is!"

"I know," said Susan, "but you should see it as well, Jim, when the tide's up. We must come back to this spot, if we can, at high water, and see how different this place looks!"

Jim looked at the rough stone road which forded the channel to Horsey Island, and saw that it was like a narrow bridge over a sea of mud. Looking at it carefully, he noticed that at intervals sticks had been planted beside the road to show where the edge was when the road lay under a shallow cover of water. He tried to picture in his mind what the place must be like at high water when, presumably, there would be no sign of the road other than, perhaps, the tops of the sticks marking it; and the sea of mud would be replaced by a lake of tidal water stretching from the mainland dyke to the distant island dyke.

"How far is the Island from here?" he asked Susan.

"About three quarters of a mile," she said. "Come on, Jim, we'd better get started."

They walked down the slope of the dyke and onto the beginning of the causeway over the mud.

"It's a good, solid road, and not as muddy as I thought it would be," said Jim.

"Wait until we get near the middle of the channel," said Susan.

"The road gets much muddier further out; but, yes, it is a good solid stone road underneath the mud and water."

"Have you been this way often when you used to live at Soken Hall?"

"Yes, Paul, Denise, and I often used to walk over here to the Island when we were children. And once, I remember, I walked across and back alone."

"Is it a dangerous thing to do?"

"Potentially, yes, this is a very dangerous place. If you were to misjudge the time badly you might easily get trapped in the middle of the Wade by the rising tide."

"Have you ever had any narrow escapes here?" asked Jim.

"Yes, once or twice we cut it a bit fine on the time for the walk back to the mainland from the Island . . . Look here, perhaps we'd better go a little faster, although it's not quite half past nine yet, so we've really got plenty of time. And perhaps we'd better walk in single file until we reach the Island."

They had been walking quite slowly, hand in hand, but now Susan set off at a brisk pace, and Jim followed closely behind her. It seemed that she did not wish to talk at that time about previous crossings of the Wade causeway; and he, of course, knew that there was no time to waste, even though there was no real need for hurry. The road was at first reasonably dry if one avoided treading in the many puddles left by the receding tide. To either side of the road there was green slime, and there were many pools of stagnant water, but Jim saw that the predominant colour of the whole place was a shade of brown; doubtless there was a thick layer of soft, oozing mud everywhere except on the road, where there was not nearly as much mud as he had been lead to expect.

He saw a little way ahead of them a narrow ribbon of shallow water which crossed the road.

"How many channels do we have to cross?" he asked, trying to remember the relevant details of the map.

"There are two main channels," said Susan, "but I don't think this little trickle ahead of us is one of them."

They soon found that the ribbon of water over the road was little more than a wet place, and not a real channel of water. They splashed through it, and it barely came up to their ankles. Then Jim saw that there were two broad arms of tidal water which joined across the road almost like a river ford.

"I think we're coming to the main channel of the Wade," said Susan, "the deeper one of the two." But they found when they came to it that it was not much deeper than the shallow splash they had already crossed.

"That presented no problems!" said Jim cheerfully; "but it *is* much more muddy out here. It's not so easy now to see where the road is, to keep walking on it."

"Be very careful that you do keep on it!" warned Susan. It gets easier again after we've crossed the other channel."

"Thank goodness we've got our Wellingtons on! I say, Sue, could we stop here just for a minute so that I could take some pictures?"

"All right."

They paused, and Jim drew his camera out of a jacket pocket. He turned round to look back towards the mainland, and stared intently for several seconds in the direction of the village of Kirby-le-Soken.

"There's a church tower over there," he said.

"That's Kirby Parish Church," said Susan

"But can we see Soken Hall from here?"

"Yes, you can see a glimpse of it just to the left of that tower; that bit of a hill with trees on it . . ."

"Got it! I'll take a picture of the view from here, but the Hall will be too far away to show in the photograph."

When Jim had clicked his camera shutter he turned again to face the Island shoreline. Almost straight ahead on the low green outline of Horsey Island he could see the red roofs of the Island farm and its outbuildings. He took a second picture.

"We'd better be getting on now," said Susan, beginning to walk on again.

Jim hurriedly stowed his camera in its case, pocketed it, and hurried after her. He did not, however, try to run as there was a thick layer of very wet mud deposited on the road, mud which had already splattered itself all over his black boots; clearly it would be easy to slip and fall down in it, which, he thought, would not be much fun.

When they reached the Island they sat down to rest for a few minutes on the dyke. At that point the slope of the dyke was strengthened by a retaining-wall, and it was on this sloping stone surface that Susan and Jim sat down when Jim had taken a quick glance at the interior of the Island from the top of the dyke.

"It seems rather a dull place," he said. "Just fields and that farm inside the dyke."

"And saltings and mud outside the dyke," said Susan. "Yes, I told you it was dull."

"It's so different from the Hebrides," said Jim thoughtfully.

"Yes, except for the sea. We were usually by the sea, or near it, when we were on the Isle of Skye.

"Oh, it was so lovely meeting you there that day!" said Jim happily. "And isn't it strange to think that if I *hadn't* met you at Loch Brittle that day - if Sam's plan hadn't worked for some reason - we wouldn't be sitting here together now on Horsey Island!"

"It's so beautifully quiet and peaceful here," said Susan dreamily. "Just the two of us!" She smiled at him, and he put an arm around her shoulders. "The peacefulness is like it was at Loch Brittle too," she continued, "only it's even better here, as there seems to be no one else about . . . just you and me."

"Oh, Sue, my darling!" breathed Jim, pulling her lovely head closer to himself so that their faces were almost touching. "We belong to each other now, Sue, darling!"

"Ah, yes . . . ! I love you, Jim, my darling . . . I love you so much . . ."

Their lips met, and then for several minutes they were kissing passionately, forgetting everything but each other's presence. They forgot where they were, and Jim even forgot their happy meeting at Loch Brittle, which he had just been thinking about. It seemed to him that nobody could be more beautiful, or more wonderful, than his beloved Susan; and as they kissed and held each other tightly he thought that she had already become a part of him, as if the two of them were melting into one another.

Presently, however, Susan, remembering the time and where they were, whispered to Jim: "I think we ought to be moving, my darling! We must remember the time!"

"Oh . . . ! But I don't *want* to move!" said Jim. He was still spellbound, staring into Susan's dreamy dark eyes, as he continued to clasp her tightly. "I'd like to stay here with you much longer! But, if we *must* move . . ." Reluctantly he released Susan from his loving embrace, but took her hand as they stood up together.

"It's rather cold, actually, sitting down here this morning," said Susan, "although I didn't notice it until just now. Shall we take a look-out from the top of the dyke?"

A moment later they were standing hand-in-hand on the broad, grassy top of the Island dyke.

"It looks finer," said Susan. "That patch of blue sky in the north is getting bigger, and the clouds seem to be breaking up."

Jim glanced up at the sky. "Yes, I expect the sun'll come through soon and warm things up," he said. He looked for a little while over the fields of the Island. Near the red roofs of the farm he could see trees and, looking carefully, horses grazing in the meadows. Then he noticed something else.

"Oh! There are people over there!"

"Where?" asked Susan sharply.

"Just over there." He pointed slightly to the left of the farm buildings. "In that meadow." The smile left his face, and he began to look rather worried. The last thing he wanted was that anyone else should turn up to spoil his solitude with Susan.

"I can see them," said Susan, locating three tiny moving specks on the green meadow. "It's probably only the farmer and his men, and we needn't mind them, and they won't mind us being here."

They turned to look the other way, out over the muddy Wade towards the mainland.

"Looks as if there's already rather more water in those channels," said Jim.

Susan looked at her watch. "I think it'll be all right for us to stay on the Island for another twenty minutes or so as the road over the Wade stays uncovered for about two hours after low water.

"Oh, good!"

"Then we'll walk back to New Brick Mill Farm when we're back on the mainland. Father said he'd meet us there with the car about eleven o' clock. But we could walk along this dyke for a bit now, if you like, Jim perhaps as far as the south-western corner of the Island, opposite Skipper's Island, if we walk fairly fast?"

"All right, Sue, let's do that," said Jim.

There was a good path along the top of the dyke, quite wide enough for two people to walk abreast, and they set off at once walking along it. The road from the mainland crossed the dyke and lead across the meadow to their right towards the farm, a brown, unsurfaced and unfenced muddy track. Jim and Susan, however, were mostly looking out over the water towards the mainland. They had not gone very far when they were startled by a sudden shout.

"Hi!"

Jim and Susan stopped and looked warily around them to see whether someone was hailing them.

"Hello, there, Susan!" It was a man's voice, a powerful shout, which came from somewhere behind them on the Island.

Susan turned on her heel.

"No!" she gasped. "It can't be . . . it is . . . Paul!"

The three people they had seen earlier near the farm were now close to them, coming straight across the field to meet them. They saw a tall man with dark hair wave to them. Jim now saw that the other two were a man and a woman: a brown-haired, full-bearded man, and a blonde-haired woman.

The tall man who had hailed them broke into a run, and with a few quick athletic strides he was close to them. The other two strangers followed him more slowly.

"Well, Susan, fancy meeting you here!" said the tall man cheerfully.

"Oh, Paul!" said Susan incredulously, "I'm absolutely amazed . . . How on earth have you got here?"

The tall man hugged Susan, and gave her a quick kiss. "By boat, of course!" he said.

"Yes, I know obviously you've come over to the Island by boat if you haven't walked over the Wade but where did you land?"

"Just here, by this landing stage." They were standing close to the place where the farmer kept his rowing boat at a landing stage.

"Only we arrived here last night."

"Last night? You mean, you've spent the night on the Island?"

"Yes, I arranged for us to stay last night at the farm."

"Well, fancy that!" said Susan. "Jim, this is my brother, Paul, who's just turned up out of the blue here on Horsey Island."

"And this is my wife, Kirsten," said Paul Ardell, indicating the blonde woman, who was now standing rather shyly at her husband's side, holding his hand. "And this lad here is a friend of mine, an old school pal" (he indicated the other man) "Captain Rodney South."

"This is Jim Sandy, my fiancé," said Susan proudly, introducing Jim to the others. There was a general shaking of hands. Jim had guessed as soon as Susan had called the dark-haired tall man "Paul" that this was her brother, and now he remembered her telling him that, as the son of the Marquis, his title was Viscount Ardell of Harwich. He had, however, forgotten to address the Viscount as "My Lord" when he had said "How do you do?" to him; but the Viscount did not seem in the least to mind this omission.

"Ah, your fiancée, Sue!" said her brother. "I remember you telling me in your last letter that there was a chance that you might be marrying again soon. What delightful news!"

"As a matter of fact, we only got engaged last Tuesday," said Susan, "when Jim came down to Rhodes Castle from Cumberland, where he lives, to propose to me. Well, Kirsten, it's nice to see you again! I don't believe I've seen you since your wedding day as you've been living in the Netherlands since then."

"Yes, in Rotterdam, my home town," said Kirsten. "Congratulations on your engagement, Susan!" Jim thought that her English was very good, and that her Dutch accent was not very striking, but he found her appearance disappointing.

"Thank you!" said Susan. "And you live somewhere in England, I expect, Captain . . . ?" she began, turning to the Captain.

"South," said the Captain, noticing by her hesitation that she had forgotten his surname. "South, as in the compass. An appropriate name, as I always say, for a sea captain who has to spend much time on the bridge, steering by the compass. I live in Harwich, my Lady."

"And you're on holiday at the moment, I suppose?"

"Yes, I'm taking a few weeks' holiday."

"What sort of ship are you the master of?"

"Only a small cargo vessel, that can also take a handful of paying passengers. I work mostly between Harwich and Rotterdam."

"Ah, so it was in Rotterdam that you met Paul?"

"Yes, it was in Rotterdam that I met him again; before that we hadn't seen each other since school days."

"Kirsten and I are taking two weeks' holiday in England," said the Viscount, "so, as Rod was in Rotterdam recently, and also on holiday, we all came over from Holland together.

"On Captain South's ship?" asked Susan.

"No, on the night ferry from Hook of Holland. Then we travelled up to London by train from Harwich."

"I heard from Mother that you were in London," said Susan. "But when did you leave London to come here?"

"Yesterday afternoon we travelled from Liverpool Street on a Clacton train as there wasn't a direct train to Walton when we needed one. Then we took a taxi from the station at Clacton, and were met by arrangement at the Yacht Club at Walton to be taken over by rowing boat to the Island."

"I told Paul that I wanted to see Horsey Island, you see, so we came here," said Kirsten.

"I see," said Susan. "Well, it's a lucky thing, in a way, that we've met you here as Mother wanted to get in touch with you last night, but didn't know where you were, so she couldn't ring you up. You see, as Jim and I are here to discuss our wedding plans, Mother is thinking of having a family re-union party on Sunday evening, and, of course, she wants you and Kirsten to be there and I expect it would be all right to bring Captain South along too. You'll be calling at the Hall presently?"

"But of course," said the Viscount. "We were thinking of calling at home in any case about midday or as soon as the tide is high enough to let us row over to the mainland."

"Well, you do that, Paul," said Susan, "so that Mother can invite you to come to dinner on Sunday evening; and probably she'll want you to stop to lunch today. I don't suppose she'll mind having one extra, unexpected guest."

"I can disappear if there's going to be any awkwardness about presenting me to Lady Walton," said Captain South quickly. "I wouldn't like to be any trouble, you know."

"Oh, don't say that!" said Susan. "Mother would *like* to have an extra guest, I'm sure and Paul will explain, of course, that you're an old friend of his."

At this point in the conversation a frown appeared on Jim's face. He had been standing at Susan's side in glum silence, listening to the talk of the others, and wanting only to be rid of them as soon as possible. He had taken a particular dislike to the Captain, having noticed the way he kept looking at Susan. Jim could not have failed to notice the hungry look of love or lust which was in the Captain's eyes as he kept glancing at Susan; obviously he found Susan an extremely attractive woman. Jim realized that Captain South was probably an eligible bachelor, perhaps on the look-out for a pretty wife. He seemed, Jim thought, quite young to be a captain; he was perhaps no more than about forty but there could be no doubting what his glances into Susan's face meant He fancies her, damn him! he said to himself, and he felt that a seething jealousy was beginning to rise up within him. Now he felt almost angry that Susan seemed to be encouraging him to think that he should be invited to lunch at Soken Hall, and to the planned dinner party there on Sunday evening. Jim did not really mind the appearance on the scene of Susan's brother, Paul, and his wife, Kirsten, although he felt rather peeved that his walk with Susan had been quite spoilt by meeting with these people. Paul Ardell, he thought, was a very handsome man who looked very like Susan, his sister. Jim had noted particularly that he had the same very dark and very beautiful eyes as Susan's; like her's they were large and more or less black in colour.

He did not care much for Kirsten. Her blonde hair was cut in a fringe over her big blue eyes, and hung in untidy golden tresses over her shoulders. She was an inch or two shorter than Susan, and several inches shorter than her tall husband; and Jim felt that she could not be more than about thirty years old. But not much of a figure! He said to himself. Female figures were always important to Jim.

Lost in thought, he had missed a little of what Susan and the others were saying. The Viscount had asked how long Susan and Jim would be staying at the Hall, and Susan had told him that they would be leaving by train on Monday afternoon to return home to Rhodes Castle, and that Jim would be travelling back to Cockermouth soon after that.

She said that by the end of the weekend the main plans for a wedding early in the New Year should have been settled.

"Mother thinks it would be better to wait until after Christmas and the New Year to get married," she said, "instead of trying to rush things by thinking of having the wedding in October or November. I agreed with her that we'd want to avoid a wedding in December, when the days are so short and dark, so I think we'll settle for a date in late January or early February of next year, perhaps the thirtieth of January, or the sixth of February, or the thirteenth Valentine's Day is on Sunday next year, we discovered, so the thirteenth would be the nearest we could manage to it." Then Susan told her brother that they were thinking of having the wedding, at her mother's suggestion, in Walton Parish Church instead of at Rhodes Church, so that they could have the reception afterwards at Soken Hall. "It's handier for Harwich, so that we could slip away quickly to the Continent for our honeymoon," Susan had told her brother, as Jim and I like the idea of going over to Holland for our honeymoon, and maybe we'll go further afield, Belgium or Germany, but we haven't really thought about that yet have we, Jim, darling?"

"No, not really," said Jim, coming out of his daydreams with a start. His frown slowly disappeared from his face. "But we'd like to visit the Low Countries."

"Then it's certainly a good idea to have your wedding here, rather than in Dorset," said the Viscount.

"You and Kirsten will come, won't you?" said Susan.

"Oh, I think we'll manage to come over for your wedding if it's here as Soken Hall is so near Harwich."

"Oh yes, of course we must come!" said Kirsten.

"That'll be the next family gathering, then," said the Viscount.

"Kirsten and I won't be coming over for Christmas, of course, if you're having your wedding in January or February. By the way, are we likely to be seeing Denise and Rupert this weekend?" Rupert Allerby was Denise's husband.

"Denise is definitely coming to the Hall today, but Rupert's probably not coming," said Susan.

"Staying at home to look after the children?"

"That's what Denise said when Mother rang her up last night."

"Where does your sister live, Sue?" asked Jim. "Somewhere quite near?"

"Yes, at Colchester, which is not far from here. Denise and Rupert have two small children, a girl and a boy." Suddenly remembering the time, Susan looked at her watch. "I say, Jim, we must go we must go at once!"

"Are you going to cross the Wade on foot?" asked her brother, glancing at the muddy boots Susan and Jim were wearing.

"Yes, we walked here, and we're walking back over the causeway.

Come on, Jim we'll have to run!"

"Look here, Sue, we could row you over to the mainland later, if you like? But I'm sorry if we've upset your plans by stopping here to talk."

"Oh, it doesn't matter," said Susan, "but I think, perhaps, we'll stick to our plan to walk back over the Wade?" She looked at Jim to see what he thought about it.

"Yes, we're going to walk back across the Wade!" he said firmly, very relieved to know that he and Susan were at last going to get away from the tiresome people who had spoiled his peaceful walk with his fiancée.

"Good-bye, Sue" said the Viscount; "but we'll be seeing you again at the Hall later on."

"Tot ziens!" said Kirsten, relapsing for a moment into Dutch.

"Good-bye!" she added quickly, in English.

Jim and Susan said a quick "Good-bye!" to Paul, Kirsten, and Captain South, and a moment later were setting off at a brisk jog along the dyke to regain the road over the mud.

"We're not going to be too late to get across?" asked Jim as he ran.

"No, we'll be all right!" said Susan. Half a minute later they were back on the road, and running down the slope onto the causeway.

They slowed down to a fairly fast walk to avoid splashing mud unnecessarily.

★

About ten minutes later Jim and Susan found themselves approaching the dyke of the mainland at the southern end of the causeway. There had been more water in the channels in the middle of the Wade than they had encountered on their outward journey, but again the crossing had presented no difficulty.

"We've made it all right, safely back to dry land!" said Jim, completely cheerful again now that he and Susan were once more on their own.

"Yes, we've done it all right, with quite a few minutes to spare, probably," said Susan; "and now you've seen the Island."

"Ah, here's the sun!" said Jim. As he was speaking the sun slid out through a gap in the thinning clouds overhead. "I think it's going to get out quite sunny. Look, Sue, let's sit down, shall we, on that old landing stage while we take off our muddy boots?"

There was a ricketty old wooden landing stage beside the road beneath the mainland dyke. With no more need for hurry, Jim and Susan sat down on it together, and began to remove their muddy rubber boots, and to change them for their walking shoes.

"I'm going to take off my socks as well, as they've got wet and dirty, and put on the clean ones I've brought with me," said Susan, peeling off a muddy sock as she spoke. "I'd advise you to do the same, Jim."

"I shall," he said. On Susan's advice they were both carrying with them in their pockets a clean pair of socks.

It feels nice and warm now in the sun! I don't think we'll suffer from cold feet!"

"I hope not!"

"I say, Jim, I hope you weren't too upset by what happened on the Island? They did rather spoil our walk, didn't they?"

"Well," said Jim, "I *was* a bit upset by the way that Captain kept looking at you lustfully!"

"Oh, Jim! I hardly think you need be worried by a little thing like that!" Susan laughed, and then added, in a rather more serious tone: "Actually, I could see from your face, Jim, what you thought about Captain South. I don't think his look was really lustful. He probably just found me rather attractive to look at. And why not?"

"Why not? Because you belong to *me* now, Sue, and I belong to *you!*" He was now smiling broadly at Susan as he added: "So no one ought to look at you in that way, Sue except me!"

"Oh, Jim!" said Susan, and laughed again; and then Jim laughed too, thinking of himself looking lustfully at his fiancée. "How sweet of you to say that!" she continued when she found that she could speak again in her usual voice. She put her arms around him for a moment, and they kissed; but a minute later they were walking slowly, hand in hand, up to the top of the dyke. Then, after a last look-out over the muddy Wade towards the Island they set off up the road to meet Lord Walton at New Brick Mill Farm.

CHAPTER FOURTEEN

Susan and Jim, riding borrowed bicycles, found their way barred by a gate closed across the road. Susan had borrowed her mother's bicycle, and Jim had borrowed one which had once been Paul's and after lunch at Soken Hall they had ridden these bicycles down to Quay Lane in the village. They were on their way to the Ardells' boathouse, which was close to the old barge quay at the end of the lane, and their plan was to spend the afternoon until tea-time sailing in the Ardell's sailing dinghy, <u>Daisy</u>.

There was a notice on the gate which proclaimed that the road beyond that point was a Private Road, and underneath this it added that no cars and no cycling were allowed.

"What do we do now?" asked Jim.

"We'll push our bikes through," said Susan; "and don't worry about that notice - it's *our* private road!"

They went on, and found that <u>Daisy</u> was waiting for them, tied up at the old barge quay at the head of Kirby Creek.

★

Before tea at Soken Hall Jim met Susan's sister, Denise Allerby, in the library.

Susan and he had returned to the Hall soon after four o' clock after they had spent a very pleasant afternoon sailing the dinghy, <u>Daisy</u>. Susan had already explained that, because of the tide, it would be necessary to get back to the boathouse soon after half past three;

otherwise they might not find enough water in the creek to allow them to row back to the quay.

However, their time in the boat had been spent without any mishaps; and at twenty minutes to four they were setting off on the borrowed bicycles to ride back to the Hall. Susan had said as they rode that she expected that Denise, who had not been there at lunch time, would have by now arrived at the Hall. She had earlier told Jim that her sister was the owner of a ladies' fashion shop in Colchester, and had spoken of buying a dress there for the wedding. "But it won't be a white dress, of course, because I'm a widow, so I'll have to choose something else to wear for our wedding." *Our* wedding! Jim had thought happily. How splendid it sounds to hear Sue speak of *our* wedding!

Soon Susan and Jim were riding the borrowed bicycles up the tree-lined drive of the Hall and across the great sweep of gravel in front of the house, where Susan noticed that her sister's car was parked. Soken Hall was a handsome Georgian house, not particularly large for a stately home, but it had an imposing, north-facing front, in the centre of which was an elegant classical portico over the front door. They propped up their bicycles by the portico, meaning to put them away later, walked up the stone steps, and entered the house by the front door.

They soon learned that afternoon tea would be ready for them in the Drawing Room in about ten minutes. Susan stayed in the Drawing Room to talk with her mother, while Jim went upstairs to his room to take off his jacket, and to remove his camera from his jacket pocket. A few minutes later he descended the grand staircase from the first floor as far as a landing, off which a door gave access to the Library. Here he paused. A huge, arched window let in a good deal of light, but the view through it was disappointing. Soken Hall was built on gently sloping ground, the back of the house being rather higher than the front, and this south-facing window looked out onto a grassy bank and the top branches of a small ash tree; beyond the grassy bank lay the parkland which surrounded the

Hall. Jim looked out for half a minute at the ash leaves seen against a clear, blue sky - it was clearer now outside than when they had been sailing - and he thought it was a pretty sight, framed in the elegant arched window. Then he opened the door of the Library. He entered the large, square, high-cielinged room, and at once noticed a woman reclining on a couch at the far side of the room.

"Hello!" The woman on the couch, who had been reading a book, at once put it down, noticing Jim at the same moment as he noticed her. He saw that she was a tall, strikingly beautiful woman with long red hair. "You must be Jim Sandy?" she said, rising to her feet to greet him. "I'm Denise. How do you do?"

"How do you do?" said Jim, shaking hands with her. He had expected Susan's sister to be beautiful, yet he was pleasantly surprised all the same by Denise's appearance. She seemed to him very tall, although he learned later that at five feet, eleven inches, she was only three inches taller than Susan, but a long neck, and long, glittering ear-rings appeared to add emphasis to her height.

"Have you been out in the dinghy with Sue?" asked Denise.

"Yes, we've just come back," said Jim.

"I've just arrived here from Colchester within the past hour, having left my husband and family at home there. Did you go far in the dinghy, Jim?"

"Not very far, but we've had a very good afternoon. We took the Daisy down Kirby Creek as far as Hamford Water, and sailed a little way up it as the tide was still coming in. Then we had to come back to Kirby Creek to be there before the tide left it."

"Of course," said Denise. "Sue knows all about the tides and channels round here. Well, I must say, it's great news that you and Sue are going to get married! Have you a date in mind yet?"

"Probably it'll be in January or February."

"Early in the New Year would be a good time, I should think, for a wedding. Ah, here comes Sue! Hello!" The library door had opened again, and there was Susan standing in the doorway.

"Hello!" said Susan. "So Jim's found you in here?"

"Yes, and we were just talking about your wedding," said Denise.

"Well, look here, come down to the Drawing Room, you two, and we'll talk about it there while we have tea. They've just brought it in."

Afternoon tea in the Drawing Room was like it had been the day before, except that the Marquis was not there, and in his place was Denise. Lord Walton had gone off sailing in his yacht, *Pegasus*, with a friend. As on the previous day the tea had been brought in by a footman on a magnificent silver tray, from which Lady Walton took a silver tea pot and hot water jug, and began to pour out cups of China tea; there were dainty pieces of very good cake to eat with it, served on elegant gold-rimmed tea plates. During tea talk continued on the subject of the forthcoming wedding. Lady Walton, sitting in the best armchair in the spacious Drawing Room, expressed her opinion that they should not plan for a wedding which would be too grand, ot too elaborate, since Susan was a widow. "Even though you are a Countess, my dear, I think we should stick with convention and have a simple ceremony."

"Oh yes, Mother, Jim and I entirely agree with you on that point," said Susan "don't we, Jim?"

"Yes, we do," said Jim seriously. "We'd like to keep the ceremonial trappings to a minimum."

The sofa on which they had been sitting was near the door, but there was another sofa at the far end of the large room, by the windows which looked out over the gardens and parkland in the direction of the Walton Backwaters. As they moved across the room Jim happened to catch Denise's eye for a moment, and saw her smile at him. Denise was standing by the fireplace, chatting with her father, the Marquis. She had seen that Jim and Susan were being bothered by the unwanted attention of Captain South, and had just suggested to her husband, who knew the Captain quite well, that he should intervene to separate them.

Kirsten and Paul were standing by the window, looking out, when Susan and Jim came over to the window sofa to escape from the Captain.

"Hello, Sue!" said her brother. "Ready for some more sherry?"

Susan's glass was empty; she had just drunk the last mouthful of sherry in it.

"Just half a glass, please," said Susan, handing her glass to her brother. "You're not ready yet, Jim, for more sherry?"

"I don't think I shall want any more sherry, thank you," said Jim politely, but with a smile at Susan. He was not used to drinking dry sherry, and did not really care much for the taste of it, although he knew that it was the kind of drink which the aristocracy took on such occasions.

The Viscount took Susan's glass and his own to be re-filled to the side-table where a smartly dressed footman was in charge of a glass sherry decanter.

"There is a nice view from here," said Kirsten to Susan. "I have just been admiring the lovely garden and, how do you say it, the park?"

"Yes, we call it the Park, the land round about the Hall," said Susan, "and it does look very beautiful, seen from here."

"But you can't see that Island from here, where we met you yesterday," said Kirsten.

"No, you can't see Horsey Island from here, as these windows aren't quite high enough, but you *can* see Kirby Creek and the islands from the upstairs front rooms. Look here, shall we sit down, Kirsten? There's room on this sofa for three."

Jim politely waited a moment while the two ladies sat down on the sofa, leaving room for him to sit in the middle between them. Just then he saw Captain South glance towards him and Susan. Aha! thought Jim, he can't talk to Sue now! He sat down on the sofa, and the Viscount returned with the sherry glasses and, having handed them over, pulled up a small chair beside the sofa.

"Have you done any sailing since we met yesterday?" he asked.

"Yes," said Susan. Jim and I went out in <u>Daisy</u> this afternoon."

"You didn't go far, I expect?"

"No, we didn't go very far, because of the tide."

"Of course," said the Viscount. "Naturally you had to be careful not to get stuck in the mud."

"I should think it would be awful to be stuck in the mud for hours in a little boat," remarked Kirsten.

"On my own yes, it would have been awful," said Susan.

"But I was with you, Sue, so being stuck in the mud would have had its compensations!" said Jim, and there was general laughter at his remark.

Then Susan said that Jim had done very well on his first sailing lesson. "That was yesterday afternoon," she said, "and then we went out sailing again this afternoon; but this morning, as it's Sunday, we went to church with Father and Mother."

"I liked Walton Church very much," said Jim. "I certainly think it's a better place for our wedding than Rhodes Church."

"So do I," said Susan.

Soon after that the butler came into the room to announce that dinner was served. Lady Walton asked her guests to follow her into the Dining Room.

She had given a great deal of thought to the business of making the right seating arrangements at the Sunday evening dinner table. There were seven guests that evening, of which four were men, and three were women, so that, no matter how they might be arranged, two men would have to sit next to each other. Lady Walton wished that she could have had one more female guest, so that a perfect alternation of seats between men and women would have been possible right round the long rectangular table in the Dining Room. But she had devised what she thought was the best possible seating arrangement for her odd number of guests. Jim, of course, was her most important male guest as the dinner was being held in celebration of his and Susan's engagement, and so his place at the table was at Lady Walton's right-hand side. Susan had been allowed to sit next to Jim, and Lady Walton had made Captain South sit to her left much to Jim's relief. It would have been too bad to have had him sitting next to Susan, he said to himself, as he sat down beside Susan at the beginning of dinner.

At the further end of the long table, on which many candles were burning in beautifully polished silver candlesticks, sat the Marquis in his special chair. Lady Walton had judged Kirsten to be her chief female guest, and so she was sitting to the right of the Marquis.

Denise was sitting on her Father's left, and the Viscount, Paul, was sitting between her and Susan. Denise's husband, Rupert, was sitting in the one remaining place, between Kirsten and Captain South. Kirsten, the Viscount, and Captain South had arrived for the dinner party in the Viscount's hired car. He had left his own car at home in Rotterdam, maintaining that it was easier to travel by train from Harwich on arrival in England, and to hire a car when he wanted one (his own car, being a Dutch model, was adapted for Continental driving on the right-hand side of the road).

It was nearly the time of sunset when they sat down to dinner, but there was still plenty of daylight in the sky, and the candles burning on the table were as yet having no effect on the illumination of the room. Looking round the table at the other guests, Jim had no doubt that Denise was wearing the most startling outfit, although everyone present, including himself, was smartly dressed; he had borrowed a dark suit which had once belonged to the Viscount. Denise's dress was of a bright pink colour, which Jim thought went surprisingly well with her red hair. The colour, he thought, was perhaps a trifle "loud" for such a formal occasion, and the dress itself, which had a daringly low front, did not seem to be a proper evening dress.

Afterwards Susan told him that she thought her sister's choice of such a gaudy dress for dinner was positively vulgar. "Something she's brought with her from her shop, no doubt," she said, "but it was more like something to wear at the seaside than an evening dress, in my opinion!"

Jim could find no fault either with Susan's dress, or with those of the other ladies in the Dining Room. Susan had borrowed a dress from her mother; luckily she and her mother were about the same size and was looking, Jim thought, lovelier than ever in a simple dark blue evening dress with a low neckline. Lady Walton was wearing a long and very elegant evening dress of dark red material; round her neck, and displayed on her chest where the dress left her shoulders bare was a sparkling diamond necklace, Kirsten's dress, a white sundress with a black belt, also revealed bare shoulders

The meal began with a small hors d' oeuvre, followed by a fish course, stewed eels ("a local specialty," explained Lady Walton). Then the main course, roast venison, was brought in. After this they were offered a choice of sweets, and cheese and biscuits to finish with.

Servants waited on them unobtrusively while they ate and talked, taking empty plates away from the table, and bringing in new dishes at the right moments. Jim noticed that a maid remained in attendance in the background all the time, ready to do anything which might need doing.

He had not himself sat down to such a meal before, but the arrangements were more or less familiar to him from his days as Guide of Rhodes Castle. He saw that Captain South kept glancing across the table at Susan whenever he could, and his eyes would gleam with pleasure as he did so. This annoyed Jim, but he told himself that it did not matter as the Captain, being polite, could not very well talk with her across the table; also he noticed that Susan was in any case taking no notice of him.

It began to grow dusky outside the windows as they drew towards the end of the main course, but the light did not fade rapidly as the sky was clear after a fine, mainly sunny day. Lady Walton refused to have the curtains pulled, saying that it was not yet dark enough for curtains to be pulled across the windows.

When they were waiting for the servants to bring in the sweet course Lady Walton, who had for some time been chatting with the Captain, turned to Jim and asked him about his plans.

"What do you propose to do, Jim?" she asked him.

"I'm staying on at Rhodes Castle until the fifteenth, my Lady," said Jim. "That's next Saturday. Then I'll have to go home to Cockermouth to go back to my job as a porter."

"Yes, I dare say you'll have to do that, but what I really meant was, what are your long-term plans? You'll want a job in Dorset, of course, when you're living with Sue at Rhodes Castle."

"Oh, we've got all that fixed!" said Jim happily. "I'm going to be the Estate Manager for the Castle."

"My word, that's a very responsible job, isn't it, for a young person like you?"

"Yes, I suppose it is."

"Jim will manage it fine, I'm sure he will," said Susan. "Remember, Mother, he already knows a great deal about how we run the Castle.

Major Ambrose taught him a lot before he left - before Jim left, I mean."

"Oh yes, I wasn't suggesting that Jim wouldn't make a very good manager," said her Mother tactfully. "I think it sounds like an ideal occupation for you, Jim, if you think you can do it."

"I'll learn as I go along," said Jim. "Major Ambrose is still at the Castle, living in the Inner Lodge, and he'll help me, and keep me right in the job."

"Isn't he retired?" asked Lady Walton.

"He is, but he says he's going to help Jim all the same in managing the estate," said Susan. Major Ambrose had been the Estate Manager at Rhodes Castle in the days when Jim had worked there as the Guide.

"That sounds like a sensible idea. Now then, Jim, which would you like next: sherry trifle with cream, or strawberry ice-cream?" The sweets had been brought in, and laid out on the sideboard.

Jim had found out earlier what was going to be served for the sweet course, and now he had no hesitation in accepting the trifle.

When they had finished eating Lady Walton rose from her place, and suggested that the ladies might like to retire from the Dining Room, while the gentlemen remained there a little longer.

"See you soon, Jim!" whispered Susan as she rose from her chair.

After Susan and the other ladies had left the room Jim felt that he no longer minded that Captain South was still there, facing him across the table and smiling at him in a way which Jim knew meant: "I like your fiancée!" A bottle of port was now brought in and set on the table before the Marquis, and small wine glasses were set before the male guests. The Marquis invited them all to drink a little port to round off the dinner, but Jim politely refused it when it was offered to him. He felt that he had drunk enough alcoholic drink for that evening; there had been a good wine served with the dinner.

"Well, Jim," said the Marquis when he had taken a sip of his port, "what are your plans for the morrow? You and Susan are returning to Rhodes Castle sometime tomorrow, I believe?"

"We're not leaving here until tomorrow afternoon, sir," said Jim. "I think Sue wants to go shopping in Colchester tomorrow morning."

"To look at dresses for the wedding in Denise's shop?"

"Yes, that's the idea, sir."

"Ah, yes, I heard my wife say she was thinking of driving you two to Colchester tomorrow morning, if you want to go there. You'll find it a charming old town."

"Roman, isn't it?"

"Yes, Colchester was *Camulodonum*, a Roman town, but it's reckoned to be pre-Roman as well in fact, they call it the oldest town in England."

"How interesting!" said Jim politely. But he was really not very interested in such matters of history.

"And what train do you reckon to catch tomorrow afternoon?" asked the Marquis.

"The four twenty-six from Clacton. Sue said there wasn't a direct train from Walton when we needed one. She rang up the station yesterday to ask about trains to London."

"No doubt my wife will be taking you to Clacton station tomorrow?" said the Marquis.

"She did say she would."

"Won't it be very late by the time you get back to Rhodes Castle?" asked Paul, the Viscount.

"Yes, it will be quite late, but we don't mind," said Jim. "Sue says we'll be able to catch the seven ten from Waterloo, as the train from Clacton gets into Liverpool Street at, I think, five fifty-nine - around six o' clock anyway."

"What time should you reach Sherborne?"

"At about half past nine, so we hope to be back at the Castle by ten o' clock."

"Do you enjoy travelling by train, Mr. Sandy?" asked Captain South. It seemed that he had been waiting for a chance to get into the conversation, and that now he was seizing an opportunity to do so.

"Yes, very much, on the whole," said Jim, "although one can sometimes get rather bored by a long train journey, especially in the late evening."

"And rather tired too?" suggested the Viscount. "You'll have to be careful not to be asleep when your train reaches Sherborne."

"That'll be all right. Sue says we could ask the guard to give us a call in our compartment about ten minutes before we get there."

"A wise precaution," said the Marquis. "Well, I hope you've enjoyed your visit to this corner of Essex?"

"I've enjoyed being here very much indeed, thank you, sir!" said Jim. "I've found it really delightful country round here, with all these creeks and islands to explore. "It's a most fascinating place!"

"But you probably haven't had time to explore the whole of the Backwaters yet?"

"Well, no, we haven't," said Jim.

"Then you and Susan must come here again sometime soon," said the Marquis, "and have a longer stay here. Three days really isn't long enough to explore all the creeks and backwaters on this part of the East Coast."

"Thank you, sir!" said Jim. "That would be very nice." Indeed, he thought, it really would be very nice to come here again to stay, with Sue as my wife and another time Captain South wouldn't be here.

Later that evening, when the party was over, Jim told Susan something of what he felt about the Captain. They had met upstairs before retiring to bed, and Susan had told him that her brother would be leaving straight after breakfast the next morning, taking Kirsten and the Captain with him. "We'll probably never see the Captain again after that," she said.

"Good!" said Jim. "I hope we don't!"

Susan looked at him for a second or two before answering; but then, with a smile twinkling in her eyes, she said softly: "Good-night, my darling!"

CHAPTER FIFTEEN

Jim was spending the day at his father's mine near Keswick. Soon after midday, feeling tired of wandering about the spoil heaps, looking for good mineral specimens, and not having found anything worth taking away, he approached the little office building. He opened the door, and entered the office, and found, as he had hoped, that Jackie Rothwell, his father's pretty secretary, was at the desk.

The Leadthwaite Mine was one of the last of the old fell mines of the Lake District still in operation by August of 1964; it produced the white mineral, barytes (barite), for commercial use. However, as Jim knew, it had been started in the sixteenth century as a lead mine, and over the centuries it had been worked extensively for ores of lead and zinc. By the latter part of the twentieth century it had seemed that the ores of lead and zinc were virtually worked out, and the mine, having become uneconomical, had closed down. Then in 1959 a small private company had re-opened the mine, employing Arthur Sandy as the manager. The company's business was now to mine barytes, of which there was a great deal in the mineral veins of the hillside. On the site were various old stone buildings which were nowadays mostly used as storage space for equipment, and for mined barytes awaiting transportation away from the site by the company's one large wagon; and there was also one newer building, the office. It consisted of two rooms: the office itself, a large rectangular room, well lit by large windows, and a small room at the back which was the toilet. There was a table in the middle of the office, and a large manager's desk at one end of the room. Two chairs were drawn up to this desk: one, a heavy wooden chair, was Mr. Sandy's personal chair, while the other, a revolving metal chair, was the secretary's seat; it was drawn up to one end of the desk. One of the walls had some maps and plans fastened to it by drawing pins.

This was the place where Jim found himself that Monday, having travelled to the mine with his father by car that morning. He was not due to start work again at the station until the next day, as the first day of his holiday had also been a Tuesday (August 4th, the day he had travelled down to Rhodes Castle to propose to Susan)

Two days earlier Jim had bid Susan a rather sad farewell, and had left Rhodes Castle to travel back to the North by train. But his sadness at the parting had been tempered by the knowledge that on this occasion his separation from his fiancée was to be only a very short one. Susan was coming to Cockermouth in two days time, on August 19th, to spend a few days with the Sandys.

Jim had been delighted that he had been able to persuade Susan to adopt this plan before he had left Rhodes Castle. Of course, it had been a great disappointment for both of them that it had not been possible for both of them to travel north together on the same day, but Susan had told Jim that she had an engagement noted down in her diary for Tuesday, August 18th. It was, unfortunately, a very important engagement, which Susan felt compelled to honour by her presence. On that day she was to formally open a new technical college near Sherborne, the John Dalmane College, named in memory of her dead husband, by the unveiling of a brass plaque in the new building. It was to be the culmination of a project in which John Dalmane, the late Earl of Saint Helens, had been closely involved; and Susan knew that she had to be there on that Tuesday to unveil his plaque. The next day she would be following Jim up to the North, travelling alone in a first-class compartment of the "Pines Express", and changing at Crewe, just as Jim had done on the Saturday, except that he had travelled second-class.

That morning as Jim and his father were motoring to the mine, Mr. Sandy had told him that he would only be doing half a day's work there.

At lunch time he was to meet a very distinguished professor of geology at the Keswick Hotel, where he would be lunching with him. "I'm looking forward to meeting Professor Wadden, I can tell you, Jim, and I expect we'll spend all afternoon after lunch discussing plans for further prospecting for zinc and other metals." Mr. Sandy was himself a qualified geologist, a very knowledgeable man in matters of mineralogy and mining.

"Won't the professor want to come to the mine to have a look round?" Jim had asked.

"Not on this occasion, he won't, as I understand it," Mr. Sandy had answered. "I'm sure he'll want to come to Leadthwaite soon for a good look at things, but this afternoon there'll only be time for talking at the hotel. I've a lot of papers to show him, and there'll be a lot to be discussed."

"What time are you to meet him?"

"One o' clock, we said, for lunch in the Keswick Hotel, the one next to the station, so I'll need to leave the mine soon after half past twelve."

"Oh yes, I see."

"But I don't expect to be coming back to the mine after that," said Mr. Sandy, "so, if you like, I could give you a lift into Keswick at half past twelve, and then you could find a bus or a train to take you home. Or, if you want to stay at the mine this afternoon, I should think you could get a lift back to Cockermouth with Jackie. She finishes work at five o' clock."

"I say, that's a good idea!" said Jim, his eyes suddenly lighting up with excitement at the thought of sitting beside Jackie in the front passenger seat of her car.

"Well, ask her then. That way you'll be back at home by about half past five, and I should be back about the same time, or rather earlier, but at least by six o' clock."

★

Jim closed the office door behind him. There was no one there except Jackie, who was busy typing at the desk, but Jim was expecting that Mr. Cole and his Father would soon come in. Bob Cole was the deputy manager and foreman of the small workforce.

"Hello!" Jackie hardly bothered to raise her head from the typewriter as she paused in her work only for a second to greet Jim.

"Hello, Jackie," said Jim. Realizing that at the moment she was busy typing a letter, he did not attempt to make any further conversation. We'll talk presently during the lunch break, he thought, and then I can ask her for a lift home at five o' clock.

In addition to the two chairs at the desk there were in the room a few other light wooden chairs; Jim sat down on one that was drawn up to the table. Then he opened a little paperback book on minerals, which he had brought with him, and began to read from it; but at once he found that it was hard to concentrate his thoughts on reading with Jackie in the room.

Jim was a little worried by his strong reactions of attraction to Jackie Rothwell. He thought that, as he was deeply in love with Susan, and was now going to marry her, he should find no other woman attractive. At least, he said to himself, that's not really possible, but I shouldn't be at all interested in any other women who do look attractive to me like Jackie. The thought then came to him that, in fact, his partiality for beautiful women was a serious weakness in his character. Damn it all, he thought, if Sue means *everything* to me, how can I want or need any other woman? Why should any other woman excite me?

He tried hard to lose himself in his book, but it was very difficult for him to ignore completely Jackie's presence at the desk. He tried to force his eyes not to look up at her, but found that somehow he could not do this. Why am I so weak, he said to himself angrily, that I have to keep glancing at Jackie? But to this question there seemed to be no answer. From where he was he saw her, when he looked that way, sitting half turned away from him, in profile, concentrating on the letter she was rapidly typing. The typewriter clattered away noisily, but he hardly heard it.

His gaze kept coming to rest on the round outlines of the full bust which was so clearly visible under the blue jumper she was wearing. He would not admit to himself that she had a marvellous figure.

A few minutes later Jim heard the paper being taken out of the typewriter, and, glancing up at Jackie, he saw put the completed letter down on the desk. Then, for the first time, she turned and smiled at him.

"There, that's it finished," she said. "Now we can talk. Congratulations on your engagement, Jim!"

"Oh, thank you!" he said, feeling that he must be blushing slightly.

"And *we've* named the day too!" said Jackie, her eyes sparkling.

"Your wedding day?"

"Yes, of course! Your Dad and I are going to be married on the twenty-sixth of September."

"Oh, how lovely!" said Jim, wondering why his father had not given him this interesting piece of news. "Where will you be married?"

"In the Registry Office in Cockermouth."

"Oh not in church?"

"But, Jim, we *can't* have a church wedding because of your father being divorced. It has to be a civil ceremony."

"Oh yes, of course," said Jim. "I'd forgotten about the divorce."

Jim had already known that Jackie was soon to become his stepmother. His father had told him before he had travelled down to Rhodes Castle that the divorce from his mother was at last a *fait accompli*, but he had said nothing about a wedding except that he would be marrying Jackie "very soon". Jim had for the moment forgotten about asking her for a lift home that evening, and was thinking of asking whether they had only just decided on the date for their wedding, when the door opened, and in came his father and Mr. Cole.

"Hello, Jim!" said Bob Cole. "Your Father's got to go now, but we'll start our lunch break, eh?"

"Yes, it's time I was setting off for Keswick to meet Professor Wadden," said Mr. Sandy, who had gone over to his desk, sat down, and opened a briefcase. "Jackie, my love, have you managed to get that plan of the Cobalt Mine finished?"

"Yes, Arthur, it's all finished!" said Jackie, smiling merrily at him. "Are you going to show it to the Professor?"

"I thought I would, and tell him your theory about that place if I may?"

"Please do! Perhaps he'll want to go up to the Cobalt Mine himself one day to see what there is there. But, of course, my idea could well be all wrong, and the zinc veins may not extend right up there."

"I'm pretty sure they do," said Mr. Sandy. "Thanks, Jackie!" She handed him a large sheet of paper from her end of the desk, on which she had drawn a careful plan in different pencil and ink colours. "My word, you've made a beautifully neat job of it, my darling!"

"Well, you see, Arthur, I've used different colours to show up the different mineral veins," said Jackie. "It's based as far as possible on what we definitely know about the courses of the veins, but where they're hypothetical I've used dotted lines . . . to show the probable courses."

"I see; and you've shown the lead-bearing veins in black, the zinc veins in red, and the supposed cobalt vein in blue. It makes it very clear. Look, Jim, Jackie's produced quite a masterpiece here!"

Jim was looking over their shoulders at the hand-drawn plan lying on the desk.

"What is the Cobalt Mine, Dad?" he asked. "I've never heard of it."

"It's an old mine right up on top of the fell, above our mine here around two thousand feet above sea level, near Scar Crags. The

Keswick Mining Company had an idea of mining erythrite, cobalt ore there, but the project was an expensive failure from what I've read."

"Aye, it were a flop, that old Cobalt Mine," said Mr. Cole, who had sat down at the table, and had started to eat a pile of sandwiches he had brought with him for his lunch. "They took a gamble, no doubt, that they'd make a fortune out of cobalt, but it didn't work. There's not much to see up there nowadays."

"All the same, Bob, I wouldn't mind going up there sometime to have a look round," said Mr. Sandy. "If Jackie's theory is right we ought to be making some exploratory drillings for zinc up there."

"I'll tell you what, Arthur," said Jackie, "I'll have a walk up the fell myself this afternoon, if I may, to make a preliminary inspection of the old tip heaps and adits. I haven't got anything else to do unless you want me to do some other work here?"

"No, no, there's nothing else I'd like you to do," said Mr. Sandy.

"Then I think I'll do that. It should stay fine, I think, and the climb up the fell would do me good – would help me to work off a bit of excess weight!" she laughed.

"Oh well, it would be good exercise for you, no doubt, but I should be a bit careful, Jackie, if I were you. The fellside is very steep; don't over-strain yourself, my dear, clambering up there. And now heavens, I must go! I'm forgetting the time, stopping here to talk." Mr. Sandy had just looked at his watch, and had seen that it was after half past twelve. "Jim, you were thinking of a lift back to Cockermouth with Jackie, weren't you?"

"Of course you can come with me in my car," said Jackie. "Climbing up to the old Cobalt Mine won't take all that long; I'll be back by four, I expect."

"Do you think I could come with you up the fell?" asked Jim suddenly, looking at Jackie, his eyes sparkling.

"Why not? I'd rather climb in company, Jim, than go alone, if you've nothing else to do." Jackie rose to her feet, seeing Mr. Sandy take his briefcase, into which he had packed her plan of the Cobalt Mine, and move towards the door. "You're off now?"

"Yes, I must be off now," said Mr. Sandy. "Be good with Jackie, Jim and enjoy yourself!" He winked at his son, who grinned back at his father. What a brilliant idea of his it was to spend the afternoon climbing the fell with Jackie!

"I'll just see you off," said Jackie.

Mr. Sandy held the door open for her, and followed her out. Jim knew that Jackie had gone outside so that his father could kiss her before he got into his car to drive away. He took out from his provision bag the packed lunch picnic he had brought with him, and unfolded a packet of cheese sandwiches.

"Would you like some beer with your sandwiches?" said Mr. Cole.

He had two bottles of beer standing on the table, and had already poured himself out a mug full of it.

"Oh, thank you very much, Mr. Cole!" said Jim. "I'll get myself a mug; I know where they're kept." He went over to a wall cupboard and opened it. "What about Jackie?" he asked.

She doesn't drink beer, but she'll have a coffee, likely, so you could bring out two mugs"

Jim brought two mugs to the table, and Mr. Cole poured out some of his beer into one of them.

"It's best bitter, this," he said.

"Super stuff!" said Jim when he had drunk a few mouthfuls of the beer. "Ah, there goes Dad." They had just heard the engine of Mr. Sandy's car started, and now Jim, looking through the window, saw him swing the car round through a half-circle, wave his hand to Jackie, and drive away. Then the door opened, and Jackie returned.

"I don't understand how this professor comes into things," said Jim a minute later, when Jackie had settled down to eat her sandwich lunch at a space cleared on the desk. "Is our company paying him to help?"

"That's it, Jim," said Mr. Cole. "The R.T.Z. Corporation has engaged him to advise us, and they've arranged for him to have this talk with your Dad." The R.T.Z. Corporation owned the small company which ran the mine.

"Does he live locally?"

"I don't really know. Arthur only said he was staying in Keswick at the moment," said Mr. Cole.

"He lives in Leeds," said Jackie, "and has a holiday cottage in Keswick, and he and his wife and family are up here on holiday until sometime next month, I believe. Arthur, your father, says he's a Professor of Geology at Leeds University. He sounds a nice enough chap from his letter of introduction, apparently."

"I expect Dad will get on well with him, talking mining and mineralogy," said Jim. "By the way, what did he mean when he said he'd tell the Professor your theory about the Cobalt Mine?"

Jackie seemed a little embarrassed as she answered him evasively:

"Oh, nothing much! It was just an idea of mine."

"What sort of an idea? Do tell me, Jackie."

"Oh well, if you must know I'll tell you, as you're coming up there with me this afternoon. We'll bring geological hammers with us, and do a little prospecting."

"That'll be great fun!" said Jim, his eyes gleaming in anticipation of a most enjoyable afternoon. "But what about this theory of yours?"

"In a word, it's zinc. I believe there might be workable deposits of sphalerite up there, particularly where the north–south lead vein intersects the zinc vein which heads west from here. Look here, I can show you better what I mean on the big map."

A six-inch Ordnance Survey map of the immediate locality of the Leadthwaite Mine was pinned to the wall behind Jackie's chair. Many geological notes had been added in ink to the printed map. Jim took a partly eaten sandwich with him, and came over to study the map carefully with Jackie, who turned her chair round to face the wall.

"Now, we're here," said Jackie, taking a pen, and pointing with it to the Leadthwaite Mine, where it was marked on the map. "And the

Cobalt Mine, you see, is right up there, where your father's written in the name 'Cobalt Mine'."

"Gosh! What a place to work a mine!" said Jim. "Why, it's right up near the summit of Sail!"

"Between Sail and Scar Crags, actually; pretty high at about two thousand feet above sea level. It'll be quite a tough climb, I should think, and perhaps it'll be nearer five o' clock than four o' clock by the time we get back here."

"We'll get a jolly good view from up there!"

"No doubt we will. Well, you can see we've added the mineral veins in ink, and it's around here that we're interested in, the place where these two veins intersect."

★

Half an hour later, having finished their sandwiches, Jim and Jackie set off from the Leadthwaite Mine to climb the fell. They had taken careful note from the six-inch map of the best route for the ascent, and were first going to follow the steep path up to the top of Coledale Hause; then they would make their way southwards around Eel Crag, and so hoped to reach the Scar between Sail and Scar Crag. It would not be the shortest possible route, but they were both agreed that it looked like the easiest and most sensible way for two people who were not expert mountaineers. Jackie had taken her geological hammer, and had issued Jim with a spare hammer from the stores room; and so they had set off.

At first their way was not unreasonably steep, but the path quickly became steeper as it skirted a vertical rocky drop by a series of zig-zags. After about ten minutes of climbing they paused for a short rest.

"I must stop . . . just for a minute or two," panted Jackie.

They sat down on a large flat rock conveniently near the footpath. Jim was not yet feeling breathless with the exertion, and Jackie, he noticed, recovered very quickly. The sun was shining, although there was quite a lot of cloud in the sky; they could see the clouds moving across the sky in a brisk westerly wind from which they were well sheltered by the steep fell behind them. They were looking down on the buildings and outworks of the Leadthwaite Mine, and Jim thought that it looked as if he could almost have thrown a stone onto the roof of the office.

"There's a good view already," he said.

"There is, but let's get on," said Jackie, rising to her feet.

They had only been sitting down for about a minute. "This climbing is just what I need to get me into training for the Grasmere Sports," she added as they set off again, walking up the steep, rough footpath.

"The Grasmere Sports? Are you taking part?"

"Yes, in some of the field and track events."

"And the Guides' Race?"

"Oh, good heavens, no! That would kill me, I reckon!"

"When are the Sports?"

"This Thursday."

"Gosh! This Thursday, the twentieth, you'll be at Grasmere! Will you be running, Jackie?"

"There's not much else . . . a woman *can* enter for," said Jackie, beginning again to be a little breathless as she spoke. "Apart from the Guides' Races, and the hound trails, it's mostly wrestling as you probably know and that's only for men and boys."

"Yes, the men's and boy's Cumberland wrestling," said Jim, who was familiar with the events held at the annual Grasmere Sports.

"I've entered for the Half-Mile Race, the Hundred Yards sprint . . . and the High Jump."

"Gosh! I didn't know you were keen on athletics, Jackie."

"I like keeping fit that way at least, I *thought* I already was fit enough . . . but scrambling up here is making me a little . . . breathless!"

"I think it's talking at the same time as climbing that does it," said Jim, "makes one short of breath. But perhaps we needn't try to go up quite so fast." He was beginning to feel breathless himself as he said this, and now, although they had not been hurrying, they slackened their pace slightly. They climbed in silence for a few minutes.

The Grasmere Sports were held on the third Thursday in August at the village of Grasmere, in the Lake District (they are now held on the Sunday of the Late Summer Bank Holiday). The Sports are a colourful event, a mixture mostly of athletics and hound trailing, with the Guides' Races, in which runners have to race up the fell overlooking the Sports Field. Jim, thinking about the Sports, found himself wishing that he could go there on that Thursday to watch Jackie taking part.

Presently he heard her speak his thought aloud.

"Any chance that you could come to Grasmere on Thursday?"

"I hardly think so," said Jim, "because I start work again at the station tomorrow, so I couldn't go to Grasmere, unless . . . unless I were to ask the Station-Master for a day off work on Thursday. Yes, I could do that, Jackie. He's a pretty decent chap, the Station-Master—might easily let me have the day off work."

"It would be nice to have your support, Jim," said Jackie.

Jim decided that he would ask the Station-Master for the day off work on Thursday so that he could go to the Sports, if he could persuade his father also to take the day off, and drive them there; but that, he thought, should be easy. Dad's sure to want to go there anyway to watch Jackie, he said to himself. Then he remembered that Susan was coming in two days time, the day before the Sports. It would be an excellent thing to take her out for the day on Thursday, especially if it turned out to be a nice day. Good, he thought, that settles it: I must take Sue to the Grasmere Sports.

They climbed on, occasionally taking short rests, and presently came to the top of the pass, where they began to veer to the left away from the main footpath. Now, still ascending, they were following a vague path towards the summit of Sail, a peak in the Grassmoor range.

They stopped close to some dark crags on their left.

"Are you sure we're heading the right way?" asked Jim.

"Yes, I think we must be right," said Jackie. "This is obviously Eel Crag to our left, and it looks as if this path will take us up it, bearing to the right, to keep those cliffs on our left."

"Look, the summit of Grassmoor's gone!" said Jim, pointing to his right. Over that way, a few minutes ago, they had been looking at the long, flat-topped mountain called Grassmoor, which around its summit is levelish and grassy. Now it was entirely hidden from them under cloud.

"The clouds are coming down," said Jackie, "or perhaps it's just that we're getting nearer the clouds, up near the summits of these fells."

"I wonder if it's covered the top of Sail too? We can't see it from here, though."

"I think we soon will see it," said Jackie, "when we get to the top of this steep bit of the ridge. My word, it *is* steep here!" She and Jim were scrambling up the hillside on all fours for greater safety.

"But we seem to have lost the path," said Jim. He kept slipping back, a few inches at a time, as small stones shifted under his feet and rolled down the steep slope, which was now more like a patch of scree than a steep path, as it had been. He watched Jackie, who was a few yards ahead of him, as she kept pausing for a second or two to look round, as if she was trying to find the easiest way up the screes.

"We should have made a detour round this scree," she panted a few minutes later, "but we're . . . almost at the top of it now."

"Yes, there's the path, marked with a cairn," said Jim, pointing ahead and to his right to a small pile of stones which indicated a path. "I say," he added, "Look at the mist swirling around those crags to our left."

"It's getting rather misty here," said Jackie, "and it's certainly not as warm as it was either. Perhaps we should turn back now, Jim, if we think that the mist's going to come down thick?"

Jim looked up into a cloudy white sky above them, and noticed that the sun had almost disappeared in the thickening mist. They could still see where it was, a dim, misty circle of brightness.

"Don't let's turn back yet," he said. "We must be very nearly there, and this mist's not really very thick."

"No, I suppose it isn't. We might as well get to the top of this ridge, though, and then we can look round and see what it's like around Sail . . . but then we'd better turn back if we can't see our way ahead."

"I suppose so."

"Well, you see, Jim, we'll never find the old mine if we can't see our way because of the mist."

"Didn't you bring a map?" asked Jim.

"I didn't bother to, as I thought I'd studied the six-inch map on the office wall well enough to be sure of the way . . . but we never thought it would get misty."

"No . . . but did you bring a compass?"

"Damn! of course I should have brought my compass! No, I've gone and left it in the drawer in the desk. We'll just have to manage without a compass."

Five minutes later they stopped, and stood side by side in the mist. They had now reached the top of the patch of scree, and had regained a path which lead uphill on a fairly easy gradient.

"I can't see the next cairn . . . if there is another one," said Jim, peering intently ahead. About a hundred yards away the path vanished into thick mist.

"We must start back at once!" said Jackie suddenly. "Sorry, Jim, but we'll have to give the Cobalt Mine a miss."

"Oh, I say, what a pity! . . . when we've struggled up all this way!"

"We'd never find it with the mist getting thicker all the time . . . and anyway we'd just get lost if we were to try to go on any further."

Jim began to wonder whether they were going to get lost in any case, even if they were to try an immediate descent of the fell.

However, far from feeling dismayed at the prospect of being lost in hill fog with Jackie, he was aware of a rapidly mounting excitement. If they were lost anything might happen to them. He turned suddenly round to look back.

"I can't see our way back," he said.

"Damn! I can't either. We've left it too late!" Jackie was staring helplessly back into the mist with Jim. "We should have turned back five or ten minutes ago. Now we can barely see about fifty yards of this path, and we can't see where that vertical drop is."

"It wouldn't do to stumble over the edge of those crags," said Jim thoughtfully.

"It would *not!*"

They were still standing on the path near the little pile of stones which could be seen dimly about ten yards away. Beyond it the path faded into an atmosphere of universal whiteness, obscuring all topographical details of the hillside.

"It's as thick as a real fog!" said Jim, hoping that he sounded alarmed rather than excited.

"It certainly is! But we'll just have to manage as best as we can."

"What do we do now?"

"Press on. It's nearly four o' clock now, so I still think we should make it back to the car by five o' clock—if we can find our way without too much difficulty."

"Then we'd better stick to this path, for a bit anyway."

"That's right," said Jackie. "We've got to remember that somewhere over there"—she pointed into the fog—"are those cliffs which we mustn't stumble over, and we want to avoid descending that steep scree too. It was a sort of short cut when we were coming up, but we'd better detour around it to the left. You'd better keep fairly close to me, Jim; we don't want to lose sight of each other in this fog."

We certainly don't! said Jim to himself as he set off, following a few paces behind Jackie. The path sloped gently downwards, and soon they passed a second small cairn at the side of it.

"We'll have to turn to the right presently," said Jackie a minute later, "but hopefully this path will join the other one, so that we could turn right at the junction."

"We can't have skirted round those steep screes yet," said Jim.

He tried very hard to see where the screes were, somewhere away to his right, but the mist was now very thick, and they could see little more than ten yards in any direction. Jackie was also straining her sight to try to see a little further than the steamy atmosphere would allow them to see.

Suddenly she checked.

"What is it?" asked Jim, also stopping.

"Why, look, we've lost our path—the path we were following!" said Jackie.

Jim, looking down, saw a small sheep track at their feet. It did not run straight across the short, boggy grass of the fellside; near the limit of their foreshortened vision they saw a large grey rock sticking out of the grass, and the sheep track, they noticed, took a wide detour around it.

"We don't want to go *that* way," said Jackie, pointing towards the rock. "That track seems to be leading uphill—going back nearly the same way as we've come down."

"How have we managed to lose that path we were following?"

"It must have turned suddenly to the left, but I didn't notice, and went on, following this sheep track instead."

"Are we lost now?" said Jim, after another look round into the fog, in which no definite landmarks were visible.

"We can't be," said Jackie. Look here, Jim, we've just got to keep our heads, and use our brains, and keep going in roughly the right direction."

"Which would you say *is* the right direction?"

"That way!" said Jackie decisively, pointing ahead into the fog. "Come on, follow me, Jim, I feel almost certain we're going the right way."

Jim, however, was moderately certain that Jackie was mistaken in her choice of the direction in which to walk; but he said nothing more about it. An idea was beginning to form in his mind: a vague, imprecise idea, yet it was causing a feeling of excitement to arise within him with every step he took. They were lost, and perhaps they would walk the wrong way, and presently find that they had descended the wrong side of the mountain. He was not yet quite sure what would be the use of allowing such a mistake to happen—if it was a case of *allowing* it to happen—unless it was simply that in this way he could look forward to a much longer evening in Jackie's company. If they found themselves in the wrong place when the mist cleared they would have to walk all the way back again to regain Jackie's car. Then he thought that perhaps Jackie would feel too tired to do that. She had said nothing yet about tiredness, but to make another climb and descent of the high pass might prove too much for her, and he too would probably find such an effort very exhausting. In that case, he thought, it might be better for them to walk on until they should come to a road where they could try to hitch a lift back home to Cockermouth. Jackie at that time lived in a house in Cockermouth which she shared with two girl students of the local college of further education in Workington.

As he walked Jim was considering these points, and wondering whether he ought to think of deliberately leading Jackie astray, so that he could remain with her for longer. The idea made him smile a mischievous smile, but he had no thought in his mind of any improper behaviour with his companion. Then he remembered that he could not be sure which way they were heading; it might be towards the Leadthwaite Mine, or it might not be, but they were certainly going downhill, and that made him feel that, if they were not heading for the mine, they must be heading for the valley of the Gasgale Gill. The path upwards from the Leadthwaite Mine lead over the pass called Coledale Hause to descend into the Gasgale Gill valley, a steep-sided defile between the Grassmoor and Whiteside ranges of hills. Jim, as he followed Jackie down a rough, pathless slope, was keeping a sharp eye open for any familiar landmarks which might give a clue as to where they were, and in which direction they were heading. But he could see nothing but mist and a few yards of rough, grassy fellside with, here and there, loose patches of stones and boulders. He admitted to himself that he was temporarily lost, and hoped again that Jackie had been mistaken when she had said "follow me" as if she had been convinced that she knew the way down to the mine.

CHAPTER SIXTEEN

"There's a path!" cried Jim jubilantly. "It looks like the main path."

"Good! All we need do now is to follow it down," said Jackie.

It had been some five minutes since Jackie had suggested to Jim that he should follow her as she set off to lead the way down the trackless hillside relying, apparently, on an intuitive sense of direction to guide them through the fog. Now, quite suddenly, the visibility had slightly improved, and at the same moment they had both noticed a path to their right, a well-trodden path which seemed to run parallel to the direction they were taking. They moved slantwise across the hillside to gain the path.

"Hello!" said Jim, slackening his pace as he came to the path.

"What's that moving down there?"

"Only a sheep," said Jackie.

"So it is—at least, there are several sheep." Jim had noticed something which he had taken for a grey rock, sticking out of the grass, but it had moved, turning it into a sheep. Now they saw a number of moorland sheep coming up the path towards them, before they turned aside to the right of the path.

"Come on!" said Jackie. "Don't let's hang about here watching these sheep. Let's get on."

"All right, let's. I say, it's getting pretty cold up here, isn't it?"

"Very cold," agreed Jackie, "and rather damp too. Perhaps it'll rain when this mist lifts."

"It's practically drizzling now, but the mist already has lifted a little."

They hurried on down the hill on a wide stony path. The gradient was at first moderate, but it soon became steeper. They felt a light, cold breeze blowing in their faces, and saw that the mist was being blown along the ground towards them in thick, curling wisps, like steam coming off hot water. It was certainly possible to see a little further, but still they could not determine their position by any definite landmarks. The summits of the fells to the right and the left were still hidden in the mist.

"Ah!" said Jim a few minutes later. "We're coming to that really steep bit of the path where we had to come up on hands and knees, in places."

"We'll get down all right on our feet if we tread carefully, taking care not to slip," said Jackie. "Keep a look-out for the summit of Sail to our right, Jim, and then we'll know that we're in the right way."

Jim thought that he heard a note of doubt in her voice as she said this. A dim, dark hillside was now coming into view on their right, sweeping up towards cloudy, unseen summits. I wonder, he said to himself, if that *is* the side of Sail? I don't believe it is. It wasn't as close to the path as this on our way up . . .

By now it was becoming decidedly cold and wet; and although the drizzle had not yet turned into proper rain, their anoraks were wet, and droplets of water were in their hair. Jim suddenly thought that it would be good to be back at the mine, where they could warm themselves, and have a cup of tea before setting off for home in Jackie's car; now he hoped that they were not on the wrong side of the pass, but he began to be increasingly suspicious that they were.

Their doubts were settled for them a quarter of an hour later, when Jackie suddenly stopped.

"What is it?" asked Jim, coming up to her.

"We've come down the wrong side of the fell," she said grimly. "I'm pretty sure we have."

Jim did not at first answer her. He peered carefully through the thinning mist, and knew in his heart, as he looked at the shapes of the nearby hillsides, that she was right.

"Can you be sure?" he asked.

"Well, not perhaps really *sure*, but—just look around, Jim! Look, the mist's lifting! We're in the wrong valley."

"I say," said Jim, "I believe we are!"

He was not sure whether he felt pleased or disappointed, but there was really no longer any doubt about it. The mist was lifting as suddenly as it had descended, and they were able to look a long way down a narrow valley, hemmed in by steep mountain slopes on both sides. Near them, on their left, a small beck was making its way down the valley. They had already heard the noise of running water, and now they were able to see the course of the small stream.

"There's no sign of the Leadthwaite Mine here," said Jim after another careful look around. "I think this little beck must be the Gasgale Gill, between Whiteside and Grassmoor."

"Have you been here before?"

"Yes, assuming that that's where we are. Yes, this *must* be the wrong side of the pass that we've come down on. That mountain on the left looks like Grassmoor . . . and this one on our right's Sand Hill . . . and there's Whiteside lower down the valley, on the right." Jim was looking up towards the summits of the hills, but above them little could be seen but cloud. The mist had lifted, but the clouds were still very low, and now the drizzle had thickened into a steady rain. "It's coming on wet," he added, pulling the hood of his anorak over his head as he spoke.

"Oh dear!" sighed Jackie wearily. "What are we to do now?" She also pulled her anorak hood over her head.

"Well," said Jim, "I suppose we ought to go back—if you're not too tired—or else we could go on. "We'll come to the Buttermere road presently if we walk on down this valley."

"I think we'll have to do that," said Jackie, "and if we can get as far as the road we could try to hitch a lift back to Cockermouth. But

I couldn't think of climbing all the way back up the fell, Jim. We've come much too far down this wrong side to do that."

"Do you feel exhausted?" asked Jim seriously.

"I do! Perhaps I'm not really fit enough, after all, to take part in the Sports on Thursday. But we'd better press on, Jim, and I'll try to keep going until we reach that road."

They began to stumble on again along the path, with Jim now leading the way; the path was too narrow for two to walk abreast. Jim, who was also feeling tired, was being careful not to walk too fast for Jackie. The rain was rapidly becoming heavier, and they noticed that the westerly wind was rising, and beginning to fling the cold rain into their faces.

Overhead there was a lowering dark sky of low clouds. Altogether the conditions were most unpleasant for walking.

After about five minutes of walking Jim, who was a few yards ahead of Jackie, suddenly checked.

"Why, look," he said, pointing ahead with an outstretched finger, "there's a house!"

"So there is!" said Jackie, noticing the small building to which Jim was pointing.

"It wasn't here the last time I came this way," said Jim, "but that was many years ago."

"Look here, Jim, we might as well make for that house and ask if we can telephone from there. I should think your Father will be back at home by now."

"Dad'll come and pick us up, of course, when we tell him what's happened. Yes, we'd better do that."

The house was only about a quarter of a mile down the valley, whereas the road was about a mile and a half away, Jim told Jackie. It comforted both of them, but particularly Jackie, to think that Mr. Sandy would come out in his car (if they could contact him by telephone), and so eliminate the need for a further long trudge down the narrow mountain valley in the wind and the rain.

"You know, I hardly think I could have made it as far as that road," said Jackie cheerfully as they strode along the path towards the house. "At least, not without the opportunity of taking a rest."

"Perhaps they may even offer us a cup of tea there," said Jim hopefully, "and then, if Dad agrees to come out here, we won't need to walk any further."

"It's nearly half past five," said Jackie. "He's sure to be back at home by now, but I hope he's had a useful talk with the professor."

The house they were heading for was a small, modern, two-storeyed building of bricks and concrete. They were cheered to notice smoke issuing from a chimney-pot, showing that somebody was at home. When they were close to it they saw that it was built beside the stream at the end of a rough car track. It had a little garden surrounded by a low brick wall.

"What an extraordinary place to build a house!" said Jackie. "It won't get much sun here, shut in between the mountains, except, I suppose, in the evenings, and maybe in the early mornings. And what a remote spot it is too!"

"Lucky for us it's here!" said Jim. "Hello, what's that notice on the gatepost?"

A wooden notice was attached to a gatepost. They went up to it, and read:–

"GHYLL COTTAGE. BED AND BREAKFAST.
Mrs. M. Lane"

"Good!" said Jim, seeing telephone wires leading from the house. "She's got a telephone."

Then they saw that there was a hand-written notice on a card displayed in a window beside the front door: "VACANCIES". If only we could stay the night here! thought Jim.

Jackie rang the doorbell, and a few seconds later the front door was opened by a middle-aged, brown-haired woman.

"Good evening!" said Jackie. "May we telephone from here, please?"

"Why, yes, by all means," said Mrs. Lane, the lady of the house.

"Come in, and I'll show you where the telephone is. You'll be glad to get indoors, I dare say, out of the wind and rain."

"Yes, thank you, we will, as it's come on wet."

"It has that!" said Mrs. Lane. "Proper nasty outside, I call it." She closed her front door behind Jackie and Jim. "The telephone's here in the hall. Would you like to take off your wet things first?"

"Well, yes, perhaps we'd better take off our anoraks," said Jackie. "I'm sorry if we're dripping water on your carpet."

"Nay, that's nowt. Folk can't help being wet when they're outside in weather like this. Do you know the number you want?"

"Yes," said Jim. "Look here, Jackie, shall I make this call, as I know our number?"

"I'll be in my kitchen if you want me," said Mrs. Lane, and left them, leaving open a door from which issued a pleasant smell of cooking.

Jackie and Jim took off their anoraks, and, noticing some coat-hooks on the wall, hung them up. The telephone stood on a small table at the foot of a narrow, steep flight of stairs; it was an ordinary domestic model without a coinbox. Jim picked up the receiver and dialled his home number. He put the receiver to his ear and heard the number ringing. The ringing went on and on for over a minute.

"Bother, Dad's not in yet!" he said quietly to Jackie, who was standing beside him. He hung up the receiver. "I wonder what we ought to do now?" he said doubtfully.

"Did you manage all right?" asked Mrs. Lane, who had clearly been listening to them, coming out of her kitchen.

"There was no reply," said Jim shortly.

"Then would you like to wait a while, and try it again later?"

Jim looked at Jackie, and saw her nod to him.

"Yes please, if we may?"

"By all means, you may. Have a seat in the lounge, won't you, while you wait?" Mrs. Lane opened a door for them. "Would you care for a cup of tea while you're waiting?" she asked kindly. "that's right, sit down anywhere you like, and make yourselves comfortable.

You look cold to me, as well as wet, and I dare say a cup of tea and a biscuit would be welcome?"

"It would indeed!" said Jim. "Thank you very much." Jackie also thanked her. Then Jim whispered urgently in Jackie's ear.

"Do you charge anything for a cup of tea?" asked Jackie.

"Nay, you can have that for nowt!" said Mrs. Lane. "But if you were thinking of staying, it's a pound each for bed and breakfast with dinner."

"That's very good value!" remarked Jim.

"But I don't think we'll be staying," said Jackie, with a glance at Jim.

"Just as you like, but I've got a room vacant," said Mrs. Lane, and left them.

"She probably thinks we're husband and wife," whispered Jim to Jackie as soon as the door was closed.

"I dare say she does," said Jackie quietly, "but it doesn't matter. There should be no need to give our names."

She had sat down in an armchair near the hearth, in which there was a small coal fire burning in the grate, but now she stood up and moved nearer to the fire. "My word, my skirt's pretty wet!" she continued. "I might as well try to dry it for a few minutes. What about your clothes, Jim?"

Jim felt his trousers carefully.

"Yes, they're pretty wet," he said, "but I don't suppose it's any good thinking of drying them . . . unless we're staying here."

"But we can't do that, Jim."

"No, but . . . but we might *have* to stay here—if Dad can't give us a lift back."

"Why should you think he wouldn't be able to?"

"Oh, well, er . . . something may have gone wrong. After all it was about half past five when we got here, and he should have been back from Keswick by then. He said he'd be back at least by six o' clock."

"You'd better ring again about six, then—after we've had our cup of tea."

"I shall—but what are we going to do if there's still no answer?"

"There will be, I'm sure," said Jackie, "but *if* you still get no answer . . . we'll have to think of some other way of getting back to Cockermouth. Perhaps Mrs. Lane could give us a lift, or Mr. Lane.

These people must have a car, living in such a remote place. I suppose we *could* phone for a taxi, but I should think that would be awfully expensive. Or we could wait . . ." Jackie left her sentence unfinished; the door had opened while she was speaking, and Mrs. Lane had entered, carrying on a tray a teapot, two cups and saucers, milk and sugar, and a plate with some biscuits. She set the tray down on a small table, and moved it so that it stood between Jim's and Jackie's armchairs.

"Thank you," said Jackie.

"Have you got your skirt very wet, my dear?" asked Mrs. Lane.

"Oh, it's not too bad, really."

"It's come on awfully wet, so I don't wonder if you've got wet clothes. You were walking, no doubt?"

"Yes, we were," said Jim.

"And did I hear you say you were needing a lift?"

"Yes, we've got to get home to Cockermouth," said Jackie.

"Well, my dear, I'm sorry, but I don't think I can help you there. Now, if you'd arrived about half an hour sooner, you could have taken a lift to Cockermouth with my maid. She lives near Cockermouth, and comes here in her own car, but she goes home about five, so I'm afraid you've missed her. But there's no car here at the moment."

"Is your husband out?" Jackie ventured to ask. She again sat down in her armchair, carefully feeling her skirt as she sat down to check that it was not too damp.

"Aye, Jack's out wi' t' car, but he won't be back until very late indeed—about midnight, maybe. You see, he's a bus driver, and he's on late shift today."

"Oh, so we can't get a lift from here—unless your father comes for us,. And if he's still not at home when you ring up after we've had this tea we'd better wait a while, and try again later."

"I'm sorry I can't be of more help," said Mrs. Lane, "But if you want to wait here for an hour or two I could give you an evening meal."

"Oh! We could have a meal without having the bed and breakfast?" asked Jim eagerly.

He had been feeling hungry for some time, but now the idea of eating a high tea or early supper at Ghyll Cottage with Jackie appealed to him enormously.

"By all means!" said Mrs. Lane. I do an evening meal for ten shillings—three courses."

"I say, that sounds simply splendid! What do you think about it, Jackie?"

"But look here, Jim," said Jackie, "if you do get your Father on the telephone when you ring again at six o' clock, and he agrees to come out immediately for us, we won't need to stay here to eat."

"No, but if I *don't* get him . . ."

"Then we might as well stay here for supper . . . and then you could ring up again after that."

They went back to the telephone in the hall when they had finished their tea. Jim rang his home number again, and this time the telephone was answered. Mr. Sandy immediately expressed his surprise that Jim had not yet arrived back home; he had just come in himself, he said, and had found only Victoria at home. Jim explained briefly what had happened. "So you see, Dad," he finished, "we were wondering whether you could come out to pick us up sometime this evening."

"I'm sorry, Jim, but that's impossible," said his Father. "I've got no car—broke down in Keswick!"

"Oh dear! Then how did *you* get back to Cockermouth?"

"Professor Wadden very kindly gave me a lift home in his car when I discovered that mine refused to start. I've left it at a garage to be repaired, so I'm not sure yet how I'm going to get to work tomorrow—as Jackie's car is left behind at the mine. But couldn't you walk to the road, Jim, and hitch a lift?"

"We're quite a long way from the road," explained Jim, "And the rain's still pouring down, and Jackie says she's too tired to walk that far."

"I see. It *is* pretty nasty out of doors. Can you get an evening meal at your B. and B?"

"Oh, yes. Mrs. Lane will give us one, if we want it, so we thought we'd stay for that."

"Well, I would do that, if I were you; and it looks as if the best thing you could do is to stay there tonight. Does this place have any vacancies?"

"Oh yes, Dad!" said Jim, trying to keep the eagerness out of his voice, while remembering the "Vacancies" notice in the lounge window. "She said she only charged a pound for dinner, bed and breakfast."

"And you could afford that?"

"Yes, I could afford that, and so could Jackie."

"Then I think you'd better stay where you are for tonight," said Mr. Sandy. "You won't have any pyjamas, or toothbrush, or any other night things with you, of course, so you'll have to rough it— but it's only for one night."

"Of course, Dad. They'll probably be able to give us a lift into Cockermouth in the morning."

"Very well, Jim, we'll leave it like that, unless I hear from you again. Good-bye!"

Jim said good-bye to his Father, hung up the receiver, and turned triumphantly to Jackie, who was waiting for him in the narrow hall of the small house.

"I agreed with Dad that we'd have to stay here tonight as he can't come for us," he told her.

"So I heard you saying," said Jackie. "But, Jim, we don't know yet whether Mrs. Lane has got *two* rooms for us." She gave him a very significant look.

"Oh!—but we know she's got vacancies at the moment—and she said she could put us up for the night for a pound each." Jim was hoping desperately that there would be only one vacant room.

"Then we'd better get this sorted out at once!" said Jackie. "I'll go and find her now." Jackie, followed closely by Jim, went up to the kitchen door, which was ajar, and tapped lightly on it.

"Come in," said Mrs. Lane, putting down a rolling-pin on the table, and wiping some flour dust off her hands onto her apron before coming to the door.

"We think we'll have to stay here tonight," said Jackie, "as we can't get a lift to Cockermouth."

"That's quite all right, my dear," said Mrs. Lane. "I have a vacant room."

"Only one room?" asked Jackie doubtfully.

"Why, yes, only one. You weren't wanting more than one room, were you?"

"Oh, well . . . no, of course not," said Jackie awkwardly. She had just glanced round at Jim, and seen the look of eager anticipation on his face.

"I'll just slip upstairs now and show it to you, if you'd like to follow me," said Mrs. Lane. She paused for a moment in the hall.

"That's the dining-room in there," she said, tapping on a door to her left, opposite the lounge door. "I'll serve your supper and yout breakfast in there for you." She lead the way up the stairs. "There's the toilet in there," she said, stopping for a moment on a landing and pointing to a closed door. "That's the bathroom and the toilet." She opened the door, inviting them to have a brief look inside the room which, they saw, was quite a large bathroom. "And the room I have vacant is the door at the end of this passage," she continued, leading the way on up another short flight of stairs. Jim felt his pulse rate increase because of his mounting excitement. Would the room have two beds in it, or only one?

"There we are!" Mrs. Lane flung open the door of the vacant room, and stood aside for Jackie to enter. Jim hurried in after her.

The second he was over the threshold of the room Jim's gaze homed in on the bed, which, he saw to his great delight, was a double bed.. It was quite clear that the landlady had assumed that he and Jackie were married.

"Will that be all right?" asked Mrs. Lane, looking at Jackie.

"Oh, er . . . ah, yes, it'll be fine!" said Jackie. She looked quickly at Jim, and saw that he was trying to conceal his excitement in an attempt not to smile too much.

Mrs. Lane did not seem to notice Jackie's hesitation in accepting the room.

"There are two clean towels here for you," she said, "and I hope you'll find there are enough blankets on the bed . . ." She pulled a counterpane partly off the bed to show Jackie what was underneath it.

"There are three blankets and a light quilt on it, but if you think that might not be enough I could get you another blanket. The nights have been pretty cool recently."

"I expect three blankets will be enough," said Jackie.

"And you've brought nothing with you, I believe?"

"Nothing. We've brought nothing with us . . . except for our anoraks and our geological hammers. You see, we set off walking earlier today meaning only to climb the fell, and return to where we started from, but a thick mist came down, and we got lost."

"And then we came down on this side of the pass by mistake," said Jim.

"Oh, I see," said Mrs. Lane. "You're not the first people I've had stopping a night here who've been up on the fells when the clouds have come down. It can happen quite suddenly in these fells, can't it?

But I'm afraid I can't do much in the way of providing things you might need for the night, beyond towels—and soap in the bathroom—but I might be able to find you a night-dress."

"Oh, thank you very much!" said Jackie.

"Right, if you'll excuse me, I'll be getting back to the kitchen.

Oh, perhaps I could ask you to sign the Visitor's Book for me. I ask all my guests to fill in their names and addresses in the Visitor's Book. People come from all over the world, you know, to the Lake District, though, of course, most of the addresses in the Book are English ones."

"Do you get many visitors here?" asked Jim.

"Oh, quite a lot in summer—and I'm only open for Bed and Breakfast from Easter to the end of September. You see, we're right on this footpath from Braithwaite to Lanthwaite Green."

"We've come from the Leadthwaite Mine," said Jim.

"Ah, have you? You were looking for mineral specimens, I expect.

Right, I'll leave you in peace now, but if you want anything you've only got to ask for it."

"Thank you very much," said Jackie.

Mrs. Lane closed the door behind her.

"Well, you rascal, look what you've let us in for!" said Jackie, keeping her voice down so that Mrs. Lane should not overhear her.

"Oh . . . ! But we had to stay here, didn't we?" said Jim.

"But a double bed! I believe you've been dreaming of the possibility of getting into bed with me since we came in here!"

"I'll be *very* good," promised Jim seriously.

Jackie suddenly sat down on the bed as she tried, unsuccessfully, to suppress a rush of giggling laughter.

"Oh dear . . . how funny!" she laughed. "It really *is* awfully funny, you know, what's happened. Mrs. Lane thinks we're married, so she's given us this double bed."

"Well, we *are* both engaged!"

"But not to each other!"

"I know," said Jim. It's extraordinary. You're about to marry my Father, and become my Step-Mother, and I'm going to marry Susan; and yet here we are together because fate has thrown us together for tonight."

"To be fair, Jim," said Jackie, standing up and suddenly sounding serious again, "I don't think it's quite true, or fair, to say that."

"How do you mean?"

"Well, it's only *partly* due to fate, isn't it, that we've been thrown together to share a bed? And partly it's been *your* decision!"

"My decision?"

"Yes, your decision! You spoke to your Father on the telephone, and decided as a result of that conversation that we ought to stay here for tonight."

"But it was Dad who actually suggested that; and you agreed with the idea of staying here tonight, Jackie, because you didn't want to walk any further."

"Yes, I know I did," said Jackie, "but don't let's argue about it. Anyway, Mrs. Lane wouldn't have offered us this double room if she didn't think we were married."

"It was a very reasonable mistake to have made, I suppose," said Jim. "After all, we are about the same age, and we arrived here together, so she assumed, when she saw us, that you were my wife. Look here, Jackie, she said we were to sign the Visitor's Book. Shall I go and sign it now?"

"And write: 'Mr. and Mrs. Sandy' in it, I suppose? Yes, why not? We can't really back out of this farce now that we've taken this room."

"Do you want to, really?" asked Jim in a suddenly serious voice. "Aren't you going to allow me to sleep in that bed?"

Jackie looked round the bedroom for a moment before answering. The room was very simply, but comfortably, furnished; a carpet covered the whole of the floor, and there were two chairs, a built-in wardrobe, and a chest-of-drawers with a movable mirror mounted on the top of it. If Jim were not allowed to sleep in the bed the only other place for him would be the floor.

"You can get into bed with me, when the time comes," said Jackie, "*but* you'll have to behave yourself—keep to your own side of the bed!"

"I shall," said Jim seriously. He opened the door and paused, his hand on the handle. "I'm going to sign the Visitor's Book now. Are you coming downstairs, Jackie?"

"I might as well, as there's nothing to do here."

Jim had already seen the Visitor's Book lying on the small table in the hall, with the telephone and the directory. He opened it at the right page and, using the pen that was lying beside it, he wrote:-

"17th Aug. 1964. Mr. and Mrs. J. Sandy, 140 Lorton Road, Cockermouth, Cumberland."

It was odd, he reflected, to think that in a few weeks time Jackie *would* be "Mrs. Sandy", but as his Father's second wife, rather than his own wife.

Then, feeling very satisfied with the pretence that Jackie was his wife, Jim joined her in the lounge, where they remained watching television until Mrs. Lane came to tell them that their meal was ready for them.

"I've got a night-dress for you, Mrs. Sandy," she added, holding out a white garment. "I should think it would fit you."

"Thank you very much; it's very kind of you to lend it to me," said Jackie.

"I'll just put it in your room," said Mrs. Lane.

Jim and Jackie looked at each other. Clearly Mrs. Lane had read their names in the Visitor's Book, and so it was now too late to retract the pretence of being married.

CHAPTER SEVENTEEN

Jim was waiting in the lounge of Ghyll Cottage to retire to bed, having given Jackie long enough, he thought, to undress and get into bed herself. He had been trying to look at some of the books which were in the lounge, but had found it difficult to concentrate on reading anything with the thought firmly in his mind of the night ahead of him.

It was now pitch dark out of doors, but it had become very windy, and he could hear rain lashing against the windows behind the closed curtains of the room. He had been eagerly looking forward to going to bed until he had suddenly remembered Susan, and remembered how deeply he was in love with her. That thought had changed his mood completely. He now remembered that it would be quite wrong for him to think of sharing a bed with anyone other than Susan, his fiancee; but, of course, it was now too late to change the arrangements for that night. Jackie would probably be lying in the double bed by now, he decided, so he would have to go and join her there.

He stood up, and put the book he had been trying to read back into its place on the bookshelf near the mantelpiece. It was time to go upstairs, and he left the room thoughtfully, and began slowly to climb the stairs; but after a few steps he stopped. The thought of what he was about to do was suddenly so repulsive to him, as he held for a moment an enchanting picture of Susan's sweet face in his mind's eye, that he felt almost nauseated. Why had he been so eager to let himself in for this adventure with Jackie? Had he not succumbed to a very basic temptation? he wondered—a crude male lust after an attractive female, when he had seen a chance to ensnare her? Surely that was how it had been. Then he told himself sharply that he was going to behave very properly with Jackie. He would not allow himself even once so much as to touch her. He would leave her alone on her side of the bed while he settled down to go to sleep: there was going to be no adventure about it, nothing exciting after all to look forward to. With that thought he climbed the rest of the stairs, knocked lightly on the bedroom door, and opened it a chink to peep around it.

"Come in, Jim!" said Jackie. "I'm ready. You can go to bed now."

Jim entered the room, and saw that Jackie was lying in the bed with the sheet and blankets pulled right up to her chin, so that only her face was visible. He closed the door, and began a little shyly to take off his clothes. It was, of course, out of the question that he should sleep in the nude, so, with Jackie's permission, he was going to strip only to his underclothes. As he did so he felt that his mood was changing once again; whether he liked it or not a feeling of mounting excitement was flooding into him.

"Could you turn the light off, please?" said Jackie. "The switch by the door. We've got a bedside light, and Mrs. Lane has lent us a torch, so we'll be able to see all right, if we have to, during the night."

"Good!" said Jim as he switched off the electric light at the switch by the door. "I'm going to the bathroom now." He took his towel and, wearing only vest, underpants, and socks, went along to the bathroom. When he returned a few minutes later, and climbed into his side of the bed, he still had the feeling that he was doing something quite extraordinary and very exciting, in spite of knowing that nothing unusual was going to happen—beyond the mere fact that he would be sleeping in the same bed as his Father's fiancee, Jackie Rothwell.

"Ready for the light out?" asked Jackie, when Jim seemed to be lying comfortably in the bed. The bedside light was on a little table at Jackie's side of the bed, while Jim had the torch beside him under the pillows. He said he was ready for the light to be switched off.

"Good night," said Jackie.

"Good night, Jackie," said Jim.

Jackie reached out a hand and switched off the lamp, and suddenly they were in darkness.

"And remember, Jim," she added a moment later, "no nonsense! Mrs. Lane may think we're married - but we're not!"

"I promise I'll leave you alone—I won't touch you," said Jim seriously.

Having made that promise Jim realized that the night was going to be really no more interesting, or exciting, than any ordinary night at home in his own bed. For a minute or two he lay quietly on his back, looking at a square of pale light which was the window. He saw that there was a fair amount of dim light in the room, as behind the cloudy sky more than half a moon was shining. The rain seemed to have stopped, and the wind had dropped quite suddenly, and it was very quiet—so quiet, indeed, that it was hard to believe that another human being was lying close to him in the same bed. Jackie had settled herself comfortably for sleep, and did not move again until she woke some hours later. Her breathing was so quiet that Jim could hardly hear it. He wondered whether she could already be asleep, and then the only thought in his mind was not to wake her, if she was asleep, by turning over too noisily. He turned onto his side to face away from Jackie—that way, he thought, he would be less tempted to reach out a hand towards her—and made the movement slowly and cautiously so as not to disturb her.

My word, he thought suddenly, will Dad mind when he finds out that I've been in bed with his girl? No, of course he won't; we're not going to do anything—we're just going to stay here, resting and sleeping.

Jackie's tired—probably she's asleep already. Jim, however, was more tired than he realized after the afternoon's long walk, and he quickly fell asleep himself.

★

"Good morning, Mrs. Sandy," said Mrs. Lane as Jackie came down the stairs in the morning, followed by Jim. "Did you sleep well?"

"Excellently, thank you!" said Jackie. "I've had a very comfortable night."

"So have I," said Jim truthfully. "Good morning, Mrs. Lane."

"Aye, it's not a bad morning, is it?" said Mrs. Lane. Outside there were breaks in the clouds, and the sun was shining. There was, however, a considerable sound of water running by as the small stream was carrying down a spate of muddy water after the heavy rain. "Now, if you'd care to wait in the dining-room, I'll bring you your breakfast in a minute or two."

They thanked her, and went into the dining-room.

When they had almost finished their breakfast they heard a car arriving. From her seat Jackie was able to look out of the window, and she caught a glimpse of a very small woman stepping out of the car. "I suppose that's the maid arriving," she said.

They were hurrying over their breakfast as they meant to be ready to go as soon as possible, so that Jim should get to the station for work without being seriously late. Mrs. Lane had offered to give them a lift to Cockermouth as soon as they were ready to leave, and they had thanked her, and accepted her offer. Jim then stood up, and went to look for Mrs. Lane to pay the bill.

"Hello!" called a voice that sounded vaguely familiar to Jim. He glanced upstairs to the landing and saw someone he recognized at once, leering at him with an evil glint in her eyes.

"Julia!" he gasped.

"Have you had a nice night in the double bed—you and *Mrs.* Sandy?"

Jim instantly knew, as Julia said this, with a particular emphasis on the "Mrs.", that she had read the entry in the Visitor's Book, and was teasing him about it.

"Oh, er . . . I'm in a hurry," muttered Jim angrily. "Can't talk to you now." He knocked on the kitchen door but, glancing upwards again, saw Julia Rose for a moment pull an ugly grimace at him, and flap a duster in a gesture of defiance, after which she promptly disappeared.

The cheeky little sod! he said to himself. He was considerably shaken by this totally unexpected appearance of Julia.

"Can we pay now, please?" he said as Mrs. Lane came to the door, and opened it.

"Yes, of course," said Mrs. Lane. "Have you had enough breakfast?"

"Yes, thank you, it was an excellent breakfast." Jim handed over the two pounds for bed and breakfast and dinner for two, and Mrs. Lane thanked him, and said she could be ready to set off in five minutes.

She refused to take any further payment for the lift, saying that she needed to go into town in any case to do some shopping.

★

Sitting in the back seat of Mrs. Lane's car, Jim said very little on the journey back to Cockermouth. He was rather worried by his encounter with Julia Rose, and decided to say nothing to Jackie about it. It had certainly been a shocking discovery that Ghyll Cottage was the house at which Julia was working as a maid. Jim had long ago forgotten that she would want a chance to even the score with him after his rude and abrupt departure from Westray Hall, but now he feared that she would not be satisfied by a few teasing words spoken that morning; she would still be looking for an opportunity to hurt him. Now he began to see how such an opportunity might possibly arise. Julia knew that "Mrs. Sandy" was in fact Jackie Rothwell as, unfortunately, she had seen Jackie just before they had left Ghyll Cottage; and Jim already knew, after his last visit to Westray Hall, that Julia knew Jackie.

The next day Susan would be arriving at Cockermouth in the evening. It was wonderful for Jim to think that she was coming to stay, but he would have to take care to see that she did not meet Julia. But that should be easy enough, he thought. I won't take Sue anywhere near either Westray Hall or Ghyll Cottage, and that should avoid another meeting with that nasty little bitch! Take Susan to the Grasmere Sports? Well, why not? With Julia working at Ghyll Cottage it would be quite safe to do that.

CHAPTER EIGHTEEN

At Westray Hall Jill was feeling depressed. She was sitting on her bed, and staring at a photograph of Jim Sandy, but in her heart she now knew that he did not love her. The door opened, and in came her sister, Julia.

"Hello, Julie," she said dreamily.

"Aren't you going to come downstairs now for your breakfast?" asked Julia, standing in the doorway, and looking round at her sister's untidy bedroom.

"I don't know whether I will," said Jill, again in an absent-minded, dreamy voice. She looked at her watch as another thought struck her. "Aren't you going to be late for work, Julie?" It was well after the time when Julia usually left the house to go to work at Ghyll Cottage.

"But I'm not working today. Don't you remember?"

"Oh yes, of course; Mrs. Lane's given you the day off today."

"So that I can go to Grasmere to the Sports," said Julia. "Look here, Jill, Mum thinks that you should come too—and so do I—a day out would do you good."

For a little while Jill gave her sister no answer. She sat where she was on the bed, looking morose and pensive, while she seemed to be considering whether she ought to go with her Mother and Julia to the Grasmere Sports that day.

Jill had several weeks ago given up her job at Penrith station on the advice of her doctor, after complaining of depression, and having told the doctor that she could no longer cope with the demands of her secretarial job because the travelling now left her feeling exhausted and frightened. The doctor had prescribed tranquillizers for her, and had advised her to stop work for a while, and to consider looking for a job which would involve little or no travelling; but Jill had made very little effort in that direction. Julia knew, however, that the whole of Jill's trouble was that she was hopelessly in love with Jim Sandy, but had realized that he was no longer interested in her.

"Well?" she said tentatively, after there had been a silence of half a minute or so.

"Jim won't be there, of course," murmured Jill in a flat, lifeless voice, looking down at the floor.

"But of course he won't be." Julia tried to answer as sympathetically as possible, knowing how painfully Jill's emotions were stirred by talk about her former boyfriend, Jim Sandy. "How could Jim be at the Grasmere Sports when he's got to do a day's work at the station here?"

"That's right," said Jill sadly; "he couldn't possibly be there because of his job. I never see him nowadays. But why should I want to go to the Sports if I know there's no chance of meeting him there?"

Julia sighed, and for a moment paused to consider how best to answer Jill without sounding as if she were losing her patience.

"Jill," she began cautiously, "it isn't good for you to be so . . . *besotted* with Jim Sandy. And you're only making yourself feel worse by spending hours gazing at that picture." Here Julia stood up, picked up the framed photograph of Jim from the bedside table, and began thoughtfully to look at it herself.

"Oh, but, Julie, how can I help it?" said Jill, also looking at the little portrait of Jim, which she had taken herself. "He is so, *so* beautiful . . . !"

"Oh, *really*, Jill!"

"But, yes, he *is* beautiful!" protested Jill, now becoming quite excited, and her voice beginning to take on an agitated tone. "Don't *you* think so?"

"Well, yes I do," admitted Julia honestly. "I find Jim a very attractive man—very handsome—but, good heavens, he's diabolically rude too!" She had not yet forgiven Jim Sandy for his insolent behaviour on that party night.

"Are you girls coming down for your breakfasts?" They heard their mother shout up the stairs to them.

"Yes, Mum, we're just coming!" Julia shouted back. "Come on!" she said rather sharply to Jill. "We're getting nowhere by going over all this again about Jim. Now, look here, *are* you coming with me to the Sports? I really think you'd enjoy yourself there, Jill. You'd . . . you'd forget about your problem for a while." Julia thought that it was risky to talk to her sister like this, but felt that a little firmness was now necessary. "Would you like to come?"

Jill hesitated only for a few seconds.

"Yes, you're right, Julie!" she said, suddenly smiling and rising to her feet. "I really *would* like to come to the Grasmere Sports. I'll come with you!"

★

"There's the Sports Field," said Jim, pointing it out for Susan, who was sitting in the front passenger seat of Mr. Sandy's car. The car was being driven fast down the hill towards Grasmere from Dunmail Raise pass.

"Yes, I see it," said Susan. "what a lovely setting for a sports ground, lying between the hills, in the valley bottom, and close to the lake!"

"You can't actually see the lake when you're on the field," said Jim, "but it *is* a splendid place for the Sports."

"Jackie'll probably be there already," said Mr. Sandy, "and perhaps she'll even be taking part in her first race by now. We're not quite as early as I hoped we would be."

"We're nearly there," said Jim. They were now less than a mile from the place on the main road where the first road turned to the right into Grasmere village.

"Are those balloons floating into the air above the Sports Field?" asked Susan a moment later. She had been staring intently at the colourful scene ahead of her, and had seen a press of cars parked on the Sports Field, and flags flying on the grandstand building at the ringside.

"Yes," said Jim. "That's the Balloon Race. It's become an annual event, like the Sports themselves. Anyone can enter it."

"Gas filled balloons, I suppose?"

"Yes, they fill them with helium, and you buy one, and a label is tied onto the balloon with your name and address on it, and then you let it go, and up and up it goes—if there's not much wind—or else it just blows along in the wind. The winner is the balloon which travels furthest."

"The wind's in the north, what there is of it, but it looks as if it's pretty light at the moment," said Mr. Sandy. "Those balloons are climbing, I should say, nearly vertically."

"The Balloon Race is great fun!" said Jim. "We must get balloons, and enter it."

"Of course!" said Susan.

Soon after that, having driven slowly through a rather congested village street, thronged with people and motor cars, Mr. Sandy drove into the Sports Ground at the main entrance, where they stopped to pay the admission charge. The official selling admission tickets directed him to park his car in a nearby parking area.

"This grass is pretty muddy, as I feared it would be after the recent rain," said Mr. Sandy. He parked his car carefully, having taken care to avoid most of the muddy tracks left in the grass by hundreds of other cars. They stepped out of the car.

"Lucky it's fine now," said Mr. Sandy. "With luck, I think it should stay fine." He was glancing up into the sky at the balloons, now drifting slowly southwards in a light breeze from the north.

"Now, shall we buy ourselves a programme, and then stand by the ringside where we can see what events are going on?"

Jim knew that his father was really in a great hurry to be at the ringside, watching the sports, although he spoke calmly enough. Dad doesn't want to miss seeing Jackie in any of her events, he told himself.

A minute later they were standing by the ringside. They were just in time to see Jackie Rothwell taking part in a heat of the One Hundred Yards Sprint. They knew already, from announcements made over the public address system, that the sprint was taking place in the ring.

Within seconds of finding themselves a good position for viewing the ring they heard an announcement which alerted their attention.

"Heat number three of the Hundred Yards Sprint will be run next," a voice boomed out over the loudspeakers in a heavy Cumbrian accent.

"Miss J. Rothwell, from Cockermouth, wearing Number Twelve, in the inside lane . . ."

The athletes on the field, who were about to run, were taking off their tracksuits and limbering up for the sprint. Jim and his father were quick to spot the girl with a number "12" on her back; she had a distinctively female shape in her white vest and shorts, and was one of only two women in the mixed heat of six runners They heard the "on your marks" command, and saw the runners take their starting positions on the track. Jim's gaze, like that of his father, was firmly fixed on the dark-haired girl with the number "12" on her back. For the moment he had forgotten that Susan was standing close to his side.

The race was a disappointment, as they saw Jackie finish in fifth place.

"Never mind," said Mr. Sandy, by way of consoling himself. "The High Jump is really Jackie's forte, rather than the running events."

"Come on, Sue," said Jim, "let's enter for the Balloon Race. The High Jump won't start for at least another twenty minutes, and the Cumberland Wrestling goes on all the time." A bout of wrestling, in another part of the ring, had just ended, and they saw the contestants shake each other's hands heartily, and walk off the field, to be replaced at once by two more wrestlers.

"All right," said Susan. She had enjoyed watching the wrestlers in their colourful costumes, and had been paying but scant attention to the Hundred Yards Sprint. Now she and Jim walked away from the ringside to make their way through the crowds towards the Balloon Tent, which was clearly marked by the balloons floating above it, tethered to the tent on long strings. Mr. Sandy remained at his position at the ringside.

Jim handed over some money to a man behind a rough wooden counter in the tent, and two belloons were filled with helium for them from a massive gas cylinder. He wrote their names and his address on both the labels, which were then tagged onto the balloons.

"I've written our address in Lorton Road on both of them," he said, with a grin at Susan.

On his advice they released their gas-filled balloons a little way off from the tents, at a spot where the crowds of people were thinner.

Then they stood side by side, staring up into the sky at their ascending balloons. Jim could see that his balloon was taking a less vertical path than Susan's; there seemed to be hardly any wind, but one balloon was being drifted gently towards the south in a current of light air, while the other was rising almost vertically and fairly quickly on a thermal.

Jim and Susan remained where they were for some time, watching the balloons. Jim was feeling very happy because Susan was there, but at the moment most of his attention was being concentrated on gazing at his and Susan's balloons. Susan had arrived, as planned, by train the evening before, and Jim himself had met her at the station, and had walked home with her, his work for the day then being finished.

"They're only tiny specks now," said Susan, staring earnestly up into a sky which had become rather grey and cloudy. "Gosh, all this looking upwards is giving me a crick in the neck!"

Suddenly Jim looked round on hearing a familiar voice.

"Ah, here you are! The High Jump's just going to start in a minute or two."

"Okay, Dad, we'll come back to the ringside now to watch it," said Jim. "We've just about lost our balloons by now, but I think Sue's is still leading mine." Mr. Sandy had come to look for them, but he looked up when Jim tried to point to his balloon.

They pushed their way back through the crowds, and returned to the place at the ringside where they had been before. When the High Jump competition began some five minutes later Jim forgot about racing balloons as he saw how easily Jackie cleared the jump. His father too was watching her in fascination through his binoculars (the pair they had used on the Isle of Skye), and even Susan, as the contest went on, began to watch the High Jump with more concentration. It was not a big event, with only five athletes taking part in the jump, all of them men except Jackie. The first round at the starting height saw one man eliminated for knocking the bar to the ground.

"Jackie's hoping to try for the womens' record," said Mr. Sandy proudly as a second round of jumping began. "Ah, it's her turn now . . .

my word, she cleared that effortlessly, I should say!"

The High Jump contest went on for some time, but Jim, Susan, and Mr. Sandy forgot about the time as they watched Jackie's performance with increasing admiration. Presently there was only one other man left in the competition. A loudspeaker announcement told them that the height now equalled the women's record at the ground. They saw the other contestant, a long-legged, athletic-looking, fair-haired young man, not unlike Jim in appearance, run in to the jump. He touched the bar with a foot, and knocked it off as he cleared it.

"Good!" said Mr. Sandy. "That leaves Jackie the winner, if she can clear it."

Jackie ran up to the jump, and cleared it easily, with inches to spare. There was a round of applause as they were reminded that she had now equalled the record, and would go on by herself to challenge it.

"She's very good at it!" said Susan quietly to Jim. "I hope we see her set a new record."

The officials at the jump raised the bar, and checked its height carefully with a tape measure, All was ready for Jackie's attempt on the womens' record for the High Jump.

"Quiet, please, ladies and gentlemen!" said the voice through the loudspeakers. There was a sudden hush. Jim, fascinated by watching Jackie's progress, never thought of looking behind him to see who else was watching.

Jackie cleared the jump, and there was another round of applause for her as it was confirmed that she had broken the record. Then they were told that she would go on, and challenge the all-time Grasmere record for the High Jump.

Some five minutes later Jackie stood on the field, waiting to make the critical attempt at a new all-time record, having cleared the bar at an intermediate height.

"That looks impossibly high for Jackie!" murmured Mr. Sandy in a rather worried tone. Jim nodded, and suddenly thought that Jackie herself was looking less confident, and even a little tense or worried as she surveyed the new height to be cleared for a new record.

Again silence was requested, and there was an expectant hush from the many eagerly watching spectators. Then Jackie ran in towards the jump, but Mr. Sandy, staring at her intently through the glasses, detected a slight hesitation in her step.

Jackie rose into the air at the jump.

Jim, and many other spectators with him, including his father and Susan, held their breath for a moment.

"Oh!" gasped Mr. Sandy.

There was a momentary yelp, either of frustration or of pain, from Jackie as she struck the crossbar awkwardly with her legs. Down came the whole jump, posts and crossbar, as Jackie landed in a collapsed heap on top of it. She did not immediately rise to her feet, but remained where she had fallen, apparently writhing in agony from the injuries she had sustained.

Jim looked round to see that his father, wasting not a second, was already breaking the rules for spectators by hurrying out onto the field, having vaulted over the crush barrier.

"Gosh!" said Jim. "She looks badly hurt!"

"Yes," said Susan, "but they're coming out to give her first aid." Two men from the First Aid tent, wearing the uniform of the St. John's Ambulance Brigade, came hurrying out to the scene of the accident. Jim watched his father running out to help Jackie, who still had not moved from the wreckage of the jump.

Mr. Sandy reached her, and knelt down beside her, just before the first aid party arrived, but Jim could not see what happened next.

"It looks as if Miss Rothwell may be badly injured," the voice through the public address system was saying. "What . . . ? Do they need a doctor? Eh . . . ? Is Doctor Bottomley there?" The man seemed to have forgotten that he was speaking into a microphone, addressing the whole crowd, and was temporarily carrying on a conversation with someone at his side. But Jim was not really listening to the loudspeakers. He and Susan were staring fixedly towards the scene of the accident, waiting to see what would happen next.

A doctor, carrying with him a black bag of medicines, ran out onto the sports field.

"Hi! Jim!" shouted a woman's voice suddenly from somewhere behind him.

Jim immediately turned to see Julia Rose wave an arm to attract his attention. He caught sight of Jill, standing beside her, looking, he thought, pale and worried. The crowd had thinned out between Jim and the Rose sisters, and Julia was close to him in a second.

"Is your wife badly injured, Jim?" she shouted.

Jim stared at her in stupified amazement, not knowing what to say.

"Your *wife*, Jackie," she continued, talking unnecessarily loudly, and pointing to the spot where Jackie Rothwell was lying on the ground, being attended to by the doctor. "Aren't you going to go and help her?"

"Why the hell should I?" shouted Jim furiously, finding his voice in a sudden rush of bad temper. Julia dodged nimbly out of the way of a blow aimed at her head.

"Ha, ha, Jim!" she laughed, as she quickly ran away from him. "Cat's out of the bag now, isn't it?"

"How *dare* you say that?" said Jim, who felt himself shaking all over with rage. "You *know* she's not my wife, you filthy little gossiping bitch, you . . . !" He checked himself, seeing that Julia, still laughing, had run off into a crowd of people, snatching hold of her sister, Jill, as she fled. With a great effort of his willpower Jim calmed himself a little, remembering that Susan was still standing by his side. He was so angry that he would have liked to dash after Julia, and perhaps even to knock her down, or beat her senseless, but in any case it was now too late to do anything of that sort, as she had disappeared.

Jim looked round at Susan. Their eyes met.

For several seconds neither spoke.

"Well?" said Susan at last. Jim thought that there was something about her expression which he had never seen before. There was a hint of a frown on her forehead, and the usual warm, dreamy look in her dark eyes had taken on a hard, cold aspect, almost an icy look.

"Oh dear!" sighed Jim. "That was really awful!"

"But what was it all about?"

"Oh, well, nothing really," muttered Jim rather sulkily. He was in no mood to explain the situation to Susan, as he was still feeling very shaken on account of his sudden necessary burst of temper.

"Nothing?" said Susan quietly, raising her eyebrows slightly.

"But, Jim, what did that woman mean when she spoke about your wife?"

Her dark eyes were looking keenly straight into his eyes.

"She just wanted to be beastly to me, because . . . because I'd been rude to her before; but it's a long story, really. Look here, Sue, I'll tell you all about it later. This is hardly the place to explain now what she meant."

"Very well, Jim," said Susan soothingly, "you can tell me later.

Obviously you're very upset about it, so it would be sensible if we were to try to forget about it now, and talk about other things. Anyway, her tone struck me as being very offensive."

"It certainly was!"

There was a short break in their conversation. Yes, Sue will understand, Jim told himself. He had seen her expression soften a little, and he thought that she had even given him just the faintest hint of a smile with her last remark. She will understand, he thought; but damn that woman for what she's blurted out about my wife! Now I'll have to explain to Sue about how I came to spend that night in bed with Jackie . . . but, hopefully, she'll forgive me when she understands that I did nothing wrong.

"Your father's coming back," said Susan. "I wonder what could have happened to Jackie?"

"I don't suppose she could have been really seriously injured by that jump," said Jim. "Well, Dad, what's happened?"

"She's not really badly hurt," said Mr. Sandy as he reached the barrier, and climbed over to regain the right side of it. "At least, it's not as bad as I feared it might be. The doctor says she's broken a collar bone."

"Gosh, that's bad enough, isn't it?" asked Jim.

"It must be agonisingly painful, but that sort of fracture is, I believe, one of the less serious ones. She'll have to wear her left arm in a sling for a while. And she has some bad bruises, particularly to her legs, but the doctor said he thought there were no internal injuries."

"They'll take her to hospital, I suppose?"

"Oh, yes, of course they will, for a complete check-up, and to set her arm in a sling. Look, the ambulance men are carrying her away now."

They looked, and saw that Jackie was being carried off the Sports Field on a stretcher by the men from the St. John's Ambulance Brigade.

"Poor Jackie!" said Susan, watching the ambulance men and the doctor, who was walking with them. "What a most unfortunate thing to happen to her!"

"Particularly as she might have set a new record with that very jump," said Jim.

"It would have been a horrible accident in any case," said Susan, "whether or not she'd been trying to break any record."

"I'll have to tell her landlady that she won't be in tonight," said Mr. Sandy, "but I can tell her when we get back to Cockermouth. Shall we go now? Have you two seen enough of the Sports?"

Jim looked round for a moment before answering. He saw balloons rising into the air by the Balloon Tent, but now the thought of the Balloon Race held no interest for him. However, he saw no sign anywhere of the Rose sisters, or of Mr. or Mrs. Rose, and that, he thought, was some slight comfort. Damn that nasty little woman! he said to himself again. She *has* let the cat out of the bag! Sue will have to be told the truth when we get home . . . He looked at her to see whether, like himself, she was ready to leave Grasmere to return to Cockermouth.

"What about you, Sue; do you want to go now?" he asked.

"I don't mind, really, whether we stay a bit longer, or whether we leave now," said Susan unhelpfully. "But what do *you* want to do, Jim?"

"Oh, well, I . . . began Jim, and stopped. He could not very well say that he was longing to get away from the place as quickly as possible, lest they might meet Julia Rose again. He glanced at his father. "*Ought* we to go now, Dad, do you think?" he asked hopefully, knowing that his father was also eager to leave the Sports ground after Jackie's accident.

"My word!" said Susan. "Those two wrestlers are pretty good! Gosh, he almost went down that time, the one in the red shorts!" She was watching two heavy-looking men wrestling. The Cumberland Wrestling had been going on all the time in another part of the ring.

Mr. Sandy said that they might as well stay a while longer at the Sports, as Susan was enjoying watching the wrestling. Jim at once gave in gracefully, and agreed that they should stay.

Mr. Sandy reminded them that one of the main highlights of the Sports was the Senior Guides' Race, and pointed that they had agreed before that they ought not to miss seeing it.

The Guides' Race, when it began later in the afternoon, proved so fascinating to watch that even Jim soon forgot his uneasiness, and stopped looking round every other minute to see whether Julia Rose was anywhere near them. There had been no more sign of the Rose sisters, but Jim had been dreadfully upset by Julia's jibe about his "wife", and, although his bad temper had more or less passed, he was still feeling very glum at the thought that he would now be forced to tell Susan things which he had meant to keep secret from her.

When the Guides' Race was over they returned to Mr. Sandy's car and set off for home. They were all glad that they had stayed at the Sports ground for the Guides' Race; the favourite had come in first, but it had been a very close race, and the winning margin had been narrow. The talk in the car on the return journey was all of the Sports: of the events they had watched, and of Jackie's great misfortune in breaking a bone on her attempt to set a new record for the High Jump. Susan and Mr. Sandy were doing most of the talking, but Jim was joining in; however, whenever there was a silence his thoughts reverted to the confession to be made when they should reach home. He wanted to talk to Susan on her own about that night at Ghyll Cottage, and he reckoned to be able to do that while his father was busy in the kitchen. They would be back home, probably, about an hour before either Carol or Victoria came in from their work, so he thought that he would sit for a while alone with Susan in the sitting-room. He almost managed to convince himself before they came back to Cockermouth that Susan was going to understand his explanation of the events at Westray Hall on the night of Julia's party, and of his adventure with Jackie at Ghyll Cottage, and that she would forgive him for his night in bed with Jackie. We didn't do *anything* in bed together—except sleep, he reminded himself, so I don't see how Sue could possibly be seriously upset when I tell her about it. But with confession still to be made, Jim remained tense and worried, and knew that he was in a hurry to get home, and to tell Susan what he had to tell her.

CHAPTER NINETEEN

Jim was surprised and dismayed when he woke up the next morning to find how depressed and gloomy he was feeling. It was rather like waking up at the end of a bad dream; he was vaguely aware of a feeling of being involved in some catastrophic disaster even before he had properly woken up from his sleep. But the memory of what had happened the evening before very quickly came back to him, and, as it did so, his spirits sank even lower than before. Yes, it really had happened: Susan had broken off their engagement, saying that it was unthinkable that they should get married, seeing that he had been "having an affair" with Jackie. There was confusion in Jim's mind, as well as great dismay, because he had indeed woken up from a very worrying dream in which this disastrous quarrel with Susan had featured very painfully; but now the realization came to him with sickening certainty that a serious break with his love had indeed occured.

Presently he sat up in his bed. It's not fair, he thought, Sue saying that we can't get married because I'm "having an affair" with Jackie. "Having an affair", indeed! How could she possibly say that when I'd carefully explained to her that I never once touched Jackie while we were in bed together—never even looked at her—unless it was to punish me? But had I done anything wrong? Could things have been done differently that night?

He stepped out of his bed, went to the window, and savagely pulled back the curtains. Then for a moment he stood looking out at a grey, cloudy morning, which seemed to be in sympathy with his grim mood. Could things have been done differently that night? he wondered again. Why, of course they could! As Susan herself had remarked, he could have walked on from Ghyll Cottage, cold, wet, and tired though he had been, leaving Jackie to spend the night at the cottage by herself. Yes, on reflection, perhaps he should have done that. Yet, after all, Susan had forgiven him—or at least she had said, "Yes, I forgive you Jim"—but had she really meant it? He remembered that the tone in which she had spoken that sentence had been decidedly cold and lifeless, not sounding at all as if she was forgiving him with all her heart. "Oh dear!" he sighed sadly, *why* has all this happened to me . . . ?

Something reminded him of the time at this point in his cogitations. He looked at his watch, and saw that it was a quarter to seven. He was going to be late for work, if he did not buck up. And that wouldn't do, because I had the whole of yesterday off work, he reminded himself. But what will Sue do today, I wonder, with all of us out until this evening? I hope she doesn't meet that wretched captain!

Susan had startled Jim very much on the car journey back from Grasmere by suddenly mentioning Captain South. "Well," she had said, "we didn't see Captain South at the Sports anyway."

"What!" Jim had said. "You don't mean to say that *he's* up here in these parts?"

"Yes, I believe he must be in the Lake District now." Susan had gone on to explain to him that on the last day of their stay at Soken Hall she had learned that Captain South and his mother were going to spend the last fortnight of August touring the Lake District by car, until the Captain's holiday was over for that year. Jim had forgotten all about Captain South, and had found it not at all pleasant to be reminded about him again, particularly when he already felt so ill at ease after Julia's outburst. Then, later that evening, he remembered, Susan had said: "Perhaps I'll meet Captain South tomorrow," in such a way that had sounded as if she had *wanted* to meet the Captain. In any case, he now reflected, it was very out of character for the Susan he knew and loved to say such a thing. They had, of course, been aware, even before Susan had come north to spend two days with the Sandys, that the days would present a problem, with everyone out at work. The Grasmere Sports had solved that problem well enough for the Thursday of Susan's visit, and, for the Friday morning, Mr. Sandy had offered her a lift to his mine, in case Susan should care to spend the day, or part of it, walking in the fells. Susan had thanked him, but had not commited herself to that plan. Now Jim feared that if Susan could manage to meet Captain South and his mother somewhere in Cockermouth she would spend the day with them. Perhaps it had been privately arranged before that the Captain would be in the town on that particular morning, Friday the 21st of August.

As he considered these points Jim was hurriedly dressing himself. However, before he went downstairs for a quick breakfast he paused a moment, and remained absolutely still, listening. There was, however, never a sound to be heard through the wall from the spare room which was now Susan's room, next to his room. Jim thought that as it was still early she must be fast asleep. Even if she was hoping to meet the Captain later in the morning there was clearly no need for her to get up for another hour or more..

★

While Jim was listening, and thinking that she was fast asleep, Susan was lying in her bed wide awake, and thinking. She had been almost as much upset as he was over what he had told her the evening before about his night with Jackie Rothwell. But Susan was not suffering from jealousy; she knew that Jim was still in love with her as much as ever, but she felt that she had to punish him a little for that escapade, and it was this resolve which was causing her great distress. She longed to jump out of bed there and then, and to rush into Jim's room, to greet him warmly with a hug and kisses, and to assure him positively that he really was forgiven for his night with Jackie.

At last she could bear it no longer. It was still too early in the morning, she thought, at ten minutes to seven, for her to get up, but she knew that she would sleep no more that morning. She was far too wide awake, thinking about Jim, for sleep to have a further chance with her, so she suddenly sat up in bed. Quick, she thought, I must slip into Jim's room *now* before he goes downstairs, and then goes off to work at the station. Or am I already too late to find him in his room? She hastily stepped out of bed, siezed her dressing-gown, draped it loosely over her shoulders, and crossed the floor. She opened the door of the spare room a little, and stopped, looking out into the passage, uncertain once again of what to do next.

At that moment the two conflicting ideas in Susan's mind were evenly balanced: she longed to be bold enough to knock on Jim's door, and to go in there to tell him that all was forgiven, but at the same time she felt very strongly that she must on no account do this. The passage outside her door was deserted and quiet; there was no one there to see her standing in the doorway, her desires finely balanced on a knife-edge of uncertainty. I did say I'd forgiven him last night, she thought, but I dare say he didn't believe me. I don't suppose I sounded as if I really meant it. Oh, poor Jim, he sounded so miserable last night when I said good-night to him, after I'd said we'd have to put off our wedding. Did he think that I was saying I was breaking off our engagement? Well, I suppose I was meaning that, in a way . . . but only postponing it for a while, for a few months . . . Oh, damn it all, what nonsense! Why shouldn't I marry him as soon as possible? What on earth's the good of punishing him by saying: "We can't get married when we'd planned to, Jim, but later on we will be married"? What would that achieve . . . ? Ah, what was that?

Just then she thought she heard a dim sound of voices from downstairs, in the kitchen. Yes, Jim and his father must be down in the kitchen. The two contrary plans in her head were so finely balanced that it needed only one small idea to push the balance one way or the other, to make her decide to see Jim, or not to see him.

The sound of voices from the kitchen at once made her decide to give up any idea of talking to Jim that morning. If his father was also in the kitchen it was already too late for any private talk with Jim. Susan now headed for the bathroom instead of for his bedroom door.

★

Later that morning Susan was slowly drinking a cup of coffee in a cafe in the Main Street of Cockermouth when she heard a man's voice address her:

"Good morning, Lady Dalmane!"

Susan turned her head sharply.

"Oh, good morning, Captain South!" she said. So she had met him after all, as she had vaguely hoped she would. With the Captain was a white-haired lady who might have been in her sixties, clearly his mother. The two of them were standing a little behind the table where Susan had sat down; they were looking around the rather crowded cafe.

"This is my mother," said the Captain at once. "And, Mother, this is Lady Dalmane, whom I met when I was at Soken Hall."

"When you were taken there as Paul Ardell's guest?" said Mrs. South. "How do you do, Lady Dalmane?"

Susan shook her hand, and then shook the Captain's hand.

"Would you like to sit at this table?" she said politely. "I don't know whether you'd find two seats at any of the other tables."

"That's very kind of you, Lady Dalmane," said the Captain. "Yes, we'll sit here, thank you, but first I'll go up to the counter—I see it's self-service here—and order our coffees. Would you like anything to eat with your's, Mother? A piece of cake, perhaps?"

"No, I think I'd rather have a biscuit with mine," said Mrs. South. "But what will you have, Rodney?"

The Captain was already looking over the contents of a display cabinet on the counter, where customers were invited to help themselves to cakes and biscuits.

"I think I'll have a piece of apple-cake!" he said gaily, as his eye alighted on some pieces of home-made apple-cake. "There are the biscuits, Mother, towards your end of the counter."

"I'll have one of those large plain ones with my coffee," said Mrs. South.

The Captain took a tray and went up to the counter, while Susan moved her chair forward a little so as to make it easier for Mrs. South, who was a rather large lady, to get in to the table, and to sit down beside her.

"Thank you!" said Mrs. South. She set a bag down on the floor beside her chair, and then sat down beside Susan at the table, which was laid for four people. "It's got out nice, hasn't it?" she said by way of starting a conversation.

"Yes," said Susan, "it's very nice outside now that the sun's broken through the clouds." She remembered that it had been grey and cloudy in the early morning, and thought that the unexpected improvement in the weather promised well for the rest of the day.

"Ah, here comes Rodney with the things on a tray," said Mrs. South.

Susan had not been very keen on the idea of asking Captain and Mrs. South to sit with her, but out of politeness had found herself forced to do so. Now she would have to sit there and make polite conversation with them, perhaps for some time, and this thought did not very much please her, even though earlier she had thought that she had been hoping to meet Captain South.

Susan had been given her breakfast just after eight that morning by the twins, Carol and Victoria, Mr. Sandy and Jim both having left the house to go out to work by the time she had come downstairs. Then, after a hasty washing-up, Carol and Victoria had also left the house to go to work in their respective shops, leaving Susan alone in the house.

She had sat in her room for about three quarters of an hour, reading a novel, but had then decided to go out, as she was beginning to feel lonely sitting in the relative quietness of the empty house. She had locked the front door with the spare key she had been given, and had set off to walk slowly down Victoria Road and over the river bridge, and so into the town via Lorton Street. She had been pleased to feel, as she sauntered along, that it was becoming quite warm as the early morning clouds dispersed, and the sun began to shine out. To fill in some time she had first visited the bookshop where Carol Sandy worked as an assistant, and had spent some twenty minutes in the shop, browsing in various books as if she were a genuine customer, although she had no intention of buying anything. She also had a word with Carol, in between serving other customers, but when she left the shop at half past ten she felt that it was time for a mid-morning cup of coffee, and so went along to the cafe.

Captain South unloaded the things off his tray, put the tray down, and then, his eyes alight with pleasure and excitement, sat down opposite Susan.

"Well, well, what a pleasant surprise this is, to meet you here, Lady Dalmane!" he said. Susan knew that he meant it.

It seemed to her that they sat at their cafe table for a long time, eating, drinking, and chatting. The Souths talked at some length about their holiday, but Susan was not very forthcoming about what she was doing. She learned, among other things, that Mrs. South was a native of the Lake District, having been born at Ambleside, and so understood that coming up to the Lake District had a particular significance for her; she had lived at Ambleside, she said, until she was in her twenties.

"And when does your holiday end?" asked Susan presently.

"At the end of this month," said the Captain. "My ship sails for Rotterdam on the thirty-first, which is a Monday."

"Oh!" said Susan.

"I beg your pardon?" asked the Captain politely.

"Oh, I only meant that, as it happens, I *might* be going over to Holland at the end of this month . . . to Rotterdam."

"To stay with Paul and Kirsten?"

"Just so," said Susan. "They pressed me to come over and see their house that time when we were all at Soken Hall; they pressed me to come, if only for a few days. So I said that perhaps I might come over to Rotterdam for a few days at the end of this month, or around the beginning of September."

"Then why not come over the North Sea with me, Lady Dalmane?" The Captain leaned forwards in his chair towards Susan a little more, and she saw that his eyes were sparkling even more than before. "I could offer you a cabin on board the <u>Dutch Maid</u> on the night of the thirty-first, if you'd like one?"

"But when does your ship return to England?"

"We're due to return to Harwich on the third of September."

"Oh . . . I see."

"I think you'd do well, if I may say so, to travel on board the <u>Dutch Maid</u> if you're thinking of going over to Holland, Lady Dalmane," said Captain South. "The fares are quite expensive on those North Sea ferries—but I could take you across and back for nothing!"

"Oh, Captain South, but I couldn't do that!" exclaimed Susan. I'd *insist* on paying my fare if I were to travel on your ship."

"Very well, Lady Dalmane, shall we say . . . you could go there and back for ten pounds? Would that suit you, my Lady?"

"That's a much cheaper fare than you'd pay to go by one of the regular passenger ferries to the Hook of Holland," interposed Mrs. South.

Susan felt that intense pressure was being put on her to accept this offer of a cheap trip to Holland, but she was not at all sure yet whether she would be going. The Captain, she thought, was really rather like an excited schoolboy: his eagerness to have her on board his ship was so obvious. She knew that Jim had been right when he had maintained that he had a crush on her; that, too, was clear enough. For a moment she hesitated, and did not answer the Captain. A ten pound return fare from Harwich to Rotterdam was a very tempting offer, but, of course, Jim would want her to say a firm "no, thank you" to it. But after last night . . .

"Well," she said at last, "that's a wonderful offer you've made, Captain South, but . . . I'm not at all sure whether I'm going. I haven't made up my mind yet."

"Of course, Lady Dalmane," said the Captain soothingly. "I don't want you to feel I'm rushing you into deciding anything. But I could keep a cabin vacant, if you like, until the afternoon of Monday the thirty-first—Monday week—in case you want to come."

"Well, thank you very much!" said Susan.

"You'll find the <u>Dutch Maid</u>, by the way, berthed at the old quays at Harwich, not at Parkeston Quay—that's if you should want to cross on my ship. She'll be moored in the dock close to Harwich Town station. Do you know where I mean? If you're coming by train, don't get out at Parkeston Quay station, but go on to the terminus, Harwich Town. You'll find the ship there."

"I see," said Susan. "I know where you mean."

A little later on in their conversation Susan revealed that she had nothing particular to do that day.

"Then why not come motoring with us?" said the Captain eagerly, again siezing an opportunity to spend more time in Susan's company. "We've plenty of room in the car, and we'd love you to come with us—wouldn't we, Mother?"

"Oh yes, indeed, you'd be very welcome to join us, Lady Dalmane," confirmed Mrs. South. "Do you know the Lake District at all?"

"Hardly," said Susan, "although I have been here on holiday before."

"We're thinking of going to Ullswater today, and then over the Kirkstone Pass, and down to Ambleside," said the Captain. "Do you know Ullswater, Lady Dalmane?"

"No, that's a lake I've never seen."

"Well, it's a very beautiful one, and now that it's come out sunny it'll look better than ever. I think you should come with us, Lady Dalmane."

"I don't want to be a burden to you," said Susan.

"Oh, you won't be that, Lady Dalmane; you won't be a burden at all. We'd be delighted to have you with us, if you'd care to come."

"Well, thank you very much," said Susan. Again the Captain's eloquence seemed to be putting her under pressure to accept his invitation; it would have been hard, she thought, to have said "No, thank you" to it. Jim will be annoyed, though, when I tell him this evening that I've spent a lovely day being taken to Ullswater by Captain South, she thought. But after all, why not? Let him be annoyed, if he wants to be! It wouldn't really be much fun to stay here in this town all day with nothing to do.

Susan was drinking the last mouthful of her coffee (which was now cold) while these thoughts passed through her head.

A few minutes later the other two were also ready to leave the cafe. They walked out into warm sunshine as Mrs. South lead the way to the place in Main Street where her car was parked.

★

As Susan had foreseen, Jim was angry when she told him that evening that she had spent a very pleasant day with Captain South, being taken to see Ullswater, the Kirkstone Pass, and Ambleside. Although he tried carefully to conceal his feeling of anger, Susan was aware of the awful jealousy she had aroused in him, but her day had been so pleasant that her tone had been quite flippant in telling him about it; and now she thought that she hardly cared what he thought about it.

They had very little to say to each other that evening, and presently Jim retired to bed feeling very miserable indeed. Was there nothing he could do to put right again his loving relationship with Susan before she left in the morning to return to Rhodes Castle? It would be more than he could bear, he thought, if she were to set off for home without forgiving him properly, leaving him to wonder when, if ever, they could mend their damaged relationship and marry happily. But Susan also lay in bed awake for hours that night, thinking about Jim. She knew how miserable Jim must be feeling, and that knowledge pained her very much. Anyway, she said to herself, what's the use of my behaving as if I were jealous of Jackie when, in fact, I'm not jealous of her at all? Jim was surely telling me the truth when he told me he never touched her in bed. There's nothing between those two except some infatuation on Jim's part—and what is that to me? Why, nothing—it's not important at all. What *is* important is that he loves me very much; I *know* he does, or he wouldn't be so upset now. We must put things right in the morning.

However, when the time came for Susan's departure by the 7.25 train from Cockermouth, she found that her resolve to "put things right" had weakened considerably, as doubts had again crept into her mind. They had walked to the station together almost in silence, telling each other only that it was a nice morning, as indeed it was. Each of them was conscious that a gulf had opened between them, and each knew that the other was also aware of this; but each was also thinking that the gulf between them was really quite insignificant, and could be bridged by a few kind words.

As the early morning train to Carlisle came into the platform, and drew to a halt, Susan was saying to herself, I *must* punish him now. I mustn't let him kiss me. Before Jim had had a chance to do it for her she had opened a door, and stepped hurriedly into the train.

Then she turned to receive her suitcase from him, but as, for a moment, she smiled at him her heart was beating very fast from the pain which, she knew, she was deliberately inflicting on him.

"Thank you, Jim."

"Good-bye, Sue, darling!" said Jim huskily. His heart was also beating very fast. They had exchanged no kiss; and now—could he hope that she would ever forgive him?

"Good-bye, Jim darling."

Susan was already moving up to the empty first-class seats at the front of the train. She quickly chose a seat on the left-hand side, nearest to the platform, and sat down in it, having deposited her suitcase on an adjacent seat.

Jim waited on the platform, hesitating. Susan was not looking at him. Did she want him to go away without a final parting wave? And then the guard blew his whistle, and the train at once began to move. As the leading carriage drew away from him Jim waved his hand in a last desperate attempt to get a response from his sweetheart. *Surely* she'll wave to me, he said to himself desperately; but Susan was looking away from him, and did not seem to notice his wave. Then she was gone.

Jim felt crushed, dumbfounded by what had happened. As he stood where he was, staring up the line after the departed train, he felt that he wanted to sink into the earth, to die upon the spot. Tears slowly filled his eyes as the bitterness of the parting gradually came home to him. He had failed after all. He had not been forgiven.

As they had walked up to the station together he had been pinning all his hopes on a parting kiss of reconciliation, a kiss which would have assured him of her love for him, but that had not happened. And now it was too late—when would he see her again—if he ever saw her again? His thoughts became all bitterness, all despair. Even the thought that she had smiled at him, and had said "darling" to him, now brought him very little comfort. He knew instinctively that her parting smile had been little more than a faint-hearted half smile, not her full, warm smile of reassuring love; he could not deceive himself on that point; he was not mistaken in thinking that she had left him without forgiving him. Their relationship had come to an end.

That evening, on his father's advice, Jim sat down in his bedroom, and wrote a carefully worded letter to Susan. The day had been one of the most miserable days he had ever known; it had seemed to him endlessly long, weary, and painful—working at the station he had been continually reminded of his parting from Susan—but now, having had a heart-to-heart talk with his father, he was feeling a little more hopeful. Dad's quite right, he said to himself as he sat down to compose the letter; the main thing is to assure her that I still love her very much, and that she means far more to me than any other woman in the world. Then, perhaps, she'll write back, saying that I'm forgiven.

Well, there's nothing to be lost by trying it anyway. With these thoughts in his mind he drafted his letter, and addressed it to Rhodes Castle, meaning to post it the next morning.

The next day was a Sunday, but Jim nevertheless posted his letter, reckoning that it should reach Rhodes Castle at least by Wednesday of that week. In fact, the letter was delivered to Rhodes Castle on that Wednesday morning, but Susan never received it. What he did not know was that she had left the Castle early that same morning, before the postman had come with the mail, to go to Soken Hall to spend a few days with her parents before she travelled over the North Sea to Rotterdam.

After a few days of uncertainty and deliberation she had finally decided to take up the Captain's offer of a cheap and convenient crossing on board his ship. She had rung up Paul and Kirsten at their home in Vlaardingen, the suburb of Rotterdam where they lived, to let them know that she would be arriving on the morning of the first of September.

Waking up on that Sunday morning proved to be a devastating experience for Jim. The previous evening, talking with his father, and writing his letter to Susan, he had been feeling almost hopeful, but now he awoke to an instant sinking feeling of overwhelming depression. The feeling came over him, in fact, so quickly that he seemed to be immersed in gloom and hopelessness even before he was fully conscious. This he found not a little frightening; he had heard of depression as an illness, but he had never before experienced it; now he began to suspect that he was about to become a victim to severe depression. What alarmed him most was the speed at which the feeling engulfed him. To feel that he was being sucked down, like a man falling into quicksands, into a dark pit of despair, even before his brain had had time to remember what catastrophe it was that had befallen him—what could that mean? Could it be the first stage in the development of a nervous breakdown? No, it simply meant that he was extremely upset because there had been no reconciliation with Susan.

The days passed slowly, sometimes painfully slowly, while he wrestled with his feeling of increasing despondency, but presently he began to look for, and to expect, a letter from Susan in reply to his letter. He looked for his letters when he came home in the evenings, as he always had to leave for work in the mornings long before the postman brought the mail. On Thursday evening, August 27th, there were no letters for him, although he had been hoping for, and half expecting, one from Susan on that day. Never mind, he thought, perhaps a letter from Sue may come tomorrow. But on Friday there was no letter from Susan, and it was the same on Saturday, and then it was the weekend. *Surely*, he thought, I'll get a letter from Sue on Monday! But he did not get one, and now his sinking feeling of depression was certainly becoming worse. The early mornings were always the worst time of the day for him. Later on he would manage to bring a little hopefulness into his thoughts.

When Thursday evening came, however, and there was still no letter from her, Jim felt that he could wait no longer. He decided to ring up Rhodes Castle at once to find out whether Susan was there. Perhaps she's gone away somewhere, he thought.

It was Samantha Burton who answered the telephone when he rang up.

"Rhodes Castle. Hello?"

"Is that you, Sam?" said Jim, recognizing her voice. "It's Jim here—Jim Sandy. Is Susan at home?"

"No, I'm afraid she's away, Jim."

"Oh, I rather thought she might be."

"She's out of the country at the moment—spending as few days in Holland."

"Holland!" gasped Jim in amazement.

"Yes, she's in Holland, staying with her brother in Vlaardingen, in the outskirts of Rotterdam. She crossed from Harwich on Monday night in Captain South's ship, the <u>Dutch maid</u>."

"Oh, no! Not on Captain South's ship!" groaned Jim in dismay.

"Why, yes. What's the matter, Jim?"

"Oh, well . . . well, I don't *like* Sue being with Captain South. He . . . he fancies her. I don't like the way he looks at her!"

"Oh, don't be absurd, Jim!" said Samantha. "I've never met this Captain South, but Sue said that she met him first with you at Soken Hall."

"We did meet him there," said Jim, "and then he went and turned up in Cockermouth on the second day when Sue was staying with us, and, would you believe it, Sam, he had the impertinance to take her out for the day in his mother's car—while I was doing a day's work! Don't laugh, Sam!" He could hear Samantha laughing at her end of the telephone line.

"Oh dear, how funny you are!" laughed Samantha, "when you talk of his impertinence at taking her out while you were working. You must be *frightfully* jealous, Jim, when this Captain's around!"

"Well, I dare say I am!" said Jim rather angrily.

"But, Jim, I don't suppose you really need be upset because Sue crossed to Holland on his ship—at a cheaper fare, she said, than the regular passenger fare. She'd have had her own cabin, I expect, and probably never saw the Captain at any time during the voyage."

"I bet he did manage to see her!"

"Well, so what if he did? It was only one night, anyway, and probably she won't meet him again."

"But she's got to come back," said Jim.

"Ah, but apparently she won't be travelling back on Captain South's ship. She rang me up yesterday from Holland to say that she's made a change of plan. You see, the <u>Dutch Maid</u> was crossing back to Harwich today, the third, but now that she's at her brother's house she thinks she ought to stay there for a little longer, having travelled so far to get there. So she's going to return to England on Sunday night, she said, travelling on the ordinary ferry from Hook of Holland."

"Oh, I see."

"I'm expecting her back here late on Monday evening, so if you want to talk to her you could ring up again on Tuesday of next week."

"Yes, I might do that," said Jim. "Actually, Sam, I'd written a letter to her, and posted it well over a week ago—on the Sunday before last—and I've been wondering why I've had no reply."

"A letter? Ah, yes, I believe a letter for Sue with a Cockermouth postmark came on the morning when she left home—but she didn't get it as the postman came after she'd gone. But I'll make sure that she sees that letter, if you like, as soon as she comes home."

"Thanks a lot, Sam." Jim hesitated a moment, and then continued. He remembered that he ought not to make too long a telephone call because of his father's telephone bill, but he thought that if anyone could help him to mend his broken relationship with Susan, Samantha was that person. "I say, Sam, I wonder if you could help me," he continued rather uncertainly. "It's about Sue and me. She's broken off our engagement, and I've been feeling very depressed about it."

"Yes, of course I'll help you, if I can," said Samantha seriously. "Actually, I've gathered from Sue that there's some trouble between you, but Sue was very close about it, so I don't know yet what's happened, unless you'd care to tell me."

"I will tell you," said Jim, and he proceeded to do so, keeping his account of his night spent with Jackie as brief as possible. Then he told her of what Julia had said at Grasmere.

"I see," said Samantha. "So this other woman, Julia, found out about your night in bed with Jackie Rothwell, and blurted out the guilty secret to you and Sue while you were at this sports meeting?"

"That's right."

"What a very spiteful, nasty thing to do! I suppose she had a grudge against you for some reason? Or is it that she doesn't want you to you to marry Susan because she'd like to marry you yourself?"

"No, I don't think it's that," said Jim, "but she does have a grudge against me, because earlier I'd been rude to her at a party I went to at her house; but I needn't tell you about that—it's not really relevant."

"If you say it isn't relevant, Jim, then I dare say it isn't.

Anyway, she called Jackie your 'wife' because you'd written 'Mr. and Mrs. Sandy' in the visitors' book at this place where you stayed the night? I've got that right?"

"Yes, that's right," said Jim, "and, of course, Sue's very upset about it."

"Have you confessed the whole episode to her?"

"Yes, I had to. Sue wanted to know what it meant when Julia shouted out 'Is your wife injured'—meaning Jackie."

"Yes, of course I can understand that you'd have to give Sue an explanation afterwards," said Samantha; "and of course she must be very upset about it. But it's a dreadful thing, Jim, if on that account she's said she can no longer think of marrying you."

"But she really has said that," said Jim wretchedly, "so we *must* get her to change her mind—and that's where I need your help, Sam. I'm sure you can influence her—make her understand that there's really no reason why we shouldn't get married."

"H'm, yes . . . I'll see what I can do," said Samantha thoughtfully. "Yes, of course I'll help you all I can, Jim, to get this difficulty smoothed over."

"Thanks ever so much, Sam!" It's really very good of you!"

"Not at all, Jim, not at all. As I see it, it's just a matter of making Susan see sense, and do the sensible thing—forget all about this unfortunate episode, and marry you as soon as possible."

"Oh, how splendid it'll be, Sam, if you can persuade her to do that!" said Jim happily. "And my letter to her should help. I've told her how much I love her in it."

"That's right, Jim, that's just what Susan needs to be assured of. Very well, then, I'll see what I can do for you when she comes home on Monday evening. And why not give us another ring presently— say in a week's time? Things should be looking much brighter by then, I should think."

"Yes, I'll do that," said Jim "Thanks very much, Sam, for your help! I'd better ring off now. Good-night!"

"All right, Jim. Good-night!"

He hung up the telephone receiver, feeling very much happier than he had been before he had made the call. It had been a long one, but, he thought, very well worth while.

CHAPTER TWENTY

On the morning of Wednesday, the 9th of September, a letter for Jim was delivered to his home in Lorton Road, Cockermouth. He found it as soon as he arrived home from work in the evening, and, seeing the postmark, and recognizing Susan's handwriting, he tore the envelope open at once. He took out of the blue envelope a letter from Susan, and at once began to read it.

Rhodes Castle,
Tuesday morning, Sept. 8th.

My dear Jim,

Sam gave me your letter as soon as I got home yesterday evening; apparently it had come on the very day I left for Soken Hall.

I've had a very nice little holiday in Holland, staying with Paul and Kirsten at their house in Vlaardingen. Captain South took me over to Rotterdam on his ship, as I expect you've heard. When I came on board at Harwich he greeted me personally, and showed me to my cabin, and after that we had a very smooth and pleasant voyage. Paul and Kirsten were there to meet me with their car when the ship docked in the morning in the Maashaven, on the south bank of the river. Then we drove through the Maastunnel, and through central Rotterdam—which was pretty busy in the morning rush hour—and so out into the suburb of Vlaardingen. Paul and Kirsten live in an attractive house, right on the edge of the built-up area, beside a small canal.

From my spare-room window upstairs I could look out over the canal at the end of the garden over wide, flat fields—altogether a delightfully Dutch scene.

Practically all the Dutch people seem to get about on bikes, so they hired one for me. Paul, Kirsten, and I spent a lot of time cycling—all the roads have excellent cycle paths beside them—but I took the train with Kirsten one day to go into the city for shopping and sight-seeing, and had a delightful boat trip round the docks.

The Weather's been good most of the time, and altogether it's been a super little holiday.

With my love, Susan.

Jim was very disappointed in this letter, as he read it through with increasing gloom and irritation. It particularly annoyed him to think that Susan had been having a delightful time without him. He read through bits of the letter a second time. "I've had a very nice little holiday in Holland." Was it nicer without me? he thought bitterly.

"Captain South . . . greeted me personally." "Damn him, I knew he would, if he had a chance to!" he muttered under his breath. "It's been a super little holiday." But why tell me these things, unless it's to annoy me? he thought irritably. This letter is nothing more than an account of her damned Dutch holiday! There's not a word in it—apart from "with my love" at the end, which really doesn't mean much—to say that she loves me, or to assure me I'm forgiven. And she's signed it "Susan" instead of her usual "Sue".

There was no doubt about it in Jim's mind: the tone of the letter was cold and unloving. With a frown on his forehead he pushed the letter back into its envelope; and at that moment Carol appeared out of the kitchen.

"Hello, Jim!" she said. "Is something wrong? You're looking very grim."

"It's this," said Jim. He was still holding the envelope in his hand. "A letter from Susan."

"Oh! Bad news?" Carol looked, and sounded, concerned. She tossed her long brown hair out of her eyes with a characteristic flick of her head.

"W ell, not really bad news," said Jim. "She just says in this letter that she's been on a little holiday in Holland, staying with her brother." Carol looked puzzled, so Jim went on quickly. "Look here, Carol, I'd rather not talk about it now. I must tell Dad I'm in."

"Very well," said Carol. "Oh, by the way, Jackie's here for supper tonight. She said she'd like a word with you in private, Jim. She's in the sitting-room."

"Okay, I'll talk to her," said Jim. He had been standing in the hall, reading Susan's letter, and talking with Carol, but now he put his head round the kitchen door, having thrust the envelope into a jacket pocket.

His father appeared to be very busy cooking the evening meal, with several pans together on the gas cooker.

"Hello, Dad, I'm back!" he said.

"Ah, hello, Jim," said Mr. Sandy. "How's it been today?"

"Oh, not bad," said Jim vaguely. He would tell his Dad later, perhaps, about Susan's letter. He had confided only a little of his misery in his sisters, and rather more in his father, but he had told the full story only to Samantha over the telephone.

"Did Carol tell you Jackie's here?" asked his father.

"Yes, she did, and I'm going to have a word with her now. Or do you need any help in the kitchen, Dad?"

"No, no, that's fine; I don't need any help now. You can talk with Jackie now, Jim."

Jim went into the sitting-room, and sure enough there was Jackie, sitting in a straight-backed chair, reading a book, her left arm still in a sling. It was the first time he had seen her since the day of her accident, but he had heard that she had been back at work two days later. She rose to her feet as Jim entered.

"Hello, Jackie," he said. "Do sit down, please." Jackie sat down again. "How's your poor arm?"

"It was my collar-bone, actually, that was broken," Jackie reminded him.

"So it was; but how's it mending?"

"Very well, thank you. The doctor says it's mending quickly, and I should have my arm out of this sling pretty soon."

"That's good! But what an unfortunate accident it was, just when you were trying for the record."

"I know," said Jackie. "It was most unfortunate; but there it is—it's happened, and that's that." She motioned to Jim to sit down in an armchair beside her, and he sat down. "That's right, now we can talk comfortably. I hear you've had great trouble, Jim, following my accident at Grasmere." Her tone was now more confidential. "Trouble, I mean, between you and Susan. I hope you don't mind me knowing something about it, but Arthur did tell me that. He said you were extremely upset about whatever it is that's happened."

"I am," said Jim seriously. He went on to say that he did not at all mind that she had been told something about it, but he soon discovered that she did not understand what, in fact, had happened. He told her briefly about Julia's outburst, and its disastrous results. She was very sympathetic when she heard that his engagement to Susan had been broken off, and tried to think of something kind and helpful to say to him.

"I'm very, *very*, sorry this has happened," she said, "but perhaps it's been my fault in a way—for encouraging you to stay with me at Ghyll Cottage."

"Oh, no!" said Jim. "It wasn't your fault at all. It was partly *my* fault, I'm sure. I should have left you to spend the night there, I think, and walked on myself to hitch a lift back to Cockermouth. It's all right, Carol." Carol had at that moment opened the door, and put her head round it. "You can come in if you like. Our talk isn't private now."

"Do come in!" urged Jackie.

"Oh, thank you, but I just wondered whether whether Vicci was there," said Carol.

"I don't think she's back yet," said Jim, "although she's late today. But I haven't heard her."

"She's back now!" said a voice as the front door opened at that moment, and Victoria herself entered the hall, a little breathlessly. She also put her head round the open sitting-room door. "Good evening, Jackie! Hello, Jim!"

They returned her greeting. Carol beckoned to her sister, and the two of them went out into the hall, and closed the door behind them.

"Jim's had a letter from Susan today," said Carol quietly, "and he seems very upset about it."

"Oh dear!" said Victoria. "It's really dreadful for him that his engagement's been broken off. We *must* try to think of some way of helping him, Carol. Clearly the letter he's had was not good news."

"Yes, it must mean that the engagement's still off," agreed Carol.

They wanted to be helpful, as did Jackie, but for the rest of that evening Jim received plenty of sympathy, but no really constructive help.

★

The next day, according to the agreed plan, Jim again rang up Rhodes Castle in the evening. He waited for a few very tense seconds while the number was being rung. Would Susan herself answer the telephone if she were now at home? Or would he get Samantha? Or perhaps some other, lesser servant? He felt his heart beating rapidly because of his nervous tension; would it be good news, or would it not?

He had nearly half a minute to wait until the ringing stopped, but it seemed much longer than that. Then, suddenly, he heard a familiar voice as the telephone was answered.

"Hello, Sam, is that you?" he said. "It's Jim Sandy here."

"Hello, Jim!" said Samantha cheerfully. Jim could hear the happiness in her voice, and suddenly knew that everything was all right again. "I'm so glad you've rung up now. I've got some *very* good news for you!"

"Oh!" gasped Jim eagerly. "Has Susan really forgiven me?"

"Even better than that, Jim! Yes, Sue says she *completely* forgives you—and she wants you to marry her as soon as ever you can! And she hopes that you'll forgive her for her strange behaviour of late."

Jim was so overjoyed by this staggering news, and had such a feeling of sudden relief, that he almost wanted to jump into the air to give vent to his emotions, but he controlled himself as best he could.

"*Wonderful!*" he breathed. "Oh, that's simply wonderful news! Forgive Sue? Yes, of course I'll forgive her! Where is she anyway, Sam? Is she not there?"

"Oh yes, she's here somewhere in the house," said Samantha, "and, of course, she wants to talk to you herself. I must go and have a look for her in a minute or two!"

"This is such splendid news I can hardly take it in!" said Jim joyfully. "Sam, you're an angel to have managed this—although how you've made Sue change her mind, I can't think!"

"Oh, it really wasn't very difficult."

"But how did you do it?"

"Well, Jim, Roger and I are going up to Scotland shortly for our holiday, and, after spending a night in Edinburgh with my Mother, we're going on north again, bound for the Outer Hebrides. I have an aunt who lives near Stornoway on the Isle of Lewis, so we're going to stay with her, and go touring about on the lovely Isles of Lewis and Harris. So what I've been doing is simply telling Sue what I know about Lewis and Harris, telling her what places we hope to visit, and what sights we hope to see. I've gone on and on, whenever I had a chance, about how beautiful it is out there in the Western Isles. 'Even more beautiful,' I told Sue, 'than the Isle of Skye'—because you know how much Sue loved being at Loch Brittle on the Isle of Skye. You see, Jim, what I wanted was to make her feel very envious of Roger and me, when she thought of us going off to such a lovely place, while she would be left behind at Rhodes Castle."

"So that she would want to come too?" said Jim. "Yes, I see that, but how does it affect me?"

"I'm coming to that," said Samantha. "You see, I'd made her very envious of Roger and me, and in fact she said: 'Gosh, I wish I could come with you Sam!' So I simply said, by way of reply, 'Why don't you and Jim slip up there for your honeymoon in the last two weeks of this month, Sue? You *could* do that,' I said, 'if you were to marry Jim straight away, say on Saturday week?' Well, of course, Sue's first reaction to that was, predictably, that she could do no such thing. But I knew, Jim, that really she was longing to do that; the idea of a honeymoon with you in the romantic Isles of Lewis and Harris was, you might say, infinitely attractive."

"My word, yes!" said Jim. "I bet Sue thought that when you put it to her like that. And you managed presently to talk her round into accepting that idea?"

"That's right, Jim, that's how it was. My suggestion had, as it were, struck a chord that was really in harmony with her own secret desires. I thought it was inevitable that she would agree to my plan— and she did!"

"Like last time!" laughed Jim.

"Yes, it was quite like last time, when I got her to agree to all my plans to sail to the Isle of Skye. And, you see, I made the honeymoon idea in the Western Isles sound quite innocent—as if I had no idea that you'd made some other plans. Hadn't you actually planned to go to Holland for your honeymoon?"

"Yes, we had, but that was before all that disaster at Grasmere.

And now, of course, Sue's just been to Holland, and come back, so presumably she wouldn't want to go there again for the honeymoon. I think it's a much better idea to head for the Outer Hebrides."

"I'm glad you think so," said Samantha.

"Well, the most important thing is that we're going to get married —at the end of next week! I can hardly believe it! So all is really forgiven?"

"Sue will tell you it is! Ah, here she is, Jim! She's just come into the room, so I'll hand over to her now . . ."

Samantha said something to Susan, but Jim did not catch the words. He waited for a few breathless seconds, and then heard Susan's voce at the other end of the line.

"Jim, my darling!"

"Oh, Sue, darling, how lovely to hear you!" said Jim. "Have you really forgiven me for that night?"

"Absolutely and completely, my darling, so you needn't think about it any more! But I ought rather to be asking *your* forgiveness, Jim. You must have been thinking that I've been acting very strangely lately?"

"Oh, that's quite all right!" said Jim soothingly. "I'm just so happy that everything's right again! And you want us to get married pretty soon?"

"Yes, next week, if you can make it down here for Saturday week, the nineteenth. How much notice do you have to give to end your porter's job?"

"A week."

"Well, if you could give your notice when you go in tomorrow . . ."

"I will, I will!" said Jim eagerly. "And then—I say, I'll have to travel down to Rhodes Castle on Friday week, the eighteenth, and it'll take all day."

"I know," said Susan, "but as tomorrow's Friday you'll have to make Thursday of next week your last day's work at the station; but the Station-Master will surely allow you to do that when you tell him that you're getting married on Saturday week, and that you've got to travel down to Dorset on Friday week."

"Dorset? So the wedding's to be in Rhodes Church?"

"No, we can't have it in church at such short notice. Listen, Jim, we've booked it for eleven o' clock at the Registry Office in Sherborne on the nineteenth. Do you mind it being at the Registry Office? Because, if you do . . ."

"No, no, I don't mind at all," said Jim quickly.

"Are you sure, my darling? We could postpone it, you know, and have the banns read out in church, and then have a church wedding later. I'll do whatever you say, Jim!"

"Bless you, Sue, darling!" said Jim lovingly. "Let's stick to the first plan so that there's no delay. Couldn't we have a Service of Blessing in church later?"

"We could indeed, and I think we should—after our honeymoon."

"Our honeymoon! What a lovely idea of Sam's that we should go to the Outer Hebrides!"

"You like the idea of our going there, Jim?" asked Susan, a little anxiously, he thought. "Of course, that wasn't our original plan, you remember."

"Oh, but I'm longing to see what the Isles of Lewis and Harris are like! We could go to Holland some other time, Sue."

"Yes, we could go there next spring, perhaps, when the bulb fields are in bloom. But, Jim, I'm sorry I dashed off there on my own. You must have thought I was being perfectly beastly to you?"

"No, you weren't, Sue," said Jim reassuringly. "Your brother had invited you, so you went there."

"Paul and Kirsten actually invited *us*, Jim, to stay with them—not just me on my own. And they thought it rather odd that I had left you behind, but I made the rather lame excuse that you couldn't come because you were working. What they thought about that I really don't know."

"Oh well, we needn't talk about that now," said Jim. "I'm all for the Hebrides for our honeymoon, and for Holland next year. But how will we be getting there, Sue?"

"To Stornoway? On board the Osprey, I thought."

"Gosh, sailing in the Osprey! Why, that would be *much* more fun than if we just took the ferry from wherever you do take it from!"

"It sails from . . . Where does the Stornoway ferry sail from, Sam? . . . Oh, from Kyle of Lochalsh, Sam says. But I think we could manage Osprey on our own, Jim."

"Oh yes, I'm sure we could," said Jim. Really he was not particularly sure how well they would manage sailing the yacht on their own, as he knew that his own knowledge of sailing was still rudimentary. However, he realized that it would involve living in intimate nearness to his wife, as Susan would be by then, for a good long while. "It'll be wonderful sailing all that way just with you," he said. "I'm *so* looking forward to this—and to our wedding day, of course!"

"Well, Jim, darling, once again we owe a great deal to Sam for these plans. When I came back from Holland I wasn't thinking at all of marrying you, but Sam persuaded me to be sensible—didn't you, Sam? . . . She says, Yes, she gave me a bit of straight talk: what was the use of delaying, when really I was longing to become your wife?"

At his end of the telephone Jim smiled as he heard Susan say this. Good old Sam! he thought. He tried for a moment to picture the scene at the other end of his telephone conversation. Susan and Samantha must be sitting together in the Green Drawing Room of Rhodes Castle, Susan sitting on the chair by the little telephone table, while Samantha would be close to her, probably sitting on the sofa.

There had been a momentary pause in the telephone conversation. Now Jim heard Susan's voice again.

"Well, Jim, my darling, I suppose we'd better ring off now, as we've had quite a long talk, but we'll need to discuss a lot more over the phone before you come down here. But it's been lovely talking with you, my darling!"

"And it's been so lovely to hear you, Sue, and to have all this wonderful news! I can hardly wait for Saturday week, though! I wish we could get married tomorrow!"

"That's just how I feel!" said Susan cheerfully. "But, never mind, the days will pass quickly as there's a *lot* more planning to do!"

Then Susan again told Jim that it was time that they rang off. She handed the telephone over to Samantha for a moment, and Jim said good-bye to her, and thanked her very much for all her help, and then she handed the telephone back to Susan again for a final word with Jim. They said their good-byes when Jim had said that he would ring her up in a day or two to talk of further plans.

He hung up the receiver, and for a minute or two remained where he was at the telephone in the sitting-room. He was feeling almost light-headed after receiving so much good news so suddenly. He felt that he needed a few minutes to sit quietly and think about what lay before him and Susan. They were going to be married at the end of next week! It was almost unbelievable. They would be setting off for a honeymoon cruise to the delightful Western Isles. Oh, it's wonderful, *wonderful*! he repeated to himself.

Suddenly he got up from his chair, smiling broadly. Now I'll tell them the good news! he said to himself.

★

Susan was sitting at the cabin table of the <u>Osprey</u>, poring over a chart of the approaches to Stornoway Harbour, while Jim was steering the yacht northwards along the rocky east coast of the Isle of Lewis. He was feeling a little uneasy, although he knew that the yacht was sailing in deep water, and that the water would remain more than deep enough for the yacht until they were very close in. Susan had given him a course to steer, the wind was light and from the north-east, the sailing easy, and, with no other vessels in sight, there was no danger of a coolision with anything. However, in spite of all these factors which combined to make his present job at the tiller a straight-forward one, Jim's uneasiness remained.

Jim's anxiety, in fact, simply proceeded from the fact that this was the first time on the voyage that he had been left in sole charge of the ship, with Susan in the cabin, rather than beside him in the cockpit. She had said, when the yacht was well clear of the small islands round the mouth of Loch Erisort: "Here you are, Jim! You can have a go at sailing her now yourself while I go into the cabin to study the chart for a bit. Just give me a shout if anything happens, and I'll come out at once." So Jim was feeling that he was well and truly the master of the ship, at least temporarily; and although that thought gave him a definite thrill, it also brought with it the anxiety of a heavy responsibility. If the ship were wrecked, having run into a rock, it would be his fault, he reckoned. But he knew that this could not happen if he continued to hold the <u>Osprey</u> on her right course; Susan had assured him that this was so, and he had complete faith in her judgement.

"Sue!" he shouted presently, half turning his head.

"Hello!" he heard her shout back from inside the cabin through the open door. "Has the wind changed?"

"No, I don't think so. It's just that we've passed that small headland that was on our left—on the port side, I mean—and I can see that another inlet of the sea runs in there."

"That must be Loch Grimshader," said Susan, after a look at the chart, "if we've passed Raerinish Point. We'll have to alter course a little when we've covered another mile or so, to come into the harbour roughly on a north-north-west bearing. I'm coming out in just a sec, Jim, to have a look round when I've done ruling these lines."

Jim turned right round for a moment to glance right into the cabin. He saw that Susan was busy using a pair of parallel rulers to draw a light pencil line on the chart. As well as the chart she had a nautical almanac open on the cabin table. Then he quickly looked ahead of the ship again.

"I say, the land right ahead looks quite near now," he said. "It looks like low, sandy cliffs." He picked up the ship's binoculars, which were lying beside him on the steersman's seat, and put the glasses to his eyes. "Yes, I can see low sandy cliffs, and sand—and some houses inland."

"That'll be the eastern suburbs of Stornoway," said Susan. "I'm coming out now. My word, it's really gorgeous out here! What fantastic colours!" She emerged from the cabin doorway, and stood in the cockpit with Jim, looking round at the sea, the sky, and the land, all lit up by brilliant sunshine.

"Yes, the colours are superb in this beautiful sun," agreed Jim "But it's hard to believe now that we had so much rain yesterday."

"H'm, yes—yesterday was our wettest day so far, but this is by far the most beautiful we've seen it. I don't think I've ever seen the sea looking quite so blue as this off any British coast—it almost looks like the Mediterranean!"

"Is it time to change course yet, Sue?" asked Jim. Although he had been listening to her, he was concentrating very hard on his job of steering the yacht by the compass.

"No, not quite yet," said Susan after a careful look round. "Keep her as she's going, Jim. The course is still due north."

"Due north it is!" replied Jim in the proper nautical manner.

For a minute or two they sailed on in silence, Jim mostly watching the compass card, and Susan mostly watching the land on the port side of the vessel, where cliffs of dark rock rose up from the smooth blue water. Inland from the cliffs the land looked bleak and treeless. They were not moving very fast through the water in the light wind, but the flood tide was helping them on their way, running north up the coast, while they were moving with it.

★

"Here we are at the Lewis Hotel!" said Susan cheerfully. "Sam said it was close to the quay."

"It certainly is!" said Jim. "Shall we go in now?"

"We might as well."

The <u>Osprey</u> lay at anchor in the inner basin of Stornoway Harbour. They had hauled in the dinghy, climbed aboard her, and rowed ashore. It had been too early to think about having lunch so they had taken a leisurely stroll around the town centre to fill in some time before heading back to theLewis Hotel, which they had seen by the quayside when they had anchored the yacht.

They pushed open the door of the hotel, saw before them a flight of stairs, and wondered whether they had come in by the right entrance. They climbed the stairs to the first floor, came to a landing, and were wondering which way to turn when a smartly dressed waitress appeared from a door on their left. Looking past the waitress, they saw a room which looked like the dining-room. The waitress stopped short when she saw that Susan wanted to ask her something. She was a young, blonde girl, wearing a pale green blouse and a black skirt.

"Good afternoon. Can I help you?" she said politely

"Good afternoon!" said Susan. "Can you give us lunch? Is that the dining-room in there?"

"Certainly, madam, you can order lunch any time you like up to two o' clock in the dining-room—in there—or you can have a bar lunch at any time. The bar's just along the passage here, so, if you want to eat in there, you can follow me now."

"Oh, thank you!" said Susan. She noticed the way that Jim was looking at the waitress (who was certainly a very attractive young woman), but decided to say nothing about it. She was in a happy, carefree mood, and knew that Jim had received punishment more than enough for his night in bed with Jackie. "What do you think, darling?" she asked. "Shall we go into the bar first?"

"Let's do that!" said Jim.

They walked down the passage after the waitress, and noticed a long mirror on the wall on their left and some coat hooks on their right; but they had nothing to hang up, and so passed through the swing door into the Public Bar. Here they saw another woman standing behind the bar, and noticed that she also was wearing a pale green blouse and a black skirt. Susan, however, was more interested in looking round the room than staring at waitresses. She noticed a couple at a table in a corner of the room, who had their backs to her, but she saw that the woman had fair shoulder-length hair, and that the man was tall and had black hair. Something about them arrested her attention at once: *could* they be Samantha and Roger? She knew they were also on holiday in Lewis, but had not really expected to find them drinking in the bar of the Lewis Hotel. After she had stared at the couple for a few seconds she gently nudged her husband.

"Jim," she whispered, "isn't that Samantha over there in the corner, with her back to us?"

Jim had hardly ever seen Roger Burton, but he thought that the woman with shoulder-length blonde hair must surely be Samantha. "Yes, it must be them," he said in a hushed voice, "but they haven't seen us yet. Shall I get you a drink, Sue?"

"Yes, indeed you could! I'd like some beer—a half pint of bitter!"

"I'll have one too," he told her.

"Where shall we sit? Over here on the left?"

"All right, Sue!"

At that moment, however, the woman with shoulder-length blonde hair turned her head and recognized them.

"Why, hello, Jim!" she said cheerfully. "Hello, Sue! They're behind us, Rog."

The man turned his head. Jim saw a neat, black moustache and a small goatee beard; he was Roger Burton, with his wife, Samantha. They rose to their feet, and Susan and Jim also stood up, and went over to their table. There was a general hearty shaking of hands.

"Well, well!" said Samantha. "Another Hebridean Meeting!—only this one was partly planned."

"Like last time!" laughed Susan.

"You two have kept very quiet, haven't you?" said Roger. "We never noticed anyone come in after us."

"Why not bring your drinks over to our table, as there's room here for four?" invited Susan. "And then we can talk for a while before lunch. You're staying for lunch?"

"Oh yes, we are," said Samantha. "We're going for the bar lunch in here. Are you?"

Susan confirmed that she and Jim were also going for the bar lunch. Just then Jim saw the pretty young waitress re-appear, carrying a tray of food for the dining-room.

"That's my cousin, Margaret MacAllen, the girl you're looking at, Jim!" said Samantha gaily. (Jim instantly shifted his gaze.) "She's my Aunt Mavis's daughter."

"Gosh!" said Jim quickly. "I remember now you telling us that she worked here."

They had forgotten about Margaret MacAllen, and it came as a shock to Jim to realize that this attractive young woman was related to Samantha. He thought, however, that since Samantha was her aunt she would probably wait on them.

"How long have you been staying with your Aunt Mavis?" asked Susan.

"Well, we got to Stornoway on Thursday of last week," said Samantha, "and we were met off the ferry by Aunt Mavis, and then she drove us home to Glen Tolsta, and we've been staying there since then. It's about eight miles away. I hope you two are coming there?"

"We might," said Susan, "but, you see, we've got the <u>Osprey</u> to think about. She's moored in the harbour here."

"But couldn't you sail round to Glen Tolsta in the <u>Osprey</u>? The cottage is only a few yards away from the sea."

"Well, that's an idea," said Susan, "but how would I know the way without a map? We've got a chart for sailing, but no map."

"We've got a map," said Samantha, "but we've left it in the car. But. . . I know—we'll ask Margaret! She's almost sure to have a map of Lewis!"

"But surely she won't have one *here?*"

"Ah, but she lives-in here during the week to save travelling every day to and from Glen Tolsta She has her own little room here. I'll ask her the next time we see her."

They only had some two or three minutes to wait until Margaret MacAllen re-appeared in the bar. She came straight up to their table to take their order. Samantha quickly waylaid her.

"Hello, Aunt Sam?"

"Margaret, I must introduce you to these two friends of our's," and proceeded to introduce Susan and Jim. There was more shaking of hands. Jim, thinking of Susan, was careful not to look her in the eye as he shook her hand. "Now then," continued Samantha, "have you by any chance got a map here, Margaret, a local map? We need to consult it, if you've got one in your room here?"

"I have got one," said Margaret. "I could get it for you now, if you like?"

"Could you, please? You could bring us the map with our food."

Margaret MacAllen took their orders, and again disappeared. In a moment of silence Roger Burton whispered in his wife's ear, but Jim could not catch his words.

"Go on, Rog!" urged Samantha. "Tell them!"

"I reckon that's a *third* Hebridean Meeting!" said Roger, smiling broadly.

"Why, so it is!" said Susan joyfully. "Well, fancy that!"

"It *is* a third Hebridean Meeting!" said Samantha. "Well, Jim—what do you think about it?"

"Me?" said Jim. "I reckon that three Hebridean Meetings *must* be lucky! It's a good omen!"

★

The <u>Osprey</u> was anchored in Glen Tolsta Bay, a small inlet on the east coast of Lewis, a little way to the south of Tolsta Head. Jim and Susan had shared an evening meal in the cottage with Ian and Mavis MacAllen, their hosts, and Samantha and Roger, and had now returned to the <u>Osprey</u> to settle down for the night. Jim, as he lay quietly in the bunk, pressed closely and lovingly beside Susan, his wife, felt incredibly happy. True, he had been slightly worried by the unexpected and sudden appearance of Samantha's young and attractive cousin, Margaret, but it was perfectly clear to him that this meeting had not upset Susan in the very slightest. He knew only too well that the incident of his "wife" at Grasmere had brought his loving relationship with Susan perilously close to total disaster, and now he was very keen to avoid any further risks of that sort.

Now all was well once again. . . very well indeed! The night was perfectly quiet. The <u>Osprey</u>, lying at anchor in the sheltered bay, lay in almost dead calm water. Everything was at peace. And just as no clouds of anguish now separated him from Susan, so in the clear sky above them there were no clouds to obscure the shining of the stars of heaven.

THE END

Lightning Source UK Ltd.
Milton Keynes UK
UKOW04f0621220215

246599UK00002B/113/P